DINEH

An Autobiographical Novel

DINEH

An Autobiographical Novel

Ida Maze

Translated from the Yiddish and with an afterword
by Yermiyahu Ahron Taub

White Goat Press
Yiddish Book Center
Amherst, Massachusetts

yiddishbookcenter.org

 Grateful acknowledgment to William Shaffir for kind permission to translate.

This book was translated thanks to the generous permission of Ida Maze's son, Irving Massey.

Yiddish Book Center
Amherst, MA 01002

Printed in the United States of America
10 9 8 7 6 5 4 3 2 1

Paperback edition ISBN 978-1-734872-9-2
Hardcover edition ISBN 978-8-9852069-0-6
Ebook edition ISBN 978-8-9852069-1-3

Library of Congress Control Number: 2022931563

Book and cover design by Michael Grinley
The type is set in Baskerville and Kabel

Cover illustration by James Steinberg

Publication of *Dineh*
was made possible with support from
Lori and Michael Gilman
Muriel and Laurence Gillick

---

*The Yiddish Book Center's translation initiatives
are made possible in part through the generous support of
The Applebaum Foundation, Inc. and
The Alice Lawrence Foundation, Inc.*

Table of Contents

Introduction

by Emma Garman

At once an enchanting coming of age tale and a superbly crafted portrait of Jewish life in turn-of-the-century tsarist Russia, Ida Maze's *Dineh* engages the reader with an immediacy made ever more potent by its undertow of wistful melancholy. Maze (pronounced MAA-zeh) was in her early teens when she emigrated from her native White Russia, escaping the pogroms and spiraling anti-Semitism. After a brief spell in New York she settled permanently in Montreal, where she wrote *Dineh* from a distance of many years. Yet to turn this book's pages is to be transported to the vanished world of Maze's Yiddish childhood: a pastoral idyll, full of harshness and wonder. A remark made by her son, the literary scholar Irving Massey, offers a clue to how Maze achieved this feat of remembrance. "My mother never really left Europe . . . she made incessant references to the old country. She sang the songs in Russian and Belorussian and Yiddish that she'd learned as a child."

The novel is set in the region around the towns of Kapyl′ and Slutsk, south of Minsk in modern-day Belarus, where Dineh, the sixth child of a tavern keeper, is born in the last decade of the 19th century. The time-honored rhythms of rural Jewish life—of work and family, religious observance and education, birth and death—structure the story, which assumes an almost documentary quality in its survey of Dineh's community, in all its joys and struggles. Among the many vividly sketched characters are Roda, who runs away from an unwanted wedding, learns to fend for herself in Kapyl′, and marries the perfect man, only to find he's not all he seems; Shprintse, a talented dressmaker with enviable panache and an enigmatic past; Hinde, torn between family expectation and a romance with a gentile nobleman; and tiny, blind Soreh-Rokhl, who can, it is said, exorcise the evil eye's curse: a valuable skill in a culture where every compliment or expression of pride is followed, reflexively, by "*Kinehore*—no evil eye."

Behind the narrative's apparent simplicity is an astute feminist sensibility. Maze questions the practice of arranged marriage, celebrates the vital fellowship of women, and laments the unfairness of prioritizing boys' education. Dineh, who from a young age is deeply curious and eager to learn, feels physically ill when her brother

Itshe tells her: "A girl is not allowed to know what boys study." She barters candy for religious stories, and she persuades her mother to teach her to read Hebrew under the pretext of helping her younger brother, Daniel, with his studies. Eventually she joins the *cheder* classes held in her home for Daniel and other Jewish children from nearby villages. (Maze herself, according to Massey, obtained a Hebrew education by listening at the door while her brothers were taught.) For Dineh, to learn new words is to be "enriched on a daily basis."

Dineh's household, as one of two Jewish families in their small village, maintains close ties with their gentile neighbors. Her father, Sholem, employs local men to work on his land, while her mother, Peshe, is relied upon to assist with difficult childbirths. Yiddish-speaking Oliana, sturdy and ample-bosomed, is a second mother to Dineh and her siblings and also acts as the family's "Sabbath goy," carrying out crucial tasks in Sholem's tavern and warehouse. "Dinkele," she tells Dineh as the girl consoles her during a crisis, "not for nothing did I carry you in my own hands and teach you to say '*ha-Moytse*' when you didn't want to eat matzo on Passover."

This longstanding harmony is upended by the inexorable advance of anti-Jewish legislation and imposed hardships, the restriction of business and removal of landrights, and the very real threat of violence, all against the backdrop of the first Russian Revolution in 1905. Dineh's friends and relatives, to her dismay, begin fleeing to America. Yet this distant country, as Dineh learns in her role as multilingual reader and writer of letters, is anything but an ideal haven. Roda's son, adrift and frightened in New York, writes: "My hands did not take to the work in the shop. They told me to stay home the next day. When I sold newspapers on the street, they laughed at my side locks. The boys ripped my coattails."

Dineh, devoted to her homeland, regards the very journey "to the other side of the earth" as a dubious undertaking. Surrounded by upheaval, poised precariously between childhood and adulthood, she contemplates an all-too-uncertain future. "There was so much that was incomprehensible, so much painful sweetness laced with childish, nostalgic sadness!" Her creator's destiny, as we know, was to become a beloved literary figure, the "den mother" of Yiddish Montreal (an apt moniker, since Maze was related to Mendele Mocher Sforim, the Kapyl′-born author known as the grandfather of modern Yiddish literature). A passionate autodidact who knew more about world literature than most scholars, Maze ran reading groups and events for both adults and children at the city's Jewish Public Library. At her home on Esplanade Avenue she held an ongoing salon, nurturing writers' talents and providing advice, food, and whatever else anyone needed.

"It seemed to me," Massey recalled, "that when anyone who had even the smallest role in the Jewish cultural world (and who did not?) came to Montreal, from anywhere in the world (and they did come from everywhere), their first port of call was my parents' house." The Canadian poet Miriam Waddington, a protegée of Maze's, remembered her "beautiful low voice, full of dark rich tones, and a chanting, trance-like way of talking . . . She radiated a sibylline and mystical quality, and possibly that was the secret of the magnetism that drew so many artists to her Esplanade apartment."

Maze made her authorial debut in 1931 with a poetry collection, *A Mame* (*A Mother*), composed after the death of her ten-year-old son, Bernard. "Children are the reason that I started writing," she later revealed. "I wrote both my happy and my sad poetry to children." Altogether she published four volumes of poetry, and her poems, stories, and essays appeared in Yiddish journals and anthologies in New York, Israel, England, and Paris as well as Montreal and Toronto. *Dineh*, her only novel, was written in the last decades before her death in 1962. Thanks to the efforts of the poet M. M. Shaffir it was published posthumously in 1970. Now appearing in English in a crystalline translation by Yermiyahu Ahron Taub, this unique glimpse into a lost milieu deserves wide appreciation as a resurrected literary gem.

A Few Words

A Note to the Original Yiddish Edition

"Shaffir, we need to get together and work on my manuscript for real . . ." So confided Ida Maze, may she rest in peace, in me more than once. And for the last few decades that we knew each other, we did, in fact, *almost* take a stab at this manuscript on, yes, more than one occasion.

But there were always more urgent matters awaiting her—ones to be completed on behalf of others. For herself, she never had any time. Until . . .

Until she sensed that it was too late. She passed from this world in June 1962.

I did with Ida Maze's text what I believe we would have done had we worked on it together—namely, completed all of the tasks needed to prepare a manuscript for publication. Ida Maze might well have made changes—structural ones, for example. But I liked the novel just the way it was, and I didn't feel that I needed to, much less that I had the right to, change anything.

And another thing. There are probably more errors than we were able to spot. So we ask the reader's forgiveness, and we also ask that you correct in your mind the errors you "catch" before reading.

—*M. M. Shaffir*

THE VILLAGE

The region in White Russia where Dineh was born was quite poor. The villages—scattered among sandy, flat fields and sparse forests. Here the peasants lived in poverty and in dark ignorance, laboring for the nearby nobility as farmhands and day laborers cutting, sowing, and plowing and as workers in the distilleries, where liquor was crafted. Only when there was no more to be done for the landowner could they turn to their own allotments.

That field work consisted of gathering a small amount of hay barely enough for the scrawny cows and horses in the stables to get through winter. After threshing, the small amount of rye used for the meager bread was ground through the millstones of the hand mill that practically every other peasant had at home. Each week the peasant woman would take a small amount of rye, grind it herself, and bake bread. A peasant rarely had enough rye to transport to the miller. Only the prominent people—the rich peasants and those who had more acreage or because of certain privileges were more closely linked to the nobleman's estate—were so fortunate.

On spring days, when there wasn't yet work on the estates, the peasants did meadow work. This consisted of clearing the field, digging up tree trunks by their roots, excavating stones from an overgrown field, and thus, with yearlong effort, making available a narrow patch of field that could later feed the flock or grow potatoes or flax. In a certain sense the peasants even lived communally. They owned a granary on the outskirts of the village, where each peasant had to contribute a certain amount of rye for the year based on his field allotment. This served as an emergency food source in case of famine or fire.

In the villages the threat of fire was ever present, causing people to live in a state of perpetual fear. The houses stood in two rows, with the stables and barns behind them. The roofs were covered in thatch, and fires were common occurrences. In the summertime, lightning would strike a tree near a house or enter a chimney and ignite a roof. At that point the entire village stood on the brink of obliteration.

Winter was even worse. In the houses, the burning of wood provided the only source of light. People couldn't afford to buy kerosene. Kindling was cheaper. Each peasant could prepare long, thin, little blocks of wood that burned with a green fire and regularly sent sparks flying. The kindling was placed in a holder suspended from the ceiling so that the light would fall upon the home. Oftentimes a spark would fly off to a distant corner and smolder there until someone suddenly discovered that the house was on fire.

In addition, fires often broke out because the chimneys, built low onto the straw roofs, were poorly constructed and not cleaned. And when a spark from the oven fire leapt into the chimney and the soot caught fire, it was enough to wipe out an entire village. Such fires were more frequent in the winter, and people who were burned out of their homes had to stay in neighboring villages until the spring, when they could return to the ruins and rebuild to the extent possible.

In such cases one village helped another. The granaries with their stores of rye, to which each peasant had contributed his portion throughout the years, then came to good use. The granaries therefore had to be closely guarded. Every night two peasants stood watch. Both of them carried a small lead whistle and encircled the granary with firm, measured steps—each from either end. When they met on the other side, they blew loudly into their whistles. With those whistle calls the village was notified that the guards were now on watch. Every night two different peasants stood watch, alternating from house to house, from one end of the village to the other.

Living in such utter poverty, the peasant's life nevertheless contained ample beauty and color. Despite the long sweep of generations of suffering, the people were not coarsened or hardened. On the contrary—the lives of the impoverished Russian peasantry were rich in lyricism and feeling. They found an expression for their suffering in countless legends and folk tales, in beggar songs that could be heard near the chapels and the church thresholds. They would pawn their last shirt in the tavern and sing out and cry out their bitter fate there.

AT THE VILLAGE GATE

On summer mornings, even before the landowner's overseers had arrived on horseback in the village to hire the hay harvesters and the rye reapers, people had already gathered at the gate. There stood peasant youths with long, gleaming scythes over their strong shoulders, and peasant girls wearing vibrant head kerchiefs, white linen blouses sewn with small cross-stitches in various motifs of birds and flowers, and thick, pleated, short rainbow-colored skirts reaching above the knee. Under loose-cut bodices, firm, round maiden breasts rose and fell in the rhythmic movement of bodies in the full bloom of youth. Over their shoulders—sharp half-moon sickles.

Fused together as one, the young men and women, with gusto and post-nocturnal joy on their faces, stood and sang. And their song wafted across fields and roads, from one village to another. This was the song of field and forest. This was the song of an enslaved generation, a generation whose every wellspring of knowledge had been stopped up. And it was a song of freedom, even as it sang of enslavement. And it was a song of love, even as it wept with longing. And the song soared from the village gate until the nobleman's overseers arrived and requisitioned everyone to the fields to work. And the song resounded far and wide, as it spread out from the village to the nearby fields, and an echo remained suspended in the air until the harvesters and the reapers took to their tools, and thus was the sound of song transformed into the sound of scythe and sickle.

After a day's work they returned from the fields with the same songs, which sounded even more beautiful and sad at dusk, at first as faint echoes, then resounding as they approached the village until they had reached the gate. Then everyone dispersed to their own cottages, ate their simple, paltry meals prepared by those who had stayed at home, stretched out on the floor or the pallet, rested, washed the dust from their hands and feet with a bit of warm water from a wooden pail, the face and neck with cold water from the well, and donned warm, clean clothing. As soon as the first star appeared in the sky and the birds in the small orchards fell asleep in their nests, new sounds advanced on the village. At first a quiet song was heard coming from an individual throat, then from two and three, like the stars twinkling in the village sky that initially lit up one by one and then suddenly were many. And without even so much as a glance around them they had already mounted their horses, each one next to his own house. Then they rode as a group to the village gate.

There they assembled and stayed. Notes of love songs, songs of supplication, dirges, labor songs, and lullabies soon resounded. The band of horses stood placidly with the riders on their backs and listened to the concert.

Shortly thereafter the gate opened, and the riders—young men and women in couples—galloped away, leaving the village and heading directly to the forest until their echoes became fainter and quieter . . .

The village went to sleep. This time jagged snippets of sound came from the forest. After starting campfires, the riders dozed and warmed themselves around them while the horses grazed. Those selected to stand guard paced around to make sure that wolves didn't attack the horses and that the horses themselves didn't wander into the landowner's field and trample it. Each night a different pair stood guard. The others sang, slept, carried on love affairs, and paired up in the nocturnal summer forest.

At dawn, even before the sun appeared in the sky, the night watchmen quietly returned in haste to the village, quartered the horses in the stables, crawled onto their pallets, warmed themselves, and grabbed some shut-eye before the day's work began.

Quite early in the morning a long, forlorn, half-asleep call from a horn sounded. The shepherd went from house to house to gather the sheep and take them to the pastures for the day's grazing. He brought them to the village gate and allowed them to run freely into the fields, into the green valley behind the village.

Two shaggy black dogs with long, droopy ears followed the flock, their noses sniffing—here the field, there the flock—while looking up at the shepherd and awaiting his command.

An hour later another shepherd driving his animals stood at the village gate and periodically released a long trumpeting call from his shepherd's bagpipe. This served to notify the peasant women who were late with their milking that they needed to hurry. From the narrow, small courtyards cows began to emerge in ones and twos driven by their mistresses. The shepherd herded them all together and went out with them into the field and forest for the day's grazing.

An hour later a third shepherd drove the young horses, those who were still too young for the harness, into the forest to graze.

THE JEWS IN THE VILLAGE

Among one hundred peasant households were two Jewish families—one headed by Peyse the blacksmith and the other headed by Sholem the lessee tavern keeper.

Peyse the blacksmith's little house stood at the edge of the village, just off the village gate. Not far from the house stood a small smithy blackened from years of smoke. A thin, blue plume of smoke invariably rose from its red chimney. Visible through its open door was the bellows, which breathed with a never-ending heaviness and sprinkled sparks into the air. Passersby could hear the forceful blows of a hammer pounding on iron.

Peyse the blacksmith—broad shouldered, with a thickly bearded, round face smeared in soot—could always be found in the smithy. Sometimes his son Velvl, a young man with a pale, fragile, sickly appearance, would also be visible. He was positioned at the bellows to assist his father.

Sholem the tavern keeper's house stood directly opposite the village and its gate. A large orchard in front and a wide, enclosed garden lent it an air of wealth. It was built on a solid foundation and had a deep stone cellar, a warehouse whose sealed shelves stored dairy products, preserves, cooking fat, and various beverages. Sholem's house consisted of a large antechamber, a long kitchen, and a guest room that served as a bedroom for guests, visitors, and Jews who used to come from the surrounding villages to pray with a quorum.

For the High Holidays, families came from far-flung settlements with bedding, packages, and cups. They stayed over for Rosh Hashanah, went home, and then returned for Yom Kippur.

Before Passover, the same long and wide room was transformed into a worker's cooperative, a matzo bakery. Fathers came with their sons and daughters and brought along flour, new boxes, and barrels and proceeded to bake matzos for two consecutive weeks. At this time of year the long, ceramic, blue Russian stove burned like a lime kiln. And the large lime kiln, made kosher for Passover and freshly plastered and whitewashed, discharged matzos like round, incandescent suns.

During the period leading up to Passover white bedsheets covered the Holy Ark that housed two Torah scrolls as well as the case of sacred books that included two sets of the Talmud. Hanging from the high ceiling, the large fixture with artfully spun branches provided light from its bluish-white stearin candles as spiky green flames danced and rose upward. The two carved "Eastern Wall" signs, with its Wailing Wall sewn from yarn, flanked by two slim, eternally green palm trees and guarded by two doves with lowered wings, were also covered with little white curtains.

Next to the long, fresh plank tables, the girls and the youths, their cheeks flushed, stood with rolling pins and sharp-toothed wheels in hand and labored hard on the rolling and perforation to see who could stretch the matzo dough thinner and rounder.

Here a young woman was bursting into a song melody. She felt an urge to sing. A man's voice soon supported her. The young people became cheerful. "Sing, Beyle, sing . . ."

Beyle sang a new song no one had heard before. She had brought it all the way from Minsk. There people sang it at demonstrations. Now the young people listened raptly, eager to master it. They tried to sing along. But soon an order rang out: "What's going on here? We're baking matzos! They have to be finished exactly on schedule or they won't be kosher! When you chatter, spit comes from your mouth! And the matzo can become leavened bread, God forbid. That's all we need!"

The young people went quiet. They exchanged glances, but no one protested. The matzo production continued without a hitch.

THE HOUSE AND ITS SURROUNDINGS

Two bedrooms, with windows facing the orchard, had been built onto the large synagogue room of Sholem the tavern keeper's house. During the summers, when the windows were open, the branches, along with their leaves and fruit, extended directly into the house. Oftentimes a bird would fly in through the window, perch on the tip of a branch, and break into song as if it were in the open fields or the forest. When the windows were closed, the branches were pushed back into the orchard, where they leaned against the walls and waited until the windows were once again opened.

During the winters the windows were closed with supplementary inner panes. White, fluffy insulation padding that looked like clean, freshly fallen snow was placed between the internal and external windows. Little red and green stars, startlingly delicate and cut from thin, shiny paper, adorned the fluffy white padding. Multicolored decorative flowers on thin wire stems were embedded in the padding. They looked like roses, alive in a snowy garden. And in the center of each window, between its double panes, stood a tall, high glass with oleum that sparkled like amber and was believed to serve as a remedy against the carbon monoxide that the ovens discharged during the winter days and nights.

The old house looked like an enchanted ancient castle straight out of a fairy tale. A large cellar, always full with casks of liquor and spirits, was built onto the side of the house. It was there, in the cellar, that business was conducted.

The neighboring tavern keepers came to Sholem to buy liquor.

But Sholem didn't earn a livelihood from the cellar alone. He really didn't care for the business at all. The only thing he loved about the liquor cellar was the aroma of the ninety-proof spirits. And he did, in fact, love to drink a cup of the strong, fiery liquid on his own. But even more than having a drink on his own, he loved to drink with someone else—to make a toast, in the traditions of fraternity and brotherhood. After such a toast, the tongue becomes a bit looser in the mouth and the heart begins to open, speaking out about what lies there, heavy as a stone. Because Sholem himself was someone descended from generations of good, honest settlers who loved the earth and the smells of the field and stable; he was diligent, hardworking, and without ulterior motives.

But in his youth he had committed something of a blunder. Now it cost him dearly. He paid his debt in a quiet, honest way, refusing to turn it into a tragedy. The field was wide, the forest was deep, the river was full of fish, and he, Sholem, in a manner that would not have discredited his ancestors, arose at dawn and harnessed the horse to the plow. By the time the hired laborers arrived to work he had already completed his part, having plowed or harrowed a few stretches of land and recited some dozens of chapters of the Psalms all the while.

Winter's arrival brought with it the work of chopping timber in the forest. Sholem too performed his share. He even caught fish, but that was not so freely done since it was not considered a seemly activity for a Jew, a homeowner, someone with a reputation . . .

Oftentimes, when Sholem was showing the hay thrashers to his field, he would ask the peasant to hand over the scythe for a while. He would look at it, tenderly run his fingers over its blade, and then start to cut the hay—with such love and dexterity that it wasn't long before he had overtaken everyone. And when the peasant reminded him, "*Panie* Solom, I'm just standing here empty-handed. Look how far you've gotten," Sholem would stop, as if emerging from a sweet dream, and give the scythe back to the peasant, as if he had committed an offense, and say, "It's nothing. The day is just getting started."

But for Sholem, the work in the liquor cellar and at home didn't always go so well. His wife, Peshe, had to drag him back, almost violently, from his natural habitat to the world of commerce, which was alien and repugnant to him. What did he need it for—this strange world? Did he lack livelihood? A proper means to raise children? The ability to give charity when a neighbor needed something on occasion? It was for naught. All it took was a single misstep, one wrong move, but a man had to trudge on . . .

When he married Peshe, the aristocrat's daughter, he gave his word that he wouldn't remain a peasant toiling in the field. After extended, hushed conflicts, this proved to be the best compromise. After all, how long can a man make a fool of himself and run after the aristocratic daughter—his young wife—when she retreated to her parents' house? And he would plead with her, "Peshe, do the right thing, come home. Are you lacking for anything with me?" And how many times can a man try to get his wife to understand how unreasonable she was being?

Again and again—and she inevitably responded no, and no! She would not be a peasant woman.

Then Reb Yankev, the tavern keeper in a nearby village, died suddenly, and his widow and children couldn't run the liquor cellar or Reb Yankev's field. Sholem, the young newlywed, came along and, with the dowry of his young wife, took over the entire estate.

In this way life slowly ordered itself. In terms of livelihood there was nothing to complain about. Sholem was busy in the field, and his young wife worked in the tavern and the liquor cellar. A peasant couple performed the chores on the Sabbath forbidden to Jews and helped Peshe measure the liquor and conduct the operations in the tavern. Quite often Sholem himself also had to be in the liquor cellar both to conduct the transactions with the nearby tavern keepers who purchased on credit and to mix the liquor. His presence was especially needed when the tax man came. You didn't dare take any chances with the treasury. Sholem knew all too well what drink to have ready for the tax man, what fish he liked, and what coin to slip into his hand.

NOT THEIR EQUAL . . .

Over time the young, temperamental aristocratic wife mellowed and became more accommodating. Peshe stopped retreating to her parents' home at every possible opportunity. And she no longer threatened Sholem with divorce over every absurd minor infraction.

For her first childbirth Peshe returned to her parents' house. For the second child she went to a nearby shtetl. By the time the third one came around a female obstetrician was brought to the house. For the fourth, a midwife came. For the fifth a nearby old peasant woman was called, and so it went until the eighth child.

True, from time to time Peshe donned her ribbed yellow kaftan with deep, wide pleats and ordered the horses to be harnessed and the farmhand to drive to the neighboring shtetl—just like that, for no reason except to demonstrate for all to see that she was still herself, different from the other Jewish settler women.

And when a neighboring settler or one of Sholem's close relatives had to arrange a bris or a wedding, Peshe would come to bake and cook some appealing dishes, dress up the bride, or get the mother ready—and then return home alone, without even partaking in the celebration. After all, they weren't her equal . . .

for all that she prettified impoverished brides in her own clothes so they would be pleasing to the in-laws and grooms.

When a gentile woman in the village was going through a difficult childbirth, *Panie* Solomova was sent for immediately. Once she arrived Peshe lost no time. While tending to the woman in labor she heated up the oven and boiled the water. Then she heated stones, placed them into a deep washtub filled with hot water, and eased the woman into it. If that didn't help she had other methods.

If none of Peshe's procedures succeeded, someone harnessed the fastest horse from Sholem's stables and rode to the shtetl to fetch the medical practitioner.

People turned to her for other matters as well. Peshe did her part—but kept herself at a distance, looking down from on high, not allowing herself to be touched by any warmth from the Jewish settlers and the peasants.

She also conducted herself differently with her own children than the other Jewish mothers in the village did with theirs. Drawing on her fine education, she taught her children herself—from the Hebrew alphabet to the Pentateuch and the entire Hebrew Bible. When the children grew older a teacher was hired to provide instruction in the home. When it was time for the boys to study the Talmud they were taken away, first to a nearby shtetl to a teacher and, after that, to a yeshiva in a larger city.

If it had been up to Sholem his sons wouldn't have to go to yeshiva at all. As far as he was concerned they could just as well be good, honest Jews here in the village, just like he himself, his father, and his grandfathers, who all maintained a Jewish way of life while working in the field. But this much he knew to be true: you needed to know how to study the Talmud. It came to good use in the wintertime when the days were short and the nights long, when people went to bed early and got up at dawn. Since you didn't have to go to the fields, there was enough time before morning prayers both to recite a good few dozen chapters of the Psalms and to study a page of the Talmud.

Quite often a guest stayed overnight and arose at dawn. Because the night was long and because the guest and the head of the household had known each other since childhood and had even been students together in religious school, they both sat at their volumes of the Talmud until it had gotten quite light outside and the clatter of utensils and the squeaking of doors could be heard from the kitchen. At that point the men remembered that they had to put aside the Talmud. It was time to pray.

For Sholem the Talmud was like a holiday garment you needed both on the rare occasions when you drove into the city and just to keep handy at home, for when people came over . . . Of course you had to know the Talmud, but it wouldn't have made any difference to Sholem if his sons didn't know it . . . A Jew always had his prayers to complete, and he had the Psalms too—what else did he need? Every Jew needed to know the Psalms, and know them by heart, for that matter. He had to carry the Psalms with him and in him, just as he wore a shirt on his back and carried God's breath inside himself, hearing Him in all the creatures that breathed in the world.

Sholem loved the Psalms not just out of his piety; he recited and sang the Psalms as if he would find the entire redress for his life within its words. With David he lamented the misfortune that is death. He sang alongside him in praise of the beauty of God's universe, with all of the ecstasy of faith and the doubts of faithlessness:

In the netherworld, who will give Thee thanks . . .

And:

Song of ascents, I will lift my eyes to the mountains, from whence cometh my salvation . . .

The sublimity of the Psalms lived in Sholem's devout soul, and he carried their song with him when he was plowing, sowing, and cutting and on the long, quiet walks he took during the summer through the rye fields and the sparse pine forests when they were green, and in winter by frozen lakes and through those same forests when they were white and covered in snow.

A NEWBORN LITTLE SOUL

Once, on an early June night, when Sholem was returning from a nearby shtetl and had reached the small forest a verst or two from home, he heard a carriage approaching from the opposite direction. He soon recognized the voice of his older daughter, Malkeh, speaking in goyish with Vasil, the farmhand.

"There goes your father. I recognize his horse's gait," said Vasil. And Sholem heard his daughter respond, "Well, fine, if it's my father, we'll have to go back and pick up Aunt Yakhe to stay with us and then get home. My mother said she won't stay alone. My mother—she's sick."

"Sick? You're just a kid. For women, this isn't a sickness. It's probably another little Yid. You'll see—by the time we get home, it'll be shrieking and not letting anyone get any sleep . . . Well, they'll make a bris and raise a glass with a good fiery toast . . . Your father, along with everyone who comes to your house for the parties—they all just make it seem like they're drinking and singing. They pretend to get drunk. But I know how to take a swig; I know how to get drunk for real," Vasil responded.

At this point Sholem could no longer contain himself. "Vasil! Malkeh! What's going on—what's this about your mother?"

"Yes. Mama isn't feeling well. They sent me to get Aunt Yakhe to bring her to stay with us."

"Vasil, turn around and go right back. See what has to be done there. I'll go and come back quickly with Aunt Yakhe. Tell Mama we're coming soon."

Each of them turned around and went in different directions. Sholem soon reached a small, thatch-roofed hut. He approached it, knocked on the door—and a hunched-over woman dressed in village clothes opened the door. "Oh, it's you? Well, come on in."

"Good evening. Where's Leybe?"

"Leybe—when is he ever at home? He's with the cattle. His whole life is there. I don't see when he gets up or when he goes to bed. When he comes back from the field he goes straight to the stable, where he settles himself in and spends too much time. But, brother, that's not what you've got on your mind. You went to the market today, right? So why are you here?"

"Well, here's what's really going on. Malkeh ran into me and told me to come for you. Peshe probably needs you. I myself expected it. She's due any day now."

Yakhe got dressed in a hurry, grabbed a large, white apron, placed a few pointed cheese wedges—"for the children"—into a small white bag, and quickly left the house. She kissed the mezuzah, walked directly to the stables behind the house, and shouted, "Hey! Leybe!"

"What is it?" Leybe asked, trudging out of the stable. He walked forward and then, noticing Sholem, greeted him. "Any news?"

"There'll be news soon," Yakhe chimed in. "With God's help, a boy. The father, may he live a long life, doesn't have a name in mind yet. A year on the nose since the last one. Get back into the house soon. The kids are asleep. Take some supper for yourself. Enough with the horses. That's plenty. He loves that dun horse like a son who'd say Kaddish for him, if you'll excuse the comparison."

When Sholem and Yakhe stepped into the entry hall, the house was quiet except for the cries of a newborn infant coming from the bedroom. Khishe, the blacksmith's wife, was moving quietly through the house. Peshe had been quarreling with her ever since they became neighbors. She was an old, bent woman—nearsighted, with a white kerchief on her head—who now walked around the tavern keeper's house with the small, measured steps of someone who had done something wrong.

Yakhe approached her. "Good evening, Khishe. Congratulations to you! Are you the grandmother? Congratulations. A boy? With any luck there will be a bris."

Khishe stayed where she was, feeling even guiltier. "I was going about my business when Sorke came running over, crying, 'Please, Khishe, my mother sent me to get you. She's sick.' I asked her where her father and Malkeh were and, excuse the comparison, Okulina. She started crying and said, 'There's no one. My mother is by herself.' Well, a person isn't made of stone, after all, God forbid. And I thought to myself: So what if there was silliness? We didn't talk; we just argued. After all, we're not enemies, God forbid."

Sholem cut her off. "Is it a boy?"

"A girl, a little darling, may she live for many years," Khishe answered, rectifying the condition of the newborn child whom others had hoped would be a boy. "A boy? Why is lineage such an obsession for them, may they all be well? Two boys and two girls, and now a third girl. Things will be all right for Sholem. He'll have enough for their dowries, no evil eye. His daughters won't become spinsters, God forbid."

Khishe wished the mother a good night, gathered her few things, and quietly went into the other room, where the children were sleeping. She went over to the beds, made sure that all the children were asleep, and went home.

DINEH

During the Sabbath prayers, Sholem was called to the Torah for the prestigious last portion. They served sponge cake and liquor and named the child "Dineh"—after the grandfather Daniel, may he rest in peace.

Dineh was the fifth child at home, and the sixth child her mother had. The eldest child, a boy, died immediately after birth.

By that point getting pregnant, giving birth, and nursing were not particularly newsworthy for Peshe. She had the babies a scant few years apart and nursed them until the late months of a new pregnancy.

The children grew up with the help of a servant or two: Okulina, an elderly gentile woman from a nearby village, and Oliana, a tall, healthy peasant woman who had her own cottage and her own child, a little girl. Her husband, Vasil, didn't own his own field. They lived off what they could earn off the tavern keeper's property. On the Sabbath Oliana carried the keys to the warehouse and the liquor cellar and heated up the oven herself. The tavern keeper's children considered her a second mother. If the children wanted bread and butter or an apple or to go outside and play, they turned to Oliana. If fights broke out among them, the children went to Oliana to complain.

When it was time for Oliana to return to her cottage, she often took several of Sholem's children with her so that Peshe would have an easier time with the younger children. The children felt very at home in Oliana's cottage. She spoke Yiddish with them, and when they got hungry after playing in her home for a while and asked her for something to eat, she gave them bread and butter or bread with an apple. When the children extended their little hands for the bread and butter, Oliana always commanded them, "*Ha-Moytse!* Don't eat without making a *ha-Moytse!*"

Between these two mothers—the cold and strict Jewish mother, whose main tasks were to nurse the smallest child, oversee the house and liquor cellar, and tend to the frequent guests, and Oliana, the gentile mother, who washed, cleaned, dressed and undressed them, and offered bread and butter—Dineh grew up.

As a child she did not flourish. She was always emaciated. From the moment she was born Dineh didn't nurse the way she should have. It was as if something about her stern mother and the milk from her breasts didn't appeal to her. Each time Peshe lifted the baby to her breast, bundled her warmly against it, and started to nurse her, Dineh—as if she just remembered something—suddenly raised her large brown eyes, looked up at her mother, started crying, and refused to suckle anymore.

Peshe wasn't accustomed to this kind of behavior. The other children, when they were already running around the house with a piece of bread in their hands, used to approach her and ask, "Mama. Nipple." And here was this kind of demon child that wouldn't take her breast.

Peshe didn't have much time to spare. When the baby didn't drink her fill, she placed her back in the cradle, half hungry. When the baby cried, one of the older children was seated by the cradle and would dangle a piece of string into her hand, which she tugged. The older child rocked the cradle as determined by age and level of maturity.

At that time the older daughter Malkeh, who was then nine years old, studied with a teacher along with the older brother, the tavern keeper's eldest son, Faytl. Sorke, the youngest daughter, was six years old, and Itshe was three years older than Dineh. He often sat by her cradle and extended the string with great concentration until he himself fell asleep.

When Sorke came to rock the cradle, she sang to Dineh and told her stories. And when Dineh was hungry and didn't want to go to sleep, Sorke threatened her with all sorts of intimidation. "Go to sleep, Dinehle. If you don't, the Gypsies will hear you in the forest. They're going to come with their horses and covered wagons and steal you from us and throw you in a big wagon . . ."

That was how the six-year-old Sorke would talk over the cradle until she frightened herself and started believing her own story that the Gypsies were about to come. She burst into tears and ran to Oliana, hiding in the folds of her wide, pleated dress. "I'm scared of the Gypsies. They're going to come soon to steal Dinehle and throw her into their big wagon."

In her cradle, Dineh did her part, crying and thrashing her thin legs—not out of fear of the Gypsies but because of the hunger that was gnawing at her and preventing her from falling asleep.

With her mother and her mother's milk, Dineh never made peace—until they began to feed her with a nipple and a little bottle, and added to that a makeshift feeding contraption. This consisted of chewed-up hard bread with sugar poured into a thin linen tied with a thread. It was then inserted, large as a large brass button, into the baby's mouth. But Dineh didn't want this strange food that had to be sucked through a rag. When the corners of the rag dragged around the baby's mouth, she would tear it and start to cry.

When Oliana saw that Dineh wasn't going to behave properly anytime soon, she decided to render the little demon into less of a nuisance. She took the nipple, soaked it in liquor, sprinkled it with a bit of sugar, and stuffed it into the baby's mouth. This quieted Dineh. She got drunk and fell asleep.

This only helped as long as the baby was asleep. As soon as she woke up she began to show her resentment. For her part, Mama also showed hers. "This is some kind of a pest, not a child. She refuses to nurse and never stops whining. You go try and figure out what's wrong."

Moreover, Peshe had another reason for her resentment vis-à-vis the "pest" that refused to suckle her milk. She was pregnant again. This had never happened with her except after the first child that died after birth. At that time she gave birth to her second child exactly one year later. Since then the nursing had been a kind of insurance policy against pregnancy. But now—such an affliction. And Peshe was no spring chicken. It was almost unseemly, and no evil eye, there was one little one after another at home, and that one, Dineh, the little pest, just a year old and far from thriving. She still didn't walk by herself and constantly had to be rocked—and rocked some more—staring out from her large brown eyes and never content.

PESHE'S PARENTS COME FOR THE BRIS

Dineh wasn't yet two years old when long tables were covered, fish were chopped, and goose was roasted in Sholem's house. Many varieties of drinks, along with sponge cake and tarts, were set on the tables. Guests, including rabbis from the surrounding small towns, merchants from nearby forests, and innkeepers from neighboring villages, arrived in sleighs adorned with little bells. Sholem's father-in-law and mother-in-law from the Nesvizh region also came with the air of aristocracy befitting Peshe's parents.

Gitele Zshukhovitser, Peshe's mother, was a diminutive woman with sharp, biting black eyes that looked out from a handsome, intelligent forehead partially covered by a gleaming black wig. A little bonnet with all sorts of colored pearls and artfully constructed velvet flowers sprang up from the peak of her wig. Behind the little bouquet hung a tricornered piece of cloth, marvelously embroidered, made of thick, black satin with cream-colored leaves sewn with thick silk thread.

This was the renowned head covering that had been worn by Peshe's Grandmother Malkehle, the daughter of Rebe Meyshele, the righteous man of blessed memory. She was a saintly woman who lived until the age of one hundred and ten. Even when she was still alive, childless women vowed to themselves that if God would help them with a child—with a girl, that is—they would, God willing, name her Malkehle. And girls were born, no evil eye, fortunate children with silver spoons in their mouths. And thus it was said that even during her own lifetime Malkehle had an entire generation of children named after her.

Her daughter Gitele was also a pious woman but by this time more modern. She understood politics, ran the entire estate, and taught the children a contemporary curriculum. Her husband, Reb Mordkhe, was tall and thin, with a mild, handsome face, a long, white beard, and kind, soft, practically childlike eyes. He was known to be a person without malice. He never meddled in anyone's affairs. He spent all his years sitting in a small synagogue and studying. He was a rabbi, but he never occupied a rabbinate position. He lived all his life in a house near Nesvizh. Oftentimes a man or a woman who lived nearby would come to him to resolve a religious matter, but he always sent them to a rabbi. He gave anonymously to charity so that no one ever knew the source. The peasants in that area considered him to be holy, and they turned to *Pan* Mordukh for all of their needs. His wife, Gitele, guarded him and his peace of mind, making sure that nothing disturbed him and seeing to it that he would never be distracted from his studies.

Now they were coming to the village to attend the bris being prepared by their son-in-law and daughter.

Just a scant few years following the birth of Dineh who didn't take to nursing, Peshe had given birth to a boy, surely their last—one could even say a child born to the elderly—and hence such fanfare and with such grand guests. In the house Aunt Yakhe carried herself as if she were the lady of the household. Wrapped in a wide, white apron and with a white silk kerchief tied under the chin, she led the women to the new mother. The new mother's room was decorated with pieces of paper with the text of Psalm 121, meant to dispel evil spirits during childbirth, white curtains on the windows, and a large blue curtain by the bed of the new mother. In this way little Dineh remained a nickname in the house—the real name of her grandfather was borne by her brother Daniel. And he came, fully flourishing, into the world. He suckled well and slept soundly—and grew. And two years after Daniel's bris Peshe gave birth to a girl. Instead of Daniel being the youngest, Freydele was actually the youngest. She was a beautiful, healthy child, loved by everyone at home.

A STORM

The first event Dineh remembered from her childhood was a fire.

As she grew older she often heard folks at home talking about that fire—how on a hot summer day a large cloud appeared overhead, and because Mama was terribly afraid of thunder, all the windows, along with the house chimneys, were quickly closed. They said that Dineh was lying in her little bed not far from a window and, as always, crying and whining. Her older sister Malkeh was sitting by her bed. Suddenly there was a lightning flash and a thunderclap. The lightning cut through the house, passed over Dineh's bed, and deafened Malkeh. It exited through another window and immediately went into the orchard. There, behind the orchard, next to the fence, where the sand pits started, stood a small hut where a poor peasant widow lived with a houseful of children and an old, blind mother-in-law. On this bent hut with its torn straw roof the lightning spread out in a zigzag, and the entire home instantly went up in flames . . .

All that Dineh remembered was Aunt Reykhl from the neighboring village holding her by the hand, covering her with the shawl draped over her shoulders, and carrying her from the house, and that other terrified people were also holding children's hands. Dineh remembered how the smoke and the flames spread over the orchard, from the trees to the houses. A forceful downpour gushed down onto the smoke, the flames, all of the terrified onlookers, and on the orchard next to the house.

More than that Dineh didn't remember.

But from later narrations of the events she learned that people initially thought that the lightning, which cut past her bed, killed her because she just lay there, seemingly deaf, eyes closed, and inert. Her sister Malkeh, who had been sitting next to her rocking her, was deaf for several weeks from the thunder. Dineh also learned that, except for that small house, the fire hadn't harmed anyone because of the deluge that rained down after it started to rage.

Well, there was another thing that Dineh remembered from her earliest childhood years. She pondered it often and couldn't decide whether it really happened or whether it was one of her childhood visions.

In this memory, Mama, dressed in a beautiful, yellow ribbed overcoat with a thick line of black buttons and a large band on her neck, was walking with Dineh, leading her by the hand . . . It was the Sabbath . . . They were walking through a wide hayfield on the other side of the village. The hay was tall, and there were daisies among the stalks. And there was Papa, also dressed in his Sabbath best, walking alongside. From afar, on the path between the hay, appeared a great carriage driven by five white horses trotting in tandem . . . In the carriage sat a woman and a man, dressed in golden finery. The crowns on their heads shone into the sun like long, silver stalks of wheat. Next to them sat their beautiful children, also dressed in the same type of clothing, with crowns on their heads . . .

This, Dineh recalled, happened quite often . . .

The strolls through those wide hayfields with her father and mother in their holiday best and the same carriage with the white horses and the people in the carriage—all of this Dineh visualized again at home, hanging on a wall directly opposite the children's beds . . .

It was—and remained—a mystery to her. This image with the white galloping horses carried Dineh off every time to a world that was both a dream and a wondrous reality . . .

With greater clarity, Dineh remembered how Oliana carried her in her arms to her home, fed her bread, and commanded her to repeat after her word by word the *ha-Moytse*. Later she was told that it had been Passover. Dineh was three years old at the time. She was not a tall child, and she was always sickly. But no one fretted over her, unless she was seriously ill.

That Passover Dineh was unwell. She asked for bread, refusing any matzo. The rabbi was consulted. He ordered her to be taken to a gentile house and fed bread there. There were always problems with Dineh. She was both sickly and stubborn.

A WORLD OF WONDER AND TALES

After she turned four Dineh settled down and improved. Her mother could even give her small tasks to perform, such as cradle duty. She sat Dineh down next to the cradle, handed her the little string, and told her to rock the cradle. By then Dineh even knew how to get her sister Freydele to fall asleep, singing to her "Sleepy, sleepy, Feydli, be a good girlie" and other such baby rhymes she heard from those older than her who sat by the cradle. Dineh patiently rocked her little sister and loved to play with her. She also began to take an interest in what her older brothers and sisters were saying. Although it was difficult for her to absorb fully all of their words, Dineh always made an effort. And the slightest thing that had to do with storytelling completely captivated her. Just from hearing a word or two she was able to explain the rest to herself.

Sitting next to the cradle Dineh would tell Freydele a story in her own childish language. Freydele was at once the center of her fantasy world, her audience, and her inspiration. Freydele needed so many stories, and her sense of wonder needed to be captivated. Dineh began to construct the world of wonder that Freydele demanded. She found a small paper box and hid it so that no one would find it. This would be something significant that only she and Freydele knew about and needed to have . . . She found an empty, small red tin chest of tea and hid it on the blue Russian stove under the beam—only she and Freydele would know the hiding place. It was important that no one else know about it. Dineh wasn't certain what she would do with the small tin chest; it would be a mystery. Something quite useful—that was to be expected. There would come a time when Dineh would let Freydele know about the great possibilities of such a chest. Sometimes Mama went into town and brought candies back for the children. Dineh never ate hers. She hid them in the small chest. Sometimes she received a sugar cube. This too would someday be useful. Living in a village, you sometimes ran out of sugar. Freydele would always need sugar. And if they needed sugar for Freydele at home and there wasn't any Dineh would have some for her. There wouldn't be any more shortages.

The candies didn't stay long in her possession. She gave them away. Or rather, she bartered them with Sorke and Itshe. Sorke, a mere six years older than Dineh, took the candies, sat Dineh down next to her on a bench or under a tree in the orchard, and told her a story. For each candy, a story. But Dineh didn't get that much out of Sorke's stories. She spoke about faraway things that, for now, the four-year-old Dineh couldn't conceive of very well.

GOD CREATED EVERYTHING . . .

Things were different with Itshe, who was just three years older than Dineh. Itshe studied in religious school. It was he who told her that God first created heaven, then the earth and the stars, along with the sun, the moon, the people, and the animals. Dineh was pleased to learn that God had created everything, everything that was needed . . . including her brother Itshe, who really did know everything . . .

In exchange for the candies she gave to Itshe, Dineh got herself a fine bargain. She now had so much to tell to Freydele in her little bed—that God created everyone: Papa, Mama, all of the little stars, and God also created her, Freydele . . .

In her child's heart Dineh sustained a vast delight and a sense of companionship with God and with all life on earth—from the smallest flower to the kitten in their house and the white puppy, Goldetske. God had created all of them, and Dineh too—and him, her brother Itshe, who couldn't possibly be seen as an ordinary brother. He was growing big and tall in Dineh's eyes.

HEAVY AND BLACK . . .

Freydele, who still lay in her little bed and hadn't learned to walk, didn't yet know what wonderful things God created. She hadn't yet seen the newborn calf that Dineh saw early in the morning in the stable and the two new black lambs born today near the gate. Vasil carried them into the stable; they shivered so much as the mother sheep followed behind and bleated. Yes, God created all of this today . . .

Dineh climbed up on a chair with her knees. She placed Freydele's little hands around her neck, scooped up Freydele's body with her hands, and dragged her out of her little bed. As she climbed down with the child from the chair, she made for the door. And there, by the door, she tripped over the stone threshold. Freydele was under her.

Hearing Dineh's cries, Mama came running in from the cellar and Oliana from the garden. They picked Dineh and Freydele up from the floor. Blood was streaming from Dineh's nose and mouth, and Freydele was lying there as if she were dead. They shook and rattled Freydele and then poured cold water on her until they revived her.

More than that Dineh didn't remember.

From what she was told afterward, Dineh learned that during that incident she had shattered Freydele's lungs and liver and that Freydele was sick for eight weeks and then died. From the moment of the fall until Freydele's death Dineh remembered nothing. But she did remember Freydele's death. This was the first experience that she put away, stored for later. It would shape her path in later life, weighing on her like a heavy, black burden.

IN A CORNER OF THE RUSSIAN STOVE

The large, blue-tiled Russian stove was now Dineh's world. She stored her little magic tin chest under one of the beams over the stove. In a corner atop the Russian stove's bulk she sat, forgotten by everyone in the house around her. She sat there, as if frozen, with her large brown eyes glued to the little bed opposite the Russian stove. There Freydele lay, her eyes glazed over and one little hand, one little foot, and the left half of her face continuously twitching. Dineh sat there immobile, absorbing every twitch of Freydele's body into her own. She feared the very act of her own breathing, of interrupting the rhythm of the twitching that continued like a clock, without stop.

The quiet weeping of Mama, Aunt Yakhe, and Aunt Reykhl seemed to her like the moaning of an autumn wind brought to their house from nearby forests through the chimneys . . .

FREYDELE DIES

The eternity of Freydele's death, lasting from quite early on the Sabbath morning until five in the evening, came to an end. Terrified, Dineh opened her large, sad eyes and didn't know where she was or what was happening around her. The wailing of her mother and aunts and also her sisters Malkeh and Soreh and the blacksmith's wife, Khishe, woke her up. When Dineh saw that the little bed was covered up and that everyone was screaming over it, she remembered Freydele and her quiet twitching. In a state of panic she slithered down from the Russian stove and furtively approached the women at the little bed. Not finding Freydele, her panic only increased.

Dineh sensed that because of what had happened to Freydele you weren't allowed to look at her anymore—just like you couldn't get too close to the Torah scrolls that stood behind a thick curtain in the Holy Ark. When candles were lit above Freydele's covered body, Dineh felt more plainly, with even greater clarity, that Freydele had become something you couldn't approach, yes, like the Torah scrolls whose protective curtain you weren't allowed to pull aside, she thought again . . .

Quietly she snuck back to the Russian stove, crawled up, and sat back down in a corner—and from her perch there she saw the little red chest standing on the stove under the beam. She reached for it, pressed it to her child's breast, burst into tears, and sobbed bitterly. Dineh's child's heart now sobbed and sighed as quietly as Freydele's twitching. In her hands Dineh clutched the pieces of sugar she had saved and hidden for Freydele.

Freydele died during the last days of summer. After that a sad autumn crept up on the entire village, and on Sholem's house it was felt even more. Peshe lay in her sickbed and wailed for Freydele. Everyone looked at Dineh with reproach and pity. Dineh herself walked around in a dream state, despondent and lost in thought. Where was Freydele? Why wasn't she here? Why did they take her away, and her little bed too? To all the questions she posed to anyone older than her she received no answer. Died, they told her. But—where was "died"? What was "died"? The word "died" hovered unrelentingly before her, day and night. By day she envisioned that word as a beggar with a large sack who came to play his lyre behind the gate. By night it was a fiery chariot driven by white horses soaring through the hayfields with daisies. She saw Freydele herself, weeping and petrified, in the beggar's voluminous sack, and sometimes radiant in the chariot with the white horses, clothed in a golden dress with a crown of silver ears of wheat on her head . . . But once Dineh rubbed her eyes thoroughly both from her daytime and nighttime dreams and saw Mama lying and weeping, and empty space where Freydele's little bed had stood, the question began again to throb in her mind: Where was Freydele?

By this point Mama no longer went into town. For a long, long time there hadn't been any pieces of candy in Dineh's small chest. She looked for a way to approach Itshe to find an explanation for Freydele's disappearance. She had given away almost all of the sugar cubes to Soreh. But Soreh told tales that Dineh couldn't understand at all. Her stories didn't go anywhere. The characters flew in the air. Soreh's stories about "died" were just useless to Dineh.

WHERE IS "FREYDELE"?

Dineh walked around in a state of agitation and looked for a way to pose her question to Itshe.

Beautiful challahs and rolls had been baked for the Sabbath. When he was reciting the Kiddush blessing, Sholem liked all of his children to be seated around the table. The boys sat around him. On one side was Faytl, the oldest, who by then was studying in a religious school in the shtetl and had come home for the Sabbath. He already had his own little challah and recited the Kiddush on his own. On the other side was Itshe. Daniel, the youngest, also sat at the table and answered amen to the blessing. Throughout, Sholem kept an eye on Dineh. He noticed that she mouthed the Kiddush along with him word for word and answered amen with great concentration. When the challah was distributed after the *ha-Moytse* blessing, he offered Dineh a large piece of bread and listened to her recite the blessing.

"You should have been a boy," he said, seemingly to himself.

Dineh ate the smallest bite of the challah and hid her piece under the tablecloth so that no one would see.

The next day all of the children received small rolls for breakfast. Dineh accepted her roll, put her hand behind her, shuffled backward, and hid the roll with yesterday's piece of *ha-Moytse* in a cupboard drawer. On Sabbath afternoon, when her father went to take a nap and Itshe was lounging on the sofa with a book in hand, Dineh quietly snuck up on him.

"Are you sleeping, Itshe?"

"Where do you see me sleeping?" he answered.

"So then what are you doing?"

"I'm studying."

"What are you studying?"

"Would you understand if I told you? A girl is not allowed to know what boys study."

Dineh felt sick again. If Itshe said that a girl can't know what boys study, he must know what he was talking about. But she also knew that she mustn't miss out on this opportunity.

"Would you like a piece of *ha-Moytse* challah?"

"What gave you the idea that I want a piece of *ha-Moytse* challah?"

"Well, do you want a roll?"

"What kind of a roll?"

"Hold on. You'll see."

Dineh dashed out and quickly returned, holding a large piece of *ha-Moytse* along with an entire roll and two sugar cubes.

"Where did you get all of this?"

"It's all mine. I hid it for you."

"Why all of a sudden for me?"

"Well, because . . . because I want you to eat it."

"In that case—since you want me to—I'll eat it."

Dineh got closer to him and gave him the bread. She touched his head lightly, then began caressing him. "Are you eating?"

"Yes, I'm eating."

"It's yummy, isn't it?"

"Definitely. This roll is really good."

"Will you tell me something?"

"What—a story?"

"No, not a story."

"What, then?"

"Where is Freydele?"

Itshe shuddered when he heard Dineh's question. "Freydele?"

"Yes, Freydele. Where is she?"

"Don't you know already? She died."

"Died?"

"Yes. You know she died."

"But what does 'died' mean? Where is she?"

"She's in heaven."

"In heaven?" Dineh asked, happy and surprised. "How did she get up to heaven?"

"God sent an angel who took her up there."

"With her little bed?"

"No, without her bed."

"You saw this?"

"No, nobody can see such a thing."

"So where is her bed?"

"In the attic."

"And why is Mama crying?"

"Because she misses Freydele."

Dineh stopped to consider this response. "I miss Freydele too, and I cry when no one can see. But you said God sent for her. Does he really need to have her?"

Itshe stayed quiet, thought for a while, and said to himself, "It probably has to be this way." Then, looking at Dineh: "Take your sugar back. Boys don't eat sugar."

Dineh grudgingly accepted the sugar cubes from him. "I don't eat sugar either," she said. She was silent, perplexed. Then she asked, "Could I be a boy?"

"What?! You—a boy? Are you crazy? A girl can't be a boy."

"But I want to be a boy."

"Why?"

"I want to study in religious school like you. I want to know all the stories and everything God does."

"You won't really know unless Mama teaches you. She taught all of us before we went to religious school."

"Well, Mama isn't a boy, that's for sure. So how does she know?"

"Well, it was different with Mama. When Grandma Gitl hired a teacher at home for our uncles, Mama studied with them—just like a boy."

"So I'll go to religious school too and study like a boy."

"Well, then you'll study . . . She thinks studying is so easy . . . Studying is also hard for a boy; it's not just hard for a girl . . . Go away—Papa'll be getting up soon. I have to study *Ethics of the Fathers*. Get lost!"

Dineh stepped away from him, walking backward and looking at him all the while. Now she knew where Freydele was. She quietly left the house, sat under a tree not far from the house, and looked up at the sky. Heaven was so high and far away. Freydele was so far away . . . Between the branches of the naked tree, with their few, trembling leaves, the cold and distance of Freydele's new home—heaven—was reflected. At Dineh's feet, the family's little white dog foraged in the dead leaves—resembling small, dried-out human skulls—that twisted under its playful little feet.

Dineh became eerily despondent and cold. She forcefully pressed her child's knees together. With both elbows resting on her knees, she took her jaw in both of her hands as if they were a frame. Dineh looked ahead, as if into a mirror, at the leaves at her feet. Goldetske raced up to her, licked her hands, and started to kiss her face. Dineh started, as if awakening suddenly from sleep.

From the house the sounds of her father's Sabbath evening prayers drifted over to her. She reminded herself about her conversation with Itshe. He really did know everything. Only boys studied in religious school. And yet Mama also knew how to study. Only she, Dineh, still couldn't study. But she knew her father's Kiddush blessing by heart—and verses from the Psalms too. She didn't know what the words meant, but the melody was so beautiful and sad, and through the melody she sensed that the words were also beautiful and sad. She picked Goldetske up, hugging her. "Are you cold, Goldetske? You're still so tiny," she said. She let her down from her grasp. "Come into the house, Goldetske; we'll listen to Papa say Havdalah and sing '*ha-Mavdil*' and Mama . . ." In remembering her mother Dineh paused to consider, "Well, Mama will cry while she says God of Abraham."

WINTER IN THE VILLAGE

Winter began to settle in the village. In the homes the rhythms of life quickened, the mood brightened. Blue plumes of smoke wafted from the white chimneys over snowy straw roofs with regularity. Paper flowers of all colors, pressed into white padding sprinkled with thin, cut-up pieces of green paper, peered from the windows. They looked like green blades of grass on a white field . . . Coming from two drying facilities found on either end of the village was a steady stream of song and laughter of the young peasant women who worked there drying and scraping the flax. From the stables came the calls of wistful cows standing and dreaming of green meadows in the summertime and feeling heaviness in their bodies from the thrusts of the unborn calves they were carrying. Periodically, truncated, minute sounds—the bleating of the sheep in their stalls—scattered like a funny, childlike, mimicking laughter.

During the evenings the glow of a long, blue, dancing flame burned in rather close proximity to the ceiling, illuminating the little houses with a dark light.

In two of the homes, a circular, powerful light shone. Every evening the girls from the village gathered here to stretch the flax into thin, silky fibers. They moistened their fingers on their lips and quickly and deftly spun the spindles. In a mere matter of moments a long, thin fiber was spun, as if magically, around the spindle. In sync with the stretching of the flax into fibers, the song and resounding laughter coming from young maidens' throats—buttressed by the healthy, joyous voices of men—extended in undulating waves over the snow-white village at night. To those houses where gentile women of the village gathered in the winter evenings to spin flax by the glow of kerosene lamps each had brought with her, young men—both from that village and from neighboring ones—also came. There they found their sweethearts, and the couples spent time together throughout the evening and into the night.

Onto each house an antechamber, with a large bed built into the wall, had been constructed. This was where the young man brought his chosen one to spend time with her. Thus were spun the loves and fortunes of the village youth.

Into the thin flaxen fibers later woven into the fine linen for trousseaus were also woven both the song of a maiden longing for her beloved, the one to whom she had given her heart while spinning the flax, as well as her hope that she would come to sew a fine shirt from this thin linen she was then weaving as a gift for her groom.

On such winter days there wasn't much for the children to do. There were no schools for them, and there was also no work. Those who had shoes or bast shoes woven from hemp plodded through the snow building snowmen, sliding or spinning around, singing and shouting and playing with the dogs next to the houses.

JEWISH CHILDREN AT STUDY

The Jewish children in the settlements studied. Several heads of household pooled their resources to hire a teacher who taught the children of one village for half of a term and then transferred to another village to teach the children there for the other half. In the course of a single term, a teacher sometimes had to eat at the homes of four separate settlers. Wherever the teacher was, that's where the religious school was.

The teachers who arrived in the settlements were not experienced instructors but rather boys themselves who were enrolled in a yeshiva. It was hard for them to make ends meet. They came to a settlement for a term or two. Others were ordinary young men from middle-class backgrounds who studied gradually on their own and, if they didn't have anything else to occupy their time, hired themselves out as teachers in a settlement. Teachers of a higher caliber taught at a religious school in the shtetl or in town and didn't have to go to a settlement.

Religious schools were forbidden, and with study came considerable hardship and fear. At the slightest sound of sleigh bells once lessons had begun terror struck the students and their teacher, not to mention the residents of the house. They proceeded to hide the sacred books they were studying under the comforters and cushions of the beds. Of their own accord, the children scattered like peas—some under the bed, some in a closet, while those old enough to climb went up to the attic. After a few minutes of stifled sound, quiet reigned in the house, as if there weren't a living soul there. The children in hiding lay with bated breath under the beds and in the crevices until the bells went past and their echoes went silent. Only then did everyone emerge from their hiding places and return to the sacred books.

MALKEH LEARNS RUSSIAN

Since the two older boys were studying in religious school in the shtetl, there was now no teacher in Sholem's house. Over time Malkeh, the eldest daughter, had picked up from the boys—when they were home studying with their teachers—how to write Yiddish and to read from the Yiddish translation of the Pentateuch. They even tried to teach her the Pentateuch and the Bible in the original Hebrew, but it was difficult for her to absorb. Besides, Mama always needed her at home to help out with the younger children and with the liquor cellar. Malkeh was the most dedicated child at home and managed the household like an adult. So she was sent to an *uchitel* in the village, where she learned to read and write Russian. This action was taken both because Malkeh was the daughter of Sholem the tavern keeper—and not merely the daughter of Sholem the tavern keeper but also the daughter of Peshe, daughter of Gitele—and because of the family business. Sholem and Peshe could read and write Russian too, but still it really did help to have someone else at home who could sign documents when needed. And with that Malkeh's education ended.

SOREH AND THE LITTLE STORYTELLING BIRD

Things were much worse for Soreh, the younger daughter. Soreh was something of an odd child. It was impossible to knock the letter *alef*—or *beys*, for that matter—into her brain. Peshe struggled to teach Soreh for several terms before she gave up altogether. And with that Soreh's education completely stopped. Everyone knew she was a blockhead. She knew it too, but it didn't bother her. "Big deal, ha, ha, teacher *shmeacher*!" she would scoff, laughing and sticking out her tongue at the religious school students who could read.

But Soreh could throw a punch or two and beat up the strongest boy. Throwing rocks was another thing she did well.

It was storytelling that Soreh did better than anyone else. She would take all the snack portions from the other children, devour them, and promise to repay them with a story. Often she just had them sit down and wait expectantly. The children would ask, "Hey, what's going on? I gave you half my omelet, and you said you'd tell a story."

Her response was, "No, not right now."

"Then why did you eat my omelet?"

"Because I felt like it."

At other times, when she did have a hankering for telling a story, Soreh would sit down and launch into a session that lasted for hours. And even children older than her would listen in astonishment.

Her stories were always fantastical, not of this earth but of the heavens and distant lands. When she would be asked, "How do you know all of these stories when you still can't read books?" Soreh responded that she had a little bird, a little blue bird visible only to her and no one else. The bird was called Danye. Whenever she wanted a story, she went off to the graves that lay not far from the village gate, behind Sholem's gardens, and sat down under a tree and called to the bird by its name. It immediately flew over, as if it had descended directly from heaven. The bird perched on a tree branch so low that Soreh could hear every word it told her. And so it told and continued to tell the most beautiful stories until the bell of the Christian chapel began to toll. Only Danye wasn't allowed to hear the bells tolling. At the sound of the very first toll, Danye picked herself up and flew off, returning to the blue skies. She left Soreh gazing up after her and dreaming up the ending to the unfinished story that the small bird had started to tell. And that's how it always was: whenever she wanted a new story, Soreh summoned Danye the little bird.

The children listened to Soreh's narration. Even the much older ones became confused, not knowing if they should believe her. How could they not believe her when she told the stories with such certainty? Herein lay the proof: the story itself. Because who had ever heard such stories? And how could she have learned them when she couldn't even read?

In this way Soreh wielded supreme power over the children who were smart—and good students to boot. For stories, everyone went to her, and they saved the better food portions for her.

DINEH WANTS TO LEARN

However young she was, Dineh understood the difference between fantasy and serious business. For all of her stories, Soreh didn't speak to Dineh's heart as strongly as did Itshe, who was three years younger than Soreh and three years older than Dineh. She had great trust in Itshe because he studied. He didn't disclose everything, nor did he know everything by heart. When he explained or just talked about something, he did so with calmness, even when he wasn't completely sure of himself. Dineh felt that he understood the holy books that great religious people wrote—and so she felt confident in the explanations he gave.

Dineh too wanted to be able to learn and to know everything Itshe knew—and what Papa held in his mind when he so beautifully and mournfully sang his prayers. But how should she start? There was no teacher at home. When would they hire a teacher? Once she had heard Papa speaking with Mama that the boy was about to turn four, and if all went well, they would need to hire some sort of teacher to start giving him lessons next year.

"And what about Dineh?" Papa asked. "That child has a sponge for a brain. She can repeat the Psalms with me by heart."

"If I weren't so miserable I would have taught her myself. She could have mastered Hebrew long ago. But whenever I so much as look at her I'm overcome with grief."

"Well, you've got to stop thinking and talking like that. It's a sin."

"Well, so—was it her fault? But the heart doesn't want to know what the brain is thinking."

Dineh didn't understand very well all that they were saying, but what pertained to her—that they would need to hire a teacher for her younger brother Daniel in a year—that she *did* understand.

But Hebrew—what was Hebrew? Was that what Papa was saying all the time? She knew the words; the melody too. It was all so beautiful. But without her father she couldn't make out a single word when she took a prayer book and looked inside.

So on that very Sabbath evening when Dineh overheard her parents' conversation she decided that she had to know how to study and she had to find a way to reach Mama's despondent heart. Several days later—it was a quiet, white day when the snow was softly falling—Dineh was sitting, as she was wont to do on such days, with her forehead pressed against a windowpane counting the snowflakes. She was watching them fall so serenely, landing on the window for an instant and then disappearing, when she heard someone calling her. Dineh turned away from the window. Mama was calling her. "Dineh, why don't you play with Daniel? He's getting in the way underfoot and has nothing to do. Call him and tell him some kind of story or put on your coat and go out into the garden, into the snow for a while."

Dineh screwed up her courage and approached Mama. When she was right next to her, she reached out to touch her hand. Peshe looked at her for a long time and, with a heavy sigh, caressed her head. "Dinehle, do you want to tell me something?"

"Mama, I want to tell you that . . . that if you'd teach me to read—just like Itshe and Papa—so that I could read the prayer book I could then teach Daniel. We could always study together, and I'd know everything I could possibly want to know. Just like Itshe . . ."

Mama went silent for a long time. Dineh kept her eyes fixed on her and waited for a response. "Good, we'll see. It's time for Daniel to learn the *alef-beys*. The older kids had already learned it at his age too," Mama finally said.

Dineh was startled for a moment but then quickly came to her senses. "Do you want to teach Daniel and me together?"

"Let's see. I'll start with him. You could sit on the side. You'll help him if you know it better than he does. He's still just a little kid, after all."

Overjoyed, Dineh said, "I'll teach him everything. I'll teach Soreh too."

WITH THE *ALEF-BEYS*

On a Saturday evening, after Havdalah, at the start of a full week ahead, Peshe took Daniel and Dineh and sat them down at the table over a large Hebrew alphabet set pasted onto a board. Each letter looked out at them like a fully formed figure with its own special background and lineage. Dineh sat down with joy and fear in her child's heart. Her large brown eyes were moist with joy.

Daniel sat and waited for the money that the angel would throw down from heaven to the boys who mastered the Hebrew alphabet.

Mama pointed to the board. "Daniel, say '*alef*'! Call it out: *alef*!"

Daniel shouted, "*Alef! Alef!*" and kept looking up at the ceiling.

Dineh kept her eyes fastened on the letters, waiting for Daniel to return to the board and master the *alef* so they could proceed with the lesson. But Daniel was hardly interested. He looked up at the ceiling and parroted the *alef* mechanically until he could no longer restrain himself. "Where's the kopeck?"

"What kopeck?"

"The one the angel throws down from heaven when a little boy learns the *alef-beys*."

"Now look at the *alef-beys* here on the table. If you focus on the letters and really study them, the angel will throw down a kopeck for you."

Daniel lowered his eyes to the table. He looked at the *alef-beys* and shouted even louder, "*Alef! Alef!*" He kicked Dineh under the table.

"Shout: *alef!*"

And onto the table a few kopecks fell. Daniel blushed and then quickly turned pale. "The angel! I studied good!" he said, scooping up both kopecks with his little hands.

"No, Danielke, the kopecks are for both of you. One for you, and one for Dineh."

"No! The angel doesn't give money to a girl," Daniel responded.

"Yes he does. One for Dineh and one for you, because she can study now too."

Begrudgingly, Daniel gave Dineh one of the kopecks. She took the coin into her hand, looked at it for a long time, and closed her fist around it. She would hide it, she decided.

That night Dineh had a hard time falling asleep. The letters of the *alef-beys* and the kopeck under her pillow spun around before her. She had to ask Itshe: Did the angel throw down kopecks through the ceiling? Did angels in the sky have money too? Dineh might not have liked it, but who knows, maybe they did it so that children would want to study. As for Dineh, well, she would have studied without money. She really did need to ask Itshe.

When Dineh and Daniel began to study, the household was infused with a new lease on life. The days that followed were short, and with the hustle and bustle of the household concerns and chores they passed quickly. When evening came the lamp was lit, bathing the entire kitchen in a warm glow. Dineh was the first one ready for the lessons, waiting for Mama with the prayer book under her arm.

Mama finished up her household duties. Teaching the children was now a daily task for her. Her spirits were a bit better, and she was sighing less often. Both a sense of interest and a certain satisfaction were evident on her face. Just four and a half years old, Daniel was absorbing the lessons quite well. He was stringing words together and reciting the blessings by heart. Or rather, he was reciting the blessings by heart by copying Dineh. In linking the words, Daniel looked over at Dineh more than he looked down into the prayer book. The angel threw down kopecks, and occasionally a candy. After the children's beginner Hebrew lessons had become somewhat routine, the angel forgot and didn't throw anything down from heaven. When Daniel started to demand, "Hey, what's going on? I'm studying good!" a sugar cube did occasionally descend. Just as a mother weaned her child, so the angel began to wean Daniel from the kopecks until Daniel was disgusted altogether by the whole thing and stopped accepting the sugar cubes. The angel could keep the sugar for himself, he said.

For a long time Dineh had spotted Mama lifting her hand just when Daniel was looking into the prayer book and then tossing the kopecks onto the table. She felt quite insulted by the whole practice, but she didn't breathe a word about it to Daniel. On the contrary, she gave him her own kopecks. Dineh was content to be able to sit next to the prayer book and study. She felt her world being enriched on a daily basis with new words that only yesterday had been unknown to her and that she was now absorbing so fully that they were becoming a part of her possessions.

In this way, the winter passed.

At home the normal pace of life was restored. On Friday nights, when the two boys had come home for the Sabbath and Mama had baked small challahs for them to recite Kiddush, Dineh and Daniel sat with them like grownups. There was even a small challah for Daniel. Dineh sat happily, as if through her another Jew had been added to the world. That Daniel could read the words in the prayer book and knew them by heart was something Dineh had taken upon herself to bring about. It was Dineh who reviewed with him what they both studied with Mama.

After Sabbath dinner, when Dineh found Itshe sitting somewhere off by himself reading a book or just lounging on the sofa, she would go up to him and quietly ask, "Would you like to hear how I already know how to learn?"

His answer was almost always the same. "Learn? Is that what you call it? Just because you can sound out a few letters you think that's learning? Well, what about the Pentateuch and Rashi's commentary—do you know them?"

At that moment, Dineh felt very small indeed. As if to defend herself, she'd say, "I will too know. Mama's going to start teaching me the Psalms in Yiddish, and she said that in a year they'll hire a teacher."

Itshe wanted to get rid of her. "Well, good, so then you'll know."

Dineh slid closer to him. "I'm afraid of a teacher. They say he hits the kids. Does your teacher hit you?"

"He doesn't hit me."

"Why?"

"Because I'm a good student."

"And the kids who aren't good students—does he hit them?"

"He does sometimes hit them, but not hard. My teacher is sick; he doesn't have the strength to hit hard."

"Sick? So if he were healthy, would he hit hard?"

"Sure, he'd hit hard," Itshe said gruffly. "But if you study hard he won't hit you!"

"I'll study hard so he won't hit me."

Then she remembered that Daniel wasn't a good student, and she said, as if to herself, "Maybe our teacher will also be sick . . ."

A TEACHER ARRIVES

Soon after the holidays, a teacher—a blond, unmarried young man—arrived from a neighboring town to stay in Sholem's house.

The religious school group was cobbled together from the children of three villages. It was decided that during the first term the children would study in Sholem's house.

The children from the two neighboring villages who were brought to Sholem for the term included Aunt Yakhe's two children from the hamlet of Stanki, Sholem of Ostrovok's three children from the neighboring village of Ostrovok, and Peyse the blacksmith's two grandchildren.

The students were of various ages. Aunt Yakhe's daughter Rive was the oldest. The second oldest was Mirke, daughter of Fayvl the blacksmith, also from Stanki. The two girls, although they were quite big, still didn't know the *alef-beys*. Fayvl the blacksmith only had daughters. Aunt Yakhe and her husband, Leybl the tavern keeper, had sons, but they were all grown and almost all had left home—to America, to Babruĭsk, or to complete their military service for the tsar. Their daughter Rive was the youngest, and Aunt Yakhe, who didn't know the prayers herself, nevertheless wanted her daughter to know them. At long last the opportunity had presented itself for the first time for her to send Rive to a religious school.

Sholem of Ostrovok's children were all boys. Berl and Shloymke were eight-year-old twins. Berl, who was older by ten minutes, was called Young Man. He had another nickname too: Berele the Ringworm Fella. As a child, he'd had ringworm, leaving his scalp covered in bald spots. Shloymke, the younger twin, stuttered, and he was called Stutterer. And their little brother, Hayemke, all of six years old, was called Little Firehead because he had flaming-red hair. His nose was always running. Peyse the blacksmith's grandchildren were Henye, a girl the same age as Dineh, and a boy, Meyer, the same age as Daniel.

The knowledgeable students in the religious school were Sholem's two children, Dineh and Daniel. Well . . . Daniel not as much as Dineh. She pronounced Hebrew well and could recite entire chapters of the Psalms with Yiddish translation. Mama stood Dineh up in front of the entire school so the teacher could quiz her.

By nature, Dineh was quiet and shy. Now, in front of so many children and the teacher, she was even shyer. But with all of her strength and trusting child's heart, Dineh resolved to recite the Psalms and recite them well so that both the teacher and the children would be pleased. If they liked her recitation they would all study the Psalms together, with the melody and with the Yiddish translation. And it would all sound so beautiful. She inhaled deeply, like someone poised to dive into cold river waters, and began her recitation—trembling at first, and then a bit more boldly:

Ashre—fortunate is; *ha-ish*—the man; *asher*—who; *lo halakh*—didn't go; *ba-atsat*—under the influence of; *reshaim*—the wicked; *uve-derekh*—and in the ways of; *hataim*—of the sinners; *lo amad*—didn't stand; *uve-moshav*—and in the company of; *letsim*—scoffers; *lo yashav*—he did not sit . . .

And on and on, chapter after chapter. Everyone sat around the table and listened in amazement to Dineh's melodic recitation of the words. Suddenly Hayemke, Sholem of Ostrovok's son, let out a shriek and then started to cry and wail. "Shloymke—pinched—me—really—hard—on—my—leg! He kept kicking me and wouldn't leave me alone!"

From the other side, Meyerke said, "He kicked me under the table too and wouldn't let me listen . . ."

The teacher, not much older than the oldest student, Rive, looked around, in fact taking in the figure of this large, dark girl with her high bosom and shaggy, black hair, and blushed, saying, "Come on, children; you've all seen how Dinehle learns. Now we'll see who else can learn that way."

Dineh lit up with joy. "Dinehle"—no one had called her this before. She would study hard. The teacher wouldn't hit her. No, this kind of teacher—he wouldn't hit anyone. He was shy. She took out a prayer book and a Pentateuch and sat down next to Daniel. He took a look at the prayer book and at the teacher and shouted, "I don't want to learn with a teacher!"

The teacher blushed again and said, "Daniel, you need to learn with a teacher. You're a big boy now." Dineh wanted to resolve the impasse and responded to both of them, "What Daniel means is that he wants to learn with me from the same prayer book. We always study together," she said, stroking his sleeve. "Right, Daniel?"

Daniel didn't answer. The teacher began to test each student separately. It turned out that of the nine students, four didn't know the *alef-beys*. Avreml could spell words, and four of the students needed to study the Pentateuch. Dineh was not pleased; she had thought things would be different. She had envisioned before her all of the students seated around the table with Pentateuchs and Bibles in their hands studying in unison with the same melody. And now it looked like the children didn't even know the *alef-beys*. Rive was already quite big, practically bigger than the teacher, and she still didn't know anything. She, Dineh, would teach her when no one was looking. That way Rive wouldn't have to be ashamed, and she too would be able to learn with the children who were in the group studying the Pentateuch.

Henye, the grandchild of their neighbor the blacksmith, was the same age as Dineh. She never dared play with Henye because the two families were feuding. To be sure, the feud was one sided—from Sholem the tavern keeper's side. The aristocratic Peshe could never bring herself to allow her children to play with the blacksmith's children. Dineh's heart would ache with longing for the old, bent little house, the one behind their garden, to the side of the sandpits.

BLIND SOREH-ROKHL AND HER SON, LEYBKE

In Dineh's childish fantasies, the blacksmith's little house was a place filled with promise and magic. There the old woman Blind Soreh-Rokhl lived. She was the size of a ten-year-old child, and people said that she could exorcise the evil eye, a shock, or a bad stroke of fortune and roll away panic. In other words, if someone were sick from fear, she took soft bread and rolled it over the sick person's belly and chanted a magical incantation until the fear departed and he became healthy again.

People also said that Soreh-Rokhl wept away her eyesight. She had had a husband and eight children. During a period when typhus raged she lost her husband and six children. She cried so much that her eyes were ruined. But she succeeded in raising two very attractive and successful children, a son, Leybke, and a daughter, Tsipoyreh. When her son turned twenty-one, he was conscripted into the Russian military service to become a soldier. Because he was so tall and in such good health he was assigned to serve in a guard regiment.

Whenever Leybke returned home on furlough, the entire region went topsy-turvy. His old mother didn't begrudge herself the pleasure of gazing upon him. Soreh-Rokhl came up close to him, lifted her red, ruined eyes to his face and his head with its lovely forelocks, and felt his uniform, including the epaulets. She then turned to the side, spat three times, and said, "May no evil eye come to harm him . . ."

When more people came into the house, or after he had gone away and then returned, Soreh-Rokhl approached him when he was asleep to ward off the evil eye. Often, when Leybke caught his mother in the act of such "theft," he would grasp her by the hand and pull her close to give her a kiss. "What are you up to, Mama? Are you warding off the evil eye again? Even the devil himself won't take a bad guy like me."

At the mention of the word "devil" Soreh-Rokhl would shudder and spit three times. "God forbid, my child. How can you say such things?"

"Mama, you should see how the evil eye gets warded off in the regiment—with mounted Cossacks riding during maneuvers, bayonets extended, and their horses flying like demons so that the ground shakes beneath their feet. They jump over the fence just as if they were torn from the earth together with you, and there you are in unison with them, riding as one. When you're up in the air like that, you feel like you won't make it back to earth in one piece . . . At the beginning, my insides turned upside down. Now that I'm used to it, it's no big deal. I can ride with the best of them. I'll show them who Leybke is. *Zshidlik*, that's what they call me. For them, it's beneath their dignity to have a Jew in their unit. They see themselves as the real Cossacks and aren't at all pleased at having a Jew doing what they're doing."

When he suddenly felt his mother's gaunt, practically childlike hands trembling—like a fish removed from water—in his own, Leybke thought about what he'd just said and burst into laughter. "Just listen to your silly son jabbering on like a little kid. Mama, it's nothing. Why are you trembling, Mama? Don't you see how nothing happened to me? I've grown there—I'm taller and bigger."

Soreh-Rokhl spit three times and said, "No evil eye."

"Well, fine, Mama, 'no evil eye'—so be it. But stop trembling so much over me."

"Yes, my child, may everything turn out well. You don't know the kind of nights I've had since they've taken you away. Sometimes one type of dream, sometimes another. One night I see you beside me, like right now; and another time—may it happen to all empty forests. With God's help you'll serve out your military service and find yourself a good bride, get married, and replace your father, may he rest in peace, at his workbench. I just want you to have a long life. Since your father left this world the village hasn't had a proper shoemaker. When the gentile women run into me they console me, saying, 'Dearest Soreh-Rokhl, soon your Leybke will come back from military service, get married, and settle down at home. Then the village will once again have good boots, and you'll have a bit of peace in your old age.' I bless them and say, 'Amen, from your mouths, excuse the comparison, to God's ears.' May God not punish me for this. When the heart longs for a drop of comfort . . . Tsipoyrehle, no evil eye, is by now a big girl, but here we are—two females without a man at home."

"Well, good, Mama, you look for a fine bride for me here, and in eighteen months, when I get back home, everyone will see that you now have a man in the house. And the gentile women, your fortunetellers, will have real boots. It won't take me long to remember everything Papa and Benye in Kapyl′ taught me. The rich ladies and the girls with plenty of money used to go crazy for a pair of Leybke's low boots."

"Just like your father you've got hands of gold, may no evil eye hurt you, and may you live a long life."

Leybke returned to military service a happy man. The entire population accompanied him on his way out of village—both gentiles and Jews. Everyone wished him a safe return.

Only Leybke never returned.

Various stories circulated about his sudden death. One soldier—a Jew from his regiment—wrote that Leybke was killed by a horse during maneuvers. Others said that drunken soldiers beat him, shattering his lungs, and that he died three days later.

Soreh-Rokhl, with her ruined eyes, received a large envelope with a black border and two large red signatures embedded in sealing wax and a painted eagle. She was summoned to the administrative office in the nearby shtetl of Romanow.

When Soreh-Rokhl heard that she was being ordered to Romanow to retrieve an official notice, she knew it was time to weep . . .

TSIPOYREH

Thus, Soreh-Rokhl wept through the next few years—until Tsipoyreh was grown. With her daughter's maturation, the house—where the very windows, the walls, and each straw on the roof had absorbed so much lamentation over the course of so many years—was brought back to life, like an invalid miraculously healed after being sick for many years. Sometimes a voice could even be heard coming from the young woman's throat, accompanied by laughter, and from her heart—by way of a gentile love song, filled with yearning, or a Jewish folk song.

At first the windows, the walls, and the straw on the roof—like old, weeping Soreh-Rokhl herself—shuddered in shock at the young voice. But gradually they became accustomed to the young life blossoming in their midst. White curtains appeared in the windows, and when they were parted, vases filled with flowers gazed out. Tsipoyreh hung pictures in beautiful, colored frames on the walls—of old aunts and uncles, as well as a portrait of Leybke mounted on a horse dressed in his military uniform with epaulets.

Gazing upon that portrait, Soreh-Rokhl wept for so long until she reached a kind of peace. While knitting a sock for a peasant man or woman in the village, she would just sit and stare vacantly with her ruined eyes and dream . . . Everything had become all muddled in Soreh-Rokhl's mind to the point where she didn't know whether dream was reality or whether reality was dream. Tsipoyreh, who had quickly mastered sewing while studying with Sorke the tailor woman in Romanovka, was now a fine seamstress, and the gentile women adored her. She had a great connection with them: having been raised as they had been, she sang like them, and like them had a flair for material and beautiful things. She knew about their loves and tragedies. She sewed clothes for them and loved to sing all the while.

When Tsipoyreh was seventeen years old she already had a groom. His name was Perets, and he was the son of a shoemaker from another village. Perets was handsome, blond, and a good worker. They had been sweethearts since childhood. When Tsipoyreh was eighteen, they got married. Perets's parents were good, honest, poor folk who supported the match. After all, Tsipoyreh was a beautiful, healthy young woman and a good earner. From the start Perets held a claim on a work domain—a village.

Soreh-Rokhl had lived to experience a bit of parental pride in her old age. If her husband, Avrom, may he rest in peace, had lived, she thought he too would have been pleased with the match.

Avrom the shoemaker and Perets's father had been friends in their youth. They had also studied together in religious school and apprenticed together with the same shoemaker.

The wedding was a humble affair, but a lively group gathered to celebrate. People attended both out of friendship and compassion. Peasants and their wives came to wish the bride and groom a long and happy life and Soreh-Rokhl much parental pride in her old age. Each guest brought a wedding gift based on what they could afford. One gentile woman offered a piece of thin linen; another, a cup of millet. Someone gave a dozen eggs and even a living rooster and a hen to boot—so that the young couple would be fruitful and multiply . . . Other gentile women brought more refined gifts. One presented an embroidered towel; another, a piece of thin, embroidered linen for a nightshirt; a third, a lovely, pleated, colored apron, a shawl with all sorts of flowers. The Jewish attendees also gave generously, both out of compassion and because it was a mitzvah.

The couple lived in harmony, content as doves. It was bright and warm at home. In the vestibule, Perets sat in his workshop, rhythmically hammering nails and singing to himself. In the other room, Tsipoyreh sat over her sewing machine, blossoming like a young rose, sewing flowered dresses for the gentile women of the village and backing up Perets in his singing. Both were young and blond—and sang beautifully. Singing was a shared language for them, something they instinctively understood about each other. Each knew the song the other loved, and both of their voices blended together into a single song.

Soreh-Rokhl carried on with bated breath and guarded this joy with a trembling heart. Looking from Tsipoyreh to Perets with her cried-out eyes, she thanked God and pleaded with him not to disturb this joy. She prayed that her home, which had known so much misfortune, would also get to see a new generation and happiness.

On Friday night, when Perets sat down to the Sabbath table to recite the Kiddush blessing, Tsipoyreh's eyes took him in with endless love. Here was her husband making Kiddush . . . Here was her husband seated at the table . . . There was a man, the master of the house, seated at the head of the table . . .

Soreh-Rokhl thanked God that there was a man at home who could recite the Kiddush to which she could answer amen, that she could take the *ha-Moytse* from a man's hand . . . And if she hadn't been destined by God to experience this either with her husband or her son—well, thank God for this. Here was a capable, talented artisan who respected her, not so much as allowing her to place the smallest piece of kindling in the oven or carry a bucket of water. "Mother-in-Law, put it down. What am I here for? Go back to your socks, or better yet, rest up," he'd say. And he practically carried Tsipoyreh in his arms. So yes, thanks be to God. And for all his youth, he already loved to recite a chapter of the Psalms after supper.

Avrom's religious books were still at home. Perets looked in them from time to time. During the reading of the weekly Torah portion on the Sabbath, he was honored with a prestigious call to the Torah. Sometimes even with the maftir, the most prestigious reading of all.

With the peasants in the village, Perets was quite the influential figure. They turned to him like a brother and depended on him. There was never a question of bargaining with him. For them, Perets was an honest Yid. He didn't overcharge; he didn't trick them.

TSIPOYREH GETS PREGNANT

When Tsipoyreh began to complain of violent nausea and headaches in the third year of their marriage, a sense of euphoria took hold in their home. Joy, apprehension, and commotion.

"You've got to put aside the sewing and the machine," Perets shouted in a mock-angry tone. "Do you hear me, Tsipoyreh? Immediately, right here and now! What—don't I earn enough for you? Do you lack for anything at home, God forbid? Do it for me; put aside the work right away!"

Blushing slightly, Tsipoyreh said to him: "What's the matter with you, Perets? Have I ever, God forbid, complained that I lacked for anything? You're a fool, Perets. When I didn't have anything to do, I sewed. Did it hurt me? But now since you don't want me to, I won't sew anymore. I'll finish up the work I've got on hand—and that'll be it."

Perets leapt from his workshop stool, flung aside his hammer, ran over to Tsipoyreh, and lifted her from the chair.

"Put it down, Tsipoyreh. Today we're not going to work."

He embraced her, kissed her on the lips, and began to dance with her. He whirled and twirled her all over the house.

Tsipoyreh struggled in his grip.

"Let me go, Perets. Have you gone crazy? You should be ashamed of yourself acting this way in front of Mama."

Soreh-Rokhl pleaded, "Children, God is with you. Let her go. Can't you see that you're making her dizzy and she's getting nauseous?"

Perets got frightened and led her to bed. "Well, good. Sit down and rest. You're not working at that machine anymore."

Soreh-Rokhl interjected. "Don't make such a fuss. People don't have to know," she spat three times. "An angry eye, God forbid, an evil eye . . ."

"Well, how are you going to keep it a secret, Mother-in-Law? You can't hide a cat in a bag for very long."

"God willing, when there's something to see, they'll see it, but making a commotion out on the streets before there's anything to see—that's just not advisable."

"Of course," Tsipoyreh agreed, "Mama's right."

"Well," Perets said good-naturedly, "you women . . . I'd like to know when you're not right . . ."

When Tsipoyreh began to feel the first pangs of pain, Perets and Soreh-Rokhl were beside themselves. More than once Soreh-Rokhl cried during the night, pleading with God for the life and well-being of her child and the new life Tsipoyreh was to bring into the world. Gradually Tsipoyreh started feeling better, and everything returned to the way it had been. If previously it had been accompanied by the whir of the sewing machine, now the hammer was alone in its noisemaking. Its pounding could be heard with greater clarity and certainty. Covered by a white cloth, the sewing machine rested.

Perets's singing became more cheerful. Tsipoyreh didn't always join in with him. Her gaze was now directed more inward than out. The warm joy that enveloped her entire body radiated from her pensive eyes. When at times she felt Perets's eyes upon her in prolonged scrutiny, Tsipoyreh would blush and turn her head. Through her shy glances, she conveyed to Perets the gladness she carried within herself. They both felt the joy of pregnancy, the joy of the coming new life that would bind them even closer together.

OFF TO BAKE MATZOS

That year Passover eve fell during a time when the roads were not very passable. It was difficult to drive a sleigh because the ice broke in many spots and water submerged the rails. Driving a vehicle with wheels was even more challenging as the roads were slippery. Still, matzo had to be baked for Passover, regardless of whether the road conditions were good or bad.

Each year the Passover matzo baking was held in Sholem's house. People from all of the villages gathered there to bake matzos for their settlements. When the time for baking arrived Perets said he would go and that Tsipoyreh and her mother should stay at home. Tsipoyreh insisted on going too. She had time on her hands, she said; she could roll dough just like everyone else. She was just at the beginning of the ninth month, and in her case the pregnancy was not so conspicuous.

The thought of going off by himself and leaving Tsipoyreh alone did not appeal to Perets. Turning to Soreh-Rokhl, he asked, "Mother-in-Law, what do you say?"

Soreh-Rokhl too wanted Tsipoyreh to go. It would be more fun for her. She'd be with young people and get a little time to revitalize herself. "But Perets, see to it that they bake your matzos first and then come straight home for the Sabbath. And how will you travel—with a sleigh?"

"Ivan's a better driver than I am. He promised to harness the horses and take me there."

Perets left carrying a bag of flour from the warehouse. Ivan soon drove up with a wagon.

Perets and Tsipoyreh said goodbye to Soreh-Rokhl, ordering her, for God's sake, not to sleep alone but to call Paraska, the neighbor's older gentile woman servant. "She'll milk the cow and stay the night," they said. And with that they left.

The distance between the two neighboring villages was no more than two and a half versts. On the Sabbaths people went to prayer services without an eruv. When the roads were frozen children slid on the lake from one village to another in about fifteen minutes. During summers they cut through the fields shot through with springs in about twenty minutes. But now, before Passover, due to the difficult road conditions, they had to circumvent both the springs and the lake. Instead they drove through a small forest, where the road was narrower and longer but nevertheless safer because there were trees on both sides of the road and you could see where you were going.

They focused on the driving as they rode along on the road to the forest. The wheels regularly sank into the broken ice, but there was no danger. The horses were driving well, and the burden wasn't heavy. They would arrive without a hitch.

But just at that very moment, wolves—tens of them, traveling in pairs—appeared as they were crossing through from one side of the forest to the other. Ivan might not have noticed the wolves if the horses hadn't suddenly reared up and begun to turn the wagon back in the direction of home. Terrified, he let out a shout: "*Volki!*"

He quickly got down from the wagon, pulled hay from it, and lit a match.

There was smoke and then flames. The wolves quickly began to run away. Before long they had vanished into the forest.

The horses calmed down. Ivan spat on the ground after the wolves and tossed a few vulgar curses in their direction. They resumed their journey.

Alarmed, Perets glanced over at Tsipoyreh. "How are you? Should I turn back?"

"Where will you go? We're practically at Sholem's house."

"This is nothing for you?"

"It's nothing. I'll survive. Just a small scare, but it's nothing."

In Sholem's yard and around the stables, wagons and sleighs from the neighboring villages, loaded with bags of flour and new kegs, were lined up. And there were little girls and boys and young couples too—the atmosphere was festive. People were chatting, laughing, inquiring after each other's health and their families.

A NAMESAKE FOR LEYBKE

Perets ordered Ivan to stop the wagon at the house. He wanted to finish as quickly as possible and send Ivan back so he wouldn't be late in getting home.

Tsipoyreh was getting ready to disembark from the wagon when she felt a sharp back pain. But she fought it off. Turning to help her get down, Perets noticed her stiffness. "What's wrong, Tsipoyreh?"

"I don't know. My back hurts."

"Come inside. I'll ask Peshe. She'll put you to bed. It'll pass, you'll see."

"No, you don't have to. Don't say anything. It'll pass this way too. The wolves just frightened me."

He led her by the hand and they went inside.

Peshe greeted them. "Good evening. I haven't seen you in so long. Tsipoyreh, how are you? How is your mother?"

"Thank you for asking. My mother sends you regards."

Tsipoyreh wanted to continue, but suddenly she was gripped by such pain that she held on to Peshe with both hands. Biting down on her lips, she could barely manage to get out, "I'm dying."

Perets turned white with fear. He took her by the hand while Peshe held open the door of the room. He led her inside. Peshe helped her down onto the bed. "How far along are you? What month?"

"Based on my calculation, the beginning of the ninth month."

"The beginning of the ninth month? A lot you kids know." Turning to Perets she said, "Leave the room. See to it that they don't start baking. It'll be all right if they start a little later. Tell Yakhe to come here."

"Peshinke, I want my aunt Khishe. Oh dear, my mother's at home. I'm going to die . . ."

"Die, shmay! How many women's hides have you seen on fences? Die . . . nothing's going to happen to you. Enough with the fun and games. You're now in the third year of your marriage. I had my first after eleven months, may you all live long lives."

Terrible pains seized Tsipoyreh. She screamed. Soon Yakhe entered with Khishe. A terrified Perets remained behind the door. "Maybe we need the medical practitioner. Someone can go get him," he said.

"Go away. If we need you, someone will come get you. Real high and mighty, these kids today. The medical practitioner—nothing less for the likes of them. You'll have it on your own. Don't worry; you have a healthy little wife, no evil eye."

As if magically, the house turned quiet.

Everyone who had gathered to bake matzos vanished as if an incantation had been invoked. Only the quiet footsteps of the three women and the screams of the woman in childbirth could be heard in the house. Bright fires heating large pots of water blazed in the oven and the Russian stove. The women wore wide, white aprons and white kerchiefs over their hair and waited like experts for whatever was about to happen.

After a few hours of terrible pain, the cries of a newborn baby resounded through the house. Peshe came out of the room looking for Perets. He was standing in a corner of the synagogue room and shaking. She approached him and offered her congratulations.

"Come here, Papa! What did you want—a girl or a boy?"

Overjoyed and terrified, Perets said, "A boy, a girl—do I care? For me, it'd be fine to have both at once. But how is Tsipoyreh?"

"She'll be making a bris. You have a son, Perets. A fine young man."

"Thank God. Thank you, Peshe. Thank you."

"Go inside."

In the morning, the bedroom was draped with pieces of paper containing the text of Psalm 121 to dispel the evil spirits during childbirth. In the large synagogue room, folks baked matzo and whispered among themselves. One by one they went in to see the new mother and offer her congratulations.

While baking matzos, no one could make noise or carry on as usual. If someone started to sing Perets soon broke in and asked him to be quiet. There's a new mother right there, just beyond that wall, he said. They cracked all kinds of jokes with double entendres about Perets—that he wasn't good at calculating months and days and the like. In the end the mood was more festive, thanks to the new mother.

On the second day Sholem had the horses hitched and sent for Soreh-Rokhl. She arrived, barely alive, from both terror and joy.

Until she took in the young mother and child with her ruined eyes and touched them with her small, childlike hands, Soreh-Rokhl didn't believe the good news herself. When she returned to her senses from her state of euphoria, she cried softly for a little while and thanked God. Then, taking care that no one except the new mother and child were in the room, she exorcised the evil eye and placed her fingers on the pieces of paper with Psalm 121 and piously brought them to her lips.

In the ten days since Perets and Tsipoyreh had left home, so much had happened. Now Perets would be returning with a newborn son and a parcel of matzos for Passover. The path was clear—there were no more wolves coming toward them. Joy seemingly smiled back at them from the roads themselves.

Their son was named Avrom-Leyb after his grandfather and his uncle, Leybke, who had gone to complete his term of military service and was never seen again. But Avrom-Leyb was called Leybke. Leybke was easier on the tongue.

Leybke grew up handsome and clever, showing aptitude at the occupations of both his father and his mother. As soon as he began to crawl around the floor he found his mother's sewing machine. Since his mother wasn't using the machine anymore, Leybke started using it, turning the wheel, dragging down the band, pulling everything out of the boxes—until they had to take the machine out of the house and store it in the attic. But Leybke hated to go empty-handed. Once they took the sewing machine away from him he went straight over to the tools of his father's trade. He crawled over to the workshop, took the shoemaker's thread, and dragged down the box of nails, scattering them all over the floor. When they took the nails away from him he starting making a racket—until his father found a solution. Perets took Leybke onto his knee, banging the hammer and singing. Leybke enjoyed this very much indeed, and he tried to sing along with his father. Tsipoyreh sang along with them, and all was merry.

But Perets had to work. And banging the hammer with Leybke was not going to get boots made. They tried a variety of ways to take him out of the workshop. But Leybke was determined to find a trade. Going empty-handed simply went against his nature. And if it wasn't going to be his father's workshop, then it could even be his grandmother's trade: socks and knitting. As soon as he saw his grandmother dozing at her work or that she had put the sock aside for a while, Leybke materialized on the spot. He dragged out the knitting needles down to the very last one and unraveled the entire sock, pulling the wool as quickly as possible. Before he would be caught in the act . . .

In this way the house was full with worry and laughter because of little Leybke. They practically shouted at him. "Oh, Leybke, what're we going to do with you? What a rascal!"

When she heard those words, the boy's grandmother started to tremble. "What do you have against the child, poor thing?!"

When Leybke studied well in religious school, Perets said, "Well, Mother-in-Law, I'm afraid that Leybke won't be a shoemaker . . ."

When she heard that, Soreh-Rokhl responded: "Whatever he'll be—it doesn't matter. As long as he's an honest Jew. His grandfather, may he rest in peace, was a shoemaker, and you, Perets, are a shoemaker too. As long as you have a long life and good fortune, being a shoemaker is nothing to be ashamed of."

"Who said anything about shame? Am I ashamed of my profession? God forbid. I just mean that the child has a good head on his shoulders. He'll probably go to the *gymnasia* and become modern."

"Modern?" Tsipoyreh interjected. "And what will the modern folk do without work? They want to rebuild the world, after all, because there are so many scoundrels, so many *darmoyedas*. They want everyone to work."

"Yes, for that we need big thinkers, sharp minds. Learned people have to be free of the *darmoyedas* in order to establish a new world order."

"Can our Leybele help establish a new world?" Tsipoyreh asked, as if in a dream.

"Who knows?"

"May no evil eye harm him," added Soreh-Rokhl, spitting out three times.

THE LITTLE GIRL WHO WOULDN'T BE BORN

Eight years had passed since Leybke was born on the eve of baking matzos in Ugli. Everything was going smoothly in Perets's house when, once more, Tsipoyreh didn't feel well. "There's a dull feeling below my heart," she complained. Joy once again swept through the house.

"It's time, isn't it?"

By this time Leybke was in religious school in Romanow. Time passed, and before they knew it, it was time to get ready. This time Tsipoyreh didn't give birth on the eve of Passover. There was no need to leave town.

It was the beginning of June. The cherry tree behind the little house was blossoming. The scent wafted all the way into the house itself.

The cradle was taken down from the attic, washed, and set up so that everything would be ready when needed at the happy time.

The good hour finally arrived. It was a Friday night. Tsipoyreh felt the first pangs of pain. Soreh-Rokhl did what was needed. It took a long time. Tsipoyreh's uterus had been sealed for nine years.

"It'll be harder. Daughter, we'll have to wait."

Tsipoyreh steeled herself, speaking words of self-encouragement in the process, but the long, dry spasms of pain were relentless. Soreh-Rokhl told Perets to call in Ivan's wife to light a fire on the hearth and boil some water.

Daylight came. Tsipoyreh hadn't moved at all except from the spasms of pain that gripped her for a long time, leaving her soaked in sweat and anxiety. It was Sabbath morning. Someone went into the next village to call Peshe. She came on foot. After taking one look at Tsipoyreh, Peshe ordered someone to go to the shtetl to fetch the unlicensed medical practitioner. As soon as he arrived the medical practitioner tried one procedure after another, to no avail. He declared the situation very grim.

Perets was sent back to Ugli to recite the Psalms at prayer services. On Saturday evening someone ran to a larger shtetl to fetch an obstetrician. When he arrived he said there was nothing to be done. The expectant mother screamed but no longer with all of her strength. Her screams were becoming wilder. Her entire body was now blue and her face spasmodic, swollen. Her eyes were bulging and bloodshot. The veins in her arms jutted out like blue whips. She wept and pleaded for relief. Gradually her voice became weaker and weaker. From time to time, an animal scream erupted from her throat, as if it were trying to rip through the very earth itself to reach the deepest depths of the Great Abyss. And then she would quiet down and fall into a soft wailing. This continued until midnight, until the good Mother Earth yielded and opened her gates for her exhausted child.

On Sunday morning the expectant mother was taken to Romanow for burial. The rabbi decreed that she had to expel the child she held in her womb. If not, she couldn't receive a Jewish burial.

The dead mother was not so willing to separate her child from her womb. Three times, the rabbi repeated the harsh words that she, Tsipoyreh, daughter of

Avrom, would not be granted a Jewish burial until she relinquished the child from her womb. After that they brought over a large, deep trough from the room at the cemetery used for the ritual purification of the dead before burial. The expectant mother was placed in hot water, and lit black candles were placed around her head. Pious female community functionaries gathered and wept, imploring God to release a pure Jewish soul who had perished in the agonies of labor before her womb opened—and to allow her to receive a Jewish burial.

As the flames started to flicker and go out and the women's weeping strengthened, the body of the expectant mother was taken from the trough of boiling water and laid on hard straw on the ground. There a stream of blood poured out of her and her face smoothed out. Along with the blood, the leg of an infant swam out and remained there, stuck like a bloody tooth.

The female functionaries breathed easier and devoutly wiped their noses. "Thank You, God, for hearing the plea of a sinful woman. We're grateful that our tears reached Your holy throne," one of them said.

They bent down to the expectant mother to prepare her for a proper burial and removed the child from her—first the second leg, then the entire little body that had been turned around in the mother's womb and which now came out of her feet first.

A girl. She was buried with her mother.

A few years after Tsipoyreh's death, Perets contracted typhus and died.

All Soreh-Rokhl could do was weep. Her eyes could barely make out the light of day.

LEYBL

When Leybl came home for Sabbath, he sometimes took Soreh-Rokhl by the hand and led her outside. After making her comfortable under the cherry tree, he would tell her what he had learned that week and the kindnesses people had shown him. He was given meals in the finest homes, and he even had a few groschens of spending money. He knew Russian and gave private lessons, and he assured her that when he grew up, he'd give lessons to the poor—without demanding payment. He would take her, his grandma, with him, he said, to the big city. There he would give her all that was fine and good . . .

Soreh-Rokhl listened and remained largely silent. From time to time she wept, the tears rolling out of her half-blind eyes. And in this way, time passed.

The women who lived nearby—both gentile and Jew—did not abandon Soreh-Rokhl.

Leybke grew up handsome and clever. At age sixteen, he was already in *gymnasium* in Minsk, supporting himself by tutoring others. He sometimes sent his grandmother some of his earnings. When he was a guest, he wore a red shirt with a black belt. He spoke to the gentiles in his village, trying to convince them to free themselves from bondage, stop working for the nobility, and demand schools for their children. He also traveled to the surrounding villages to spread those same ideas. The gentiles were unsettled by such talk.

When he was eighteen years old, Leybl became involved in some kind of conspiracy. Together with his comrades, he was captured and sent to prison. And after that, yet another letter—with a black border, stamped with two red, signed seals and adorned by an illustrated eagle on the envelope—was delivered to Soreh-Rokhl. Once again, she traveled to Romanow to retrieve the official notice—and this time she wept out the last drop of light from her eyes with tears that dampened this letter that contained such large, important signatures.

It was then that Soreh-Rokhl's sister, Khishe, the blacksmith's wife, took her into her poor, crowded little house, and it was there that she remained, sitting behind the oven, day and night, summer and winter, knitting needles in her small hands. She didn't trouble anyone for help, unless a stitch slipped off and she couldn't catch it and realign it back onto the needle.

Soreh-Rokhl earned money for her expenses not only from the socks she used to make but also from something else altogether: warding off the evil eye.

When a gentile woman came for such an exorcism, she packed something in her bosom for Soreh-Rokhl: eggs, a package of flax, thread, a small piece of linen, a little bit of millet.

Khishe, herself old and stooped, with half-rheumy eyes, cared for her sister as if she were another child in the house.

VELVL AND ITKE

Besides Soreh-Rokhl, there were other figures in the blacksmith's house that sparked Dineh's curiosity.

These included Khishe's daughter-in-law, Itke, who churned out a household full of children until she lost use of a leg in her most recent pregnancy and from then on had to walk around with a crutch. She was a young woman—beautiful and healthy. Prior to her misfortune, Itke had been an itinerant peddler who traveled around with a large pack of sewing merchandise on her shoulders—both in her own village and in neighboring ones. This was how she helped support the house filled with little ones, whose numbers kept multiplying year after year.

When the misfortune struck, Itke stayed in bed for a year. After that she reappeared in the village, albeit with a smaller pack on her shoulders and with the crutch under her left arm. She would hobble from courtyard to courtyard, often hitching a ride in a stagecoach to a neighboring village too. She would stay there for a few days if the opportunity allowed it and then hitch a return ride home.

At every opportunity, Dineh followed poor Itke with her eyes until she entered the house. Dineh was frightfully eager to stand next to her, to touch with her own hands Itke's crutch, from which were suspended the weight of half of her body and the heavy pack on her shoulders.

But Peyse the blacksmith's house was forbidden territory, a site for Dineh's longing. So many wonderful people could be found there. There was also Velvl, Itke's husband, who helped Peyse in the smithy. He was tall, pale, with an honest, sickly face, and he suffered from a terrible condition of hiccups. Whenever the hiccups seized him he'd start crowing like a rooster. His face would turn completely blue until he vomited, at which point he could breathe easier again.

Dineh often heard Velvl lose his breath in the hiccupping fit until he started to crow. The hiccupping would overtake him mostly after eating. During summers Khishe often took him outside behind the house and sat him down on the earthen bench so that he could inhale the fresh air scented by the fruit trees of Sholem's orchard. From there Velvl's crowing and hiccups could be heard quite clearly through Sholem's windows. Sometimes Dineh snuck into the orchard to a large pear tree and listened to the hiccups with bated breath and a pounding heart. When Velvl's fit came to an end she breathed freely, wiping the anxious sweat from her child's brow. Dineh would stare at his handsome, pale face and his thin, short, jet-black beard that seemed to be a thin, black frame to his pale martyr's face.

There was something else that drew Dineh to Velvl. He often led the congregation in prayer—at their house, in fact. He had a sad, very sweet voice. On the Ninth of Av he recited the Book of Lamentations. This was the most beautiful thing Dineh had ever heard in their home. His mother, old Khishe, sat and wiped her eyes, speaking quietly to the few women around her: "He should only be well—my only son. His prayers are like piroshkis in the mouth."

PEYSE THE BLACKSMITH AND KHISHE

When Khishe had married Peyse and come to stay at the home of Peyse's parents after traveling from a distant settlement, she was a beautiful, young woman—a child, really—and Peyse a vigorous young man. Even now, in their elder years, he was a bear of a man—large, healthy, shaggy. Khishe did not fare poorly with Peyse's parents. She quickly took over running the household. Whenever she had a spare moment, she went about the village with cutting tools and a bag on her shoulders. When she returned, it was full. From one gentile woman she had bought a bit of flax; from another, some sixty eggs; from yet another, a few swatches of linen. Peyse was an honest, industrious person who worked in the smithy, creating shoes for the horses and sharpening the plow irons and the harrows. In the evenings he went home, taking work with him.

Khishe's troubles began when it came to having children. She had no children to raise. She gave birth to three, but two died. She had another two, and these two also died. Velvl was their only living child until she gave birth to a girl later in life. For good luck, the child was given the name Alte, meaning "old one."

Alte was a tall, thin, pale, and very quiet girl. Everyone fretted over her. They didn't let her do any heavy work. When Itke joined the household and gave birth to a healthy child every other year or every year and a half, it was always fondly welcomed into Peyse's house. A spirit of unity and a quiet, respectful love reigned in the home. Because both Velvl and Altitshke, the two trembling children, knew how to pray and write Yiddish, the grandchildren were also sent to religious school, especially since it was held in Sholem's house and would only cost a pittance.

Although Itke herself was crippled and unskilled at writing, she did everything she could to ensure that her children weren't in tatters, that they had clean clothes. She bought prayer books and notebooks for them so they wouldn't be ashamed in front of the other children.

Henye was the oldest grandchild in Peyse's household. Following her was Khashe, a pale girl who had difficulties. She wasn't sick, but she didn't understand what was being said to her. Meyer was a dynamo. He was Itke's third child and very clever. After him were twins, a boy and a girl, and then another pair of twin girls, and then the last child—the youngest—a boy named Fayvele.

With her large, brown eyes filled with longing, Dineh stared intently at the blacksmith's extended brood, considering their appearance and their outfits. She stared at them from the moment they left religious school until they reached the gate and the door of the blacksmith's house, a gate that opened so accommodatingly and then closed as directed by their hands. But for her, for Dineh, the little house remained forever the magic castle with a locked gate, for which she sought the key . . .

RIVE

Dineh was none too pleased with the religious school and her studies. All that she had imagined had come to naught. The three boys from Ostrovok were always fighting and didn't learn a thing. She tried to teach Rive, but the girl only looked back at Dineh uncomprehendingly and talked all sorts of nonsense—about the teacher and getting married, in fact.

Dineh looked at Rive with pity and explained to her: "If you can't learn, no one will want to marry you, and the teacher will hit you."

When she heard what Dineh said, Rive burst out into a fit of raucous laughter. "He's gonna hit me? I'll knock him out cold with my pinky," and with that, she once again laughed coarsely. "Now that's a fine story. Him—hit me? I'd like to see him try! You know something, Dineh—the strongest goyim in our village are afraid of me. I punch like a man," and here she made a fist and offered it up under Dineh's nose. "See? Strong as iron. They're all afraid of me."

"You're not at all like the Jewish girls," Dineh declared.

"Why am I not like the Jewish girls? My mother doesn't know the prayers either—and didn't she get married? And Mariana, Todosya, and Aksenka—well, they've all gotten married."

"So then why are you going to religious school?"

"How should I know? They really laugh at me."

"Who laughs?"

"My *podruzhkas*."

"You mean—the gentile girls?"

"Well, yes, the *podruzhkas*. They all say, why do you need to write letters to your groom?"

"So you do have a groom?"

"That's actually why they laugh. Where do I have a groom? Where? This is what I tell my mother: marry me off, I say. At my age you were already nursing a son. She screams at me, telling me I have to go to religious school and learn a Yiddish word and be with Jewish children and not be so ignorant. She tells me to stop running around with the goyish girls, and that if I don't she'll kick me out of the house, pack me off to her brothers in Babruĭsk, where there are Jews. And maybe there I'll find a practical purpose in life."

"Practical? Like what? Study?"

"Go on, that's ridiculous. For a girl, practical means getting married, finding a man."

Dineh considered this response and said, "If that's the case, Rive, you really do have to learn how to write."

"For what?"

"So that you can write your groom a beautiful letter. You'd please him."

"Go on. Dineh, you're a fool." She thought for a while and then said, "If I get myself a groom in Babruĭsk, I'll bring him here and show him off to everyone."

"He's going to want you to know how to pray."

Rive became sad. "If I give you half of my omelet each day, will you teach me?"

"Yes, but you just have to review. You see, our Soreh also has a thick skull, but she's ashamed that she can't understand, and she doesn't want to learn from the teacher. She says he's a brat. It's beneath her dignity to learn from him. So I teach her. She can already spell words and knows half of the Grace After Meals by heart."

"What does she pay you with for teaching her?"

"With nothing. She tells me stories."

"I hate stories."

"But Soreh can tell really beautiful stories, and she carries me like a ram. She takes me up on her shoulders and walks me back and forth across the kitchen while I say Grace After Meals, and she repeats after me."

"Like a ram? I can carry you better than she can. I'm as healthy as that light bay horse of ours." Then Rive caught herself and said, "Papa is always shouting at me for saying how healthy the light bay horse is. He said we should say 'No evil eye' right afterward."

She grabbed Dineh, lifted her onto the bench, placed her on her shoulders, and ran with her across the house, stamping like a horse.

"You see how healthy I am, Dineh? I barely feel you on my shoulders. Will you teach me?"

"Yes. I'll teach you at night."

Thus the days in religious school passed. Daniel was revitalized. He played horse-and-rider with his gang of pals, getting into fights with them. They stole away from the teacher, played hooky, and climbed trees. They had themselves a grand old time!

HENYE

Slowly, Dineh was also dragged into playing with the boys. She didn't find studying in the religious school terribly interesting. The lessons weren't difficult for her. She knew everything that was being taught. She turned to Henye, slid over to her, and looked in her prayer book and notebook. "Henye, if you'd like, I'll teach you how to write 'p-o' and spell 'Mama.'"

Henye looked around as if she were afraid. "Your mother won't shout?"

"Why should my mother shout? She'll just be happy. I teach Soreh and Rive."

"But it's different with them."

"Tell me, Henye, why don't we ever go to your place? Why doesn't my mother want us to play with the kids there?"

"How should I know?"

"You don't know?"

"No, I don't. My grandpa says it's because your mother thinks she's a noblewoman, and since we're blacksmiths, she thinks we're too low-class to play with her kids."

"My mother's bad."

"Nah, your mother's not bad. She's just stuck up. When Fayvele was born and Mama was very sick, your mother never left our house. She did everything that had to be done. She always went herself to fetch the doctor in your coach. She took care of Mama until she was able to get back on her feet. And then after that she stopped talking to us—as if we were strangers. My grandpa says she's temperamental. He says that's how rich people behave."

"You're poor?"

"Who said 'poor'? Grandpa works day and night. Grandma and my aunt Soreh-Rokhl too. And Mama does what she can. We aren't poor."

"Will you take me to your house sometime?"

"Well, will your mother let you come?"

"No, Henyeke, take me with you so my mother won't find out."

"I won't do that. My grandpa will yell at me."

"You can say that I came on my own."

"My grandpa knows that you wouldn't have come on your own."

"Well, what if I do come?"

"Well, then you'll come."

"Will you show me your mother's crutch?"

Insulted, Henye said, "What do you need my mother's crutch for? Do you want to learn how to walk with a crutch?"

Feeling guilty, Dineh responded, "I want to see how your mother walks with it. It must be hard for her."

"We don't even think about it anymore. It's just become a normal thing. At first it seemed weird for all of us. My mother used to cry all the time until my father came to quiet her down. But now no one gives it a second thought."

"Well, will you show me your aunt Soreh-Rokhl?"

"What do you mean, 'will I show you?' Is she a piece of wood or a toy to show off to you?"

Once again, Dineh felt guilty. "I mean—can I see her up close?"

"Why not? If you get up close, you'll see her up close. She's not a bear."

"Is it true she can't tell whether it's day or night?"

"How should she know if she can't see? She's blind."

"So how does she know when to go to sleep and when to get up?"

"Actually, she doesn't know. She always sleeps a little bit at a time during the day, and then she's up at night. It's only when we all go to sleep that she goes to sleep too. When we get up, she gets up."

"And how can she get outside?"

"She feels her way with her hands until she gets to the door, and sometimes she takes a kid outside. And when she loses a stitch when she's knitting, we put it back on the needles. Then she tells us beautiful stories."

Amazed, Dineh asked, "Beautiful stories?! She can tell beautiful stories?!"

"Beautiful and very sad. Grandma says she makes them up herself, these stories, and then she weaves them together with her own experiences."

DINEH VISITS THE NEIGHBORS

That same evening, when everyone was sitting in the blacksmith's narrow, warm little house and resting from a hard day's work, Dineh quietly opened the door. Everyone's face turned toward the door. Dineh stood frozen, one foot on the outside of the threshold and the other in the kitchen.

The first to greet her was Khishe. She approached, observing her with her nearsighted eyes, and called out, "Well, look who we have here—what a guest! Come in, Dinehle."

Everyone in the house stared at Dineh in great surprise. As if talking to himself, Peyse said into his beard, "Isn't this something! Wow! To what do we owe such an honor? That the noblewoman would permit such a thing . . . Well, come over here. Why are you being shy, standing over there like that? Come closer. No one's going to bite you, God forbid."

But Itke interjected, "Father-in-Law, you should only be well, but what are you saying? Peshe probably sent the child over to get something."

Here Khishe added, "Come here, Dinehle, don't be afraid. I was your midwife. It was just me and your mother—there was no one else at home. When your father and Aunt Yakhe—we weren't even expecting them—got there, it was all over. Your birth wasn't hard for your mother; if only the same could be said for all births. Just as long as they're not worse, God forbid . . ."

"Well, did your mother send you to get something?"

Dineh was confused and frightened.

"Yes? For what? Does she want to borrow something? The chopping bowl? The grater? Or a frying pan to make latkes?"

Dineh looked over at Henye, pleading with her eyes for her help, but Henye kept her head lowered and wouldn't look at Dineh. "The . . . the chopping bowl," Dineh stammered.

Khishe took her by the hand. "Come here to the table. You'll see how we cut the wicks. Tomorrow we'll start to make the candles and dip them in the first tallow."

Dineh furtively approached the table, looking all around her. Soon, however, she was immersed in the work around the table. Everyone was seated. First they measured a thick, twisted, soft string, then they twisted it around a small board. After counting out a certain number, they cut it with a scissors. It was then tied with a small knot, and the process of measuring and twisting began all over again.

The long table, with Peyse—with his great head of thick, white hair and his full beard and his hardworking hands—at the head, and with everyone else involved in the rhythm of the work, made a great impression on Dineh. Blind Soreh-Rokhl sat among the children as well, twisting the wick, counting, and cutting the string.

Dineh stood and considered these heroes of hers of whom she'd dreamt for so long. She forgot where she was and that she really did have to get out of there as soon as possible. But then Khishe came over to her with the bowl and reminded her. "Here you go, Dinehle; your mother must definitely need this bowl if she sent you over for it," she said.

Dineh started as if from a state of sleep. It was only when she stared at the large wooden bowl that she realized what she had done. What would she do with it? Where would she put it? How would she go home with it?

But staying here any longer wasn't an option either. Totally at a loss, she took the bowl from Khishe's hands and snuck out of the house without even saying good night.

Once outside of the house, Dineh stood there with the bowl in her hands. She'd go through the orchard and hide the bowl under a tree in the snow. She would leave a telltale sign for herself so that tomorrow she would know where to find it and then she would return it.

She hid the bowl well in the snow under the thick pear tree. She tore out a dead twig from elsewhere in the orchard and then brought it over to the spot where her sin lay buried.

She went quietly by herself through the back door on her tiptoes, took the Pentateuch, and sat down to review the weekly Torah portion.

That night Dineh had terrible dreams. Mirke the stable man's girl, who slept with her, woke her up from her sleep and asked, "What did you dream about? Why are you screaming?" But Dineh was afraid to tell her about her dreams because it involved Peyse the blacksmith's little house and the wooden bowl now buried like a criminal's loot under the snow in the orchard.

The next day Dineh sat leadenly in religious school, as if in a daze, unable to make out the words in front of her or the teacher and the other students. As if through a fog she saw little candles with thin flames and many large round wooden bowls spinning before her eyes. At first she didn't dare look at Henye. When she did finally steal a sideways glance at her, Henye lowered her eyes as if Dineh hadn't meant her, as if to convey that she hadn't seen her at all.

In the evening right after supper, after a fire was lit, Dineh breathed a bit easier. All of the childish worry that had weighed so heavily on her throughout the night and all of the day went up as if in a cloud of blue smoke. From that thin blue smoke sprung new hopes, new expectations. Peyse the blacksmith's home—the children around the table, the wick that would be dipped in the first round of tallow, tiny Soreh-Rokhele with her childlike hands and eyes blind from weeping, Itke, who hopped around on her crutch, and the entire household—all of it sprouted before her like a magical wheel with thousands of fantastical stories . . .

Dineh waited until everyone else had finished eating their supper, recited Grace After Meals, and left the table, each returning to his work. Papa went to the stables to check on the cows, horses, and sheep. Mama went to the tavern to check if there were any customers waiting there for a flask of liquor or a keg of beer. Malkeh gathered the dishes. Soreh was busy with Rive and Mirke. Daniel, as usual, was busy with Sholem of Ostrovok's three boys. They hitched each other up to a horse's harness and were goofing around.

Dineh snuck out of the house and ran into the orchard and over to the pear tree. The twig was gone! Apparently the wind had tossed it around in the snow that had fallen during the night. Now it was covered.

Her heart beating rapidly, Dineh lowered herself into the snow that was piled around the tree and began to rake through it with her fingers. Every second stretched out into an eternity. What would she do if the bowl had also vanished? Anxiety gripped her.

But with her right hand Dineh finally struck against the hard corner of the bowl. She felt an immense sense of relief. Pulling it out of the ground, she held on to the bowl with both hands and ran straightaway to Peyse the blacksmith's house. Unlike yesterday she didn't hesitate. She didn't measure her steps or hem and haw about whether to enter. She ran right in as if someone from the outside had been chasing her or like someone carrying a hot, burning coal in her hands who wanted to toss it away from herself as quickly as possible.

The door of Peyse's house opened quickly. Dineh entered, holding the bowl in both hands. Everyone in the house turned to look at her. Khishe came close, considering her. "Is that you, Dinehle? Your mother sent the bowl back?"

When Dineh answered yes it felt as if the words weren't coming from her own mouth, and she handed the bowl over to Khishe.

Khishe saw that the bowl was full of snow and ice. "Did you fall on your way over here, Dinehle? Did you hurt yourself?"

"No."

"Well, come inside and warm up. You're just in time to see the first round of tallow dipping."

With measured steps, Dineh approached the long, narrow trough filled with tallow. She saw that almost all of the children were working with the candles. They took the wicks that were now hanging on rods and individually separated them. Then they took the stalks by their ends and dipped the wicks in the tallow. They lifted them out, held them in the air for a short while until the tallow stiffened, and then suspended them between two long tables in rows.

Dineh greatly enjoyed this work.

Henye approached her. "Aren't you afraid?"

Summoning up her courage, Dineh said, "Well, I came."

"Do you want to dip the candles?"

Henye gave her a rod with wicks. Dineh took it with trembling hands. She dipped the wicks into the tallow, held it with the others in the air, and suspended it between the rows of candles between the two long tables. She took one rod and then another, and everything hummed along smoothly. Dineh worked with everyone, doing what they were doing. She chatted with Henye, Khashke, Meyerke, and everyone at once. Everyone was so warm and welcoming to her. She felt that this should have been her home.

Why didn't they make candles at her house? Mama recited the blessings on the Sabbath candles, and on Hanukkah and all of the other holidays they used so many candles! This was such beautiful work! How beautiful the candles looked hanging in rows!

With such thoughts going through her mind as she worked on the candles, Dineh heard Peyse say, "Why don't you see to it that the child goes home? It's already late. After all, over there they won't know where she's gone to."

"What do you mean—they won't know? Peshe herself sent her here to bring back the bowl."

Dineh started awake, this time as if from a pleasant dream. She did have to get home right away. She put on her coat and started to go. The curly haired little boy Fayvele and the little girl Tsirl ran after her. "Come tomorrow, Dineh. We'll make candles again."

Forgetting herself, Dineh said, "You can also come to us . . ."

"Good, we'll come."

Dineh felt that she had made a stupid mistake. Ashamed, she ran out of the house without saying good night.

AUNT SOREH

When Dineh returned home, Malkeh asked her, "Where were you?"

Dineh played dumb. "Nowhere," she responded.

"You don't come back so late from nowhere. Look how frozen she is! Her face is burning. You'll catch a cold. We'll have to take you to the doctor. That's all we need."

"I'm not cold at all. I'm going to bed now."

Soreh approached Dineh in bed and wanted her to read the Shema bedtime prayer with her, as they always did before going to sleep. Soreh already knew both the Grace After Meals and the Shema by heart, as Dineh was well aware. But whenever Soreh started to say it for herself, she'd mix up the words and the order of the verses and couldn't disentangle herself. With Dineh at her side, Soreh felt sure of herself.

When Soreh started to recite the Shema, Dineh asked her, "Soreh, why don't we make candles like they do at Peyse's house?"

"How do you know they make candles at Peyse's house?"

"If you swear you won't tell anyone, I'll tell you how I know."

"I won't say a word, but if Mama finds out you were there, she's going to give it to you."

"Why can't we go there?"

"I don't know why. But we had a falling out with them. Sometimes when Khishe leaves the village in the evening, me and some of the other kids chase her and throw little stones at her. We always hit the sack she carries on her shoulder, and we shout at her: 'Little donkey! Blind donkey!' Once she came to complain to Mama. But Mama just said she didn't believe that her kid would shout after a peddler lady, even though I knew for sure that Mama knew that I ran after her and threw stones, along with the other kids."

"So why do you do it?"

"Because that's just the way we play. Everyone does it. Why does everyone throw stones at Aunt Soreh, the way she lugs herself from one village to the next?"

"Aunt Soreh is crazy . . . I'm so scared of Aunt Soreh . . . When she comes here, why does she always sleep by the oven? Why doesn't she sleep somewhere else?"

"Because she's related to Papa. I mean, she's his aunt by blood!"

"Does that mean she's also our aunt?"

"Of course she's our aunt!"

"So then why do you throw stones at her?"

"It's nothing. People throw stones at all the lunatics. They don't remember a thing."

"Yes, but they still feel pain."

"Well, listen to you sticking up for her! She once stole Daniel out of his cradle, and Papa, the farmhands, and all the goyim in the village went out to look for her. They finally found her sitting deep in the rye fields, holding him in her arms. She was singing to him and feeding him stalks of rye . . . If they hadn't heard her singing from the road, they wouldn't have found them, and she would have choked Daniel."

Trembling, Dineh said, "She could steal her own kids."

"Her own kids? They're all grown. Even the youngest girl—the one who drove her crazy when she was giving birth—is also grown up by now."

"Why doesn't she live at home with Uncle and her kids?"

"Because Uncle divorced her and got married to someone else, and so they don't let her into the house. A few times she stole Beylke, the youngest girl. They looked for her and took her back. Uncle beat her so hard that now she's afraid to go there."

Dineh felt a tightening in her heart, and she burst into tears.

Soreh calmed her down. "You're a fool, Dineh. Why are you crying? Aunt Soreh's a lunatic. She doesn't know anything. When you hit her, she doesn't even feel pain."

Sobbing, Dineh asked, "Will she never be able to die?"

"Why not? She'll die."

"But if she never feels pain . . ."

While still crying, Dineh recited the Shema bedtime prayer with Soreh, snuggled into the cushion—and into Soreh—and fell asleep.

The blacksmith's grandchildren showed a voracious yearning for study. It wasn't long before Henye was reading the Pentateuch and even the rest of the Hebrew Bible with Dineh. It brought Dineh great joy to help Henye with her studies.

On several occasions Peshe remarked, "Why are you pushing everything you know into Henye? Soon she'll know it better than you."

"Well, then she can help me out. She's older than me, after all. She should know more. By the way, it's easier for me to review with her. First I quiz her, and then she quizzes me."

"Well, how come you don't review with Daniel?"

"He keeps kicking, and he doesn't want to learn. Besides, he can review with the boys from Ostrovok."

"It's true that he doesn't want to learn, but he does have a good head. He's a mischievous boy. He'll be able to learn. We should all be well."

Once, at dusk, Peyse's grandchildren came to Sholem's house. The two smallest, Tsirl and Fayvl, came.

When Dineh spotted them, she got scared and didn't know what to do. She called them into the bedroom and carried them up to the tiled Russian stove and showed them her toys. When Peshe came into the room, Dineh blocked them so her mother wouldn't see them. When Peshe asked, "Who are you hiding there?" Fayvl called out, "Tsirl brought me!"

Peshe approached, stared at the children, and with an expression of mock outrage on her face said to Dineh, "Really, now?"

To Fayvl she said, "Just come here. Let me have a look at you."

He stood up. Peshe turned him around and looked him over. "Already a big boy. And you, Tsirl? You're a big girl." To Dineh she said, "It's already late. Send them home. They haven't had their supper yet."

The children got down from the Russian stove, and Dineh helped them put on their overcoats. At the door, Fayvl turned around. "Dineh, will you give me the little red box? I'll give you my dreidel. My grandpa'll make me another one."

Peshe approached, taking two raspberry-shaped candies out of her pocket. She gave one to Tsirl and one to Fayvl.

"Wow! How beautiful!"

Each one stole a glance to check if the other one had gotten a better one.

"Go, children, and don't fall. Hold each other by the hand."

Dineh looked up at Mama with gratitude.

"What else are you going to drag into this house?"

"They came by themselves."

"Oh, sure, they came to call on me, huh?"

"They're all so nice in Peyse's house, and they make candles on their own."

"Is that so? They make candles on their own? And they're all nice? How do you know these things?

Realizing she was caught, Dineh said, "Well, I always review my lessons with Henye."

"So what? Don't you have space here at home to review? For all the other children there's enough space, and for you there isn't?"

From that point on, the thick partition between the two neighboring households became a bit thinner and more transparent.

Dineh went to Peyse's house and played with the children there. She helped Soreh-Rokhl raise the yarn back on the knitting needle whenever it unspooled and walked with her in the street whenever needed. And she asked Soreh-Rokhl—just to be sure—if she really did know the difference between day and night. Dineh sat by Soreh-Rokhl's side and listened to her tell stories to the children.

THE ORIGINS OF THE FEUD

Dineh did eventually find out how the feud between the two families began. Soreh-Rokhl told her the story:

When your mother, Peshe, arrived in Ugli she behaved like a noblewoman and was always running away to her parents. Peyse once said to Sholem, right in front of her face, "What's going on, Sholem? You've bought yourself a foreign mare who can't breathe the air in your house, huh? She's never satisfied. Is visiting a neighbor beneath her dignity? Come on in, Sholem. My wife is a common woman. She doesn't resist the blacksmith's hammer." At that moment, Peshe came home and made a scene in front of Sholem. She wept and cursed the terrible misfortune that had banished her to an island among wild creatures and vulgar youths.

Peshe puffed herself up like a turkey. At prayer services on the Sabbath, when Peyse, Khishe, and Velvl came to pray, she was even more peeved that Peyse the blacksmith, that rude young man, had looked at her with contempt. He had refused to be taken in by her airs and puffing, as if none of it was directed at him. Peyse was like a good brother to Sholem, the way a father was with a son, always stopping to give him advice, speaking with him about the plow irons and the horses that had to be shod.

All of this greatly annoyed Peshe. From her very first days in the village the feud commenced. It was one sided because Peyse's entire household—the women and children—looked at Peshe like someone of higher status.

And so time passed.

For three semesters, teachers were boarded at Sholem's house. Dineh learned a great deal during that time. Although he wasn't diligent, Daniel did have a sharp mind. Dineh's friend and fellow student, Henye, the blacksmith's granddaughter, did not lag behind. Dineh was very attached to her until eventually Henye became like one of the family in Sholem's house. She ate there and even often slept over. When someone was looking for Henye, they knew they could find her at Sholem's house, sitting with Dineh in her room poring over a Hebrew Bible or a little Russian book, reviewing their lessons.

Truth be told, the adults in Peyse's house didn't dare cross the neighboring threshold of Peshe's house freely, but they did come to inquire after a child.

They always made excuses, insisting that no matter how many times they'd been warned, children will be children and they didn't listen and just went ahead and did what they wanted . . .

At such moments Peshe pretended not to hear, as if the person weren't speaking to her. And if the situation arose when she couldn't extricate herself, Peshe would say, "Whom doesn't she drag over here? She'd bring all of the village bastards here if we'd let her."

Of course, this could only mean that it was Dineh's fault that a child from Peyse's household was here in her house.

THE RELIGIOUS SCHOOL MOVES OUT

Sholem of Ostrovok, whose three boys studied for three semesters in Ugli, insisted that he wanted to host the religious school in his house. For one thing, he had four youngsters to send to school by then, and it was hard for him to have them so far from home. For another, Gute the miller woman's two twin grandchildren—both girls—who lived just over the lake also had to go to school. They were anxious children, and the family didn't want to send them far from home.

A rabbi came to Sholem's house to deliberate over the matter. It was decided that Sholem of Ugli's two children, Dineh and Daniel, would go to Ostrovok to study for that term.

Daniel was all gung-ho for this plan. He had his gang of pals there. He could have fun and be a grown-up there—like Itshe and Faytl—who also studied away from home. And to top it all off he could slide on the lake with his gang.

For Dineh it wasn't so easy. Before the High Holidays, when plans were being made to send the children to Ostrovok for the term, she immediately began to tremble with fear. What did being sent away from home mean? And where was this place? Somewhere in the boondocks! So far! A whole three versts away! She had rarely been there. She'd passed by a few times, but no more than that. If it had been Dakhtervitsh—at least she had aunts and uncles there. But in a strange place like Ostrovok, she practically didn't know anyone at all except for Sholem's boys, whom she didn't like much . . . But she didn't dare speak out about her fears.

Dineh was also upset that she wouldn't be studying with Henye anymore. She felt that they both needed to master the stories of the Bible and the little secular books together. True, she would be coming home for the Sabbath, and she could tell and retell Henye everything she'd learned in school. But Dineh knew that sitting at the table in school without Henye and reviewing the lessons by herself in the evening would make her very sad.

The impending departure from home and journey into the unknown weighed so heavily on Dineh that she stopped eating altogether. It reached the point that they had to summon Rabinovitsh, the medical practitioner, to the house. He prescribed a drug of anthelmintic leaves. "The yellowness of the face is the main sign of worms," he said.

Dineh walked around in something of a stupor, standing for a long time and considering each tree in the orchard, each calf in the stable. She bent down to the young lambs, petting them and weeping so that no one would see. She walked to the river, where the fields split into two long, endless rows and where the exhausted ripeness of late autumn was reflected . . .

With the little white dog, Goldetske, Dineh would take long, quiet walks over the narrow path. Then when she was tired she'd sit down, take Goldetske in her arms, pet her for a long time, and gaze over the faraway expanses of the fields. Emotionally overcome, Dineh would measure the distance from her home to Ostrovok . . .

Dineh had never been anywhere, never stayed anywhere overnight away from home. She would be afraid to sleep in a strange place. She would be too shy.

During these long interludes of apprehensive reflection, Dineh felt embarrassed. She could discuss it with Itshe. But no, that wouldn't work. Itshe was a boy. He wouldn't understand. A boy wouldn't understand what it meant to be afraid. There was Daniel, younger than Dineh. But when she asked him if he were afraid of the unknown, he immediately answered, "I'm a boy! A boy isn't afraid of anything." She also remembered that Itshe had said that God is everywhere and that instead of being afraid when there was thunder you should recite the blessing on thunder. And she was so afraid of thunder that she even recited two blessings: one for lightning and one for thunder. She was sorry that she wasn't a boy.

Dineh walked around in this dream state and bade farewell to every mute thing around her. Only to the mute trees and animals could she speak from the heart. They understood her, felt what she was feeling. To the verbal human beings around her Dineh didn't breathe a word of what was gnawing at her, weighing so heavily upon her.

RELIGIOUS SCHOOL IN SHOLEM OF OSTROVOK'S HOUSE

The time had come. It was a cold, rainy autumnal day. Dineh and Daniel were dressed warmly. Their sacred books were packed in a bag along with bread and butter and other food. They were settled into a carriage with springs as Malkeh sat down in the driver's position with the whip and the reins in her hands. Before Dineh could turn around to see what was happening the carriage had pulled up in front of an old, low, stooped house. Malkeh had climbed down and was tethering the horse to the fence in front of the house.

Daniel immediately jumped out of the carriage and fell straight into a muddy puddle right in front of the house. The boys came up to him making a racket and laughing at him. It almost came to blows. But Kreyne, Sholem of Ostrovok's wife, a tall, dark woman with a wide face and shaggy locks of black hair that hung down over her brow and twisted to the sides of her cheeks, immediately lurched at the children with curses and shooed them away. Daniel remained standing in the puddle like a young rooster about to pounce on his enemy only to come to the sudden realization that the enemy was gone.

Kreyne approached the carriage, inquired after her mother to Malkeh, and helped her unload the packages. Looking over at Dineh still sitting in the carriage, Kreyne asked, "What's wrong with her? Is she not well? She looks kind of scared."

"No, she's not sick. She's too lazy to get down."

Sensing that she couldn't stay in the carriage any longer, Dineh crawled down and stood next to Malkeh and Kreyne. When they started to head toward the house, she followed them, as if not with her own legs. Once inside, Kreyne took their things, set them down, and showed Dineh where she would find what she needed. Dineh looked back at her fearfully, taking in the old, crooked shelves and the chipped cupboards stuffed with rags.

The cottage looked like a narrow shaft bursting at the seams.

The beds, the table, the teacher and students, the sacred books—all were thrown together without rhyme or reason. The steam from the pots filled with cooking food seeped into everything and everyone.

With homesick eyes Dineh looked around for some kind of corner where she could set herself apart from the others. But it was hard for her to find anything . . . until her eyes set upon the oven. There, behind the fireplace by the oven, where pieces of freshly chopped kindling were drying out, her gaze landed. She decided she could hide there and no one would find her.

Malkeh jolted her back—as if from a state of sleep—to the here and now. "Well, Dineh, be well. Take care of Daniel. On Friday we'll come back to take you home for Sabbath."

Dineh felt a heaviness in her heart. She didn't respond to her sister. Only after Malkeh had gone outside did Dineh mutely follow her. And when Malkeh shouted at her that she should go inside to study with the other children, Dineh went back into the house. She stood at the window and looked out as Malkeh sat down on top of the carriage, took the reins in her hand, steered the horse around—and gave the reins a tug. The carriage left the courtyard and disappeared in what seemed like the blink of an eye.

Dineh choked back her tears until her shoulders began to twitch. Kreyne approached to quiet her down. "Fe, such a big girl and you're not ashamed to cry? Stop! It's not pretty."

Turning from the window, Dineh went to the package of sacred books and removed the Pentateuch and the Bible. The teacher, a tall, stooped, coughing young man, approached her, looked at the books, and asked her if she studied with the boys. Dineh answered that she learned everything that her brother Daniel learned and that without her he wouldn't want to learn. The teacher told the children to go to the table and assigned Dineh a seat near Daniel. And with that the semester began.

The teacher could teach well and cough even better. Both of these things deeply pleased Dineh. She loved the teacher both because he taught the Bible with such a beautiful, sad melody and translated it with all kinds of parables and because he coughed until sweat began to pour from him.

Each time he coughed Dineh raced over to offer him a drink of water, and he took his medication from a dark bottle—a yellow fluid that had a terrible smell and probably an even worse taste. Anxiously she looked directly into his mouth and, in her heart, wished him a thousand speedy recoveries.

Throughout the first week Dineh counted the days, the hours. Today was Tuesday, tomorrow would be Wednesday, the day after tomorrow would be Thursday, and on Friday they would get to go home . . . At night, before she and Daniel fell asleep in the bed they shared, Dineh talked with him and counted down the days.

For his part Daniel had lost the desire to be in a strange, new place. The bed was terrible, and Sholem of Ostrovok quarreled with his wife late into the night. In the evenings he shouted at the children. Nor did he spare Daniel, who always seemed to be underfoot, given the crowded living conditions in the house.

Dineh always managed to stay out of the way. She sought out a corner and sat there with her Pentateuch or another sacred book. She maintained a vigilant eye to ensure that the nasty Sholem wouldn't get the big idea, God forbid, to shout at the teacher, who was now moving in a world so alien to him. This teacher who was tall, bent, pale . . . and coughing.

On the first Friday a ride home came for Dineh and Daniel. The carriage had driven from Hrozawa, where Itshe was studying in a Talmudical school.

Itshe came inside to fetch the children. Dineh was in seventh heaven. She would be riding with Itshe home for the Sabbath . . . He was coming home from school, and she too was coming home from school. She too was a student. It wasn't just Itshe who was studying; she too was studying Torah. She would eventually study Talmud as well. A girl could also study Talmud if she wanted. She saw how Itshe approached the teacher, shook his hand, and chatted with him. Her heart lifted. Dineh was proud of her brother. He was so tall and handsome. He had such striking, black curly hair and such beautiful, soft, burning eyes, and he carried himself so ramrod straight.

If the teacher didn't cough so much he too would have been as straight and tall as Itshe. But as it was, Itshe stood taller than him. The teacher walked Itshe out to the carriage. When everyone was seated, farewells were exchanged. Vasil pulled on the reins, and the carriage was off.

As they approached the barns, the stables, and the yard, Dineh's heart began to beat so wildly that she imagined everyone could hear it. When she climbed down from the carriage, Goldetske tumbled over the children. She started to yap and lick them all over. Dineh didn't know where to go first—Peyse's house to see Henye or the stables to the cows and lambs or the house to confirm that everything was still in place and as she had left it.

Throughout the Sabbath day Dineh was busy telling Henye about her new teacher and everything she had learned. She tested Soreh to see if she still remembered the Grace After Meals—and in fact discovered that she had once again forgotten it and was mixing up buckwheat with beet-leaves soup. At dusk Soreh gave her a piggyback ride in the darkening front room. While riding on her sister's back, Dineh repeatedly drummed the text word by word into Soreh's brain. Soreh repeated each word like someone who had done something wrong, with great diligence. They did the same with the Shema bedtime prayer. In a week's time, Soreh had forgotten it all. It was as if she had never learned it in the first place.

On Sunday morning the horses were once again harnessed to the carriage and the children were taken back to religious school.

This time Dineh was almost eager to go. True, she didn't like living with the host family. But the teacher, with his cough and pale face and melancholy singsong recitation of the sacred texts, made up for everything.

After Dineh told Mama about the teacher's cough and his bitter medicine, she ordered Malkeh to bring a small jar of cherry preserves up from the cellar for the teacher. Dineh was pleased. The preserves would surely make the teacher better.

Once she was back at school, Dineh presented the preserves to her teacher. "My mother sent this to you to make you get better."

He smiled sadly at her. "You're a good child. You've got a good heart and a good head on your shoulders."

Dineh felt happy, at a loss as to what to do or say, and was, in her childish way, embarrassed.

The autumn days had passed. Frost spread on the windowpanes in Sholem of Ostrovok's house and on the fields and the lake as well. The first snow fell when everyone was asleep. When they woke up at dawn they at last set eyes on a new, white world.

The children rejoiced. The mood around the school table was cheerful. When the children glanced out the windows, white rooftops, white fields, and a white lake stretching from Gute the miller woman's house with its water-powered wheel mill all the way to Sholem's house looked back at them.

Each morning Gute's grandchildren—the twins—came to school dressed in clean, warm clothes, their hair beautifully combed. By that time they had already mastered the basics of study. Their father, Gute's son-in-law, had taught them himself until the teacher arrived.

Their father was a refined young man, a scholar. The two girls looked like the children of a rabbi.

But Dineh did not succeed in befriending them. Their elegant manners didn't appeal to her, and she didn't even like their well-maintained clothes. She missed Henye and all the other children in Peyse the blacksmith's house, with their threadbare dresses and undergarments. Her heart was drawn to all that was plain, rebelling against anything that smacked of the well-heeled and rich. She was used to the ordinary, overworked Kreyne, whose husband was forever bellowing curses at her and who in turn directed those same curses at her children. Dineh had great empathy for Sholem himself. He invariably came home late at night with a meager sack slung over his shoulders, frozen and ill-tempered after a day of trudging through villages looking everywhere for someone who had a bit of flax or a dry pelt for sale.

On several occasions Dineh saw him approach the teacher with a large envelope with sealed wax stamps. She saw the teacher remove a large letter from the envelope and read an official summons in Russian to Sholem.

Following the receipt of such a summons, Sholem had to go to the rural district office. On his return home he added a few more curses against Tsar Nikolai to his standard repertoire: "What does he have against me? Well, he can have my poverty, and the two of them can go up in flames together! It wasn't enough for that bloodsucker that one of my sons had gone to serve the *Fonye* and didn't make it back alive. The second one managed to escape the murderous clutches of military conscription by fleeing the country! Oh, what do they want from me? Why do they keep sending me these summonses? What are they trying to squeeze out of me?

"Maybe Nikolai, let him go to blazes, wants me to go get my son myself so that he can kill him just the way he killed my first one. A plague on him! Everything else, yes, but not that.

"He won't get any more of my sons! And he'll just take, you say? Well, let him take! What can he take from me? The children and the rags? He can take them and be done with it. That'll be the end of hauling me all the time to the rural district office in secret to bleed my arteries dry trying to get me to tell them where my son is . . . Soon I'm going to go and serve him up to them myself! Let them just wait and see."

In the short winter days, the students also studied during the evenings. They went to bed early. In addition to the eight family members, three strangers had to be housed in the two rooms of Sholem's house.

The children slept on top of each other. Dineh and Daniel slept on a hard, narrow little bed next to the oven. Several of Sholem's smaller boys slept on top of the oven among the pieces of wet wood. On the other side of the oven was an old sofa missing a leg, propped up by a piece of wood. On that sofa the teacher coughed through the night.

AN *OBYSK*

On one such night when the children had fallen asleep and found themselves somewhere in dreamland, the sound of dogs barking rang out. Then came the jingling of the bells of a horse's harness. A loud bang on the door and cursing in Russian followed the bells in quick succession.

The entire household was soon fully awake. Fear gripped everyone throughout the home.

Sholem dressed quickly and went to the door. When he opened it, he found himself face to face with a wall of sparkling buttons, sabers, belts, and tall hats. Four gendarmes entered simultaneously and began barking orders.

"*Ogon!* Fire!"

Sholem started to call Kreyne. Then he said, "Let her stew there in sickness. Doesn't she see what's happening here? Why doesn't she get up and light the lamp?"

Kreyne emerged with a small, smoky lamp in her hands and set it on the table before the men wearing protective gear.

They wanted a somewhat bigger lamp. "That lamp is too small for a night-time *obysk!*" "*Naplevat*," said another. "We'll look ourselves."

An uproar broke out from the children in one of the beds, acting as a signal that soon spread like wildfire through the house. The children screamed "Look out! Help!" from all sides. The armored men began to swear and curse and tear up the bedding left and right.

Dineh and Daniel wrapped themselves in the covers and left the house in their bare feet. They walked across the lake and then immediately began to run to Gute the miller woman's house.

They pounded on the windows. When they were allowed inside the children were so frightened that it was impossible to get out of them what had happened at Sholem's house.

It was only the next day when Gute's son-in-law returned from Sholem's house that they found out what happened. He told everyone seated at the table that the gendarmes had come at night to conduct an *obysk* to see whether Sholem was hiding his son from military service. When they didn't find him they arrested the teacher and "registered" Sholem's only cow from its stall.

"Now Sholem himself has to bring the cow over to the regional police superintendent for the treasury coffers."

Gute the miller woman hitched the horses and drove Dineh and Daniel back to Sholem's house on her own. Both children were sick—at first from fear and the cold and then from typhus. Their teacher never returned. From his personal documents it was discovered that he was afflicted with tuberculosis and that he'd been betrayed to the authorities. He had come to the village to elude the police.

With that the semester in Ostrovok ended, even though it wasn't yet Purim.

Dineh and Daniel were bedridden with fever for six weeks. After that, others in the house also took sick with typhus. This bout lasted into spring.

DECREES

That year was full of all kinds of hardship and decrees against the Jews, especially those living in the villages.

First, there was an *ukaz* stating that the right to sell liquor was to be stripped away from all lessee tavern keepers. This reverberated like thunder throughout the Jewish population of the villages, a number of whom earned a portion of their livelihood from the sale of liquor.

It wasn't long before an excise tax was levied and the permits were taken away. Before the month was up the authorities had built large monopoly houses in the villages. They sent in young Polish or German noblemen, along with their households from the city, and resettled them in a lordly manner in houses with large windows and shingled roofs. Tall fences with green iron railings and little narrow gates were built around the houses.

On long shelves lining the walls of long corridors stood bottles of various sizes containing spirits. The long, thin-necked white bottles, with their heavy red seals, appeared like a kind of aquatic vegetation crowned by a flowering of red poppies.

Before a peasant entered a monopoly house he had to wipe off his boots—his bast shoes, actually—with considerable thoroughness. The gentiles in the village rarely owned boots. Only a few of the more eminent ones owned those, and they wore them only for special occasions, such as sometimes at Christmas carols in church or at a posh wedding when they had to dance a special dance, where heavy boots played a prominent role.

After wiping his feet off on a kind of checkered iron carpet expressly laid for that purpose in front of the door the peasant had to remove his hat immediately. A portrait of Tsar Nikolai, looking stern and commanding, was there to greet him upon entry. Hat in hand, a bit shy, the bolder peasants undertook to enter this paradise castle one by one. According to the law of the treasury it had been built specially for the *ruskii narod* to redeem him from the Jewish tavern keepers and their taverns, where he had spent such pleasant free time in the evening or on a holiday over a glass at a table with other friends, imbibing until he was plastered, singing and weeping over his bitter fate—until forgetfulness, until braggadocio, until dance and blows—and begging forgiveness and kissing . . .

The first spies who made their way into the monopoly store stood there at a loss with their sturdy, sealed bottle in hand. This had been offered to them through the bars of a small iron grate. A clean hand, decorated with a white cuff, had offered it to them after it counted out the money and slipped it into a drawer. They felt both lost and insulted. Hat in one hand and bottle in the other, they left this aristocratic outfit abruptly in a state of agitation. They didn't know what to do until, after some consideration, they thrust the bottle in their pocket, put on their hat, and spat mightily on all of the nobleman's racket. And poof . . . they were out of there and back to the Jew in the tavern.

There they took the bottle out as if they were at home. They considered it from all sides, looked at Tsar Nikolai's picture so artfully adhered to a blue paper on the red seal, spun it all the way around, and tried to open it. They couldn't . . . until someone from the tavern keeper's house opened it with a corkscrew and offered a glass to the table. Without any real appetite, the gentile sampled this government merchandise and mournfully determined that it would not do at all. The well-fed young nobleman would not live to see him standing before him a second time, hat in hand and waiting for the nobleman to present him with his goods and then—scat! But where should he go? What was he—a dog? Outside, behind the fence, or on the threshold, without a glass to drink from the bottle? No! That's not how things would go! This dog was the boss of his garbage heap. They wouldn't be coming here to teach him how and where to drink! They'd call a meeting! They'd go to the government and demand that they go back to the way they used to be! No new practice would be set up here!

The meeting was, in fact, held in Sholem the tavern keeper's house. They decided that they would go to the government and demand that it return to the peasant his rights over his own free time and his hard-earned groschens. Once again he would sit over a glass of liquor at a table with his friend in a tavern. It was his right . . .

The delegation proceeded to the government—to the regional police superintendent. They were told to leave and not disturb the peace . . .

So they returned to the village, furious. They came together and immediately proceeded to the monopoly store with stones in their pockets. They broke the window panes and did all kinds of damage.

For a short period of time the monopoly remained closed. In the village, the "high caps," the "cockades," and the "glittering buttons" arrived. They disciplined the village, ordering them to repair all of the damages and to conduct themselves appropriately. If not the gendarmes would be brought in, and the village would have to maintain them at its own expense.

With hanging heads the peasants themselves repaired all of the broken windows and everything else they had damaged. The young Polish nobleman returned with his entire household and added a large, ferocious dog that stood watch through the night while chained to the front gate of the courtyard. The dog roared like a worked-up lion and cast the fiery gaze of a tiger upon every passerby.

The gentiles got used to the new way of drinking. They bought the bottles, took them home, drank them at home, beat their wives and children, and argued with the neighbors—until . . .

NEW DECREES

Until a new decree aroused the village and pushed aside their dissatisfaction with the liquor monopoly. To the Jewish settler, Tsar Nikolai brought new decrees, and to the peasant, new gifts, new salvations. Jews were ordered to hand over every foot of land they held in their own name to the government or sell it to someone who was Russian Orthodox.

The peasants were ordered to build schools for their children, buy books, and board the teachers the government is good enough to appoint for them.

The decrees went like this:

To our Russian narod! *The government of our little father, Tsar Nikolai, hereby informs you that he's had enough of the good Russian, the salt of the earth, being kept in ignorance. The time has come to turn our children into literate folk so that they can sign their own names and read the prayers for their Tsar, the Little Father Nikolai, and the Gospel of the Holy Christ. Amen.*

At that moment, the Jews in the villages who owned their own land didn't understand the true meaning of the decree. In a state of agitation they ran to the bigwigs in the district city—to the regional police superintendent, one of whom they slipped a fiver, and another a tenner. They soon returned enlightened. Their fate had been spelled out so bluntly that soon even their wives and children knew the decree by heart.

There was nothing to be done.

The Jew, with land in his own name, searched for a suitable buyer. But just when the Jew had to sell his field there were no buyers. Straightaway the administrative officer gave a wink and let the village's mayor and elder know that they mustn't dare buy land from the Yids. They would have to leave it and clear out, and then the field would be theirs for the taking—and without having to pay for it to boot.

After the release of the decree to the peasants to build schools and to allow the Russian *narod* to learn their letters, there was no rush to obey it. After all, these weren't taxes that they had to pay the government for the scrap of land in their possession.

For not fulfilling this decree, no government official would come and take away their last cow from the stall. Just a moment ago the grandfathers and fathers had been living their lives without being able to read—and, well, their children would wait to become literate. There was no need to hurry. No one was standing there in anticipation of them coming into knowledge.

The Jewish settlers frantically searched for buyers. They rushed off to neighboring small towns to ask the rabbis what they should do. But no help was to be found anywhere. The Jews who owned a small parcel of land waited for what God would give them. Others succeeded in selling their land dirt cheap and moved to nearby shtetls to look for a means of earning a living in the markets. Still others signed over the ownership of their land to a good neighbor and waited, utterly vulnerable to his benevolence. They hoped he wouldn't send them away and claim that everything belonged to him.

THE GROUND BENEATH

For Jews such as Sholem of Ugli, this problem was difficult to solve. The regime had already taken away his livelihood—the tavern and his liquor license. Well, so be it—he would have to manage without them. After the first decree he simply missed the commotion. The doors which had seldom closed, the banging of the pitchers and the pails, the constant measuring out of liquor, the counting of the money, the chatter of the customers, and the squeaking of the wagons in the yard—all of that was now gone. All was quiet—as after a funeral. A terrible unease blanketed the house and its surroundings. After so much traffic and hullaballoo it was difficult to get used to the orphaned tables and chairs, the pitchers and pails. Having previously minded the tavern, Vasil was now without regular work, and he saw himself as superfluous.

Oliana, the Sabbath goy, also felt embarrassed. She looked down at her large, hardworking hands as if they were suddenly no longer of use.

But as time passed they began to look for other work. They got used to their lot of the quiet life in the field, the stall, and the barn.

Sholem himself wasn't all that bothered. He had enough work to do without the tavern. The field was always ready to accept an honest day's work and was grateful to the hands that tended it.

But the new decree regarding ownership of land had an altogether different effect on Sholem. What did it all mean? Would he have to sell his own field? How do you go about selling a field? He *was* the field; it was a part of his own life. Each tree in the orchard was a part of him. He had planted them with his own hands. The joy he experienced in the debut of each new fruit on the saplings was something that could not be expressed in words. Perhaps it was the joy that Peshe felt when she bore another child for him, because with the joy of new fruit Sholem could rejoice openly—before Jew and gentile alike and before God, too . . .

How could all of this be sold?

Still, when you go to sleep and the little pillow beneath your head becomes just a little uncomfortable and uncertain for the first time in your life, you really do start to think about things. And through long nights of just such reflection Sholem came up with a way out. He would travel to Minsk to see the governor himself. He would have to make a great effort to reach him. He would bring before the governor his *dyela*, this pressing matter.

Sholem drove off and was away for two weeks. When he returned his appearance—and his prospects—had changed. He now saw that the matter would have to proceed.

In fact he wouldn't be selling the field. He didn't want to sell it. And if he had wanted to sell it, who would have bought it from him? But he had a different plan. On the way back from Minsk he had unexpectedly run into a dear old friend, the Polish nobleman Marko, a wealthy, honest landowner. Over the years Sholem had often done favors for Marko and lent him a few rubles. When Sholem told him about where things stood with him and his field Marko said, "I'll help you as much I can."

Sholem discussed the issue with Peshe and with his neighbor, Reb Yoshe of Otkulevitsh. Since time was of the essence and the deadline for the decree was fast approaching, Sholem went to Marko and asked him if he would take the fields over in his, Marko's, name. Marko was not keen to do so. He was no longer a young man, and although he could vouch for himself and his own honesty, there was no way to ensure the ultimate outcome of all of this. He had young sons and daughters, and he couldn't guarantee their actions.

Sholem felt that Marko really meant what he said. He trusted him as if he were a family member. He had asked and eventually persuaded Marko to do this favor because there wasn't a better friend to whom he could turn.

Marko went with Sholem to the district city. They drew up all the necessary papers. To make Sholem feel more confident Marko presented him with promissory notes stating that he would give him eight thousand rubles. In the case of

Marko's death or if one of his children did something malevolent to him Sholem would be protected with that sum of eight thousand rubles.

Sholem returned home and life went back to normal. But the sense of peace that had previously reigned in Sholem's house gradually began to ebb. During the day, when he was busy in the field, his mind was overcome with worry. And at night—well, there was no relief from the worry then either. The ground beneath his feet had lost its solidity, and his step upon it had become full of fear. So much hard work had gone into making this place all that it was: the stalls, the barns with the hay, the silos with wheat, the orchards with fruit . . . He repeatedly drove away these thoughts that kept coming at him like wild dogs. And while they may have retreated for a brief time, they inevitably returned to rip out chunks of his peace of mind.

Sholem's insecure situation also affected the entire household. Without the tavern Peshe had more time to think, and the children came together on the Sabbath and spoke of the city and of looking for something to do.

The eldest son, Faytl, was still studying in the yeshiva. He was a young man of twenty, no evil eye, and it was indeed time for him to figure out what he was going to do with his life. Malkeh, the eldest daughter, was also grown. At almost eighteen years old she was still her parents' right hand, indispensable in running the household.

THE NON-JEWISH SCHOOL

Soreh was whiling away her days without any direction. She refused to help with the household chores or obey her mother. Instead she ran around like a wild goat, acted as stubborn as a mule, and even talked about wanting to get away from home. She said she wanted to go to Kapyl' to become a seamstress, earn some money, and become a socialist.

It was quite difficult to say how Soreh got such ideas and talk into her head. Unless, of course, she got them from the gentiles in the village, who had started to revolt over the school the government had mandated them to build and the expense of maintaining an *uchitel* they would have to pay for out of their own pockets.

At first they thought the government was only advising them, making a suggestion, if you will. But then the village constable came—once and then a second time—and sternly explained that this was an order that had to be followed. Hearing that, the gentiles began to revolt, holding meetings and demanding justice. We should build the schools? How? We don't even have enough money to pay our taxes! If the government wants to educate the folk, let *it* build the schools and pay the teachers!

But their making their case didn't do much good. After an official summons came to the village elder requiring each citizen to appear individually on such and such day in court, the village began to assemble the lumber and build a school. In fact, it was on a portion of Sholem's field, not far from Sholem's house, gate, and garden. It was a large structure with a shingled roof that followed the model presented in an architectural drawing. Inside were long tables with benches. A separate home was set aside for the teacher.

In the beginning of fall a slim young girl with a pale, beautiful face and blonde, neatly combed hair arrived. With her white, high-collared blouse and narrow black tie, she looked like a slim young man. This was the teacher.

Straightaway Soreh found a way to spend time with this young lady from the big city. She brought her bread and milk and helped her tidy up when the students left for the day. Sometimes Soreh even stayed overnight in the teacher's home.

Unexpected guests often came to the young teacher. These young people wore black blouses, high collars, and red belts; their forelocks were long and unkempt.

After such visits from these remarkable, strange guests, an odd echo lingered in the village. A packet of printed brochures was found in the mayor's house. When the materials were brought to a village meeting and their contents were dissected, the people were utterly amazed. Such honest words! To speak out so strongly against the injustices suffered by the peasants!

Several of the older peasants went as far as to wipe their eyes, while others took off their caps and crossed themselves, blessing the honesty of the government and their Little Father Nikolai. The time had come when the wretched peasant would also be treated with consideration.

Then the matter attracted the notice of the rural district—the constable and then the regional police superintendent. They came and searched, rummaging through things. How did such papers manage to get into the village? Who brought them? They told the mayor to keep an eye on the matter and to inform officials in the rural district as soon as he spotted anything suspicious in the village.

In this way time passed. The teacher taught the children—not so much about Little Father Nikolai and the New Testament as about their own difficult lives. She visited the peasant women in their homes, befriending them, helping them out when one of their children was sick and speaking with the older children. She also held evening classes for adults. The school became the hub of the village.

People thought of Helyena, this young lady, as nothing less than a god.

And the guests from the outside—those young folks in black blouses, with red belts and long forelocks—kept on coming.

Moreover, it reached the point that peasants from two villages would gather on a Saturday evening. On a table in middle of the street, one of the red-belted guests would stand up, cast his head, crowned by its long forelock, upward, and spread out his arms like two loops over the gathered audience. The audience stood there in amazement and listened as if riveted in place, with bated breath . . .

Things continued in this way until gendarmes on horseback—four riders with spurs—arrived from Romanow, a shtetl eight versts from Ugli, and sought to disperse the crowd and seize the speaker. But in the end the people badly beat up the riders and hid the speaker. When it had all quieted down the peasants harnessed two horses and drove the guests to the train.

Helyena, the young lady, went with them.

Soon after this event government officials came and ordered the peasants to board up the windows and doors of the school—and abandon for the time being the task of teaching the Russian *narod* to read . . .

Quiet returned to the village. But shortly thereafter individuals from the outside appeared from time to time. As if descending from heaven above they convened their meetings, gave speeches to audiences, left behind a packet of brochures, and vanished.

A SEAMSTRESS

People speculated that it was from these events that Soreh got the idea to go to Kapyl′ to learn to sew and to become a socialist.

On his recent visits home from Hrozawa, Itshe too would express dissatisfaction. He said he couldn't stay in the shtetl anymore. He had no one with whom to study there, and he wanted to go to Slutsk to pursue a secular education.

And so in Sholem's house, the kind of unease and discontent that appears before a storm became palpable. The birds tore themselves from the nest, each in its own way seeking to test its wings . . .

The first revolutionary steps to reverberate in Sholem's house were Soreh's.

With all of her obstinacy and primitive will, Soreh decided that she must leave to become a seamstress and a socialist. But the house was burdened with more pressing concerns and, as a result, few paid much attention to Soreh's talk . . . until she failed to appear at the table for lunch . . . or for dinner. As the family members looked around and tried to brainstorm about her possible whereabouts, a close neighbor stopped by and reported that when he had gone to market in Kapyl′ today he unexpectedly ran into Soreh behind the barns. She was carrying a small package in her hands and asked if she could catch a ride with him to Kapyl′.

Only then did things become clear to everyone. Peshe immediately began to worry that she might have disappeared somewhere.

On Thursday, when members of Sholem's household went to Kapyl′ to buy things for the Sabbath and to see if they could locate Soreh, they found her, along with two other girls, at Roda the tailor woman's table. Soreh had a needle in hand and her head was bent over a dark fabric as she sewed fine stitches.

Roda was a distant relative of Sholem, and in his house they guessed that they might well find Soreh with Roda.

When Peshe loudly shouted her tirade at Soreh, wanting to know why she hadn't told anyone where she was going, Soreh stayed silent. She didn't say a word and instead kept stabbing the needle into the fabric as if she weren't the one being addressed. When asked if she were coming home for the Sabbath she responded that she wanted to stay here, that she didn't have anything to do at home.

Roda told Peshe that she had run into Soreh standing in the marketplace, dazed, not knowing where to go, and so she took Soreh home with her. Soreh soon asked Roda to teach her to sew. The girl showed great diligence. If Peshe wanted she could leave Soreh with her. She would teach her how to sew. It would always be useful for a girl. Look how it had helped her, although in her youth she never dreamed that she would have to earn her livelihood from tailoring. Still, she didn't want to offend anyone. As long as everyone was healthy—that was the main thing.

Soreh did stay at Roda's to sew and, in fact, rarely came home. When she did come back, she was in a hurry to return to Roda's. She preferred to be in the shtetl for the Sabbath. As time went on she largely stayed at Roda's home in Kapyl′.

Each Thursday someone brought her a package of food—butter, cheese, eggs, a beautiful challah, a few rolls—from home. As for cooked meals, she ate those at Roda's.

In this way six months passed. Roda was extremely pleased with Soreh, and for her part Soreh too didn't complain. But each week, when Malkeh or Peshe came to Kapyl′, they noticed that Soreh was wasting away, that she was becoming paler and thinner. Soreh had been tan, with high cheekbones, big, black eyes, and thick, black hair that circled her forehead and ears in lovely tresses. She was sturdily built, with wide hips, an energetic step, and a beautifully developed bosom. At fifteen years old she appeared mature—a grown woman. Now thin folds of emaciation could be detected on her face, and her eyes appeared exhausted and tense.

Peshe and Malkeh became frightened. They had always been accustomed to seeing a healthy and carefree Soreh. They asked her how and where she spent her free time, whether she should be taken home for good, and whether the town air and sitting bent over a needle wasn't causing her great harm.

They made an effort to persuade her that it was time for her to go home. But their words had no effect. It was as if she and the seamstress had made an agreement, as if they were bound to one another in a longstanding love. Soreh claimed that things were good for her here, that she didn't want to go home. And Roda said, "The child feels good here. Everyone loves her. What will she do if she goes back to you in the village? And by the way, I don't know what we'd do here without her. We've gotten so used to having her, both the children and I myself. Listen, you take good care, but just leave her be."

A MARRIAGE AGREEMENT

At Sholem's house they were taken up with a much more important matter.

After all, the young Soreh was always obstinate and did whatever she wanted. When she herself got tired of living with Roda she'll come home, they figured.

The excitement in the house was over a marriage agreement and then the formal engagement contract that followed. Preparations soon began for the wedding.

The marriage agreement had been made for Faytl, the eldest son. It was quite a distinguished one with a young woman from the shtetl of Pesatshne, about a six-verst drive from Ugli. Pesatshne had a lot of sand and sand pits. Sholem would now be linked through marriage with its wealthiest property owner.

The bride was a professionally trained pharmacist who knew four languages. Having studied in Minsk, she was highly urbanized. The family drove over; the bride and groom looked each other over for the first time. The in-laws were already acquainted.

The bride was taken with the groom straightaway. True, Faytl was a yeshiva boy, but he was quite handsome, well proportioned, with a high, white forehead from under which shone large, gentle, gray eyes. And he had a beautiful, sweet speaking voice.

An engagement contract was quickly drawn up, and a wedding date was picked out for four months from that date.

Faytl didn't want the engagement, the wedding, or the highly learned, wealthy bride. He walked around in utter silence—like a mute. On the bride's side they interpreted this as shyness. On the groom's side they knew what was really going on. But they kept silent, pretending not to know.

From as far back as childhood Faytl had been in love with his cousin Mikhliye—a daughter of one of Sholem's brothers—who lived in a neighboring shtetl. She was a quiet, beautiful village girl who endeared herself to everyone who came to know her. They had loved each other since childhood, and as they grew, their love grew with them until it assumed its current, natural form.

But this was something neither Peshe nor Malkeh could bear. "This won't work. Such a thing cannot be permitted. We didn't keep him in yeshiva until he was twenty-one years old for this—to be Shimen the pauper's son-in-law and a maidservant's husband."

Shimen of Dakhtervitsh, although he was Sholem's blood brother, lived a life that was completely different from Sholem's. An honest man, without ambition, he didn't own any field land—just a small, low house with a surrounding garden, not far from the lake. The house didn't have a floor, and the roof was low. His wife, Khashe, didn't know the prayers, but she was a pious woman. The six children at home were the apples of their eye—both hers and Shimen's.

All of the children were called by the affectionate, diminutive forms of their names: Sorehle, Mikhlinke, Hayele, Motele, Khayemke, and Rivele.

It was always warm and bright in their house. The floor was swept clean and spread with yellow sand.

Shimen supported his household by driving lumber and railroad ties to the river, where they were then transported to Prussia. He was quite a hard worker and a pious Jew. Although Shimen was not learned he could recite the prayers and the Psalms—and he did so with all of his heart. He saw to it that all of his sons became artisans: the eldest was a shoemaker, the second was a tailor, and the youngest was a tanner. The daughters took in sewing at home in the village, and when there wasn't enough sewing to be done they went to Slutsk to serve in a pious, bourgeois home. To be ashamed of work was considered a sin. And although Shimen drove the railroad ties just like the peasants, he was greatly respected—by Jews and gentiles alike.

The children conducted themselves with refinement and dignity. They didn't see themselves as beneath others because of the work they did. The daughters looked like well-educated children. From their mother they inherited a lovely appearance and affability. From their father—straightforwardness and a healthy attitude toward life.

The most beautiful and beloved of all was Mikhliye. When Faytl came home for Passover or the holidays he would go over to Uncle Shimen's house and return home late at night with Uncle Shimen's children. Peshe and Malkeh stayed awake and waited up for him.

The older the children got the more strained the relations became between Sholem's household and Shimen's daughter. She was always quiet as a dove and felt guilty about the state of things.

It finally reached the point that Peshe told Mikhliye to tell her mother to get the whole notion of them ever becoming in-laws out of her head. She added that Mikhliye should find a young man—her own peer—when she was working in town and leave her son in peace.

Mikhliye was sent off to a faraway city to work. But she became sick there. So that she would breathe in fresh air that the doctors had prescribed, she accepted a position as a maid in a lumber company records manager's house situated in a forest, not far from home.

Faytl became an even quieter young man, utterly withdrawn, full of longing, forever nursing an inner, distant melody within himself. As if through a cloud of smoke his gray eyes always seemed to be looking elsewhere, somewhere far away, so as not to see the reality close at hand.

In the meantime preparations were underway at Sholem's house for the wedding.

Tailors were brought in for the occasion. For three weeks they measured and sewed. Faytl allowed himself to be measured. As he was being turned from side to side and everyone marveled at how the clothes fit him like a glove, Faytl just stood there like a mannequin, sad, lost in thought, and gazing off into the distance.

In the evenings he disappeared altogether. He returned home late, tossing and turning in bed until late into the night.

EN ROUTE TO THE WEDDING

As they were driving to the wedding in Pesatshne, Faytl took action on a decision of his own for the first time in his life. He was sitting with his two little brothers and sisters in one wagon and there was Mikhliye—right next to him. This was what he wanted. There was no time to argue. He insisted, and he saw it through.

In her child's mind Dineh replayed that journey for a long time. The older she got the more evident it all became to her. With greater clarity and precision she was able to grasp the meaning of her brother's words, spoken through tears, as well as Mikhliye's words, also spoken through suppressed tears.

The wagon was tightly packed. The road, full of potholes, stretched out long and lazy before them. They rode on and on, hour after hour. Soon it was late—night. Dineh was so sleepy she couldn't keep her eyes open. The wagon rocked from one pothole to another. As if in a dream she heard conversation . . .

"I'd rather you were taking me to my funeral."

"Oh dear, what are you talking about? May God protect you! You're not allowed to talk that way."

"Not allowed? No one is allowed to do anything . . . The sin now being perpetrated against both of us is greater than all other sins. And that *is* allowed?"

"What can we do? This is our destiny. We are poor, and you—"

Faytl interrupted her. "We? What *we*? Malkehtske—it's beneath her dignity. She simply can't stand that I love you. That everyone loves you. That you are so beautiful."

"Don't be silly. I'm not beautiful."

Quiet.

"And my mother can't stand it either. A noblewoman! I hope nothing terrible happens to me for saying this, but your mother is more of a human being than mine."

"Stop, Faytl. You're not allowed to talk that way about your mother."

They fell once more into silence. Dineh napped. The wagon lurched. She started awake and heard Faytl speaking quietly. "But you're not angry at me, are you?"

Mikhliye sighed. "No. How could I be angry at you? It's not your fault. After all, you can't do anything differently."

"You won't get married, Mikhliye? Will you wait for me?"

Mikhliye was silent.

"Will you wait for me?" Faytl asked again.

"What are you saying, Faytl?"

"Well, yes, what am I saying? You should get married. Of course you should get married. Let someone else have you, and I'll just torture myself like this."

Through choked-back tears, Mikhliye pleaded, "Stop, Faytl, stop . . ."

After the wedding Faytl and his wife lived with his father- and mother-in-law at their expense.

Sholem's house kept getting eerier and emptier. Itshe had departed on foot for Slutsk to look for work in an iron business and to pursue his secular studies in his free time. He was spoken of as if he were an adult. After several trips to Slutsk Sholem brought back news of Itshe—that he was well liked at both his place of work as well as his place of study. He had befriended the best youth in town, and he had a good reputation.

But the unease in Sholem's house only increased. The evenings stretched on. In the quiet everyone wondered: What will the future bring? Generally, the parents thought—and worried—about how to achieve a decent life for their children.

Malkeh was getting older. Matchmakers turned up. She didn't want to hear about any matches and didn't let anyone get close. She held herself stiffly and acted arrogant. Whom was she waiting for? It was hard to say. She was beautiful, healthy, and young. Young people attached themselves to her but she rebuffed them, hid herself from them, and fashioned herself into a sedate young lady.

Her parents searched for a solution for such behavior coming from a girl of her age—and couldn't find any.

Dineh and Daniel were squandering their days at home. They needed a religious school with a teacher. It was time to study the Talmud. Both children had good heads. In the case of Dineh—well, that was one thing, but Daniel was a boy. He, at least, had to be taught.

At this time things were not going so well for Soreh in Kapyl′ either. The girl was getting more emaciated by the week. They tried giving her more to eat: more challah, more butter. It was hard to find out from Roda what was wrong with the girl. She thought the world of Soreh—truly a dear child. May all good people have such an outstanding child. Her family at home knew nothing about how Soreh lived there or how she spent her free time and her Sabbaths. As for why she appeared so emaciated—that too eluded them.

SHPRINTSE

Of the two seamstresses who sewed with Soreh around Roda's table, only one was Soreh's age. This was Levi the shoemaker's daughter—a dynamo who sang songs about labor strikes and who planned to immigrate to America. The second at the table was Shprintse, one of Roda's nieces. Because of her small, delicate, almost childlike appearance, she was called by the diminutive form, Shprintsetske. She was a placid, refined creature who wouldn't swat a fly from the wall. She sat quietly, sewing her petite stitches into the fabric. When she did speak to another girl she did so only in the politest of terms: would you please, dear, and many thanks. Every word she uttered, every movement of her genteel hand served as an example to the person she was addressing, as if she were demonstrating without having to resort to speech: "This is how it should be done. This is what is correct."

Shprintsetske's look was foreign, utterly alien to Kapyl′. Each day she came to work stiffly laced up. Some said that she was wearing a stiffly buttoned-up foundation garment, while others maintained that she was actually wearing a corset, like the ladies in the big cities. The dress, which conformed closely to her small form, was made of a black material. It had a small, precise, white collar that was stiffly starched and stiff, white cuffs, which she removed for work. Under the collar she wore a long, narrow tie made of dark green silk with slight, white dots. On high heels—small, lacquered shoes. Her reddish-blonde hair was swept up in a high coiffure. At work she wore a little white apron; numerous escaped strands of curly hair floated around her neck. From her pocket invariably extended a flowered kerchief, which she would often decorously remove to wipe her small, bright-green eyes that always seemed to have just been crying. She then looked meekly and ruefully around for having done so. Immediately afterward she wiped her heavy pince-nez mounted in a black frame and hanging on a black silk ribbon. On that same ribbon also hung a small gold watch that she kept in a bosom pocket of her dress. The white lace of a handkerchief extended from her left sleeve.

All sorts of rumors and stories circulated around Shprintse. But the truth was that no one could say for certain what was true or what had really happened to her in the countries where she had lived.

This is what was known. Shprintse was thirty-two years old. She had left Kapyl′ when she was eighteen. She was enlightened, modern, and read forbidden booklets. She had gone to Minsk. From there it was said that she became a worker, a tailor—and a teacher in the evenings in a "free school" for workers. It was said that one night after a meeting she and other workers disappeared. After that she was said to be studying in St. Petersburg. Then word was that she was incarcerated in the Petropalovsk prison. Still later people heard that she had taken up with a man—a political leader—in St. Petersburg and that he had been exiled to Siberia and had died there. Others reported that she too had died.

But some six years ago, on a cold winter's day, a sleigh drove up to Leybe the sexton's home. His wife, Neshe, was coming out to see who was visiting—when soon a throng formed around the sleigh. Neshe fainted. Someone ran to get Leybe to come home from the cold synagogue. The young people didn't know the identity of the guest who was causing such a commotion. And the older folks didn't recognize Shprintse anymore. It was only when Neshe came to and began screaming "Oh my God! I can't believe I've lived to see this in my old age! My child! So this is what's become of you!" that it hit them that this must be that daughter of Leybe about whom such varied stories—some credible, some not—had circulated.

An iron trunk was taken down from the sleigh, Shprintse paid and thanked the gentile driver, and they went inside. The audience that had gathered outside began to disperse in twos. Each person had something to whisper in the ear of a companion. The basic gist was: "That poor old father."

A few weeks passed and Shprintse was, once again, standing next to a sleigh and gratefully paying a gentile. Only this time the iron trunk now found itself in a small room on poorhouse street. She was in Aleksey the caretaker's house, where the old, tidy Kulina circulated in a wide, white apron and maintained the cleanliness of her walls as her husband, the old caretaker, maintained the regional police superintendent's courtyard and orchard.

Once Shprintse moved into a gentile household, Leybe, who for years had been somewhat hard of hearing, became completely deaf and stared back like a simpleton when someone spoke to him. Neshe was more likely to be found in bed than out of it. In the women's section of the synagogue the women looked at her with pity and wiped their eyes.

Another interval of time elapsed. People noticed that in the early mornings Shprintse briskly left the poorhouse street and walked downhill to Roda. When women brought work to Roda they saw Shprintse sitting there like a laced-up doll and sewing.

Out of curiosity, housewives now stopped by more often at Roda's for all of their sewing needs and to be measured for dresses. Shprintse now wore a measuring device around her neck. She stood up on tiptoes in her little lacquered shoes with their high heels to reach tall, fully grown women or she spread out newspaper and got down on her thin, childlike knees before them to measure the length of the dresses.

These days fashion journals were making their way onto Roda's sewing table. Shprintse would sew a garment based on the fashion and presentation shown in the journal.

What compelled the eye's attention more than anything else was her white handkerchief, with which she blew her nose with great elegance. The girls thought of her as stuck up because of her refined, understated speech and because of the handkerchief so white that a blind person would have been able to see it. If it wasn't because of haughtiness, why else would someone blow their nose with a white handkerchief when it would so quickly get dirty? She wants to show us that she has big-city style. Why did she wear that watch on a black cord? Wasn't it to make clear to all that she wasn't just a nobody?

Women reported that there was a theory circulating that she had had a gentile for a husband and that she herself had converted. Why else would she need to live at the home of a caretaker?

Others went even further with their speculation. They spoke of how she behaved with small children. According to these stories, she had decorated her little room with a small, stuffed doggy on the dresser and a little doll with blonde hair wearing a green silk dress and red beads around her neck. Given all of these indicators, they said, she probably had a child of her own . . .

And they speculated further that when the child was born, Shprintse, out of her tidiness, set it on the potty to do its business and didn't keep it in diapers. Because there hadn't been pieces of paper with verses from Psalms 121 hanging on the walls to ward away the evil spirits, the child, God have mercy, was snatched away by the hands of death. She was holding on to the child's things as a memorial, and she cried her eyes out in grief.

Roda, who was Neshe's blood sister and Shprintse's aunt, treated her like a gift from God—never speaking to her without a "please," offering her a glass of chicory and a cookie in the morning and serving her lunch and supper. True, Shprintse didn't let Roda wash the dishes. That Shprintse did herself—in her own, big-city way: triple-washing them, setting them to dry off, and then wiping them until they sparkled.

RODA

For Roda, Shprintse's difficult life was an affirmation of her own fate. The two women shared much in common that served to bind them to each other.

Roda was all of ten years older than her niece Shprintse. In the small shtetl people went looking for sensationalism and invented fantastical stories to feed their famished imaginations. About people like Shprintse they concocted whatever popped into their minds. But also through Roda's life experiences the people of the shtetl of Kapyl′ were destined to come in contact with the sort of bizarre stories that Jewish daughters only encountered in the storybooks they rented for two kopecks from Elye the Redhead and read on the Sabbath after supper and over whose pages they lost themselves and spilled tears.

At nine years of age Roda had been left a complete orphan in a home of brothers and sisters older than her. An aunt from Slutsk came and took Roda home with her. This aunt maintained a tavern where soldiers would come to drink and while away the night. Roda was a pretty child. The soldiers carried her in their arms, bought her presents, and she grew up lovely and clever. The aunt made her help out in every possible way.

But when Roda was sixteen years old the aunt began to fear for her actions—the way she conducted herself with the soldiers as if she were their sister. She, the aunt, herself was elderly and wanted to find a match for the orphan. She had a matchmaker summoned to find an honest groom for her niece. She was prepared to bequeath the house and tavern to Roda, as she had no children of her own, and she and her elderly husband would live out their years here, in fact, with their niece and her future husband.

It wasn't long before the matchmaker returned pleased. He had a groom, a delightful man. And since the groom knew who the bride was—he had seen her on more than one occasion and he liked her—they would soon be able to write up the engagement contract. The wedding would take place, God willing, on the Sabbath after Shavuot.

On a Saturday evening the aunt—Soreh was her name—told her to put on the blue dress with the white belt at the waist and notified her that important people would be coming to the house and that she should offer them some sponge cake and liquor at the table. She mustn't jump like a goat and guffaw at every moment as she had a habit of doing when she was among gentiles. "An honest man will be coming here. May the merit of your poor mother's good deeds help you now. A sapling gone so early from the world. She wasn't destined to walk a single child of hers to the marriage canopy."

And Aunt Soreh sobbed and wiped her eyes.

Roda donned the blue dress, combed her lovely chestnut-brown hair, looked in the mirror, broke into laughter as she was prone to do before remembering that she mustn't laugh—and then went quiet. Before long the door opened, and the matchmaker and the groom entered.

Roda didn't grasp the full reality of the situation. She looked at the two men and offered them some sponge cake and liquor at the table, still not realizing why her aunt had told her to get all dressed up. Perhaps some other guests would be arriving. Perhaps someone that she, Roda, would want to appear dressed up for. She wanted to break into laughter, but she restrained herself. She found it so boring to hang around these old folks.

The door opened again and Aunt Soreh's relatives and their wives entered. They all sat down around the table. Words were exchanged; something was written down on paper. A plate broke, and "Congratulations!" rang out.

Roda still didn't fully understand what was happening here. And when one of the men approached her, took her by the hand, and pinched her cheek, Roda wrenched herself from his grasp, insulted. But her aunt murmured to her: "He is, after all—and to your great fortune—your groom—a man of sacred learning. With God's will things will go well for you with him."

For a moment Roda burst into laughter out loud, and then, recalling what was happening to her, she shouted: "I don't want to! Get out of here!"

And when her aunt went over to her, started to caress her, and asked her to calm down, Roda grabbed a shawl from on top of the bed and left the house, slamming the door behind her and not returning to go to bed. Her aunt found her and told her to come home. She explained to her that she was now a bride to Reb Yoshe, the ritual slaughterer. This made Roda even more furious.

Reb Yoshe the ritual slaughterer was a widower without children, a man with a great red beard and a large red nose and broad shoulders who wore a greasy kaftan. He had begun with some frequency to show up at the tavern home in the evenings to wait until Roda was finished with her work. He would sit down next to the oven in the room that was their home and listen through the wall at how Roda's laughter resounded throughout the tavern filled with soldiers. When she came home and noticed Reb Yoshe, she slammed the door and fled.

The aunt began to tell Roda that she had to comport herself in a respectable manner because, God willing, in another ten weeks she would become the wife of a pious man.

Roda realized that things were looking grim. But she wouldn't marry this man. She could accomplish more with her young heart than with her sense of reason. She packed up a small bundle for her dresses and, on a market day, made her way onto the country road, where she ran into a wagon driver from Kapyl′ who used to bring her regards from the children. She seated herself in the covered wagon and told him to consider her a passenger to Kapyl′. She offered him half a ruble.

When Roda arrived in Kapyl′ at her sister Neshe's house, Neshe was happy to see her. But when she found out what happened she became frightened. If her husband Leybe found out, he'd kick her out of the house.

Unfortunately, it wasn't long before Roda had to look for a place to stay. Neshe herself was poor and lived in a cramped house, with several children of her own to raise. Leybe shouted that she ought to go back to Slutsk and marry Reb Yoshe. "He's a fine man. What does she know, that she-goat? Since there are no parents in the picture there just isn't anyone to keep such a wild she-goat in line," Leybe said.

Roda found a position as a maid in a bourgeois household. But the family was utterly unsuitable. They had never had a servant. She was taken from service and sent to apprentice with a seamstress, and once again she stayed at Neshe's house, with its cramped interior and its poverty.

Leybe was a devout Jew and a sexton in the synagogue. However poor he was he still found a way to bring a guest home each Sabbath.

Neshe economized on everything throughout the week so as not to be ashamed when it came to the Sabbath table. There was always a bit of fish with horseradish and a beautiful challah, an embroidered Kiddush tablecloth, candlesticks gleaming in cleanliness, and the children, with their hair washed and combed, around the table.

SHMUEL-ARN

On one Sabbath Leybe brought home a strange guest: a tall, blond young man about twenty years old with a longish, pale face and eyes continually gazing off into the distance and flashing, as if they were forever engaged in a debate with someone that he—and only he—could see . . . At meals he was absorbed in his own thoughts and would answer a question as if caught red-handed in the midst of an act of theft, uncertain whether he was hearing correctly. His long black kaftan rendered his appearance even more bizarre. His body was elongated, and his pale, long face framed by the blond sidelocks gave him the look of a martyr.

Throughout the meal Roda didn't take her eyes off him. When asked where he came from and where he was headed, the young man himself couldn't really answer. Roda's youthful heart, with all of its fresh tribulations and compassion, focused on his half-baked, inconclusive answers. She kept staring at him until he felt her gaze and asked Leybe if she were his daughter.

For the first time since her days in her aunt's tavern Roda let out a joyous laugh. The children became infected with her laughter, and the guest, not knowing what the laughter was all about, took it personally and blushed. He began to fix his kaftan and tug on its sleeves. Roda noticed his behavior and also blushed—and quickly went quiet. Leybe was mortified. "What's this laughter all about? Huh? You're sitting at a Jewish table! You're not in a tavern," he said.

Neshe felt guilty and began to make excuses. "She's a she-goat so she starts to laugh. The kids don't know any better and just follow her lead," she offered.

At this point the guest felt that Roda was being insulted. So he provided a defense of his own: "When a person laughs, the sound is beautiful to the ear."

Those words resounded in Roda's ears like enchanting chimes.

When the guest left after supper to go to sleep in the synagogue a shiver went through her body. It was so cold outside, and he was so lightly dressed. For the first time in her life she contemplated the cold synagogue. Was it warm enough? And the benches were so hard—how could he sleep there?

The next morning she said to Neshe, "I'll sleep in Shprintse's bed. Maybe you could ask the guest to stay over with us?"

"How should I know? I'll ask Leybe . . . a courteous child. It looks like he's also a Talmudic student."

"He's so handsome! Such a pale face. And so preoccupied he doesn't even hear what you say to him," Roda said.

"That comes from all that Torah knowledge."

"Maybe. So you'll ask Leybe? I'll sleep with Shprintse."

On the Sabbath Roda made the whole house shine. She looked at the guest from beneath lowered eyelashes.

Leybe invited him to stay over but he refused. He would sleep in the house of study.

The guest's name was Shmuel-Arn. He stayed on in Kapyl′. He was given room and board in the most beautiful homes. Pious women gave him a shirt to change into for the Sabbath, and he sat and studied. Everyone showed him respect—both the older folks because of his sharp mind and the educated young folk because of his knowledge of politics and Hebrew literature.

He became a regular guest at the home of Leybe the sexton. And the rumor mills of Kapyl′ started churning at full speed: Who was he, this stranger? And what was he doing here? Among the finest householders in town were those who would gladly have taken him as a groom for their daughters. But he rebuffed all of their approaches. Either he was studying in the synagogue or playing chess with a good player or reading a Hebrew newspaper from time to time—and then spending the rest of his time at Leybe the sexton's house. It had to have been fated from heaven that such good fortune would come to a poor orphan girl.

Once, in a conversation with Shmuel-Arn, Leybe dropped a broad hint: "I've got her on my hands . . . a girl, an orphan. People are talking . . . it would make sense for there to be a match. Her aunt in Slutsk will surely give her a hundred rubles for dowry. She feels like a mother toward the girl because she raised her in her own home."

Shmuel-Arn sat quietly, was silent for a long time. His face became even paler. His gray eyes stared intently into the distance. A thin smile played around the sides of his mouth. Without answering he stood up, said good night, and left the house. After his departure Leybe reflected about him. "He's probably afraid. He's alone here. He'll be a rabbi in a large city yet. A dear young man."

Leybe felt sorry for Roda. If he had been a rich man and able to give her a true dowry, he would have dared to speak differently. But as things stood, alas; what could he offer the young man?

In a week's time the young man disappeared. Once again Kapyl′ became animated. Thousands of rumors circulated around him: he had seduced the orphan girl and fled; he'd become disgusted with the synagogue and studying; he was from distant lands and had a father who was a great rabbi; he came here to see how Jews lived and would describe them in the Hebrew-language newspapers . . .

Each person invented his own bright idea.

Leybe felt robbed. "How can it be? How can someone disappear like that without so much as a goodbye?"

With puzzling terseness Roda answered, "He said he had to go but that he'd come back. He didn't know when. But he said he'd be back."

Six weeks later Shmuel-Arn once again appeared in the synagogue in Kapyl′. He appeared even paler than before—and more withdrawn. His burning eyes probed as if they were seeking to elicit . . . from somewhere undetermined . . . a solution to something that was bothering him. His gaze appeared to be that of someone struggling with all of his might to accept a certain decision that was outside the bounds of religious observance. It looked like he succeeded. And then he came to Leybe and told him that he'd decided to marry Roda and that they needed to pick the right day.

The wedding was quite joyous because both bride and groom were complete orphans, may other children be spared such a fate. Therefore, all of the very respectable homeowners of the city got involved. The synagogue courtyard, where the wedding canopy stood, was packed. Young girls looked at the couple, and more than one of them wished for the sort of groom that had been fated for Roda. People gave substantial wedding presents. Aunt Soreh and the sick Uncle Mikhl were the main hosts of the joyous occasion and gave Roda two hundred rubles as dowry. Aunt Soreh brought along two pillows, a good blanket, a feather bed, and a few household items: a meat dish, a small salt board, and four lovely brass candlesticks. If God was helping Aunt Soreh give away the youngest child of her sister lying, alas, so young in the ground, and if God hadn't preordained her to have children of her own to give away in marriage, then may she, Roda, have good fortune—Aunt Soreh considered the bride to be her own child, for she had raised her in her own home.

Aunt Soreh forgot all about the earlier marriage plan with its shredded betrothal agreement. She wiped her eyes in parental pride as she gazed at the beautiful young couple.

Roda was flushed, looking out from under lowered eyelashes. Whenever she looked at Shmuel-Arn, a light shiver went through her body, both from joy and fear. Today he appeared stranger to her than when she had first seen him seated at the Friday night table. Back then he seemed very familiar to her, but now he was like a man far away, to whom she had no access. He looked extremely pale. To everyone's congratulations he seemed to respond only half-heartedly, with lowered eyes and a catch in his voice. Onlookers noted: "An orphan, poor thing. He must be remembering his parents."

They felt a shooting pain pierce their hearts, and all were vigilant and polite in their conversations with him.

With the money Aunt Soreh gave them the young couple bought a house. They made a down payment and the rest—promissory notes for fifty rubles a year to pay out in four installments. The house had cost five hundred rubles—a real bargain. It stood down the hill, not far from the synagogue courtyard. Above it two streets extended uphill: the poorhouse street and the ritual bathhouse street. And since no coaches drove uphill, the streets going downhill were good for village commerce. When you went to the fairs you had to pass Roda's house.

Roda took to tailoring right away. She bought a sewing machine on installment and began by sewing aprons for gentile women and inexpensive, flowered dresses for peasant girls. After that housewives began to bring in a few children's undershirts to sew, a padded blanket to stitch, or a foundational garment sewn to the body's specific measurements. Curious to see how the young couple was faring right after their wedding, young girls also came by—one with a bodice, another with a blouse. This was how Roda set up a way to earn a living. It was difficult, to be sure, but still Roda sang as she sewed . . . She kept her house sparkling clean. She tended Shmuel-Arn like the apple of her eye. Roda would look after him with pride when he left the house. He treated her with such respect. But most of the time he was sad.

On the Sabbath after the hot meal, when Roda took a walk with Shmuel-Arn on Slutsk Street or in Yanetske's little forest, everyone's eyes would follow them. "It must be wonderful to take a walk with such a handsome husband," the girlfriends would say to each other.

The boys said the opposite: "What a joy it must be to walk in the forest with a young little wife like her."

Shmuel-Arn spent most of his time in the house of study, where he met young people, studied, talked politics, and sometimes went to play chess. He built a reputation as a good chess player. Oftentimes young and middle-aged folk came to Roda's house, where they bickered with Shmuel-Arn about politics before turning to chess. They sat for hours on end over the figures, biting their lips, all the while twisting their young beards and humming a melody under their breath.

Roda sat and sewed, radiant. Every now and then she got up from her seat, dashed over to where the men were sitting, and looked over the chessboard. She invariably saw Shmuel-Arn's figures ahead on the battlefield.

With happiness in her young heart she sewed quickly, quickly, as if the stitches were letters, her needle a pen, and the fabric into which she was sewing a white sheet of paper—and she herself were writing a poem of love and joy.

When she finished her sewing Roda served tea and preserves with cookies for refreshment. The guests followed her movements with grateful glances and partook of the quiet cheer that ruled in the young couple's home.

A happy year passed in this way. Shmuel-Arn found work giving a few private sessions in Hebrew and Russian. The work fell heavily on Roda—she was in the advanced stages of pregnancy.

Shortly thereafter the family celebrated a ritual circumcision. They named the boy Yitskhok-Mendl, after Roda's father and grandfather. With the child's arrival, a new happiness came to the house. Roda went back to her sewing and took on an apprentice girl who also watched over the child. Nothing was lacking in the household. When Itshe-Mendele, as he was called, was a year and a half old, he had a little brother—Leyzer.

Now when Roda and Shmuel-Arn went on their walks, each of them carried a child in their arms.

A DARK CLOUD

On the eve of Rosh Hashanah, Shmuel-Arn went to the house of study and didn't return until after midnight. But the door squeaked as he entered. Roda got out of bed, turned the wick in the lamp, and faced Shmuel-Arn. Seeing his greatly altered face, she became frightened. "What happened?"

But she didn't get an answer. Shmuel-Arn sat down on the corner of the bench, rested his head in his hands, and sat, like a man frozen stiff, drilling with his eyes into his own thoughts. Roda sat opposite him on another bench and shivered as if from the cold until tears caught in her throat and she began to cry.

"Don't cry," Shmuel-Arn pleaded in a semi-imperious tone. "Crying won't help at all."

"Something's happened to you. You look like you just escaped a fire."

"I have escaped from a fire—a sickening one."

He stood up and started to pace nervously through the house, seemingly speaking to himself. "I would have had to give them a hand if I didn't come back to live under the same roof as you. I walked round and round in the streets with the children until the saints, God's thieves, fell asleep."

"Oh my God, what are you talking about? You must be sick. Go lie down in bed." She went over to him, taking him by the hand. "Come, I'll help you take off your shoes. Lie down in bed. Maybe I should call the doctor? Oh dear."

Shmuel-Arn embraced her around the shoulders with one arm, saying, "Come, we'll talk about it." He led her to the bench at the table, sitting her down and seating himself next to her. He was deathly pale. "Roda, do you remember how I told you a while ago—before I went away—that I had something to take care of?"

"Why are you bringing up something of no importance?"

"No, Roda, actually, it's not something of no importance. If only it were."

"Well, what are you talking about?"

"I left, tortured myself for six weeks, and got nothing done. But how would you understand all of this?"

"Tell me, Shmuel-Arn. I'll understand."

"Promise me, Roda, that whatever happens, you'll stand by my side, that you'll help me with these beasts, and that you won't listen to what they'll tell you to do. There must be a way out. We'll have to find a way. You just have to stand firm and not give in to their harsh words."

"Have pity, Shmuel-Arn. In all the time you've known me, have I ever done anything to betray your trust?"

"Well, all right, then hear me out. Do you remember the first time I came to Kapyl'?"

"Of course I remember."

"And at the time I said that I was an orphan."

"Of course you said that. When both of our boys were born, I asked you if you wanted to name them after your father."

"But you don't name a child after a living father."

"What are you saying, Shmuel-Arn? Your father is still alive?"

"If he would leave me in peace I would have forgotten him long ago."

"What are you saying?"

"Listen to me, Roda. I'll tell you now. When I was seventeen my father betrothed me to one of the daughters of a good friend of his, a Hasid as fervent and stubborn as he himself. My father made the match because of both the pedigree and the money. I was studying in the yeshiva. When I turned eighteen I was brought home and told that I was about to be taken to see my bride. A wagon came. My father and stepmother prepared and packed everything I needed for the journey, while warning me that I mustn't forget what happiness was in store for me. I would always have room and board. I could study as long as I wanted and become a rabbi. I went without any enthusiasm whatsoever. But when I arrived there and saw the fine, grand home, with all of its beautiful furnishings, my heart lifted for a moment. My future father- and mother-in-law sat around a beautifully prepared Sabbath table, and I was seated next to the father-in-law. Opposite us sat three young men—three sons—all handsome and strapping youths. Next to the mother-in-law were three daughters. The two younger ones were quite pretty. But one of the daughters appeared aged and sickly. One of her shoulders sagged lower than the other, and her head was turned a bit out to the side, to the lower shoulder. The two younger daughters served me and bashfully smiled at me, but the sick one held herself apart and didn't address a single word to me. The Sabbath day flew by. In the synagogue I was called to the Torah and congratulated. The father-in-law appeared satisfied; the mother-in-law looked from me to her daughters and sighed . . . On Saturday night, after Havdalah, I went back home, and on Sunday I was sent to the yeshiva again. My stepmother suddenly showed me some friendliness: 'He'll have everything he needs there. He's really struck it rich, no evil eye. Amazing! Such classiness!' My father only asked me if I liked the synagogue there. 'You'll still get to be a rabbi there. Such authority Sholem-Ber has there—amazing! It's both Torah and commerce,' he said."

Shmuel-Arn didn't respond to the words of his father and stepmother. He thought only about the two girls and wondered which one of them was to be his bride. Both had kept themselves at a distance from him; he liked them both.

Shortly thereafter Shmuel-Arn was brought home and measured for a new kaftan and new boots—and off they went to the wedding. When Shmuel-Arn went to place the veil over the bride he saw before him the hunchbacked, sick girl. He was confused. Crisscrossing flames flashed before his eyes, as if spears had crawled through his eyes and into his skull . . . He had to be held up beneath his arms and helped to the canopy. The wedding ring fell out of his hands. He recited the vows as if in a daze.

His in-laws went home after the wedding. When Shmuel-Arn's father came to say his goodbyes he was able to speak for the first time. "Papa, I'm going home too."

His father, feigning ignorance, said: "What do you mean, you're going home? Your father- and mother-in-law are providing you with room and board. You'll study here in the yeshiva. With God's help you'll become a rabbi here. You'll have everything you need here."

Shmuel-Arn responded contemptuously to his father. "Papa, are you taking me home? I'm not staying here."

His father looked at him in fury. He sat down in the wagon and left.

Shmuel-Arn didn't go home again. Shmuel-Arn tried to go after his father's wagon, but he noticed his son, got out of the wagon, and threatened him. "Go back home. If you don't, I'll smack you in the face, you brat!"

Shmuel-Arn turned around and began walking in the other direction with rapid strides—into the night, into the world, wherever his eyes carried him, as fast and as far as he could get away from the horror that was now behind him and from the strange, spinsterly daughter of the wealthy Sholem-Ber. The entire problem had assumed the face of an apparition standing like a shadow before his eyes, terrifying to behold. He had to escape from it.

And so Shmuel-Arn hid himself from the apparition, wandering from city to city, never staying in one place for very long out of fear that he would be discovered—until he made his way to Kapyl′. When he decided to marry Roda, Shmuel-Arn returned home to try to persuade his father, after long nights of quarreling and pleading, to see to it that he get a divorce. His father went to Sholem-Ber, but he was adamant about just one thing: he wouldn't grant a divorce. As long as his daughter was a deserted wife, Sholem Ber wanted to ensure that this man, may his name be erased, have no hope of rebuilding his life elsewhere.

At that point Shmuel-Arn decided to take the law into his own hands. And that's why he was sitting here next to her, Roda. According to the law he wasn't allowed to spend the night under the same roof as her.

For a long time Roda looked at him sadly. A thin smile, born of helplessness, played on her lips. She remembered her marriage contract in Slutsk . . . Quietly, speaking more with her eyes than her lips, she asked out loud, "What's going to happen now?"

Her words were like a cure. "They discovered my whereabouts. The rabbi received a letter from the rabbi in Lublin. The gist of it was to send so and so back to his wife who has been stuck for four years in her deserted status. I'll have to go back."

"What are you saying, Shmuel-Arn?"

"I'll go back to get a divorce."

"Well, that you'll have to do."

"But before I do that I'll have to divorce you."

"What are you talking about, Shmuel-Arn?"

"According to Jewish law, that's how it will have to be. If not, I can't demand a divorce from her."

"Well, then, we'll get divorced. And when you get a divorce there you'll come back."

"But in the meantime, what will you do here by yourself? Those wild animals—they'll stone you."

"Who cares about them? It's my bread earned by my own two hands. As long as I sew beautifully and cheaply the gentile women won't care."

Shmuel-Arn went over to her, took her hand, and said, "I don't remember my mother. I've also never had a sister. Only you have treated me the way a mother—and a good sister—would."

The next day Shmuel Arn got up at dawn with Roda to pack his things, and then he went to the synagogue to pray. Soon after prayers her brother-in-law Leybe the sexton and Yisroel the synagogue manager came to tell Roda what she already knew and to order her to go to the rabbi.

After Shmuel-Arn divorced Roda he went to Lublin. But he wasn't granted a divorce there. For two years he wandered to strange places until Sholem-Ber's daughter died of typhus. Then Shmuel-Arn returned to Roda and their children in Kapyl′. Their life was difficult. People avoided their house, and when they went out together into the street they were pelted with stones and bombarded with all sorts of names. People called him a bigamist and her a concubine. They suffered greatly from their surroundings. They went nowhere and saw no one. The women in town avoided the house and didn't allow their daughters to bring work to Roda. Shmuel-Arn accepted a few positions as a teacher in a distant area, but he never lasted a full semester in any one place—first because of his restless nature, and second because as soon as the parents found out about his issue they immediately sent him away . . .

All the while Roda sat through the night and sewed. They had five children, five little blond heads on tidy cushions—four boys and their fifth child, their only daughter, Rivl, who had a stunningly beautiful pale face, long flaxen hair, and deep-set gray eyes like Shmuel-Arn. The children were smart, gifted at study. They couldn't find a teacher for the older two in the small shtetl. The oldest child, Itshe-Mendl, went to study in the yeshiva in Valozhyn, where he was spoken of as a great student.

Shmuel-Arn was often at home. As time went on he had given up on making a living as a teacher and devoted himself to his own children. And just as all things get worn out over time, so what had happened to Shmuel-Arn in his youth faded, little by little, in the minds of the Kapyl′ residents. And because his successful children were such highly welcome guests of the young people in town, they would come to them for books and advice about matters of learning. It got to the point that quite wealthy homeowners sent their sons to study Hebrew with Shmuel-Arn while he was teaching his own children.

Shmuel-Arn noticed that one of his sons, Leyzer, had great talents. He sent Leyzer off to Minsk, where he found several opportunities to teach lessons, instructing others while attending courses himself. The three younger children—Motl, Noske, and Rivele—were still quite young and were taught by their father.

Roda hired three female workers, and with the help of her niece Shprintse the family lived well and peacefully. The old wounds were covered up with a new healthy skin. Shmuel-Arn applied himself in the house of study, debating with others in matters of learning. Once again people came to their house, staying long into the night, playing chess and talking politics. A sense of assurance, stemming from great unity, was palpable in their house. In the meantime their eldest son, Itshe-Mendl, received his rabbinical ordination. Their younger son Leyzerke finished university with great honors and was sent by the government to study in Switzerland.

But then a major change happened in Itshe-Mendl's life. He veered off into political activity and abandoned his studies. He was soon arrested on a political charge and served half a year in prison. When he was released from prison he returned home. Roda and Shmuel-Arn were terrified every time he left the house. They weren't sure he would come back because by that time there was considerable political movement in the shtetl. The *strazhe*—police guards—descended, and arrests became commonplace.

LETTERS

Years earlier, one of Roda's sisters had immigrated to America, where she lived a hard life. Roda also had other relatives in New York. Having heard of Roda's problems with Itshe-Mendl and wanting to save him from danger, they sent him a boat ticket. With great effort Roda gathered together the few necessary rubles and sent him off on his journey to America, where his life would at least be safe. She pined for her two sons, the two apples of her eye, one now all the way on the other side of the ocean.

The mail carrier became the focus of her life. With both sons gone from her she placed her chair, upon which she used to sit and sew, next to the window opposite the synagogue courtyard—because the mail carrier went there every day . . . Roda couldn't read, but she could recognize Leyzerke's or Itshe-Mendl's handwriting on the envelope. Leyzer's handwriting was clear, with large, sharp letters; Itshe-Mendl's was rounded, with uncertain, small letters. Her sister in America's handwriting was pointed, with tense lettering, as if penned by an exhausted hand. Roda recognized all three and held each letter with a different kind of trembling in her heart. She held each for a while, staring at the script before bringing all of them over to the nearest person available in the house to read them to her.

Shmuel-Arn had his own routine. He would read the letter to himself first and only then read it out to Roda. This didn't sit well with her. So Roda selected her own reader. Soreh read her the letters. Truth be told, Soreh read quite badly in the beginning, but her vast curiosity helped a great deal. In her hand she was holding a letter that had come from so far away, traveling over oceans and after that in trains . . . The powers of her imagination ignited her young blood. With all of her powers Soreh strained to know what was being written from such a distance. For her part Roda dragged the words out of her mouth, helping her by heart, guessing what the next word needed to be. Thus, out of these two different senses of curiosity, the letters acquired their sought-after flavor and enhancement. In this way a great friendship was sealed between the lovesick mother and the curiosity-smitten Soreh. One longed for her children and the other—for all that was far away, for the dream of ships and seas and trains and big cities, about which you could fantasize for so long that you became lightheaded . . .

Roda sewed, did the housework, and still found enough time to think about and yearn for the two who were not by her side. But life had taught her to see things for the good. She felt herself to be one of those people who received more than she deserved. Who was she to have such a husband? A simple seamstress, and yet what woman in town had what she had? Her children were her pride and joy, and she therefore felt a profound gratitude for her life. Each child was a distinct jewel to her. And for each day, God was to be thanked.

The Kapyl′ cemetery was located downhill, at the gate of the shtetl, and most of the funeral processions passed Roda's house. And in a small shtetl, funerals did not occur frequently. When someone died the news spread, and practically the whole town attended the funeral—just as they attended weddings. People are greedy for a change that breaks the monotony of gray daily life. With open arms they took in the buzz of a funeral—the elderly women performing a mitzvah by weeping, the young waxing philosophic and serious, the mischievous boys just running around and wondering how they could be carrying someone on a board in broad daylight over their shoulders while he lay there and was silent . . .

SHMUEL-ARN COLLAPSES

It was the morning of the Ninth of Av. Roda hurried into the kitchen to prepare something to eat for the breaking of the fast. Shprintse, Soreh, and the little children were in the sewing room. Through the window Soreh saw a large crowd suddenly coming down from the synagogue courtyard—as if it were a funeral. She called out to Roda and asked, "Who died?" No one knew. The women and children gathered around the window to see what was happening. The crowd was getting closer to the house. It did look somewhat like a funeral procession—and yet not. Someone was being carried on something, but not on a stretcher for the dead. People were hurrying. People were running. Roda's curiosity mounted. She raced to the door; everyone else was right behind her. She saw the crowd turning toward her house. She opened the door and ran out—it was Shmuel-Arn who was being carried! They brought him into the house and lowered him onto the bed. Dr. Rabinovitsh arrived. He danced around on two crutches, jabbing Shmuel-Arn with a needle in his feet, his hands. He shouted to Avreml the medical practitioner to run and bring him this and that from the pharmacy. They made injections, placed boiling compresses. One hour went by, then another. The crowd dissipated. Those who remained: the doctor, the medical practitioner, the rabbi, and Leybe and Neshe. People sat and waited without speaking. Every now and then the doctor sprang up to the bed—and back again to his medicine bag. Suddenly he called out: "He's moving his right hand and foot . . . his left side is completely dead. Paralysis."

In the meantime Roda ran from the room to the kitchen, tearing at her hair. The fingers of one hand frenziedly twisted and seized those of the other, and she burst into a quiet lament. Before long she straightened up, made herself presentable, and went back to where the patient was lying. She approached the bed, bent over, and quietly said to the sick man, "Can you see me, Shmuel-Arn?"

He responded with wheezing, half-intelligible words: "Yes, my darling."

"The doctor says it's nothing. With God's help, you'll get better."

Once again Shmuel-Arn didn't hear anything, fixing his glazed eyes overhead. On his half-twisted mouth a white foam bubbled. He murmured something unintelligible. The doctor held his hand, searching for a pulse. Roda went outside and gathered the children. She created sleeping places for them in the sewing room, on the couch, and on the ground and then put them to bed. She returned, pulled a chair up to Shmuel-Arn's bed, and sat down. Everyone had left. Roda stayed with Shprintse and Leybe, sitting through the night. Teary-eyed, Soreh went to sleep over at Shprintse's.

On Thursday, when Sholem and Peshe came to Kapyl′ and saw what was happening at Roda's house, they ordered Soreh to pack her things.

Soreh was frightened and felt superfluous in a house where such a great misfortune had happened. Her home had narrowed, since Shmuel-Arn had taken over the room where she and the children slept. She definitely didn't want to go back home to Ugli. Feeling as if a sentence had been handed down to her, Soreh asked Shprintse what she should do. Shprintse told her to go home for the time being. Soreh trudged through the house, gathered her few things into a parcel, and mutely bade goodbye to everyone in the house. Roda went over to her and gave her a kiss. "You'll come back, Sorehle," she said. "You're my right hand."

With the bundle under her arm, Soreh snuck out of the house, settled into the wagon, and like a small child burst into tears. Peshe tried to calm her, but Soreh would have none of it.

Sholem told Peshe that he heard how it all happened. Immediately after prayer services Shmuel-Arn had had a heated debate with the rabbi regarding a Torah matter. Suddenly he was unwell and collapsed. Everyone thought he died on the spot, but the doctor discovered that his heart was beating and that he was paralyzed.

THE TABLECLOTH AND THE DRESS

When Soreh returned home the gang was happy to see her. Coming from a city, Dineh thought, she'd surely have stories to tell.

But Soreh surprised the adults as much as the young people. It was a long time before she started to unpack her bundle. Malkeh kept circling it and then asking: "What does she have in there?"

Soreh gave her standard response: "Nothing. What should it be?"

Finally, she let the cat out of the bag. Undoing the bundle, a lustrous vision unfurled before the eyes. There before them was a woolen tablecloth made of many colors, and beside it was also a marvelously beautiful navy-blue dress with flowers and red pearls sewn on its front. And around the edges of its wide sleeves, more flowers.

Malkeh stopped in her tracks as if dumbfounded. With bated breath she kept looking back and forth from the tablecloth to the dress and from the dress to the tablecloth, and after that—at Soreh. Soreh stood her ground. She lowered her head a little so that no one could read what was hidden in her eyes: the secret of these sewn articles that she had brought back from the city to the village. But truth be told, pride and victory shone in Soreh's eyes. Had Malkeh ever seen anything like these things? Never. Had anyone in Ugli seen or even dreamed of anything that could compare?

Malkeh's stiff fingers slowly started to move, and as if of their own accord they reached out to touch the wonder-things that lay before her. Gently and carefully she caressed the miniature, multicolored round saucers from this dazzling tablecloth and then the red pearl flowers of the dress. Quietly, as if to herself, she asked, "Who gave them to you—Roda?"

Soreh defiantly lifted her face and met her older sister's gaze. "What do you mean—Roda? Why would she have given them to me? And how would Roda be able to give away such things?"

"So where did you get them?"

Soreh feigned ignorance. "Where did I get them? As long as I have them, what difference does it make?"

Malkeh called out to Peshe: "Mama, look what Soreh's got here."

When Peshe took it all in, she became frightened: "Where did you get it?"

Her gaze lowered again, Soreh responded, as if to herself: "I embroidered it."

"What do you mean, you embroidered it? And where did you get the money for it?"

"I earned it."

"Where did you earn it?"

"A little bit at Roda's."

"And where else? Roda wasn't supposed to pay you for the first year."

"She wanted to."

"What do you mean, wanted to?"

"She didn't pay me with money. She just sewed the dress for me. I sewed the flowers myself."

"But where did you get the money for the dress and for the tablecloth? It must have cost a small fortune."

Disoriented, Soreh said, "I took it."

"But where—did you steal it from a church?"

"I didn't steal it."

The mystery continued until Peshe threatened that she was about to hitch the horses and drive to Roda's house for an explanation. At that point Soreh had to reveal the big secret that she had hidden for an entire year from everyone except Shprintse and Roda.

When Soreh had arrived in Kapyl′ she threw herself, with all of her primitive childish imagination and her famished eyes, into scrutinizing everything that was stylish and beautiful . . . So she went with another girl on the Sabbath into Yanetske's little forest. Instead of listening to what was being said there at the *sobraniia* of the workers, she assessed each girl—her hairstyle, the dress she was wearing, the shoes she was walking in, the ribbons she had in her hair, and the beads she had on around her neck. She devoured all of this with her eyes the way a starving person eats bread. From there she started to dream day and night. Whenever she was sitting at her work Soreh saw only the dresses, along with the ribbons and beads, she had seen at the *sobraniia* in the forest. Shprintse noticed, and one day she brought Soreh a string of red beads that she'd kept in her possession for years. Since Shprintse now only wore dark clothes she had no need for the beads. With a pounding heart Soreh made a grab for the strand. Her fingers were trembling. But she quickly remembered that she couldn't take it. It wasn't hers, and she had no means to pay for it. Slowly Soreh withdrew her hand. But Shprintse started to persuade her that she was giving it to her as a gift. She said, "Well, good, Sorehle, you can pay me with a stick of butter or a block of cheese or a challah loaf that you get from home."

Soreh agreed. And so a commercial transaction plan was set in place. Soreh would give away her food to Shprintse, subsisting on whatever she could. More than once Roda and Shprintse tried to put a stop to Soreh's bartering, but it didn't help. Soreh had found a way to sell some of her food and to buy herself with those few kopecks what she found more important than challah, butter, and cheese. If she saw a tablecloth at a girl's house, she went through her days making herself sick until she had saved the first fifty kopecks and purchased a bit of wool and an embroidery needle. She started to sew through the night and before and after work. She would turn the miniature saucers, knitting and laying one next to the other: one week, green; the next, red; and after that black and white and violet—until the great wonder emerged. Every time she sneaked a secretive glance at it worlds of fantasy, fantastical lands, unfolded before her very eyes . . . Roda and Shprintse marveled at her determination and her refinement until they made their offer of the navy-blue dress. Soreh didn't accept it right away. She needed to wait. She'd consider it. Only after a few weeks of not sleeping did she agree to it. And so, by way of the challahs, cheese, and butter that she received from home, Soreh attained this great, invaluable wealth.

"Now I see why she's such a wreck," Peshe responded to Malkeh, "wearing herself out and slaving away day and night. And Roda allowed it, didn't even tell me."

Here Soreh interjected: "I made her swear not to tell anyone. She always wanted to tell you."

But all pieces of news get old with the passage of time.

From then on Malkeh looked often and long with hunger at the dresser, where the wonderful tablecloth was stored, and at the closet, where the navy-blue dress, protected by a bedsheet so no dust would fall on it, was hanging. Truth be told, when it came to sewing, Malkeh was no slouch either. She devoted her free time to sewing various wall hangings on hard and soft canvases indicating the east so prayers could be directed toward Jerusalem as well as other Jerusalem scenes. The walls of Sholem's house were decorated with them. With cross-stitches she sewed various types of lace onto towels, along with Russian incantations and poetic phrases. She even produced a tablecloth of thin, white cotton. But reality couldn't be denied: all of her work until that point and all of her things appeared insignificant in comparison to what Soreh had brought into the house from Kapyl′.

Still, Soreh remained thoroughly discontented at home, not wanting to do anything—either in the house or in the field. When she was told to watch over the workers she disappeared straight into the rye. She spread the rye out underfoot, tore off the rye blooms, and spun out all sorts of garlands. She proceeded to adorn the women reapers, whom she ordered to stand with the sickle in one hand and with the other hand placed on their hip. She then assessed them to determine whether she was pleased with the overall effect, to see whether they in fact measured up to how she had imagined them in her fantasies . . . And with the smaller children she organized all sorts of bizarre games, disguising herself as a naiad or a mermaid . . . The older family members did not consider her to be a responsible person, even though by all appearances she was a grown and finely developed young woman. If Malkeh or Peshe sometimes scolded her for not helping out in the house or if they insisted she wouldn't amount to anything, her answer was that she had nothing to do here, that she needed to go to America. Until . . .

One day Soreh vanished from the house again. They looked for her everywhere but couldn't find her. It wasn't until the evening that Uncle Shimen and others told them how they had spotted her quite early when they were driving out of the forest with the wagonloads of railroad ties. She had walked far from the village and asked to be taken to Kapyl′.

"What are you saying?"

"She's going back to sew at Roda's."

And so once again Soreh stayed at Roda's house, and even more than previously proved to be of great help to Roda. In every way she could Soreh performed Roda's chores before she could get to them and helped look after the paralyzed Shmuel-Arn as well as the children. And she sewed.

In Sholem's house the two smaller children, Dineh and Daniel, were without a teacher. No religious teacher was hired. Dineh was often left alone, and together with Henye she pored over the Tanakh and the Russian readers. Daniel, on the other hand, spent his free time playing with the non-Jewish boys in the village and was hardly concerned that he was wasting his time on pointless activity, as their mother called it. In the evenings after work, when Sholem was sitting at the table, they discussed this issue. "What's going to happen with the boy? We'll need to take the children to Kapyl′ to study."

But where would they stay? Staying at Roda's was not an option now. Where could they be placed? Dineh listened to their talk, disconcerted, frightened. She had only heard Itshe or Soreh talking about a town or a shtetl. She herself had never been to a shtetl. Only once did she remember, as if in a dream, when she was four years old and sick with diphtheria, how she had been taken, half dead, to the doctor in Kapyl′. But midway they had turned back with her because she had started to choke and they thought she was dying. But when she was back home they saw that an abscess had burst in her throat. She still remembered that Afanas, a young gentile in the village, had died right after his wedding, also from diphtheria, because his young wife had fed him hot latkes on the first day of his recovery.

And from then on Dineh had never gone to Kapyl′ again. The very word "Kapyl′" came to sound to her like a distant land. It was an encapsulation of all that Dineh couldn't perceive with her own eyes and was very far away. The clouds moved to wherever the sky set, and that's where infinity was. There the heart was drawn with dream and longing. But let it stay a dream . . . The idea of going to investigate it and discovering reality filled Dineh with fear and trembling. But whenever she heard them talking about her and Kapyl′ she would walk out onto the road that led to Kapyl′, stand next to a tree with the little dog—her Goldetske—in her hands, and gaze out until her head became muddled and she started to become lightheaded. How far it must be! Somewhere past where the sky fell away. She couldn't make it out with her eyes. Somewhere beyond the lake. She wouldn't be able to see home from there. There were so many people—strangers—there! In her great distress, she clasped the puppy close to her. She thought about Faytl, wondering how he was doing so far from home. And she thought about Itshe too—alone in such a big city . . . Ever since Itshe had left home, she thought about him with anxiety . . .

Once Dineh had seen him lying sick, and that picture remained engraved in her mind's eye. Itshe had been riding at dusk from the field, tending two horses. He was astride one of them and leading the other. Riding into the village he felt the urge to show off his tricks. He stood up with one foot on the back of one of the horses and the other foot on the other and held the reins of both horses in his hands. Everything probably would have been fine because Itshe knew his horses well and they knew him too. In Sholem's household the horses were practically members of the family. They ate out of the children's hands. But the dogs in the village weren't used to such riders, and they began to bark and chase after the horses. The horses dashed off, throwing Itshe off and down among their feet, piercing his skull with their horseshoes. He was brought home bloodied and half dead, laid down in bed, and washed. Peshe gave Dineh a red kerchief to go to Old Afanas to ward off the evil eye. Dineh carried the red kerchief in her trembling hands as if she were carrying Itshe's very life itself. When she brought it home and gave it back to Peshe and saw that it had been bound around Itshe's head, she was happy. She had brought him his cure.

Late that evening Dineh quietly approached his bed and saw that he had a swollen face. "It doesn't hurt you anymore now, does it?"

"It hurts a lot." Itshe could barely answer her because of his pain.

Dineh was surprised. "No, it only seems that way to you. It can't be hurting you anymore. You have the kerchief on your head . . ."

Through bloodshot eyes, Itshe looked at her and smiled disdainfully. "Go away, Dineh. You're a big fool."

Dineh stepped away and, in her heart, felt sorry for Itshe for his lack of gratitude. But she knew that nothing bad would happen to him now. And in fact he did regain his health. Still, Dineh could never erase that image from her memory—how she had seen Itshe lying there.

A DRIVE TO KAPYL'

One Thursday Peshe and Sholem made the drive to Kapyl'. Malkeh dressed Dineh in her Sabbath dress and seated her in the wagon. Dineh clutched her father's coat the entire time. With each passing verst that separated her from Ugli she felt as if an abyss were opening before her eyes. Her head was spinning like a mill wheel.

Sholem noticed. "Are you cold?" he asked.

Dineh herself didn't know what was the matter, but she had to come up with something. So she said yes. When they approached Stanki Sholem picked her up, bundled her in the cover that was on the wagon seat, and carried her into Yakhe's house. Peshe followed behind them. When Yakhe saw them she was frightened. "What's the matter?" she asked.

Peshe explained to her that they were driving to Kapyl′ and Dineh had somehow taken cold, even though it was warm outside. Yakhe felt Dineh's forehead and spit on the ground three times. "She should be given anthelmintic seeds. She's looking kind of green in the face. Worms. I had to give my kids anthelmintic seeds at the end of each month."

Everything in Yakhe's house was almost the way it was at home: the ritual washstand, the copper cup for water, the cat and the kittens, a small shelf hanging below the beams where triangular pieces of fresh white cheese were drying out . . . Yakhe treated them to a bit of fresh buttermilk and cut them a few slices of sheep's cheese. Then they exchanged goodbyes, put on their outerwear, and the ride resumed.

The farther they traveled and the closer they came to Kapyl′ the worse Dineh felt. When the wagon came to a standstill and she was told to exit, Dineh did so and immediately reached for Peshe's hand. Peshe pushed her away. "Aren't you ashamed? Such a big girl. Whom are you afraid of?"

They went into Roda's house. Soreh was happy to see Dineh and showed her the sewing machine that she already knew how to use and gestured sideways in the direction of the sick Shmuel-Arn with his half-twisted, pale green face. Roda approached, patting Dineh on her head. "Oh, Dineh, are you really so shy? We hear great things about you."

Shprintse also came up to Dineh and spoke with her. But Dineh could barely grasp what was happening. She followed Soreh around like someone in a daze, afraid to utter a single word in response. Afterward they left the house, sat back down in the wagon, and resumed their drive.

A MARKET!

When the wagon once again came to a halt, Peshe told Dineh to disembark. But this time she said to Dineh, "Hold on to me. This is a market. Don't get lost. Today is market day. There are a lot of people here."

When Dineh climbed down from the wagon she looked around her and began to tremble with fear. She couldn't believe her eyes. True, she had come across such things in the Hebrew Bible. She remembered the facade of King Solomon's palace, how the Temple of Jerusalem looked, how the nations went to war, how Deborah went forth and sang to her people about the great victory. And Dineh remembered too the city of Jericho. There was room for all of these images in Dineh's mind. There, in the Hebrew Bible, in her land of dreams, there was room for everything. Space . . . But here in reality she spotted a two-story, green brick building and a church with a great, shiny bell that swayed back and forth, ringing out in a terrifying racket from a high cupola that propped up the sky . . . And there were stands each one right next to the other; people crammed together, creating so much commotion; so many carts in the middle of the street side by side; cattle tethered to wagons, with frightened, sad eyes, and calves also tethered to wagons, with outstretched necks, bleating extended, mournful cries of longing for the mother cows in the fields; sheep bleating; dogs barking loudly from wagons; women running all around and carrying small sponge cakes and beans and baskets of eggs and jostling and speaking all at once, half in Yiddish, half in goyish; men rotating around the wagons and the buildings that encircled the marketplace that rose higher and higher and swam before Dineh's eyes reaching all the way to the sky—and the church bell rang out with greater strength and fury and everything spun around in a single whirlpool: the vehicles, the shops, the people, the clamor of the chickens, the whinnying of the horses, the call of the calves—everything became jumbled in one long, terrifying tumult, and the sky began to totter until it fell on Dineh's head . . .

When she opened her eyes Dineh found herself in a strange house with high shelves full of small bottles. Around her stood Sholem, Peshe, and a man in a white smock on crutches. She sensed powerful odors. She looked around her and saw pictures as if from a dream. A fit of trembling seized her. Someone quietly asked her: "Dinehle, do you want something?"

"I want to go home."

The doctor patted her on the hand: "Home, of course. You can go. There's nothing wrong with her."

Dineh sat down in the wagon and, with every stride of the horse's legs, felt the ground beneath her becoming firmer. She recognized the fence around the village and the poplar trees too. The stars, having only just emerged to face her, were her very own good acquaintances, and now there she was already out of the wagon, and there was little Goldetske jumping all the way up to her hands and licking her over and over.

For the first time in her life Goldetske's body was heavy as Dineh lifted her up and carried her into the house. With much gratitude Dineh looked at the still upright walls that enfolded her now in their embrace. To all of the questions posed by Henye and the blacksmith's other children, all having to do with how she liked Kapyl′, Dineh answered bashfully that she was afraid of Kapyl′, that there was no true Kapyl′, that she didn't know what Kapyl′ was.

For the time being the plan to send the children to Kapyl′ to study was abandoned.

GOLDETSKE, THE LITTLE DOG

Goldetske, the dear little white dog with the pointed black muzzle and nose and the charming miniature body set onto thin petite legs, was having a bit of a hard time moving around of late. To everyone in Sholem's home—especially the children—she was a jewel. But now Goldetske was in a precarious state. The whole household was worried about her. The little dog had been sent all the way from the Pohulanka estate in Nesvizh—from Peshe's parents' home—as a gift to the children. This was no ordinary little dog, and she was rigorously tended. For years she had been protected from what was now taking place.

Goldetske had mated with a bigger ordinary dog of mixed blood. For Goldetske, born of an especially delicate breed, this posed danger.

The "time" had come. In the middle of the night strangled screams of pain, like the crying of a tormented child, reverberated. When Peshe, lamp in hand, approached the little box turned into a sleeping pad under the bed next to the oven, she saw Goldetske rolling from side to side. In a plaintive, weeping voice and with bloodshot eyes, Goldetske looked up at her mistress and mutely pleaded for help. Peshe got down on her knees, placed the lamp on the ground, and caressed Goldetske on her head. The little dog licked Peshe's hand with a hot, dry tongue. Peshe stepped away and quickly returned with a heated woolen blanket. She covered her thoroughly, stepped away again, and returned promptly with a bottle filled with a green fluid. With feverish lips Goldetske drank from the bottle, like a hungry child at her mother's full breast. From the warmth and the liquid she was overcome with exhaustion, and for a while she remained quiet. But it wasn't long before Goldetske resumed her howling in that jagged, mournful voice and once again began to toss and turn.

This continued until a hot, red fluid started to leak onto the tiny white body. Goldetske's tidy white coat was covered in blood, and she started to give birth with difficulty. One by one, small, white, and spotted puppies, with thick, round little heads and snubbed noses, began to emerge from her. Five in total came out, and only one of them had a small, delicately pointed mouth and sharpened ears like its mother. Goldetske lay there, exhausted to death. She gazed—both up at Peshe who was standing over her and down to her children who were snuggling up to her and searching in the dark with closed eyes and open mouths. She blearily licked each one of them separately, all the while quietly shrieking half in suffering, half in joy, like someone whose terrible pains have suddenly abated and yet she still can't forget them.

The next morning, when they found out what had happened during the night, the family members tiptoed over to the little box that served as Goldetske's bed. Quietly they got to their knees in front of the box as if they were praying and breathlessly considered the mother and her five offspring. Emaciated and wounded, Goldetske was looking at her puppies squealing like birds searching everywhere for their lost nests and butting their round heads against her empty sides. Their eyes half open, they jostled to find a spot for themselves around their mother's hollowed breasts.

Peshe got up from her knees and stepped away. She returned with a saucer of milk. The puppies were pushed apart to the sides. Peshe placed the saucer close to Goldetske's mouth. Goldetske licked it a few times with her dry mouth, moistened her pointed little face, and looked up at Peshe with teary eyes, like someone saying, "Thank you so much, but I can't. No more."

For a while longer Peshe stayed crouched on her knees over the box. Then she left the saucer at the side and stood up. "A bitter pill to swallow. The puppies will die of hunger, and Goldetske herself isn't long for this world."

Dineh moved over to a corner, where she could look out and see directly into the box with puppies. She stood there grieving, not taking her eyes off her Goldetske. Daniel approached her. "What's the point of standing here? Come on, let's try to give her a little cold water. Come."

They both went to the well and, with great effort, lowered the bucket and dragged it back up with clear, fresh water. Dineh lifted a pottery shard filled with water to Goldetske's mouth. She licked the cold water as if she were quieting a great thirst and feeling a bit more confident. Daniel stepped away and quickly returned with a sugar cube, Goldetske's favorite food. Goldetske licked Daniel's hand, wanting to sink her pointy, little white teeth into the sugar cube. But she soon gave up. In exhaustion and sadness, she lowered her head to the puppies around her, who were still butting into her sides in search of nourishment from her small burnt-out nipples.

Their calls were becoming weaker and weaker. They were now squeaking like small mice. Their enfeebled mother looked at them and started to lick them as if that would quiet their hunger. She herself wept like someone being tortured. The puppies were too young. They could have been nursed. But they could only be nourished in the natural way—and the source upon which their lives depended was dry. The situation had degenerated to such an extent that Vasil, who minded the tavern, proposed that the puppies be taken away and drowned. Maybe then the mother would revive. The children pounced: "What do you mean—take away the puppies from their mother and drown them? How could you even think of such a savage plan?"

Dineh burst into loud tears.

Daniel comforted her. In that moment he felt like a man next to Dineh's feminine tears and helplessness. "Don't cry, silly. He won't touch the puppies. Tomorrow they'll be able to drink milk from the saucer by themselves. They'll grow up, and we'll have six little dogs."

He drew Dineh into a conversation about names for the puppies. Dineh insisted that they all be called Goldetske. To such silliness Daniel burst into laughter like a grownup: "What do you mean—call all of them Goldetske? Come on, Dineh, you're crazy. When we call to the mother she will come running with all of her puppies following behind. A fine plan . . ."

"Oh, Daniel, that would be beautiful!"

"Crazy! What would be beautiful?"

"That when someone called Goldetske, six little dogs would come and line up on their hind legs and stand ready to serve . . . Don't you think so, Daniel?"

"The things you come up with! Now I've even thought of names for all five puppies. One of them will be called Mishka, another Prince, and another Cosi, and another Bosi . . ."

"And the smallest one—the one who looks exactly like Goldetske?"

"We'll call that one Shpilke!"

"Shpilke, Shmilke! Why not Goldetske?"

"Names are given for the dead. Goldetske is still alive!"

Frightened, Dineh answered, "Well, good, let it be Shpilke. Why should I care?"

That day the family stood around the box with the puppies more than anywhere else. Throughout that time, Peshe occupied herself with the puppies, trying to nourish them, but none of her remedies were enough. In her despair, Goldetske wept and pleaded for them to save her children. She licked and stimulated them with her last bit of strength, lifting them with her pointed muzzle. But the puppies only got weaker.

Before the household went to sleep, water and bread soaked in milk in a saucer were left in the box and Goldetske was covered with a warm blanket. Peshe and the older ones at home knew that the puppies wouldn't make it to daybreak. With utter certainty, Daniel convinced Dineh that by morning she'd see the puppies' eyes open and their tongues lapping the milk in the saucer on their own.

In middle of the night, when the entire household was asleep, Goldetske began to wail frightfully. On her thin, shaky legs, she went from bed to bed, whining and waking everyone up, running back into the kitchen and then back to the beds where everyone was sleeping. Peshe turned the wick and, lamp in hand, she followed the dog. When she entered the kitchen she saw a picture that convulsed her maternal heart. Peshe burst into heaving sobs that caused everyone to come racing out of their beds to her in the kitchen. They stood there, before the threshold, as if frozen. Laid out on a white tablecloth on the ground in the middle of the room and arranged in an even row were all five puppies—dead. The little mother dog, who had witnessed their deaths with her own eyes, had pulled down a white tablecloth folded up on a corner of the table, spread it out on the ground, laid her puppies out on it—and proceeded to mourn them . . .

No one could come up with words; speech itself eluded them altogether. A sense of the futility of talk itself in the face of the profound sorrow of a little dog pervaded the room. Everyone stood and quietly rubbed tears from their eyes.

First thing in the morning Daniel dug a grave for his five dogs, placed them in a long cardboard box, and brought them to their burial. After that he looked for a long little board and, with a piece of lime, wrote out in big, crooked Yiddish letters the names of all of the puppies—the ones he had decided upon himself. He then propped the board up with stones on both sides so that it wouldn't fall down.

Dineh couldn't bear to watch. Wherever she went she had to swallow the tears welling up inside her.

And Goldetske raced around, looking everywhere for her puppies. Through the nights she didn't let anyone sleep. It took three days and nights for her to stop looking for them and to lie down and close her eyes. When Dineh brought her food, she'd open her teary eyes, stare at her, and not touch the food. Deciding that no good would come of this, Daniel forcefully took her from her box and into the field, where the sheep were grazing. There he would prod her to chase after the lambs that were wandering away from their mothers. For the first few days he wasn't able to do much with her. But when he brought her home she took a bit of milk. In this way Goldetske slowly regained her lost strength. The family members breathed easier, as if a dangerously ill patient had suddenly recovered.

Dineh thought often about the five puppies, and when no one was looking she went outside to see if the board with the names was still standing. And on one rainy night, when checking on the board, she discovered that the names had been washed away and erased; it pained her deeply. She thought, it's better to be a person than a dog after all . . . When a person dies, he's not forgotten as quickly the way puppies are—even ones who hadn't died all that long ago . . . Dineh could no longer play with Goldetske in the carefree way that she previously had. Somehow the tiny dog had become a different being to her. It had experienced such a terrible life tragedy.

GOLDETSKE FORGETS

Oftentimes Dineh would take Goldetske in her arms, stare into her eyes to see if she were still thinking about what had happened to her, about those five puppies . . . But wriggling impatiently, Goldetske would jump from Dineh's arms and start chasing the big gray cat, another member of Sholem's household with a prestigious pedigree who also came from the Pohulanka home, the very same household as Goldetske herself. The cat would walk around with a stately tread as befitting one with a great claim to Sholem's entire household. When Goldetske would chase her and want to play, she shoved her away with her front paw in a gesture calculated to insult, as if to say: Don't make a fool of yourself. Can't you see that such nonsense doesn't carry any weight with me?

But when this big fat cat with her warm coat was sleeping before the threshold in the sun, or at times during the winter in the kitchen by the fireplace not far from the tiled Russian stove, Goldetske would bend close to her and snuggle into her fur. The cat would let Goldetske rest against her side.

When Dineh saw that a carefree Goldetske was leaping in pursuit of the cat in effort to pester her into play, she decided for herself that Goldetske had probably long forgotten about her puppies. Dineh thought about the gentile women who came at dawn to the cemeteries not far from Sholem's house before heading off to their day's work. They regularly set aside some time and moved quickly to the graves of their loved ones. There they wept in such sad tones and with such refined, heartrending words . . . They spoke to their dead about their own difficult lives and lamented their fates—and then crossed themselves and departed . . .

In the evenings those same sad tones could be heard over the graves. The mothers and the wives and the beloveds took a half hour between their day and the evening to speak with their loved ones in the cemeteries. Quiet, mournful sounds extended from one side of the cemetery to the other. Over practically every grave a figure was bent, speaking straightforward, refined words and seeing to it that the grave was tended, that the "little apron" covering the crucifix by the icon was clean, that the grass over the grave was tended . . . Broad silky grasses, like striped ribbons, grew in the middle of the graves with a round, small bed of dark red velvety flowers in their midst, and all around the sides thousand-eyed, dainty nasturtiums of various colors. When it got dark and the stars appeared in the sky, the women stood up from over the graves, crossed themselves, and left quietly, with quick steps, for home. They said goodbye to those close to them for the night and left them under the watch of a quiet evening sky with trembling, green stars . . .

Dineh invariably stationed herself in the orchard behind the house where she could hear the intonations and words wafting over from the cemeteries. For her this was a wonderful evensong that connected for all eternity the lives housed in the cemeteries with those moving about the village who addressed them with such sorrowful and achingly beautiful words. Her Goldetske was not so fortunate . . . and, alas, what a great shame that was . . .

A DIFFERENT ITSHE

One evening—a Friday at dusk—Itshe suddenly returned home from Slutsk. When asked why he was back he answered, "No reason." Uncle Shimen, who was in Slutsk at the time, had come with him. They only learned the real cause when Itshe didn't go back to Slutsk and stayed at home instead. Sholem went to Slutsk, and it was there that he found out everything.

Haneh Yoshelyevitsh, the owner of the iron warehouse where Itshe supported himself, loved Itshe as if he were her own child in no small part because of his cleverness and politeness. She had no children of her own. Throughout the year and a half that he had been working for her—both at home and in the business—he grew so close to her that she wouldn't let him go home for the Sabbath or a holiday. When he began to befriend and go out with students, Haneh sat up until the wee hours of the night waiting for him to return. Only when he was back did she go to sleep. Lately she'd become very uneasy and anxious about him. There had been arrests in Slutsk. The authorities stormed into houses, carrying out raids in search of illegal literature. Haneh told Itshe to go home for a while until things calmed down in the city.

So Itshe stayed home. At first Dineh was happy that he was there, but it didn't take her long to sense that he wasn't the same Itshe. He no longer wanted to speak about God and the Torah. When she did succeed in drawing him into conversation, he spoke incomprehensibly and asked questions that were so strange and perplexing to Dineh. For example, he once asked her if she ever thought about how the gentiles worked for them in the fields all through the summers and the winters, wasted all of their money down to the shirts on their backs on drinking in the tavern, and lived in such darkness that they couldn't read or write and didn't know what was happening in the world . . . Didn't she ever think how everything was unfairly stacked against them?

Dineh fixed her large eyes on him in amazement. "Who's unfair?"

"Who? The landowners. Papa."

Dineh considered this response. "Papa is very good to them. They all love him," she said.

"A lot they know. How is Papa good to them?"

"How is he bad to them? When they work, he pays them."

"How much does he pay them?"

"However much they need."

"However much they need? If he paid them what they needed they would live like us, and we would live—like them."

Dineh stood there in confusion and looked back at Itshe. Then she stammered out: "It was probably meant to be that way."

Itshe mimicked her. "Really, now! 'It was meant to be that way . . .'"

"You once told me that God sees to everything. Well, probably if God would have wanted it to be, then it would be different . . ."

"Get out of here; you're a fool! What does this have to do with God?" And he walked away from her.

Dineh stayed where she was, dejected. Now it seemed she didn't know anything . . . and she became very sad. Her eyes filled with tears. Her heart became heavy, like someone who had suddenly lost something very precious. Itshe had once explained to her the ways of God and the world with such clarity that she could understand. And now, suddenly . . .

The longer Itshe stayed at home, the more alien his ways became to Dineh. Until one time—

ON A SABBATH MORNING

It was a Sabbath. Reb Yoshe of Otkulevitsh had come for prayer services. He, his son, and his son-in-law always came to Sholem's to pray. Now it just so happened that in order to get there they had to go through Sholem's forest, where gentiles were at work chopping wood. Sholem had sent Itshe out to see if they were all working and informed him that he should be home before prayer services were due to start.

On that particular Sabbath Reb Yoshe arrived at Sholem's home greatly agitated and immediately called Sholem over to the side. "What's come over you, Sholem? Has it really come to this? I saw your Itshe standing in the forest among the woodcutters, standing there with an ax in his hands and chopping along with all of the goyim . . . What an insolent young man! When he spotted us he didn't put down the ax. He kept right on chopping. And when I approached and told him to put down the ax, that insolent young man had the audacity to answer me: 'If I can watch over other people working for the Jews on Sabbath then I myself can work too, because directing others on Sabbath is also considered work.' That's what the big city produced for you," Reb Yoshe added, looking over at Sholem with pity. "What a time we live in! They want to remake the world, those rascals. A fine world it would be if we just handed it over to them . . ."

His head lowered and his face crimson in shame, Sholem stood there, not saying a word, as if the power of speech had suddenly been taken from him. In the meantime people from nearby villages, along with the menfolk from Peyse the blacksmith's house, had arrived. It was time to begin the prayer services. Sholem, who had to lead the services, didn't rush. He looked uneasily at the door. When the door opened and Itshe entered, Sholem approached him calmly and, without a word, gave him such a slap in the face that the young man immediately spurted blood. This was the first and last time in his life that Sholem raised a hand to a child. That Sabbath, after Havdalah, Peshe sadly packed Itshe's undergarments and a few shirts. She added a few blocks of cheese and some cookies. On Sunday morning, with his face all swollen, Itshe left for Dakhtervitsh to Uncle Shimen and went with him on the same day back to Slutsk.

Peshe was now worried, complaining about her fate, her bleak village existence. From Uncle Shimen they heard the news that Haneh wept from joy at Itshe's return. He told his uncle to tell his mother that he wouldn't be re-enrolling in his courses, and that from here on out he would remain a clerk at Haneh's iron business.

In Sholem's house there was no shortage of worry.

RUMORS AND UNREST

In addition to the overwhelming concerns about the children, other quite serious concerns arose. Rumors of social unrest in villages and small towns were beginning to spread. On Sundays gentiles came from the churches and reported how they heard that in a number of places Jews had been beaten and robbed of their property—and that the administration officials allowed it to happen. Others went so far as to say they heard that for each Jew killed the regime paid a ruble and a bottle of liquor. In the villages, where a small number of Jews had been living for many years, the news reverberated, causing immense terror and despondency. The Jews knew their gentile neighbors well, and they knew how easy it was to persuade them to do evil. They felt their distress more keenly than ever before and struggled day and night to come up with a way out.

On Shavuot Peshe and Sholem's daughter-in-law, Leyeh, came to the house. She came alone, without Faytl. Her once beautiful, healthy, round face was ruined. Her nose—pointed, elongated. Her cheeks—sunken. The luminous eyes in her high rabbinical forehead beneath thick, curly chestnut hair—tired, their light extinguished. It was obvious that the young wife was suffering. Faytl was cold to her, a stone wall. In her shy young girl's manner, she reproached her mother-in-law and Malkeh, her sister-in-law: "If you knew how much they were in love, you shouldn't have meddled . . . Now things are bad for him, and for me—even worse."

She ran into the bedroom and slammed the door behind her. Choked-back sobbing could be heard from the bedroom. Bitterly, Peshe said, as if to herself:

"He was crazy then, and he's still crazy. What would he have been missing? What? A young wife with every fine attribute imaginable—both beautiful and smart, an exceptional family and an excellent livelihood."

Here Malkeh added a word of her own. "No one else was good enough for him—only the maidservant. And she sits at home and still isn't thinking about getting married. She'll be a burden around Aunt Khashe's neck for a long time."

"You'd better keep quiet. And what about you? You won't agree to any match either. Whom are you waiting for?"

Malkeh blushed. Her eyes flashed with two stubborn tears: "That's no one's business. The right matches just aren't here for me."

"The right matches just aren't here for you? Haven't more than a few suitors beaten a path to the door? The problem is no one is good enough for her."

"There isn't a groom here for me."

"Are you going to wait for Isak, your Uncle Ruvtshe's son, from Odessa?"

"Well, what if I am going to wait?"

"You'll be waiting until your braids turn gray."

"So what?"

"Nothing less than Odessa, huh? When that one writes to her—she thinks it's the Torah from Moses himself."

"Oh, enough already."

Sighing, Peshe said: "It's just not my destiny to have any pride from my children. And here, Alte, Peyse's daughter, just became a bride. So what is she lacking? A fine young man, an artisan. She'll settle in a city and live like a decent human being."

"Well, good for her."

"It certainly is good for her. Hasn't Meyshke fallen at your feet, and hasn't Meyer implored you?"

Furiously, Malkeh responded: "You would have loved that. You'd consider it acceptable for Meyer the shingle maker's son to be my groom. That would be just great. Meyer serves my father in the forest, and his son, the harness maker, would be your son-in-law."

"If only that were true. What a young man he is. Alte will live like a countess with him, and from what I can see—when he's here, he spends more time with you than with her."

"He sings beautifully, so we sing together. How does any of this concern me?"

Impatiently, Peshe retorted: "Well, good, so you'll wait for the man from Odessa."

"Of course I'll wait for him."

The bedroom door opened. Her face washed and hair combed, Leyeh emerged singing some kind of Gypsy ditty. She approached the window and looked out. "How long have the Gypsies been staying near you?"

"They've been staying in the forest—it'll soon be two weeks now."

"Really?"

"Thank God they'll be leaving soon. They did a good job on the village, and now they're going elsewhere for free room and board."

"What a carefree people. I've always envied them. Ever since I was a kid I've been drawn to them. I know all of their songs. Whenever they used to stay in the Pesatshne forest I felt like one of their own. My mother always screamed that I must have Gypsy blood in me . . . that they must have cast a spell over me . . . When I was studying in Minsk everyone called me *Tsyganka vorozhilka*. I told all of them their fortunes by their cards. Ach, what a free life . . ."

"You call that something to be envied?"

The door opened. Gypsy women entered and asked them if they could read their palms. Peshe gave them something and told them to leave. They then approached Malkeh. She would have wanted the Gypsy women to read her fortune, but she looked over at Peshe and said, "I don't believe in such things." But Leyeh leapt up and approached the Gypsy women as if she were one of them. She took the elder woman by the hand and pulled her off to the synagogue room. She sat down on the floor in the middle of the room and crossed her legs beneath the voluminous skirt. She looked like a mischievous, insolent child. Leyeh then dragged the Gypsy woman down to the floor next to her, took a silver coin from her pocket, and gave it to her. She stretched out her right hand with the palm up and said: "Well, *pavorozhim, matushka*."

The Gypsy woman peered at her sharply, placing her thin, yellow hand with its heavily ringed fingers on Leyeh's brow and sweeping up her curly chestnut mane. She looked Leyeh directly in the eye and said: "Oh, little daughter, you're sad. Your little heart is weeping . . ."

Leyeh shivered as if to shake off the fear triggered within her. "Well, what is it, *matushka*? Is there a young man with a black mane and burning eyes who doesn't sleep at night waiting for me somewhere? Will I travel by train and then boat to a foreign land to meet him?"

By now the Gypsy woman was holding Leyeh's hand in one of her own, and with the other she traced the etched grooves of Leyeh's palm and read out the lines of her fortune. "You weep through the night," she told her. "Your fortune is bad. The one you love doesn't love you. I see a long, long path across a black sea stretching out before you . . ."

Leyeh pulled her hand out of the Gypsy woman's yellow hands. She took out another a coin, tossed it to the woman, and said, "Now read my cards."

Peshe and Malkeh looked on from the sidelines. They stood there in confusion, not knowing how to interpret the strange whims of someone who had studied in a big city and who wore a little hat and gloves on weekdays for no particular reason, even when it was warm outside . . .

Little Dineh trembled over Leyeh's bad fortune and believed every word the Gypsy woman said. Leyeh looked on impatiently as the woman laid out the cards—her card, the king, in the center, and around it, laying out black tens, black aces, black and black . . . The woman turned her head . . . but suddenly Leyeh grabbed the cards and flung them away from her. "Get out, you witch! Out!" she shouted. Then she stretched herself fully out on the floor and burst into hysterical laughter that turned into sobbing. She lay there, her body twitching in spasms.

The Gypsy woman bent over her and caressed her. "Poor thing. Poor thing," she said.

"Go now," Peshe called out. "They're waiting for you."

The Gypsy woman exited, and Peshe approached Leyeh. "What foolishness, listening to such things . . . It's not allowed. May God watch over you."

She spit on the floor. Leyeh stayed in that position for a while. Then she lifted herself lethargically from the floor, smoothed out her dress, and walked slowly to the dresser with the mirror. She looked at herself in the glass . . . Dineh shadowed her, and her feet started to tremble. Leyeh noticed Dineh and turned to her. She embraced Dineh, pressing the girl close. "What is it, Dinehle? You're still a little girl. Things are still good for you."

Dineh stared back at her, not knowing how to respond. But she pressed herself against Leyeh, hugging her and quietly trembling.

"Do you love me, Dinehle?"

"I don't know."

"Really, now? Well, then, who does know?"

"It's just that you're kind of strange."

"You see, Dinehle, you've hit the nail on the head. I am strange. A strange woman."

IN KAPYL′

Immediately after Shavuot Dineh and Daniel were taken to Kapyl′. There they were enrolled in a religious school led by Elye the redhead, who taught Talmud—to the boys—and gave Russian lessons after religious studies. They were sent to board with Shaye the water carrier up the mountain. Soreh worked as a seamstress down the mountain. For all intents and purposes Shaye the water carrier's home practically overhung Roda's little house. Dineh and Daniel were not at all pleased with the change in their lives. Nor was it easy for Soreh to get them gradually adjusted to their new surroundings. For the first few mornings following their arrival she took them to school. For meals the children went to Roda's house, where they ate with Soreh both what they had brought from the village as well as what Roda prepared for them while cooking her regular meals.

It was easier for Daniel to get used to the children in school, who were all boys. Dineh was the only girl seated at a table of boys. After lessons Daniel would go out to play with the boys in the street while Dineh, who already knew the way by herself, would walk to Roda's. During those early days she sat quietly in a corner and looked with sad, surprised eyes at Shmuel-Arn, at how he lay with a half-twisted, sore face, sort of half laughing, half crying as a result of his paralysis. She also looked at Shprintse with her high detachable collar, her stiffly laced up, practically childlike body, her small, red eyes that welled with tears behind heavily framed glasses. She often had to remove them and use two types of kerchiefs—one to wash the glasses and the other to wipe away the tears from her eyes. Throughout these initial days Dineh's gaze didn't stray from those two remarkable figures. She looked at them as if they weren't living creatures but rather some sort of objects that had been expressly prepared for her, targets of her consideration and amazement. One day, when Soreh noticed Dineh sitting there as if frozen stiff, never taking her eyes off them, she told her that it wasn't nice to do that. From then on Dineh took to sitting in a corner of the kitchen, where she didn't look over into the room where Shprintse sat and jabbed those fine stitches with a small needle or in the corner where Shmuel-Arn lay. As a result, things became harder for her . . . and she grew even more lonesome.

One day Shprintse approached her and took her by the hand. Dineh shuddered as if she had been awakened from a dream. "Dinehle, would you like me to teach you how to sew a buttonhole?"

Both delighted and frightened, Dineh didn't know how to answer and stammered out, "Of . . . of course I'd like to know."

"Well, then, come here, Dinehle, I'll show you."

Dineh followed her. Shprintse took a chair and set it down not far from her own. She removed a thimble from a small box and a needle threaded with white cotton from a needle bag. She took a scrap of blue satin, folded it in half, basted it along the edges—and with a small pair of scissors cut a long hole, a slit in the middle. She put the thimble on Dineh's finger and said, "Do you see? I could tell right away that it would fit you. It's not too small."

Holding the blue scrap between herself and Dineh, she took the needle and began stitching around the cut slit. With each stitch, she cast the white thread around the needle with a loop—until a smooth, long, thin white stripe appeared in middle of the blue satin. Dineh, who had already watched her mother and sister embroidering in the winter evenings and who could hold a needle in her hand by herself, easily took over from her. To be sure, her work couldn't compare with the model that Shprintse had made for her. But she kept stitching and learned on the various scraps Shprintse gave her. In this way a new life began for Dineh at Roda's house in Kapyl′. She became Shprintse's right-hand helper, sewing buttonholes in simpler blouses and undershirts for her. As Dineh grew more comfortable in the home she also began to approach Shmuel-Arn's bed. She would offer him a cigarette, lighting and holding it for him until he took several puffs. Then she would put it down and offer him a glass of water and, sometimes, the chess set and the board.

Roda's third son, Motl, now the oldest child at home and older than Dineh by a total of two years, showed her how to set up the chess pieces on the board for Shmuel-Arn. Slowly Shmuel-Arn came to depend on Dineh's help so much that when she was in school he would call out for her. For Dineh, Roda's home became the only anchor in her unhappy child's life. She didn't like the religious school. The lessons didn't interest her very much.

The home where she had to stay was a source of torment. Shaye the water carrier was deaf. His wife, Nekhe, a tall, dried-out, big-boned woman—constantly coughing, blowing her nose, and grumbling—was never content. Nekhe had no children of her own, and she hated children. Whenever Nekhe looked over at Dineh in the corner with her crossed eyes, Dineh felt as if her heart were being stabbed. But things were different with Daniel. He was a naughty child who indulged in mischief at every opportunity. He'd goad Nekhe in the following way. She had two hens in the chicken coop, which was both very long and very low, practically to the ground. Whenever the hens laid an egg, she would ask Daniel to crawl into the coop and retrieve the egg for her. One time he removed the egg and intentionally dropped it from his hand. It splattered all over the stone floor. That night Nekhe spewed an unending stream of invective. Another time he handed two eggs from the coop to Nekhe, shouting, "Wow, what big eggs!" Shuddering, Nekhe spit on the ground and screamed that the bastard was, God forbid, casting an evil eye, and the hens would stop laying eggs and what would she then do without eggs at home? And that's in fact what happened. The hens stopped laying eggs. Nekhe walked around in unrelenting misery. She exorcised the evil eye from the hens with an incantation and didn't let Daniel get close to the chicken coop.

Once in the middle of the night, when Daniel and Dineh were asleep on the Russian stove, they heard a terrible racket. Before they could shake off their child's sleep they felt pieces of pots, plates, and wood falling on them. The children lay there more dead than alive for several minutes before they understood what was going on. Daniel was the first to get down from the stove. His clothes in hand, he quietly called out to Dineh: "Dineh, are you alive?"

Gasping for breath, Dineh answered: "I don't know."

"What do you mean—you don't know? Take your clothes and get dressed."

"Where will we go? It's still nighttime."

"Don't be afraid, Dineh. I'll take you to Roda's."

Dineh lay there in utter terror, too afraid to budge. In the meantime, the fight in the house had quieted down somewhat. The blows and the broken pots and pieces of wood had transitioned to curses and invective and Nekhe's hoarse sobbing: "You drunk! He almost killed me. Oh, what terrible luck I have. I'm all alone in the world. If I were in my own town, my brothers would carry him out of the house in bedsheets—then he'd know not to get into a fight, that deaf boozehound, that drunkard."

From Shaye's side came the following choice, enraged words: "Pest. Stone. Cross-eyed bitch. Who needs you here? I should've divorced and gotten rid of you long ago. The 'sons' that she gave me that would say Kaddish in mourning for me! Ha! Carcass!"

From Nekhe's side the words quieted until she broke into a long, half-weeping, half-pleading, whispered monologue: "I'm punished . . . I should have expired in my mother's womb. Reduced to marrying such a hooligan . . . Not a drop of pleasure in my life. Oh, woe is me. Oh, woe is me . . ."

With those words, all went quiet in Shaye the water carrier's home. There the dwelling was attacked in the middle of the night by the same pain and fury, which, through the heavy, joyless days and nights, had accumulated in the deaf water carrier with his bent shoulders and in his wife Nekhe, with her warped fate, which together with her cross-eyed gaze mockingly disdained her life.

That morning Dineh and Daniel left for school without having had anything to eat. Daniel looked at Dineh in commiseration and tried to comfort her: "You know what, Dineh? Let's remember that today's Thursday. After school we'll go straight to the market and see wagons from home there. Maybe Mama and Papa too."

"Well, so what? We can't go home anyway. Tomorrow we have to go school."

"Yes, but tomorrow we'll be going home for the Sabbath."

That prospect lifted Dineh's spirits a little. "Let's hope they send the wagon. They don't come for us every Friday."

"Well, then we'll walk. Or we'll go with Uncle Leybe."

Dineh became sad again. "I'm afraid to go past Keylye and then through the marsh. There are always Gypsies and dogs there."

The next day—Friday—after religious school let out and Dineh and Daniel saw that the wagon hadn't come, they stepped onto the road and started walking home for the Sabbath. It was a journey of eight versts, which, when you were half walking and half running—both out of childish curiosity and, as was often the case, out of fear that Gypsies would snatch you or the dogs would set against you—could be completed in two hours' time. But sometimes when you forgot and digressed and sat down to rest and gathered berries, well, then you arrived home just before candle lighting . . .

That Friday Dineh and Daniel went home directly after school, not even stopping at Roda's to tell Soreh that they were going home. That wouldn't have helped in any case, since Soreh rarely went home for the Sabbath.

When you set out at dawn and went into the little forest that led from the shtetl directly to Stanki, you could sometimes come across Uncle Leybe, who drove an empty open-sided wagon from Kapyl′ home every Friday once he unloaded the lumber he sold. Still, his giving the children a ride invariably concluded with its own ritual: "Good morning, kids."

"Good morning, Uncle. Please let us ride home with you."

"Very well, kiddies. Come and walk alongside me. Young feet need to learn how to walk. It's healthy for the bones, kids. A cow has to be treated gently—a mute creature. It has to be protected. If you give the cow a good bundle of hay she gives you back a pail full of good milk. If you take good care of your horse through the winter it'll serve you through the summer. A beautiful day, kids. It's a pleasure to be alive on God's earth on such a day . . ."

In this way he won over the children, who followed step by step alongside the wagon through the small forest until they reached his house. There Aunt Yakhe always emerged, a wide, white apron covering her sturdy, broad belly and hips, and offered the children something to eat and told them, "Kids, go directly home from here. Don't dally by the berries in the forest. You mustn't be late for candle lighting. You mustn't make your mother worry . . ."

HEAVY CLOUDS

Summer was gone. On the autumn days heavy clouds extended over both the village skies and Sholem's house—the gate to the village. Marko, to whose name Sholem's entire property had been signed over, took seriously ill. He was taken to a big city to see a leading doctor, who diagnosed Marko with cancer of the throat. He said there was no cure for him.

This news hit Sholem's house like a thunderbolt. Nearly every week Sholem went to visit Marko, bringing various drinks and preserves that Peshe made and sealed tightly in glass jars. Each week he returned sadder from these visits to Marko. He even tried to talk with the patient about his field and the promissory notes, but Marko was so tired and sick he could barely understand what Sholem was talking about. Invariably he answered, "As long as I'm still alive, Sholem, nothing bad will come to you from my hand."

The only thing to do now was to remain silent and wait and worry through the days and nights. His tread had lost its sureness of footing, as if the very earth itself were slipping out from beneath his feet.

A WEDDING

In the meantime, however, life went on as it had. In Ugli everyone was looking forward to a wedding. Alte, Peyse the blacksmith's only daughter, was to marry Meyshke, Meyer the shingle maker's son. Meyer was a simple and honest man with a long, white beard who for years had stayed over at Sholem's and, alongside other shingle makers, made shingles in Sholem's forest. He had only one son, and he acted as both father and mother to him, since the child's mother had died in childbirth. And oh, how the father had hoped that his son, both handsome and clever, would become, with God's ongoing help, Sholem of Ugli's son-in-law. For Meyer, Sholem's eldest daughter, Malkeh, was like his own child, dear to his heart. But when Meyshke went to call on the father it became clear that this was not to be. Although Malkeh was very nice to and sang all sorts of songs with him, she had maneuvered, apparently with absolute intentionality, for Meyshke to be a groom for Alte. A nice, quiet girl—but she couldn't hold a candle to Malkeh, that's for sure. The devil only knew what she had in mind—Malkeh was probably hoping for someone else—most likely that cousin with the long cape. When that cousin had been in the area in connection with the draft and then traveled back, Malkeh became a different person altogether, living only in her dreams and just writing short letters. On more than one occasion, Peshe complained to him, to Meyer, as if he were an old, dear friend, that the girl was preoccupied with vain matters and that nothing would come of them in any case . . .

And now, since the wedding was to take place in the village of Ugli and there were no Jewish homes besides Peyse the blacksmith's and Sholem the tavern keeper's, well, it was no surprise then that Sholem's household would come to stand in for the groom's side. Preparations began in Sholem's house as if they were putting on the wedding for one of their own family members. They sewed clothes, cleaned, washed, cooked, and helped in Peyse's house with all of the necessary tasks. The wedding ceremony and the meal were held in Sholem's house. In the synagogue room long, covered tables were set, and all of the branches of the chandelier were lit with large stearin candles. Neighbors came from all of the nearby villages. Sholem's family came for the occasion. Faytl and Leyeh came from Pesatshne. Itshe came from Slutsk. Soreh, along with Dineh and Daniel, were brought over from Kapyl′. Everyone was dressed in fine, new clothes. The wedding celebration lasted for five whole days—until the in-laws, one by one, gradually departed and a post-wedding mood took hold in Sholem's house. Faytl and Leyeh returned to Pesatshne, and the younger children were brought back to Kapyl′.

Itshe had come to the wedding all grown up, like a sapling, slim and handsome, with a high head of black curly hair, a brown, round face, and very serious eyes. He kept to himself, speaking only when someone asked him a question. His responses were invariably biting and clever, even though they were offered with cheer and a smile. Whenever he wasn't busy helping around the house, he was reading two books at once. When he found something he was looking for in the books he jotted down notes on long, narrow sheets of paper. Then he hid the books back in the dresser. When Dineh wanted to see what it was all about he'd good-naturedly push her away: "Go away, Dineh, you won't understand."

Dineh felt insulted. He always said she wouldn't understand. She knew that it once again probably had something to do with God, like when he'd explained to her when she was so little that God was present in everything. She would wait. She would learn, just as she had done until this point. Someday she too would be able to read from two books at the same time and write something down on long, narrow sheets of paper, just like Itshe. In the meantime she would stand with great respect for her tall, handsome brother who had arrived from a faraway city and who understood things that were, for now, beyond her. Everything she could say she said with her eyes that gazed upon and caressed Itshe. Only he barely looked back because he was busy with more important and meaningful matters.

Itshe was studying Karl Marx. He wanted to build a new world, and the path was—risky and wonderful for a young man as slim and fleet of foot as a deer, for such a handsome young man crowned with curly hair under a sky full of sun and promise. During the course of the week he spent at home Itshe emerged as a revelation to everyone around him. People saw in him something they wouldn't soon forget. After his return to Slutsk everyone at Sabbath prayer services spoke about him and his ways. Sholem, to whom Itshe's ways were not clear or comprehensible, also reported what was said about Itshe in Slutsk—that he was a real doer in the schools for workers where he studied at night and that his woman boss fussed over him . . .

After all of the children left the anxiety in Sholem's house once again began to hum. What was going to happen to them? Since she hadn't been home in a long time Peshe figured this would be a good time to go home and spend time with her parents, who were themselves far from young. At the same time she could consult with her father and her brother about their property, which now lay so arbitrarily in the hands of strangers. Besides, the roads were clear and there wasn't that much work to be done in the winter months.

So they harnessed two horses, dressed warmly, packed food, and headed out onto the road. It was a two-day drive from Ugli to Nesvizh and Pohulanka. Along the way they stayed at the home of Uncle Mesele, who lived in a village at exactly the halfway point of their journey. While there they spent time with the family, inquiring after and speaking about kinfolk and discussing the decrees that were becoming more severe and difficult by the day. Around midday on Friday they arrived in Pohulanka. Peshe's mother, the elderly Gitele, was delighted to see her daughter and son-in-law. Reb Mordkhe, who at one hundred and two years old still studied in the small synagogue, emerged from the house unbent and white-haired like a snow-covered tree. Beaming radiantly, he greeted his son-in-law, kissed his only daughter, and inquired how they were. When asked how he was he replied by thanking God for his health—may it last and not deteriorate. For someone of his age each day is a gift . . .

REB MORDKHE'S LAST SABBATH

The mood that Sabbath was upbeat. Uncle Mesl, Reb Mordkhe's brother, had ridden along with them, eager to get the latest news.

"At my age, what you don't grab with force—you won't have," contended Uncle Mesl to his wife and children, who tried to dissuade him from setting out on the road on cold days. Reb Mordkhe's two sons from Horodishtsh were also on hand to see how their parents were doing. Around the table at meals the atmosphere felt simultaneously like the Sabbath and the holidays.

Gitele wore her Sabbath kerchief, a satin dress, and a string of pearls. Reb Mordkhe himself was cheerful, smiling to everyone individually and singing the hymns in unison with everyone. On Saturday night he recited the Havdalah, holding the large silver goblet filled with wine, and then wished everyone a good week. Afterward he went into his bedroom and called to his son-in-law. "Listen, my child, you're a man, after all. See to it that the women don't get scared and make a fuss. Go get Borekh the miller. The time has come. I want you to call the children in."

Sholem helped him undo and take off his clothes, laid him down in bed, and called in all the family members. "Father-in-Law isn't feeling his usual self. He's asked everyone to go in quietly."

When everyone gathered in the room they found Reb Mordkhe lying gently and peacefully with his face up and his snow-white beard outspread. He gestured for his neighbor, Reb Borekh, to come forward, and told him to recite the *Vide*. Reb Mordkhe repeated each word after him—in case he stumbled on a word. He repeated the words in a quiet, clear voice. At the last word of the *Vide* he closed his eyes, like a child falling asleep. Reb Borekh and Uncle Mesl bent over him and called out in a distinct voice: "Blessed be the True Judge." All the others supported their call with their own response: "Blessed be the True Judge."

After Sholem and Peshe returned home, Peshe observed the seven days of mourning. But before she began the observance she placed a small package over the Holy Ark under the beam. Dineh first found out what this was when her Aunt Yakhe, Aunt Reykhl, and other women came to pay a bereavement call. Mama spoke to them at length about the death of Dineh's grandfather and his funeral. All of Nesvizh, both Jews and gentiles, had crowded the streets where the body was carried. Mothers carried their sick children, jostling closer and pleading for the merits of the great saint to protect their unfortunate babies. Crippled people sprang after the coffin on their crutches. All of the poor crawled out of the poorhouse and followed the funeral procession. The linen and soap used to wash the deceased were cut up into small pieces, and close family members took them as a remedy, God forbid . . .

Dineh's eyes turned from Mama's lips, where she had kept her gaze fixed, and looked up at the Holy Ark, the beam above it, and the small package hidden there. She looked up for a long time. In her child's imagination and heart it seemed to her that a great treasure had come to them. The house, the Holy Ark, and the beam above it were transformed into holiness. In it she conjured an enchanted wheel, and at its center—her grandfather with his kindly, luminous face, his white beard, his long white side locks, the long, black kaftan on his refined, slim body, the long belt that hugged his narrow hips and hung down with long fringes down to the soles of his feet, his soft slippers. Dineh saw all of it clearly before her. Her grandfather had died. Now she knew all too well what the word "died" meant. "Died" meant: separating only in body from the living, and the soul went straight to heaven, where all souls were waiting for it and where no soul would ever have to be separated from another. Her holy grandfather had become even holier now. He had gone to heaven to be among the angels. But his holiness also remained here among the living. The small package there above the Holy Ark under the beam was now a remedy against all the evil that could befall a living person.

RIVE BECOMES A BRIDE

Aunt Yakhe's daughter Rive never did become literate. All of the effort that Uncle Leybe had put into driving her to religious school and all of Aunt Yakhe's insistence that she must learn how to pray and write a Yiddish letter hadn't helped. Rive had little respect for the teachers. And when she was laughed at and called blockhead it hardly bothered her. With great self-confidence she would reply with the following defense: all of her girlfriends—Todosya, Alina, and Katerina—couldn't write. And her older sister Yudes had married someone from Babruĭsk and then moved there, and she couldn't write either . . .

Yakhe was afraid that her youngest child would coarsen and, God forbid, come to disgrace in the village with the gentile girls and youths. As a result she sent her to Babruĭsk to be with her elder siblings.

So Rive stayed in Babruĭsk for the winter. When she came home for Passover she wasn't alone. She brought along a groom—a quiet, refined, pale young man who followed her every move with pining, black eyes. Rive, all of sixteen years old, was fully developed, with a high bosom; fine, swaying hips; a full, dark face with red cheeks and red lips; thick, curly hair; and large, black eyes. About being shy she knew nothing. She went by herself with her groom to visit all of her aunts and uncles. She also went to the *podruzhkas*—the gentile girls—and bragged that she had a groom.

After Passover the pale young man, Alter, went home, immediately homesick for her. On the Sabbath after Shavuot Rive was driven to Babruĭsk with a trousseau of pillows, comforters, and a few rubles of dowry. There, in the big city, she was married, and there she lived along with her brothers and sisters. As for writing to her parents back home, it wasn't Rive but rather Alter, the pale young man with the black eyes who was now her husband, who wrote the letters. These letters weren't very frequent, but each one contained a piece of good news worthy of congratulations, such as: "We're writing to let you know that Rive was fortunate enough to give birth to a son." Another letter contained the piece of good news that "Thanks be to God, we are the parents of two dear children." And so it went with a few more such letters.

UNCLE YANKL

Through the years Sholem's youngest brother, Uncle Yankl, had been poor—but cheerful too. His tall body, in its ease of movement, deflected the mundane concerns that crouched all around him awaiting his attention. His head, with its thin, black hair, never rested in one place for very long. Whenever possible he turned around to gaze out with his kind, almost mischievous eyes, like someone expecting a rider to fly in and bring him good news. He waited his entire life for this good news to come from somewhere. His gleaming black beard was never stationary. He was forever holding or brushing it with his thin, refined fingers while singing all the while.

He spent all his years in the old tavern in Dakhtervitsh that his parents had left him. The tavern was propped up on all sides with old, wooden support poles. The roof was more holes than straw. Inside utter poverty reigned. Descended from a distinguished family, the lovely, fragile Reykhl was more bedridden than mobile. She suffered from consumption. When she was young Reykhl had traveled every summer to her parents' dacha located in a pine forest, where she drank rush. But over the course of time her parents died, and the estate was given to a miserly brother and an evil sister-in-law.

Practically every year Reykhl gave birth to another child. Their poverty grew stronger—and she weaker. She lived quietly in her want, with nary a word of complaint to anyone. Quite the contrary, in fact. If Peshe or another family member came over with some kind of help, they didn't know how to offer it in a way that wouldn't cause the fragile Reykhl pain.

Yankl, on the other hand, floated about, ever happy and upbeat. The gentiles in the village—and even in surrounding ones—loved him. When spirits were still being sold in the taverns, Sholem always sent him a barrel. Yankl was able to make a living from it. What they were missing to go with their bread a gentile man or woman brought under their fur coat or apron. They'd say: "Here you go, Yankl," and offer a bundle of flax, a bowl of millet, and at times a dozen eggs too. The perennially cheerful Yankl was always the jolly good fellow ready to raise a glass and make a toast. Whenever he traveled to a neighboring village the gentiles immediately sniffed him out and called him over for a glass of whiskey, like a good guest. For Yankl's part, there was nothing to stop him. He always had time—both for the glass with a good neighbor as well as to coax out a melody with the peasants gathered around the table with their drinks. And when it happened that his fellow revelers succeeded in getting him to guzzle yet another glass, beyond the two that were his usual limit, Yankl allowed himself to be persuaded to dance the Roskamarushka after much pleading. At first the audience clapped and sang, providing encouragement. Then he quietly and slowly removed his kaftan and hat and parted his beard into two halves. With slow, rhythmic movements Yankl clapped his hands to the beat of the foot tapping and singing of everyone around him. Gradually he picked up speed, going faster and faster, whirling on his tiptoes or his heels around the table in a circle—until gradually the table was set to the side of the room, flush against the wall. Soon the peasants too were against the wall—standing on the table and chairs. Everyone sang and clapped along, and Yankl was transformed into a whirlwind, spinning in a circle dance, now on his tiptoes, now in squatting whirls near the ground.

On the days after such antics Yankl walked around feeling somewhat guilty.

With sheepish eyes he looked at the fragile Reykhl and tried to smooth over the gray reality with pleasant, farfetched plans. While he was blathering on a quiet and weary Reykhl thought of the children, may no evil eye befall them, who were abundant as beans and lived on top of each other in their home.

She looked at him, Yankl, as if he were one of her children, and without reproach asked: "Yankl, I always come back to the question: What will become of all of you?"

Hearing such words, Yankl felt utterly lost. He knew all too well where the question was targeted. But he didn't allow himself to stay lost for long. "You'll see, Reykhl, this summer I'll take you to the dacha in the Pesatshne forest. You'll drink rush and get well there. You'll see."

Only Reykhl did not get well.

One Passover eve she grew very feeble. The doctor called Peshe to the side and told her that this time Reykhl's pregnancy had put her in danger. As a result he advised her to be taken to Slutsk to the *bolnitsa* while there was still time. She really was in a bad way.

Peshe came home and discussed the matter with Sholem. The next day they hitched the horses, placed soft bedding in the wagon, and drove Reykhl to the *bolnitsa* in Slutsk. She remained there for six weeks. As she was giving birth to her eighth child Reykhl died from a hemorrhage.

Yankl returned from Slutsk with Sholem's horses and wagon, and Peshe brought home the infant—a boy with a starved little body forever screaming and searching the air with his mouth. Whatever came close to his mouth he latched on to and suckled.

The oldest child in the house was Beyle, a fourteen-year-old girl—tall, slim, proud, and quiet. She now grasped everything with an adult's awareness. In almost total silence she assumed her mother's burden. Even when her mother had been alive Beyle acted as the mistress of the household. She cooked, cleaned, looked after the little children, washed, and even mended an article of clothing or two. Now suddenly she became even more serious and took upon herself the role of mother.

At home practically nothing had changed. When Yankl came home from the village or a nearby shtetl at dusk he found a small portion of cooked food waiting for him. All of the children were asleep. If he came home at dawn the children were in the street, playing with other youngsters of the village, plucking fruit from a neighbor's small orchard, or returning home from nearby fields and forest, sometimes carrying berries, mushrooms, nuts, or chestnuts.

So yes, very little had changed.

Until one day Yankl drovc off to a fair all the way to Polesia. He lingered there for an entire fortnight. Nothing was heard from him for all that time. As a result his return shook up not just his own crowded house but all of the surroundings. He came back on a Thursday and brought with him a middle-aged, short woman with sickly red cheeks, teary eyes, and hands painted the seven colors of the rainbow. With this woman's arrival into Yankl's cramped house also came two boys and a tall, thin, forever coughing, hunchbacked girl. A stunted cow with long udders and half-moon horns across was tied to the wagon. A calf, four bound hens, bundles of rags, and old pots and plates were in the wagon. Yankl had finagled a bargain at the fair. Over a glass of liquor his drinking mates cooked up a deal for him so that he wouldn't go home empty-handed.

From that moment on Yankl's house was transformed into a living hell. Kreyne the dyer—as Yankl's wife was known—woke up every morning with new worries and troubles. She had been a widow for seven years. To survive she dragged herself to each fair looking for something to dye—and a piece of thin bread for her three orphans. She had been looking for a way to make her life easier—but she was deceived. Each morning she had to go out over the neighboring villages to look for work, to re-dye old clothes. When she came home with her bundle, utterly exhausted, the children fell upon her from all sides. His children beat up hers; her boys beat up his smaller girls. The house was in a tizzy. Each one tried to outshout the other, and it turned out that there was nothing to eat. Yankl, never much of a homebody to begin with, now began to avoid the place altogether. He would disappear for a month, sometimes two. Kreyne had the hell all to herself. She cursed her years and days and those who had caused her such unhappiness, luring her with enticing words and predictions of golden fortunes . . .

With the arrival of Kreyne into Yankl's house life became harsh for his children. The older children felt it the most. So Peshe drove over to Reykhl's family. A sister took in Khayeh-Sorkeh, a girl of seven. A brother—wealthy—who didn't have children of his own took in Goshke, a boy of nine. Hershl, the oldest boy, was given to an artisan in Kapyl′. Mikhl, an eleven-year-old boy, was given to work for Sholem in the forest to shadow the shingle makers and eventually become a shingle maker. One fine day the oldest child, Beyle, picked herself up, packed her paltry rags, and left home. She hitched a ride to Kapyl′ with a gentile and then went on to Slutsk. There she went into service with her mother's relatives. Two years later Beyle went to Minsk and became a maid at the home of a Jewish doctor, where they weren't allowed to speak Yiddish but only Russian, German, and

French. She stayed in Minsk for four years and then returned home.

When she returned to the village Beyle looked urbane—a fine lady. She wore beautiful clothes, lacquered high-heeled shoes, a cape, a hat, gloves, and carried a parasol. She only spoke Russian. When Beyle went for a walk in the evenings everyone gaped at her as if she were some bizarre bird with golden plumage who had washed up on these shores through a fluke error.

Beyle returned to the village on Shavuot. As it turned out she had been homesick. When the doctor and his family went abroad for the summer she went home and planned to return to work after the Jewish holidays. But Beyle quickly became miserable in the village and in her father's house, where Aunt Kreyne was now the mistress over such abject poverty. Shortly thereafter she went to her Uncle Sholem's house, where she spent a few weeks before heading off to Kapyl′ to visit her mother's sister. During her evening strolls in Kapyl′ her developed figure and gleaming, flowered parasol made her a sensation—just as she'd been in the village—with the gentile youths and girls. When the young men and girls approached to get acquainted they spoke only Russian to her. Oftentimes they brought her the Russian newspapers to read. Beyle was delighted. "This takes me back home, back to the city, with all of its energy . . ."

And so the summer passed.

But when Beyle received a letter from her boss, the doctor's wife from Minsk, the aunts and uncles and her father, Yankl, too began to question the direction of her life. What was the point of all of this? Being in service to strangers for so long and then going back there—still as a maid? When would enough be enough? She was a beautiful girl, to be sure, but an orphan, a maidservant—and in a city where she didn't know anyone.

Aunt Brokheh, Reykhl's sister, had a plan up her sleeve. Brayne, the baker, owned a building in the market located on a plateau and made an excellent living. Brayne's only child was a son. When Brayne passed away, both the building and all of the estate would be inherited by her son. What Jewish daughter wouldn't wish for such good fortune? The young man himself was handsome, a good earner, and had a pair of golden hands—he was a harness maker who made the best horse collars. There was a bit of a drawback: he was deaf and mute. But not from birth, God forbid. His condition had come from a fall when he was a little boy. But who was Beyle, after all? An orphan in service to strangers. Had her father prepared a dowry for her? Here she would be entering a situation with everything all set. The house had everything anyone could possibly want. A brick building like that in the market in such a prominent location—nothing to sneeze at! Brayne wouldn't live forever. She was already an older woman.

And, incidentally, Brayne herself had sent the matchmaker to Brokheh's house. "Brayne," said Getsl the matchmaker to Brokheh, "likes your niece. She's a healthy girl who can ease the burden of Brayne's struggle in her old age. Yudl likes her too. Yudl is a smart young man, a good wage earner. She would have a good life with him. He wouldn't take a penny of dowry from her; he'd take her just as she was. Brayne would pay for all the wedding expenses herself. And she'd also buy the candlesticks for the bride."

Beyle didn't want to hear anything of it. She packed up and rode back to her father's house in the village, where her dresses wrapped in a bedsheet were hanging over a bed. She intended to pack these into a suitcase, say goodbye to her brothers and sisters, and return to Minsk. But at home, they—her father, Aunt Kreyne, Aunt Peshe—tried to convince her not to go. All of them pressed her hard. Here she had an opportunity to marry Yudl, the son of Brayne. She could be the mistress over a building with a large bakery. She would live properly, like all Jewish daughters—with her own home, with a husband. God would help her, and she would have her own children. What was the alternative—to be a maid for a doctor in Minsk and serve his wife and raise someone else's children?

Beyle fought back for so long she became depleted. Through her tears she finally told her father that he could do whatever he wanted. She had no strength left to listen to anyone's arguments. And who knows? Maybe this was her destiny . . .

On a Saturday night the in-laws came from Kapyl′, and the reception with sponge cake and liquor was held at Sholem's house. The engagement contract was drawn up, and the wedding was set for a month later. Each Sabbath the groom came to visit Beyle in the village and never failed to bring her a gift: a watch, a ring, beads, sweets. Beyle accepted it all with tears in her eyes. She took walks with him, and on Sabbath after the main meal visited Uncle Sholem, Uncle Shimen, Aunt Yakhe, and Aunt Golde. Folks warmly welcomed them wherever they went. They looked at Beyle as someone who had made a sensible decision—even as their looks were laced with pity. She was saddling the years of her young girlhood to a deaf-mute she didn't love.

The wedding was held in Brayne's house in Kapyl′, and so Beyle stayed in the red brick building in the market on the plateau. She worked hard alongside her mother-in-law, kneading the dough in the kneading troughs and baking the bread. The customers praised Brayne's young daughter-in-law both for her round, well-kneaded loaves of bread and her good cheer. She laughed with everyone and was as delighted with each customer as with a welcome guest. Yudl worked on his horse collars and returned home each evening a contented man, carrying small packages under his arms and in his pockets.

One year after their wedding Beyle gave birth to a girl. She brought over her youngest sister to take care of the child when she was otherwise occupied with baking and selling bread.

Yankl was now quite the regular visitor to Beyle's home. He always returned home with bread and bagels—and a few kopecks to boot.

A FIRE IN KAPYL'

It was a Saturday night. Sleep was hard to come by in Brayne's household. All through the night they stoked the oven and then baked the round loaves of bread, the braided challahs, the bagels, and all sorts of sponge cakes that were needed for the Sunday fair. As was their custom the peasants from the surrounding villages would be coming to town for church services. Afterward they would bring their wagons to a stop before the large courtyard in front of Brayne's red brick building and walk through the side gate of the courtyard to the bakery that had been added onto the back of the building.

On Saturday nights Beyle stood by the oven, her white sleeves rolled up over her young, healthy arms and a kerchief covering her dark, thick hair. The oven's flames reflected on her longish, dimpled cheeks. She was always tidy and attentive, her ears ever alert. With every creak of the door her lovely eyes looked up, as if she were expecting someone. People came to see Beyle, even late at night—one person forgot to prepare bread for lunch; another came for no particular reason, just to while away the time and have a chat or crack some jokes with Beyle. Her big city ways hadn't worn off, even here in Brayne's bakery.

Brayne started to rest a little, relax her old, worn-out bones. She could no longer stand in front of the oven for very long and often went to lie down to take a nap.

Among the customers and others observed coming into the bakery was a young Pole. He came later than everyone else and was the last to go.

More than once, Brayne asked Beyle: "What does he want here—this young nobleman? Sure, he's buying, but why is he dawdling and getting underfoot?"

Beyle didn't answer, pretending that Brayne was addressing her questions to someone else.

It sometimes happened that Dineh and Daniel didn't travel home for the Sabbath. On such Saturday evenings Dineh would play with Beyle's little girl and also various games, such as jacks, with Beyle's younger sister, Hayeh-Soreh. She felt relaxed and comfortable with her. Both of them talked about home: their homesickness for the village, its quiet atmosphere, the small orchards abundant with cherries and gooseberries. They'd chat this way late into the night—and then Dineh would sleep over in the same bed with Hayeh-Soreh.

On one such Saturday night, when Dineh was sleeping with Hayeh-Soreh, terrible cries—from Beyle—rang out: "Get up! Hurry! Get dressed! Run! Fire! Fire!"

Beyle grabbed the child from her cradle and bundled her up, running all the while to Yudl, Dineh, and Hayeh-Soreh: "Hurry, children, hurry! Mother-in-Law, for goodness' sake, hurry! Run! We're going to get burnt alive!"

Dineh got out of bed. What was happening here? In the darkness visible outside the windows she could make out heavy plumes of smoke penetrated by long tongues of fire. Smoke and fire crackled loudly. Beyle kept screaming, "Hurry! Run! We're doomed! The roof is about to come down!"

Half naked, carrying their clothes in their hands, everyone made their way to the door. Into the open doorway that the family needed to escape a cloud of smoke and fire was advancing. Choking and gasping for breath, they were barely able to push their way out to the courtyard and the street. Beyle ran from house to house, banging on the doors and windows. "Get up! Fire! You're going to get burnt alive in your beds! Get up!" she shouted. Brayne and Yudl also ran and banged on windows.

This happened on a late autumn night. The wind whistled and raged from all sides and drove the heavy clouds of smoke and the tongues of fire over the roofs. Whenever they heard a loud crackling sound—like the cracking of a thousand whips—they knew that another roof had collapsed. And so it went from roof to roof. The powerful plumes of smoke quickly surrounded the entire high market. In the middle of night's darkness it had become a fiery day. The wind insolently whistled and raged and, as if with long, fiery arms, embraced the city from all sides. Into the fire and wind came the frightful tolling of the church bells, at first slowly, then faster and stronger until they overpowered the night with a deafening din.

The *pozharnaia komanda* that conducted fire drills every two weeks and diligently crawled up ladders, in brass hats, red epaulets, and shiny, yellow buttons, now set themselves to work. But the firefighters were barely visible. It was all well and good when it was a lovely, sunny day with the youngsters running after them and staring at the stunts of the *pozharnaia komanda*. But on such a dark night, against such a wild wind that was breaking trees and ripping off roofs with fiery hands, the *pozharnaia komanda* looked pitiful indeed. More than anything they looked like drowning victims, clutching at straws.

"Quiet! Leave it!" came the cries. "Make way! The *pozharnaia* are coming!" But soon people despaired and ran yet again to the wells to drag water in buckets and tubs to pour onto the dancing flames. But it was like oil on the flame . . . As if with mocking laughter, the crackling tongues of fire only seemed to welcome the water, swallowing it and licking their lips in the process.

It wasn't long before people gave up trying to put out the fire. They sensed that human hands wouldn't succeed in impeding its march. Everyone took to saving whomever they could—both the lives in the houses and those of poor defenseless animals in the stables. Throughout the burning streets resounded the squawks of awakened hens, the bellowing of sleepy cows and calves, and the screams of tiny children carried in the hands of their terrified mothers. Hitched wagons with bundles and packages as well as weeping women and children on board, as if riding on high, broken springs, began to materialize. Everything went up—now in the air and now, with a bang, back down.

Dineh pushed her way through the crowds in the burning streets and tore herself free from the members of Beyle's household. Her goal now was to get to Shaye the water carrier's house and wake up Daniel. She had to see if he were still alive or if he had been burnt. She had to see what had happened with the paralyzed Shmuel-Arn. Where was Soreh? Where was Shprintse?

Dineh ran through the streets crashing into wagons, people, packages. She fell, fainted. People pushed against her. She wanted to get up and run. She screamed in terror, as in a nightmare. "Daniel! Where are you?"

A small hand took firm hold of hers. "Dineh, I'm here. Get up. We'll run downhill to Roda's."

Dineh didn't believe her own eyes.

"Dineh, come quickly, let's run to Roda's to help her pack and carry out Shmuel-Arn from the house."

"Where's Soreh?"

"She's there, helping to pack. I came looking for you. I was barely able to find you. The fire actually started at Brayne's house. I thought you got burnt . . . Run faster, Dineh. Soreh's crying. She doesn't know I found you . . ."

When the children arrived at the synagogue courtyard the entire downhill expanse spread out before them like a bed of fire. All of the homes were ablaze. In the light of the flames they made out Roda's home—not yet on fire—and Shmuel-Arn lying on the bed outside in front of the house right by the road. Over Roda's house—uphill—stood narrow, shabby cots with people in them. These were the sick who had been carried out of the poorhouse. Among them was Itshinke Kaminar, the epileptic boy who had lived all of his life in the poorhouse. No one could take him in because of his illness. He was now lying on the ground near the cots and writhing, like a snake, in convulsions . . .

When Dineh and Daniel approached Roda's house Shprintse came running toward them, calling out, "Here they are!" Soreh whimpered and embraced the children without speaking. All the while the fire continued to spread. The sick—Shmuel-Arn among them—had been placed on wagons conveyed to the scene, and with measured steps people followed the wagons out of the shtetl. After the wagons bearing the sick came pedestrians and—again, wagons with packages, and on the packages, women and children, geese, cats, hens—and after them, the men leading the cows and calves tethered by rope. In this way Kapyl′ moved out of its own walls, accompanied by smoke and flames, and through the dark night, onto the road to wherever the eye might show a way.

At daybreak it began to rain. Riders and wagons came from the surrounding shtetls and villages and tended to those who were burned out of their homes. They divided them up—this many to be taken in by one city or village, this many by another. And so it went well into the day.

KAPYL′'S RESIDENTS RETURN, BEYLE ISN'T AMONG THEM

Kapyl′'s residents didn't stay away for long. They returned home, living four families to a single house—that is, in those houses that had remained whole. The usual demarcations between yours and mine no longer existed. Houses, one after the other, were built. As long as a structure had walls with the promise of a roof and holes for doors and windows, people moved in and carried on with their lives.

Roda's house was still standing. The poorhouse remained intact too, only it looked even shabbier and more broken than it had before the fire.

The foundation of Brayne's building stood in the middle of the tall market like a scarecrow. Its bricks were blackened from smoke; the doorways and window apertures opened from all sides onto black caves. The bakery was completely burned down to the ground. Brayne whirled through her days, now haggling with a glazier, now with a carpenter.

Utterly desolate, with wild eyes red from not sleeping, Yudl, the deaf-mute, frantically searched for his wife and daughter. Both had disappeared without a trace. He had already searched for them at his father-in-law's house, but Yankl, embarrassed and distressed, flailed his arms and shook his head as if to say "No, I don't know" in response to Yudl's silent questioning. Yet deep down they both knew what they wanted to hide from themselves. Both of their hearts were pounding . . .

AUNT GOLDE AND ALTKE DIE IN THE SAME MONTH

That autumn, Kapyl′ wasn't the only place where a sad chain of events occurred that was remembered for many years to come. In the village of Dakhtervitsh something happened that shook the entire area. When people spoke of sad news they let out long sighs—from deep within themselves—over the misfortune that happened there.

Meysl was a learned man and a bit modern. In addition, he was actually from a faraway region. When he came to the area he ended up staying as a resident—but by accident. As a young man he had come as a tutor to Dakhtervitsh to Reb Hayem, Sholem's father. In a large family full of young people, the youngest daughter was Golde. She was a dark, short girl with large, black eyes and a broad, resolute figure, agile and talkative. Golde spoke so quickly that only she herself understood what she was saying. Nobody could follow her stream of words. Everybody was fond of her for her high spirits and chatter that provided laughter and amusement. She never took offense and laughed raucously along with them. Meysl was an orphan and a poor boy. He liked Golde. Reb Hayem discussed the matter with his clever wife, Soreh, and a match was made.

After the wedding it soon became apparent that Meysl had a quick temper. People tried to excuse it by saying that he was a Kohen—of the priestly line—but that didn't help Golde any. Meysl often cursed and abused Golde to her face in front of strangers. For the two years that the couple lived off the room and board provided by Reb Hayem, Meysl did absolutely nothing. When Reb Hayem once asked, "Meysl, what do you plan on doing?" he replied that he wanted to be a tutor elsewhere, away from home.

And that's what happened. Meysl left to be a tutor. Reb Hayem built Golde a home in a corner of the village by a garden, and that's where she lived.

Golde's life was difficult. Meysl only came home twice a year—for the holidays. Every eighteen months, Golde gave birth. With Meysl's earnings, she was barely able to make ends meet. The small amount he did earn he didn't give all to her. He enjoyed being a dandy. Whenever he came home for the holidays he had something new to show off to the village: a new kaftan, a handsome walking stick, an odd tobacco pouch that opened from two sides . . . He interacted with Golde and their children as if he were a stranger to them. At the most minor offense he grew livid and agitated, playing the martyr who had the misfortune to fall into a net tightening ever more around him . . . During his semiannual visits, the children saw their father as an angry nobleman to be greatly feared.

Once so full of high spirits, Golde aged quickly. For days she trudged through the villages, looking for work. Sometimes she was able to buy from a gentile woman a dozen eggs, a little thread, and a bundle of flax and bring it to her brother Sholem and in exchange get a loaf of bread, a pound of cereal, and a bit of kerosene for the lamp. She was proud by nature and didn't want her brother to give and give. As she herself said: "It's hard to cram a bag full of holes."

The children grew in the house like mushrooms after a rainfall—all of them clever and beautiful, with black eyes and curly hair. Only one of them—the oldest daughter, Altke—resembled the father. She had a long, pale face, a high forehead, and deep, pensive eyes with a faraway gaze.

Years of drudgery and slogging through the villages foraging for a wretched piece of bread had made Golde sick. She had contracted a severe cough that impeded her breathing, which the medical practitioner in Kapyl′ called "*zadishke*." Rather than prescribing medicine, he told her that she really had to take care of herself and live a stress-free life. But after a day of combing the villages, Golde came home choking from her cough and unable to catch her breath. Soon her ankles began to swell.

When Meysl came home for Passover, his brother-in-law Sholem had a frank conversation with him. Sholem told Meysl that he really had to give up the tutoring far from home. He had to find a way to earn a living nearby and lift the heavy burden of supporting the family from Golde. But Meysl claimed that he had no trade or skills. Sholem had a plan ready: Meysl would become an orchard keeper. Plenty of Jews earned a living from such work. He had enough of his own friends who would look out for him, gather the fruit, and take them to be sold. It wouldn't be hard for him. And as for the few rubles needed to get started? Well, he could borrow it. Everything would go smoothly. He, Sholem, knew of two fine orchards actually not far from here—in Ostrovok. Each year they made a fine profit. No one had ever lost money there. Sholem knew the owner well. He would drive over with Meysl—today, as a matter of fact—and give a down payment, and may good luck reign.

Meysl went with Sholem as if he were going to a stranger's wedding, but from then on he stopped being a tutor and became an orchard keeper and somehow managed to make a living from it.

Golde could barely stand on her feet. On rainy or cold days she didn't get out of bed at all. The oldest girl, Altke, was deeply attached to her mother and tended to her every need. Even at night, when it was hard for Golde to lie in bed, Altke would sit next to her, raising her head with extra pillows and offering her a drink of water.

With a distant look in her eye, Golde would contemplate her quiet, delicate daughter and sigh without saying a word. This inevitably meant: oh, my child, before I close my eyes, it would be good to see you settled in life. At least that.

Meysl would often take Altke away from home with him to one of the orchards to stand guard and make sure that nothing was stolen. But Altke impatiently counted the days until she could leave. She longed for home.

One day Golde called Altke over to her and told her to put on her Sabbath dress and comb her hair. "The in-laws are coming today."

Altke started to tremble with fear. Her characteristically pale face became white as lime. "Mama, that's not necessary."

"What do you mean—that's not necessary? I've had to work so hard to convince your father to make this match. Let's just hope it goes well—and that the groom likes you."

That evening the prospective in-laws came from Slutsk—with a widower, a man living in a non-Jewish area, tall, with broad shoulders and heavy, dangling arms.

He sat down, his head lowered, and when no one was looking he cast glances at Altke, who hovered around in the corners of the room not knowing what to do with herself.

The wedding date was set for autumn when the harvest from the orchards would be finished. When the soon-to-be-in-laws departed, a pleased Golde, despite her poor health, began to prepare household items for Altke. She refilled the feathers in the cushions and little pillows, hemmed linens into bedsheets. She did it with every last bit of her strength, barely able to stand on her feet.

As for Altke, she approached the whole matter like someone in a dream state. Silently, her pale face, with deep, black circles around her eyes, followed her sick mother, who coughed, clutching at her heart and barely able to catch her breath.

One time, when Altke and her father were in Ostrovok, a rider came to summon them home. Golde had suddenly become gravely ill. The next day she died. Following the seven-day mourning period, Altke stayed home and assumed the duties of running the household. Her groom had learned of Golde's death and came to visit one Sabbath. He consoled Altke and promised her that he would soon take her home. All would be well for her. In fact, he wanted them to get married shortly after the thirty-day mourning period. Altke told him that it was impossible to leave the house so soon after her mother's death. How would her father manage the children by himself—without a woman to run the household? The groom departed, having secured a promise from Meysl that the wedding would take place once the thirty-day period after Golde's death had concluded.

It was an early autumn day. Altke went to Ugli to Uncle Sholem's house to talk things over with Aunt Peshe—and from there she would either go by foot or transportation to Ostrovok, where she would stay over to look out for the orchard. Peshe examined Altke closely, scolding her for not taking adequate care of herself and noting her overall pallor. Altke didn't answer, bursting instead into tears. Peshe told Malkeh to ride with Altke to Ostrovok and stay there overnight with her. The two should return together the next day. Peshe placed some food into a small basket and quietly told Malkeh to talk with Altke and find out what was causing her such stress. She told Malkeh to distract her a little—Altke really was a frightful sight.

So Malkeh rode with Altke on a small, tottering carriage harnessed to a dun-colored horse, whom no one was afraid to drive. The three-verst journey from Ugli to Ostrovok passed entirely through the forest. It was a quiet, sunny autumn day, ripe for exchanging confidences. The two young cousins opened their hearts to each other. The older of the two, Malkeh, had secrets of her own, and Altke was curious to hear what her cousin had to tell her. For Altke, Malkeh's secret was news, hardly to be believed. She hadn't known that Malkeh was romantically entangled with a cousin from Odessa—the one with the long, chestnut hair and the wide, black cape who had served in the military . . . Altke was even afraid to look at him. He was so odd, so urbane . . . Did Malkeh really think he would bring her to Odessa and marry her? She herself would be afraid to ride to such a big city—and so far from home to boot . . . Malkeh told her that as soon as Isak sent for her she'd go to him straightaway. Besides, soon Altke herself would also have to go to unfamiliar surroundings—to a village on the other side of Slutsk. It may not have been Odessa, but it still wasn't home. At this Altke turned pale and tongue-tied. Then she grabbed Malkeh by the hand, looked deeply into her eyes, and blurted out, weeping: "I won't get married . . . I won't leave home. I'm afraid of him, just like I'm afraid of my father . . . I've been afraid of him my whole life—since I was a child, since I got scared . . ."

"What made you so scared? What did your father do to you?"

"He didn't do anything to me but to my mother. He hit her, and she ran from him and hid in our bed . . . I slept with Neshke and Yudes . . . They were still really little . . . She hid behind my shoulder. He chased her, dragged her by the hair from the bed . . . She cried, begging him to take pity on her. She told him that he was going to kill her, that the children would be orphans . . . He trampled all over her and kept beating her . . . This was when my mother got sick . . . But he kept beating her . . . If I get married my husband will beat me too . . . I won't get married . . . Do you hear me, Malkeh? I won't!"

Frightened, Malkeh tried to calm her: "Come on, you're being silly, Altke. Your husband won't beat you."

"Since my mother died I've been afraid to be alone in the house. At night my mother comes to me in my dreams. She cries out to me. She wails . . . I always see her choking on her cough. I want to help her . . . but I can't."

Altke was quiet for a while and then reached for Malkeh's hand again. "In my dream I came to an agreement with my mother that I wouldn't get married. I cried and told her I was afraid that he would beat me the way my father beat her . . . She wiped away my tears and said, 'I will take you away to me, and then no one will beat you.'"

Malkeh shivered and said: "What are you talking about, Altke? How could you have talked with your mother? I mean—after all, she's dead."

"That was nothing unusual. I speak with her every night . . ."

Looking around, Malkeh saw that they had passed the orchard. She shook herself as if waking up from a bad dream: "Oh, Altke! Look, we've gone too far!"

They turned the carriage around and drove into the courtyard of the orchard. After hitching the horse, they set out to work.

Under the trees, apples had fallen. They started to collect those apples into the baskets and carried them into the hut. Having gathered the fallen fruit, they sat down and mournfully gazed upon the vanishing day. In her reflective mood Malkeh was drawn to the horizon, to the flames of the setting sun. Altke sat there, her gaze frozen stiff; it was hard for her to know what she wanted. A sense of bleakness pressed upon her soul.

"We have to go in and get supper ready," Malkeh suddenly said.

They stood up and went to the front room in Maxim's house. There Maxim's wife stood around the oven, busying herself with the dairy after the milking. Seeing the girls, she fixed her broad, white apron, wished them a good evening, and asked if they needed anything for dinner. They'd need milk, Malkeh replied, but the rest of the provisions they'd brought from home. Shortly thereafter Meysl arrived from the other orchard with his three boys. With them were two fruit merchants from Hrozawa. "They'll stay here overnight. Tomorrow morning they'll see what they want to buy."

The girls quickly peeled potatoes, cut herring, and asked Maxim's wife to boil some eggs. They spread a tablecloth on the table, and everyone ate dinner together. They went to sleep in the barn, on fresh hay. In the fresh autumn air, they soon fell asleep. Malkeh and Altke made their bed far from the menfolk, at the other end of the barn.

The girls talked for a long time before they fell asleep. The men and the boys had long been snoring while Altke kept talking . . . She was afraid to sleep because she was afraid to see her mother. Whenever she saw mother in her dreams, her mother was always in a state of torment. Malkeh calmed her with soothing words, telling her that she mustn't think that way, that it would be better for her to dwell upon the living, that things would still turn out well for her. If she recited the Shema bedtime prayer and the *ha-Mapil* blessing she wouldn't have dreams. And if she did have dreams they would be good ones . . .

Altke embraced Malkeh stiffly, and they both recited the Shema and whispered the *ha-Mapil* . . .

THE OTHER SIDE OF THE WALL . . .

Altke was the first to fall asleep. Malkeh was a bit disturbed by all that she had heard that day from Altke. Still, she was pleased that Altke had fallen asleep. Malkeh shifted over from her, covered herself up, and fell asleep too. She couldn't be sure exactly how long she'd been asleep—whether it was minutes or hours—when she was awakened by a terrible scream that cut through the darkness above the high bale of hay like a knife. Malkeh remained horizontal, feeling groggy. She sat up and realized that it was Altke who had screamed. Malkeh began to awaken Altke and try to pull her over to herself. Only Altke wouldn't budge; it was as if she had been chained to the wall. Malkeh couldn't revive her.

Altke let out wild, animal-like cries.

It wasn't long before the men, with a lantern lighting the way, were standing over Altke, rubbing her with alcohol. They tried to have her sit upright so they could then carry her into the house to get warm. But Altke resisted with an animal strength, screaming that they were dragging her from the other side of the wall—that she had struggled all night, but now it was too late—and she could no longer budge from the wall . . .

Maxim and his missus came from the house with a son and son-in-law. They all started to lift Altke up and then carried her down. It was as if she had been stuffed with lead and welded to the wall, and she wouldn't let herself be touched. With great effort they brought her down into the house, lowered her into bed, and placed hot water on her feet. But Altke kept shivering and screaming.

At dawn they brought Altke home and set her down in Golde's empty bed. One doctor after another was summoned—but for three days in a row she kept screaming without permitting a drop of water to reach her lips. On the third day, at exactly midnight, Altke sat up in bed, looked far overhead, stretched out her arms as if she wanted to embrace someone, then fell backward—and died.

Countless tales spread throughout the surrounding villages and small towns. Everyone offered something different to say about what had happened, a distinctive interpretation of events. Who knows how long folks would have spoken about this calamity that happened in the far-flung village home if another calamity hadn't caused an even greater sensation—greater because the story had to do with love and life instead of sadness and death.

A GREAT TERROR—AN ATONEMENT

It took place in a home all of one verst from Meysl's house of misfortune. In this home lived a respected, handsome man with a long, white beard, Reb Shiye the miller. Reb Shiye was descended from an old, pedigreed family. He himself was quite learned. He rented out the water mill from the Dakhtervitsh nobleman and, as a result, really did live at a "court," in a grand and beautiful home. His wife, Soreh, was a small, pious, and nearsighted woman. There were only two children in the house: their son Shimshl, a young man of twenty-two, and Hinde, a girl of seventeen, their granddaughter from their eldest daughter who had died in childbirth when Hinde was born. Hinde was blonde, slim, and luminous. She conducted herself like a young lady. She studied together with the nobleman's own children—and also danced, sang, and went on walks with them, wearing hats under pointed silk parasols.

Hinde was the apple of her grandparents' eye. They were anxious about her; they were afraid to get their fill of looking at her. The spitting image of her mother, Soreh thought, wiping her nearsighted, teary eyes. Reb Shiye would consider her from the side of the room and sigh deeply within himself. He was afraid to allow certain thoughts—the ones that crept into his mind at night when sleep eluded him—to take center stage in his mind: she was an orphan girl without parents—who knew whether she was on the right path in life? But there she was—again and again—spending time with the nobility. They really did need to get her married as soon as possible.

Shimshl followed Hinde with sadness and longing. He swallowed every glance she sent his way like a man desperate to quench his thirst. He tailed her at a distance when she spent time with the young nobility. Whenever she put on her white dress with the pink belt and went to the fine halls to dance with them, Shimshl would pace in front of the house, like a shadow, in his long, black kaftan . . . And when Hinde joyously came back out, accompanied by one of the gentlemen, Shimshl would hide behind the wall and follow them at a distance so they wouldn't spot him. As they were approaching the mill, he hid behind a bush. From there he watched as his niece kissed the gentile nobleman. On the nights of his spying excursions Shimshl couldn't sleep. He tossed and turned in bed as if snakes had bitten him. The next day he didn't eat anything and walked around like someone with a fatal illness. Soreh followed him and told him to bend down a bit so she could feel his forehead with her lips to see if, God forbid, he had a fever.

No, Shimshl didn't have a fever. But ever since that night when he saw Hinde kissing the gentile, sleep eluded him altogether. He shadowed her every move. Hinde, preoccupied in her youthful romance, didn't see what was happening around her. She was intoxicated from her own joy and oblivious to everything else. Her grandparents, too, stopped sleeping. The three of them lay in their beds thinking of only one thing.

Hinde herself was also unable to fall asleep—but out of joy. The tall nobleman stood before her in her mind's eye, sprinkling her with tender words.

For a long time the elder folk carried the pain within themselves, afraid to allow the first word to cross their lips. But the mute sighs they exchanged in their sleepless beds screamed out the secret of which they were both all too aware. During the day Soreh's tearful eyes avoided Reb Shiye's prickly gaze that bore into both of their hearts like a drill.

One Sabbath afternoon, as Hinde was getting dressed to go for a walk, Reb Shiye called her over and ordered her to stay home. He and her grandmother had something to discuss with her.

Hinde cheerfully glanced over at her grandfather: "No, dear Grandpa. I have to go now. They're waiting for me."

"Who's waiting for you?"

Hinde blushed: "What does it matter? Fyodor is waiting for me."

Sternly, Reb Shiye responded: "Shimshl will go over and tell him that you need to stay home."

"No. I have to go."

Reb Shiye gestured to Shimshl with his finger and said: "Son, go and tell them that Hinde can't come. And you, Hinde, come here."

Hinde approached her grandfather who was sitting at the table, his head supported by both of his hands. Soreh sat down next to Hinde. "Don't be afraid. Grandpa won't do anything to you."

Reb Shiye lifted his old, white head and looked at Hinde: "We need to talk, Hinde. I believe it's time to discuss your path in life. I realize you're still young, but a Jewish child must go in a Jewish direction . . ."

Reb Shiye grew quiet, contemplative—and resumed speaking, more to himself, than to Hinde: "Who knows? Here I am busy day and night . . . I ought to have paid more attention . . . and your grandmother," and here he looked over at Soreh, "gave in to you too much . . . and now? It's better to prevent a sickness than to heal one . . ."

Hinde was quiet but feeling impatient. "What is it that I'm doing, Grandpa? Why are you so worried?" she asked. "I'm not sick. I don't lack for anything."

"No. Thank God, you're healthy and beautiful, but there are different types of sicknesses. It's best that we not discuss them . . ."

Seeing that Hinde was looking in the direction of the door, Reb Shiye straightened up and pulled his chair closer to Hinde: "You don't remember your mother or your father, may you live a long life. But your father, may he rest in peace, has a sister—Leytshe's her name—who immigrated to America. Surely you remember Leytshe."

"Well, so?"

"Leytshe writes that she's doing quite well there. She's gotten married. Her husband is a fine man who earns a good living. And, no evil eye, they have a few little children . . . She writes that she would really like for us to send you to America, that you would be like one of her children . . . Until now, we didn't want to talk to you about all of this. Your grandmother forbade it. Hinde, you're like our own child to us in our old age. And it's true that Shimshl is your uncle, but according to Jewish law, an uncle is permitted to marry his niece . . ."

Frightened, Hinde looked around and stammered, without any audacity: "No, Grandfather, no . . . I already have a groom . . . I don't need to go to America. Things will go well for me here . . ."

Reb Shiye and Soreh were struck with terror as if a heavy load had been placed onto their heads. Reb Shiye was the first to find words: "What are you saying, child? Who is your groom? Do you mean Shimshl?"

Soreh eagerly grasped at this straw. "Of course she means Shimshl. Everything will turn out well . . . God willing, you'll be the mistress of every last scrap we have," she said, wiping her eyes. "You're my only ray of hope in my old age . . . I cried my eyes out enough at night so that, God forbid, your poor dear mother wouldn't be ashamed in her grave . . . Since, praise God, we were thrown here to earn a bit of bread among the gentiles . . . I wanted to give in to you so that you wouldn't be sad. You were raised in the nobleman's house, with his own children . . . But with God's help everything will still turn out all right . . ."

Hinde looked over at the door impatiently. "May I go now?" she asked.

"You may go," Reb Shiye answered. "Go, my child, go find Shimshen, and both of you come home for the third meal."

"No, Shimshl will come home himself . . . I'm going for a walk," Hinde said and went over to the door.

"You'd better come home with Shimshl, do you hear me?!"

Hinde left. Reb Shiye crossed over to the other side of the room, tugging on his beard, as if by doing that he could elicit a solution to this vexing question that refused him a moment's peace. He went back to the table and sat down not far from Soreh. She sat over a thick Pentateuch translated into Yiddish. Her glasses perched at the tip of her nose, her eyes lowered close to the letters, Soreh searched for the words that were hard to find—"Oh, dear God!"—and she wiped her eyes with her white apron.

"Do you hear, Soreh? We've waited here long enough. Maybe too long. But God willing, we'll quickly write up the betrothal agreement and set the wedding date for Lag BaOmer. Do you hear me?"

"I hear. What else am I doing? Let's just hope it all goes well..." Soreh responded. She wanted to confide in the tall man with bushy eyebrows who was her stern and good husband. But somehow she couldn't find a way to start. In relation to him she was forever the bashful child. She always seemed to lack the right words to begin.

Accustomed to her stammering, Reb Shiye handed down his orders and outlined the plans: "You'll prepare sponge cake and liquor. We'll invite a few neighbors and write up the engagement contract. Shimshl will stay home. He won't go back to study. He'll slowly learn the work around the mill, and we'll study together in the evenings."

Soreh wiped her eyes: "Hopefully it will all go well . . . May the merit of our daughter who passed away so young protect her . . ."

"Well, I know this much. A young goat . . . We'll teach her respect. You'll order a wig for her. Cut off her braids. Don't let her walk around with a bare head. You see to it. She comes from a Jewish home . . . God willing, she'll be a fine Jewish daughter. But she just has to get married. And when children come she'll forget about all of this foolishness. A young goat—well, a young goat is jumpy. Don't worry. We have to trust in God."

"From your mouth to God's ears. I'll give charity in the name of Meyer Baal ha-Nes. I'll fast for her. And may He, whose name I don't want to mention, help me correct what I've overlooked up until this point."

At the third Sabbath meal Shimshl came home by himself. Where was Hinde? He hadn't seen her.

That night Hinde returned home quite late. The next day Reb Shiye told her she was grounded. Hinde stayed at home, not budging from the window. Holding a book on her knee, she gazed out the window. Several days passed in this way. Then Hinde was ordered to get dressed and pack a few skirts. She was going to ride with her grandmother to Slutsk to have dresses sewn for her. Hinde was going to be a bride for Shimshl. In fact, shortly after the engagement contract was drawn up, they would, God willing, be married.

Humiliated, Hinde looked at her grandfather with a sidelong gaze and tried to speak, but her words got lost on her grandfather's gloomy face . . . Feeling sad, she folded her few skirts and left the house with her grandmother. A hitched wagon was waiting in front of the house. A driver—Antosh, the day laborer from the mill—helped the two women get settled. And off they went.

When Antosh was ready to make the return drive home, Hinde approached him in the wagon. She slipped a sealed letter into his hand and said quickly: "Deliver this. Don't forget."

"I'll give it to the sir. But you're not allowed, Hindula. Your grandfather will get angry. He'll start pulling on his beard."

Hinde pressed Antosh's hand. "The gentleman will reward you, Antosh."

Hinde went into the house, where her grandmother Soreh was waiting for her. For several days Soreh rode with Hinde to the stockrooms to purchase satin and ribbed fabric for dresses. They went to the tailor woman, Malkeh Kharash, the most accomplished needlewoman in town, and placed an order to have the clothing sewn. Soreh stayed in Slutsk and waited for the seamstress to finish the alterations. Afterward they would go home. She was old and tired. When Hinde advised her grandmother to stay inside and assured her that she would see to the alterations on her own, Soreh allowed herself to be persuaded. Every time she went out Hinde was tardy. She returned home pleased and excited.

During the several nights that Hinde and her grandmother were away from home, the two of them barely got any sleep. Hinde tossed and turned. During the day she didn't stay inside. When she did come back and Soreh called her in to eat, Hinde sat at the table, dispirited . . . Soreh thought that the child must be having difficulty just thinking about her rapidly impending marriage to her Shimshl. She was afraid to discuss it with her. Soreh caressed her granddaughter with her near-sighted glances as she brought her a superior portion of food: "Eat, my child. With God's help, all will be well . . ."

Her grandmother's quiet words jolted Hinde awake as if from a dream. Shivering lightly, Hinde shook off the thoughts that had been tormenting her.

The day of their return journey had arrived. All of the clothes were finished and packed. Antosh arrived with the horse and wagon. But Hinde was nowhere to be found. "Where's Hinde?"

She'll probably come in any moment now, they thought.

Seconds stretched out into minutes—and then hours. And Hinde still hadn't turned up. The day was gone. Dusk was on the way. They looked for her everywhere they could think of: at the seamstress, at a girlfriend, at a female relative—but she wasn't in any of those places. The grandmother began to wring her hands and feel faint.

Night. And then the next morning. Still no Hinde.

Barely alive, Soreh sat down in the wagon and told Antosh to drive home. Maybe Hinde had gone home? What could she, an old wreck, do? Soreh's anguish was so great that she was barely conscious of sitting down. She couldn't get clear in her mind whether this was reality or, in fact, a terrible dream that would soon be over. She had only to open her eyes and spit on the ground three times, onto all the desolate forests, and everything would be as it had been. She could see Hinde walking around, singing, preening before the mirror, or sitting in an alcove reading a storybook . . .

The wagon rocked like a cradle rocking a crying child.

She had fallen asleep. She only woke up when the wagon had come to a standstill before the mill. When she saw her husband and Shimshl approaching with quizzical looks, everything that had happened flooded back to her . . . She began to rub her teary, nearsighted eyes and then burst out loud into tears.

Approaching Antosh, Reb Shiye asked, "What happened? Where's Hinde? Why is she crying?"

"*Yey Bogu, Panie Shiye, ne znayu . . .*"

"What do you mean—you don't know?"

"Oh dear, something terrible has happened to me! She vanished from my hands. I've gone through the entire city—and it's as if she's disappeared without a trace!"

"What do you mean? Did you go to the rabbi? Did you ask his advice? Did you go to the police?"

"I thought I was going to pass out . . . I didn't know what to do . . . And somehow I got the idea that she had gone home."

Reb Shiye stood there tugging on his beard and murmuring to himself. "Get out of the wagon. I'll go to the landowner and find out where Fyodor is . . ."

Reb Shiye returned home, utterly transformed as if he had endured a long illness. He braced himself for evening prayers like someone sentenced to death. After the service he told Soreh to pack his prayer shawl and something for the road and Antosh to hitch the horse. Reb Shiye bade Soreh and Shimshl a good night, kissed the mezuzah, and left the house. Soreh went after him, and in a pleading, broken voice, called out: "Where are you going? Do you know something?"

Reb Shiye said to himself, into his beard: "God's punishment in my old age. We're all in God's hands . . . And maybe God will still help us save her from gentile hands . . ." With that he crawled into the wagon and drove away.

Reb Shiye was away from home for two entire weeks. The mill and the house stood mute. Shimshl and Soreh wandered about like shadows, not speaking to each other, even avoiding each other's eyes. All around the muteness of the mill and the house, the voiceless secrets of the calamity were transmitted, as if shadowy trees around a river had shaken them from their branches and handed them over to the wind who was now, in turn, dispersing them across the entire neighborhood to nearby houses. Old and young alike steered the secrets onto their tongues—and a whispering campaign commenced. It wasn't long before the whole neighborhood was speaking openly about it. People shook their heads with sorrow over what had besmirched a fine Jewish home. Jewish mothers kept a more watchful eye over their children to ensure that, God forbid, they didn't stray from the right path. Gentiles sympathized with the old, honest miller and cursed—the devil take their fathers!—the nobility and their debauched, impudent sonny boys.

Reb Shiye the miller returned home at dawn. His appearance had changed so drastically in those two weeks that it was impossible to recognize him. His formerly steady gaze now wandered, searching, never resting for a moment on one thing, as if there were all sorts of danger crouching in wait for him on all sides. But he wasn't lost for long. There was a decisiveness in his gaze when he turned to Soreh one day and said: "We'll need to go to Sholem in Ugli and talk it over with Yankl, Shimen, Peyse, and Velvl. God willing, we must return to Slutsk. I'll take along local men from there; if we need them, there are enough Jews in Slutsk . . . If God gives me back my child without any fuss—all well and good. But if we need to we'll wage war over this . . . And you, Soreh, pack up a few of her skirts and blouses."

Without saying anything in return, a weeping Soreh did as her husband ordered.

That night three wagons left Reb Shiye's home. In them were some dozen Jews from the area—old, middle-aged, and a few young, healthy fellows. By Sunday night the Jews were back in their homes, except for Reb Shiye and Sholem of Ugli. Everyone in the entire area went through their days with a kind of bated breath, whispering among themselves as they anticipated the return of the two men.

On the following Thursday the two wagons they'd been waiting for finally arrived. Reb Shiye could barely drag his exhausted body to bed. He told Soreh to place mustard on his heart, and he asked for some whiskey and a sour pickle. After the fine piece of work they'd completed, he deserved a good stiff drink. And may she go in good health . . . shipped across the border, bought a ship ticket, settled onto a ship, and lo and behold, off to America. There she'd forget all this foolishness . . . how she cried and how she kissed her grandfather! They had turned her head: monastery, conversion . . . But the minute the door closed on her, she began to scream and cry that she wanted to go home . . . They promised her a thousand fortunes, but she held her ground. Good thing the monastery is under the control of the city . . . When the nuns saw so many Jews they got frightened, and Hinde herself, seeing her grandfather, began to scream . . . and before you knew it, she was with us in the wagon, and off we went!

"Hopefully everything will go well for the old folks . . . What a wreck he had become!" Peshe said, letting out a heavy sigh.

A letter arrived from Hinde in America. She was with her aunt, and, thank God, all was well. But she missed her grandparents very much and begged their forgiveness for what she would never forgive herself for as long as she lived . . . And she asked for Uncle Shimshl's forgiveness too. New York was such a vast, beautiful world . . . one that can only be seen in a dream . . . She was already enrolled in night school and hoped to master English. Her aunt and uncle and their little daughters sent them warm regards. Shimshl read out the letter. When he finished Reb Shiye called out: "Thank you, God. *Shivtekha u-mishantekha, hemah yenahamuni* . . ."

Soreh took the letter from her son's hand, touched it all over, and brought it to her lips: "My child, my child . . . I wasn't destined to see a bit of parental pride in my old age . . ."

Before anyone even had a chance to get back to normal following this event, something else happened on the estate in Dakhtervitsh that captured everyone's attention for a while.

MARIA ANDREYEVNA AND HER DAUGHTER, PAULA

On his estate, Kiriakov provided support for a pair of distant relatives: Maria, a widow, and Paula, her only daughter, a young girl with blonde braids and a slim, charming figure. The mother was the housekeeper and practically managed the entire household. She herself owned very little. Very little indeed. She shared a room with her daughter, maintaining an ever-vigilant eye on her. She watched over and schooled her in all of the ways of refined living. Every morning and evening, they went to the small church on the estate, where they got down on their knees before the Holy Maria. There, she asked Her to extend Her protection and light over her one-and-only abandoned lamb . . . Together with Paula, she invariably recited a prayer for her deceased husband, her dear daughter's father, now in Paradise.

The blonde Paula grew like a delicate, well-tended white flower. Beneath the veil of love and piety her mother cast over her, she grew as if in a more beautiful and exalted world. Clad chiefly in white, Paula moved quietly and politely through the world. On her long, white, girlish neck hung a thin, black cord that lowered a golden crucifix over her heart and between her firm breasts. Everyone on the estate reserved a special kind of love for Paula. The servants saw her as a holy woman. The children in Kiriakov's household also treated her politely. Although they were deeply convinced that they were the ones who were truly in charge, they understood, too, that, for all the pageantry of their balls and for all the distinction of their chambers, there was still something about Paula they could never attain.

Paula spent her time reading the Bible. When her mother finished with her work, they would both go past the graves and into the church. And so it was, every evening, and every morning before the mother's work day began.

On the estate, it was known that Paula was preparing herself to become a nun. But since she was still too young and it was so hard for her mother to part with her, Paula's leave-taking was postponed until she turned nineteen. Meanwhile, the mother watched over Paula as if she were an exalted being who had been entrusted to her.

For mother and daughter, time passed quietly, and with pragmatic optimism. The church and daily work filled their days. The church, with its wonderful dreams about the young, crucified Lord, with whom Paula would oh-so-soon be forever linked, and with whom she, along with another dozen young nuns, would be able to prostrate themselves in sacred prayer, also occupied Paula's days and nights. And she walked about as if she were in a dream state . . .

One evening at dusk in late autumn, as they were making their way home from church across the bare meadows, the mother gripped Paula's arm close to her with greater tightness than usual and informed her that she had to go away to a larger city for a short while. Something had been causing her pain in her side for quite a long time now, and the doctor said that an operation was needed. If not for the relentless urgings of both the doctor and her relative, the Countess Kiriakova, she herself might have forgotten about it, although it really did hurt, and as a result, she wasn't able to sleep at night. She had to go. They'd reserved a bed in a hospital and booked a renowned surgeon for her. She hadn't wanted to tell Paula anything about it. She didn't want her to worry for no reason. But now that she had to go, she had arranged for Paula to board in the same rooms as the noble daughters of the estate. There, Paula would eat and sleep. The Countess had demanded that she not give over the keys to anyone except Paula. For the few days that she would still be here, she would show her how to use the keys. And when she returned home a healthy woman, they would start thinking about preparing Paula for the nunnery.

A few days later, the mother left, and Paula moved in with Kiriakov's family in their fine rooms.

Maria Andreyevna expressed her worry in every letter she wrote to her daughter. The doctors said that she had to remain in the hospital for the time being, she wrote. At the outset, they had said it would be a matter of weeks. Only later did it become months.

The worry in the mother's letter focused more on her child than herself. In every letter, she reminded Paula about the church. Was she going twice a day? Was she saying a prayer for her father? And she should also say a prayer for her mother so she would regain her health as soon as possible and be able to return to watch over her child's life until she could deliver it into more secure hands forever . . .

At first, Paula's letters to her mother were punctual and regular. *Maminka, I was in church today. I lit a candle for your health. The Holy Lord, whom we love so, will help us. You will soon get better and return to me. I kiss you and plead to God on your behalf.*

But Paula's letters reached her mother like frightened geese. All that was unwritten and unsaid screamed forth from the pages. This made the mother, lying in her sick bed, even more sick and uneasy. She struggled with the doctors, begging them to let her go home. But in vain. She would be trifling with her very life if she didn't stay in the hospital as they were ordering her to do.

Paula's letters came less and less frequently. The more uncommon their arrival, the thicker and blacker the fog that enshrouded their lines, and all of the unwritten words gleamed from between them like slaughtering knives. With each passing day, the mother worsened. The hospital held her like a prisoner, against her will, as if her dark fortune had so willed it.

Until there were no more letters at all from Paula.

Maria Andreyevna wrote heartrending letters to the Countess Kiriakova. A thousand times, she begged forgiveness for her insolence—only it wasn't for herself that she was asking but for the apple of her eye, for her little orphan, for her poor, luminous Paula. She knew deep within her heart that the noble countess, herself a mother, would, with God's help, answer her request and write a few words to let her know how her little dove, Paula, was doing, whether she was at least well, and why she wasn't writing her.

But instead of a response from the noble countess, the doctor saw her on his rounds. He considered her and then said pointedly, almost in passing: "Not so good . . . It's absolutely essential that you remain here, but there's a letter—from the countess saying that you should be sent home."

With these words, Maria Andreyevna initially felt her emotions in tumult. Joy and terror enfolded her in a twin embrace. But it wasn't long before these two feelings evolved into just one: terror. Something had happened to her one and only, her Paula, alone on her own!

Shakily, she got out of bed with the help of a compassionate nurse. She straightened herself up only to fall back down. Again she steeled herself and stood back up. She asked for her clothes and then put them on. She was eased into a wheelchair and wheeled down to a droshky. From there, Maria Andreyevna was seated on a train, which took her to the small town at the end of the line. At the train station, she waited for an old servant from the estate. Spotting Maria Andreyevna barely able to descend the steps of the train and requiring the support of the train clerk, the servant, his cap under his arm, fearfully crossed himself. With considerable care, he then led her to the wagon parked nearby. She could barely traipse after him. He settled her into the wagon, covering her knees with a woolen blanket. He then climbed into the driver's seat and took the reins in his hands. But before he signaled to the horses to go, she called out to him in a trembling voice: "Vasil?"

"Yes, Maria Andreyevna, how may I serve you?"

With great effort she once again brought his name to her deathly pale, stiffened lips: "Vasil . . . ," she said, but nothing else came out. As if in fear of the answer Vasil was about to give, the question stopped in its tracks, stuck like a bone in her throat. While still seated, the elderly Vasil bowed once again to the invalid, turned the upper half of his body to her, removed his cap, made the sign of the cross in the air, and as if to himself, said: "May He who died for our sins help you . . ."

Maria Andreyevna remained seated as if turned to stone, but tears, like large, glowing drops, trickled down her cheeks and onto her hands, which lay impotently in her lap.

As Vasil drove up to the little home that had been added onto the aristocratic home, with its grand rooms, in the middle of an orchard, the countess herself came out to greet Maria Andreyevna and help her out of the wagon. After Maria Andreyevna bowed and thanked her for this great honor, the countess took her under arm and led her to her small home, where there were two fully made beds. Everything was exactly as she left it.

The countess told Maria to get out of her travel clothes and lie down on the sofa. The servant immediately entered with glasses of wine and water on a tray. As if hypnotized, Maria did everything the countess told her to do. But after a while, she asked: "Begging your forgiveness, Countess, where is my Paula? Why is she hiding from her mother?"

The countess drew her chair close to the sofa where Maria Andreyevna was lying. She took her feverish hand in her own and said, "You know we're all in the hands of God, Maria. God's will is done—we can't go against it . . ."

Maria's hand trembled in the countess's. She lifted herself up and withdrew her hand. "You must tell me what's happened to my child. I left her in your hands. If not, I would never have gone . . ." she said. She collapsed, lowered herself to the countess's feet, embraced her knees, and began to weep.

The countess carefully disentangled herself from the clutches of Maria's clinging hands. She helped her to stand and then eased her back down onto the sofa. "If you act like a decent human being, Maria Andreyevna, I can tell you what happened. There's a letter . . ."

Deathly exhausted, Maria stretched out her lost hands to the countess: "Forgive a poor mother . . . Give, give me the letter. What have I done to sin against her? Give me the letter. Have mercy on your poor servant."

The countess removed a creased letter from her purse. But before handing it over to Maria, she bent down to her and made the sign of the cross over her: "May Our Protector help you. I took this from her hand when she struggled with death. In her anguish, she asked me to give it to you. And she asked you to forgive her."

As if with someone else's eyes, Maria swallowed every single letter contained in the few lines. Again and again. She read it like someone who doesn't quite believe her own senses, who doesn't know whether she is awake or in a dream within a dream and who wants to wake up and free herself from the terrible nightmare suffocating her . . .

Before her eyes quivered these crooked, twisted lines: "Forgive me, dear mother—I could no longer———I ask God to take my soul and return it to Him———I couldn't defend myself—The hands that ruined me were like iron chains against my weak girl's hands———Forgive me, dear mother———And love me, and may God forgive my sin———

Maria was led into the aristocratic chariot and driven to their church, where Paula lay, covered in flowers. With her hair undone, she appeared under the illuminated icon as the Holy Magdalene.

Three days after the funeral of Paula, her mother, Maria Andreyevna, was also carried to her final resting place. Over the graves of both, a single large crucifix, as well as a slate board that read "Here lies loyal, beloved servants of the Great House of Kiriakov," were installed.

The second young lord—he of the curly black hair and broad shoulders who often indulged in carousing sprees at the estate, causing the girls of the village to hide in the attics and bar the doors—was suddenly spirited abroad for two whole years . . .

AFTER THE FIRE

As a result of the fire in Kapyl′, all three children stayed home for almost all of the winter.

The first to return to Kapyl′ was Soreh. The period leading up to Passover was a busy sewing time at Roda's home, and Roda let Peshe know that she really wanted Soreh to come back to work. Soreh was thrilled to get this piece of news. She was bored to death in the village. Sure, she was helping Malkeh sew, knit, and embroider—but she felt her days to be beside the point, irrelevant. She missed Roda's house, the letters from faraway countries, Shprintse, and the paralyzed Shmuel-Arn . . .

Kapyl′ was building itself back up, becoming more beautiful than ever. The synagogues were covered with shiny red and green tin roofs. There were more stone and brick buildings. On the well of the synagogue courtyard, a brand-new wheel and a new bucket were installed.

There was other work happening at Roda's. She had arranged with carpenters, who were busy all over town working on home construction sites, to build another room onto the antechamber of her house.

Roda figured that she would somehow pay for it in installments. If she could keep Shmuel-Arn in a separate room, she thought, it would be better both for him and for the entire household.

Shmuel-Arn's bed was placed near the window, where he could observe the flow of pedestrians and wagons.

In Sholem's house, the two younger children once again didn't have anything to do. There was no point in keeping a boy and a girl without a teacher. The plan to send the children back into town for religious school was revived.

Shaye the water carrier's house had burned in the fire. Unable to rebuild the house, Shaye sold the plot of land, and he, along with his tall, thin wife, went to live with someone else. Peshe consulted with Roda about the two smaller children. They decided that they should be brought to live with Roda. Since there was now another room in the house, there was more space to configure the arrangements. They would eat with Soreh. In the same pot used to cook for the household, they'd toss in a few more grits, pour in another spoonful of water, and, God forbid, no one would starve from hunger. Everything would turn out well.

Dineh and Daniel were driven back to Kapyl′ for another semester.

This time Dineh returned almost eagerly, even though it was difficult for her to tear herself away from home every time she had to leave. She longed for each individual thing at home in the village, but she now viewed the shtetl the way you would someone whom you'd left dangerously sick and then found out was recovered. You still couldn't quite believe the news and wanted to see the recovery with your own eyes.

The night she had left the burning shtetl returned to Dineh like a fiery specter: the burning houses, the packed coaches, the weeping mothers and children, the screams of chickens, cows, and calves, the flight from the shtetl into the night . . . Where had Beyle and her little girl with the red curly hair and laughing green eyes gone? Dineh would go and see with her own eyes how Kapyl′ looked now . . .

In school they went to their own teacher. The children liked living in Roda's house. Being with Soreh, they felt even more at home. Dineh made herself thoroughly useful. She tended Shmuel-Arn with utter devotion, and beat Roda to it every time. Shprintse kept Dineh by her side and taught her how to craft the delicate stitchery of fine sewing, such as embroidering a nicer buttonhole in a shirt or sewing a fine silk ribbon crowned by a flower onto a blouse.

Dineh also grew closer to Roda's older boy, Motl, who was two years older than her and Roda's third son. Since the other sons were no longer living at home, he was now the eldest at home. She went with him to gather birch leaves in the forest. As a folk remedy for paralysis, they placed the leaves in the baths they ran for Shmuel-Arn.

During her walks with Motl, Dineh told him about her home and their forest with its birds and springs. She spoke with such pride about her great property that he looked at her with a degree of pity. Motl treated Dineh the way a big brother would treat a silly little sister. Little by little he started to tell her what he knew of the world. He had already studied in Slutsk and read thick books. He was a Zionist who read his father's newspapers and knew who Herzl was. Slowly they became friends. Dineh wanted to lead Motl over the borders to her land of wonder, and he wanted to lead her to his. He reacted to her talk like an adult who keeps giving in to a small child and her play until he loses the upper hand and becomes a child himself. In his talk, Dineh saw distant, incomprehensible, unattainable, yet wonderful worlds.

Motl would often take Dineh along on his walks in the forest when he would go there with his friends: the rabbi's son, Hershl, a blond, handsome, polite boy, and Reb Yisroel's grandson, Shmuel-Leybl, a thin boy with a white, elongated face and quick black eyes and white, long, girlish hands.

These three boys were the best fellows in town. Everyone thought of them with great respect. Dineh became a sister to them. They took her with them on their outings. When they got into a heated discussion, they would often glance over at Dineh—at the way she was looking at them with such fear—and then burst into laughter at her fear.

"Don't be afraid, Dineh. We're not arguing. We're having a discussion. When you get older you'll understand too."

But when it was just Dineh and Motl gathering the leaves, she shyly asked him why he, Hershl, and Shmuel-Leybl talked so weirdly—words that were so hard to understand—and did they always have to shout when they were talking . . .

One day Dineh went walking with Motl to fetch a basin of water from the synagogue courtyard. While carrying the water downhill—with Dineh walking in front and Motl behind—the basin slid down on the two poles all the way toward Dineh's end. Dineh lost her balance and fell. The basin fell on her feet. They weren't far from home. Her left foot quickly became swollen. The doctor said that a bone had cracked and immediately set it in a plaster cast. And Dineh was confined to bedrest. She was in a lot of pain. But she didn't cry or complain. Motl felt so guilty for not being the one walking in front and for letting Dineh fall that this alone caused Dineh to forget her sharp pain. Whenever he approached her bed to ask her if she was in pain she answered, with a smile, that it was nothing, she wasn't in any pain at all . . .

For the Sabbath Dineh was taken home, where she was made to stay in bed for two months. During the first week Dineh was in great pain. One Friday evening she heard Daniel's voice through the window speaking with Motl. Soon Motl was in the house asking Peshe if it was all right that he had come. Peshe received him with great warmth. "If it's all right that my three children stay with your mother, then it's more than all right that you come to us."

The boys entered the room to see Dineh. She blushed with joy and didn't know what to say. Motl offered her his hand. "How are you, Dineh?" he asked.

Bashfully, she gave Motl her hand in return but didn't answer his question. Then she asked Daniel: "Did you show him the calves in the stable? And the big pear tree in the orchard? And the footbridge that we swing from?"

"Hold on. We just got here."

"You walked?"

"No, we came with Uncle Leyb."

All three of them laughed out loud at the same time.

"But he himself walks . . ."

"We picked berries on the way and ate them."

"And you weren't scared of the Gypsies in Keylye and their dogs?"

"No. Why should I be scared? We often take a stroll to Keylye on the Sabbath—me, Hershl, and Shmuel-Meyer. We go to Reb Elye's kids, and we know the Gypsies."

From then on Motl traveled to Ugli for each Sabbath, often bringing his two friends.

After two months Dineh was healed, and she returned to Kapyl′.

THE TATARS' CURE . . .

One day, while sitting next to the window in Roda's house, Dineh saw a group of people running from the synagogue courtyard downhill. Daniel and other boys from the religious school were running behind them. When she got a better look Dineh saw a young woman in flight with long, unkempt hair and wearing a torn shirt. On her heels a man with a dirty face and hands was flogging her half-naked body with a heavy leather strap. The woman was screaming and desperate to break free from the adults and children surrounding her. Dineh burst into loud tears. Soreh, Shprintse, and Roda came running toward her—and, utterly horrified, they all ran out into the street.

The young woman was Crazy Soreh's youngest daughter. When she became pregnant with her first child she lost her mind. Her husband and father brought her to the Tatars in Kapyl′, hoping they would beat the craziness out of her.

The Tatars had a custom of pouring buckets of water on the patients, and they would beat them with thick leather belts. The young pregnant woman was quite strong. When they poured a bucket of water on her she became terrified. When they started to beat her she knocked down the two Tatars standing over her and fled. Now she was being driven back, downhill, to the Tatar street, where the Tatars lived and worked at their tannery. (The place forever reeked of the heavy odor of hides being worked, and the cries of the sick being flogged could regularly be heard. Their small prayer house with the half moon atop the minaret was also there.)

Witnessing this scene, Dineh was so disturbed that she once again took ill and had to be taken home for a few weeks. Daniel would tell her about how he, along with the boys from religious school, would go to the Tatar alley and hear the lunatics screaming when they were beaten.

They beat Crazy Soreh's daughter for a long time until they beat all of the madness out of her. They came to bring her home . . . She sat on wagon, pale and quiet as a dove. Dineh was happy that the woman had gotten better, but she still couldn't make peace with the Tatars, with their thick, wet straps and the buckets of cold water they poured over the sick.

BEYLE FINALLY TURNS UP

One day Uncle Yankl breathlessly appeared in Sholem's house with the following news: "I was in Kapyl′, and look what I got in the mail—a letter from Beyle in New York, from America. She's there with the child and the blond young nobleman. Things are going well for her. She sent me twenty-five dollars. Here's the money." And he took a wallet filled with bills out of his pocket to show them.

"And what does she write from America? What was she doing running away with a gentile, and then—?" asked Uncle Yankl.

"Here, go ahead and read it," Sholem said. "It's not just from her; he writes too. He says he wants to convert to Judaism. He wants Beyle to extract a divorce from Yudl. If that can happen he'll marry her. And she writes that he's better to her than a real father, and he loves her. And he's a fine person—and very good to the child. Go figure."

Based on that piece of good news, Yankl made a toast with a few drinking mates around the table and returned home late at night in a jovial mood and altogether refreshed.

CLOUDS CREEP CLOSER

It was the eve of Passover in Sholem's house. Like any other year, the premises were cleaned, polished, and purified for the baking of matzos. The wagons were parked closer together in the barns to make room for all of the neighbors' vehicles that would be coming for the matzo baking.

But during the past few years much had changed in the appearance of Sholem's house and yard. The income from alcohol sales had been taken away. Ever since Sholem signed away all of his holdings to the nobleman Marko, the entire household—both the homeowners and the servants—walked around as if there wasn't ground beneath their feet, as if they expected what was hanging so heavily in the air to fall upon their heads—if not today, then tomorrow. The mood of the residents was palpable all throughout the property.

In addition to these worries, there were others that cast black veils over Sholem's house. Faytl's life with Leyeh in Pesatshne had not improved. Leyeh was due, but her face was streaked with tears. She hoped she wouldn't live to see the birth. Faytl, quiet and stubborn, moved through life as if he were in alien surroundings. He performed his job in the shop like an underling and came home late at night.

From Itshe came the sort of tidings that caused his parents sleepless nights.

The young man, not yet sixteen years old, was as developed as an adult—both in physical appearance and in understanding. The lofty, boyish head of black hair, the prominent forehead, and the sharp, clever eyes were now set atop a pair of broad, healthy shoulders. Itshe had matured like a handsome, unbent tree.

When Sholem came from Slutsk, he had much to report about Itshe. However, Itshe himself was rarely seen at home or even in Slutsk, where he was supposed to be working and studying. Mrs. Yoshelyevitsh was forever complaining to Sholem, as if her own child's life was in danger: "What's to be done with the child, Reb Sholem? I've gotten old and sick because of him. What'll become of him? They use him to stop up all of the holes. Wherever there's a gathering, wherever there's a dangerous mission—in Minsk, in Riga, in Babruĭsk, anywhere in the entire world—they send him there. No matter how much I plead and no matter how much I talk to him, he looks at me as if *he* were right. And when I press him to slow down, ask him to tell me what he thinks and whether he doesn't know how this will all end, he smiles and says, 'Well, someone definitely has to do it . . . And what if what may befall me happens to someone else?' Go try talking to him."

Things had gotten so bad that Peshe wrote about her trouble to her brothers in

America. They sent back a letter and a boat ticket. And as hard as it was for Sholem and Peshe to send such a young child across the ocean, they nevertheless decided that, around the time of the Jewish holidays, they would send him—together with another group of people who would be leaving from Slutsk to America.

When Sholem was in Slutsk a few weeks before Passover, he told Itshe that he must come home for the holiday. His mother said he must come, he said, and he, his father, was ordering him too.

In his quiet, confident way, Itshe responded: "There's still time before Passover . . . If I can get away, I'll definitely come . . ."

In the smallest towns, even in the villages, an atmosphere akin to the foreboding before a storm prevailed. Clandestine meetings were being held everywhere.

On the peasants' houses, signs were repeatedly found. The signs called out to the population: "Russian people! Free yourself from your yoke! The time is nigh! Do it now! We're with you in your struggle! Brothers! Onward to uprising!"

Furtive hands completed the work without being seen. Everywhere people whispered to each other, buzzing like bees around a beehive. As if descended from heaven, riders, armed with unsheathed swords at the sides of their blue and red striped trousers, suddenly appeared. People were whispering, "They're afraid of an uprising. The tsar is about to issue new decrees . . . All political prisoners will be freed . . . There will be *svoboda* . . ."

In the small towns and the villages all sorts of unbelievable, bizarre news tidbits floated. The echoes from the big, distant cities had been muffled and transformed into inexplicable rumors by the time they reached far-flung corners . . .

Ugli was a center of revolutionary activities. Much of the region was covered in forest. One of the largest forests near Ugli belonged to the wealthy timber merchant Yankev Gurevitsh. He was an ordinary Jew who was once an oxen driver and then became a timber merchant through some cause or other. He had three sons and a daughter. During the summers he would bring the entire family to that pine forest. Tsipke, his small, gaunt wife who had small, red eyes, gussied herself up in the latest Parisian fashion and spoke a very broken Russian. Yankev, a big man with a wide belly and broad shoulders who wore a shiny top hat and carried a cane, looked like a wealthy butcher. But he was amiable to everyone and loved to have a drink with any peasant he encountered. Because of this all of the peasants—and the nearby Jews as well—loved him. In an emergency, you could turn to Yankev Gurevitsh. He hardly addressed anyone in the formal mode "*Ir.*" He often drove abroad to carry out big business deals with Prussians over railroad ties and other types of lumber products, even entire forests. He was believed to be a millionaire.

His one and only daughter, Fanye, who, by the way, was his youngest child, rode a slim, brown horse. Her two governesses, one German and one French, rode on either side of her on small, fleet-footed horses. Fanye alternated between speaking French or German, and she conducted herself as a true child of the aristocracy. But as a result his three sons, students in the Minsk *gymnasium*, were totally devoted to the socialist movement. When they were in the forest they chopped down the trees and cut the timber alongside the woodcutters. They offered the woodcutters cigarettes and told them about the new laws and decrees. They handed them leaflets to take home. The sons would often go by themselves to the peasants' houses and spend evenings there. The oldest, Naum, was married and had a child but behaved like a boy and was deeply devoted to the cause. His wife, who with her short haircut looked like a blond boy herself, was the daughter of a rabbi. She helped distribute the propaganda. In Minsk she was well known in the movement.

In Sholem's house all of them felt at home. Yankev Gurevitsh and Sholem didn't address each other in the formal mode. They had been friends since childhood.

Yankev Gurevitsh's sons wielded great influence over Itshe, and they too thought highly of him. Together they traveled to various cities and villages to carry out propaganda work. They invariably brought Sholem regards from Itshe and added that he would be a great man someday, that he was a born leader.

They spread the word that the liberation was nigh. Everyone was told to go to Minsk for a great holiday to greet the newly freed political prisoners. Anyone who was able to travel did not stay at home. They went to the larger cities to spend the holiday. Yankev Gurevitsh's three sons, along with his blonde daughter-in-law, went to Minsk too. Workers from small towns traveled to the bigger cities in contingents while singing "The Marsellaise" en route. People traveled from the villages in wagons to the smaller towns to witness the amazing sight of the *Batiushka*'s generosity and how he would liberate his *narod*.

But the Jewish parents, whose children were mixed up in this holiday, weren't happy. Quite the contrary, really—their hearts trembled with a premonition of doom . . . The elders sat around the ovens and on the earthen benches outside their homes and waited for their children to return, unharmed by the big cities and their enormous newsworthy events.

Like the jolt of an earthquake causing widespread chaos, the bloody news ripped through the entire region. The workers had been enticed into the cities to gather on bridges and in the middle of marketplaces to hear speakers hired to agitate them to a fever pitch. They were then surrounded by riders and cannons who shot at them and blew up the bridges, causing thousands to fall into the rivers.

Blood flowed in the streets.

So it went for a day and night until everything was quiet. But the stench of blood and burnt flesh hung over the streets. Then the merciful powers that be once more allowed the *narod* to go to the marketplaces to identify the dead and bring them to *pohorony*. The streets needed to be cleaned. People didn't have to be asked twice. Only instead of young footsteps resounding with song there now came stooped, wailing mothers and fathers in search of the torn remains of their children. It was difficult to identify your own child. Most went unidentified.

Yankev Gurevitsh found his youngest son Binyomen alive. The two older sons, along with his daughter-in-law, were found with pierced skulls.

ITSHE, IN THE BALANCE

Itshe made it back home with Yankev Gurevitsh's youngest son. They were together in the marketplace in Minsk. Cossacks rode over the two youths but they survived.

Itshe returned completely changed. A cough had taken hold of him. Whenever he coughed he clutched his chest. The doctor said that this was the result of a terrible blow. His heart had been dislocated.

Itshe was put to bed.

The clouds blanketing all of Russia darkened and thickened. During nighttime raids youths were pulled from their beds and never seen again. In cities and small towns people were afraid to be seen together in groups of three for fear they would be suspected of political activity and carted away.

A nocturnal darkness descended on Sholem's house.

Soreh, Dineh, and Daniel were brought home from Kapyl′. With the windows and doors shut, the family members sat day and night in fear of every sound they heard outside. Itshe lay on a long, narrow bed, his body on fire. He periodically jolted awake, and looking into the distance with his burning gaze and his proud, young head lifted upward he would call out: "The time is now . . . Come, brothers! . . . Demand what's rightfully yours!"

It wasn't long before large drops of sweat had collected on Itshe's burning forehead. Standing on either side of him, Malkeh and Sholem eased his head back down on the pillow and tried to calm him. From time to time he covered his face with both hands and screamed, as if with a force beyond himself: "Brothers!—

Cossacks! Cannons! Run!" He continued until he was utterly spent, drenched in sweat and pleading for a sip of water.

Day and night Malkeh never left Itshe's bedside. Peshe was completely drained and often took to her bed herself, unable to rise. His black mood visible on his face, Sholem fasted and recited the Psalms while sitting by the sick youth's bedside through the nights.

Dineh occupied the same spot on the ceramic tile Russian stove from where, as a little one, her childish eyes had watched her baby sister, Freydele, die. Unnoticed by her exhausted family she sat there, never taking her eyes from Itshe. Thoughts, utterly incomprehensible even to her, floated through her mind. Everything around her grew hazy. All she could see was Itshe, the big brother who had been the first to tell her about the world and life and God and who now lay in terrible agony, screaming, so terrified, and saying such strange things.

Then these images returned to her: how Itshe had once lay with his head all bloodied when the horses threw him off . . . and how she had gone to old Afanas to exorcise the demons from Itshe—and how he had gotten better . . . She didn't understand what they were waiting for. Do they still need to wait? Would she be sent once again with a kerchief to find someone to perform the exorcism? Afanas had died. But Dineh would go to Soreh-Rokhl, who would do an even better exorcism . . . And she, Dineh, would bring the kerchief to Itshe and place it on his head, and then he would get better . . .

Throughout the day Dineh monitored Itshe's every breath. She observed how hard it was for him to breathe. She had no one to talk to or ask questions. Maybe they were so sad that they had completely forgotten about him . . .

Dusk. Dineh quietly moved away from the Russian stove. She went to the dresser, carefully opened it, and took out her mother's fringed kerchief. She hid it under her dress, snuck out, and ran over to Peyse the blacksmith's house—straight to Soreh-Rokhl, who was sitting behind the oven and resting against the wall, a sock with knitting needles dangling from her hand. Dineh realized that Soreh-Rokhl was asleep. She sat down next to her and placed her small hand on Soreh-Rokhl's hand. Soreh-Rokhl started awake. "Who is it? Is that you, Henyele?"

"No, it's me—Dineh."

"Dinehle?"

"Yes."

"How's Itshe doing?"

"Actually, that's why I came—to see if you can do an exorcism on him. He's very sick."

"May God help him. What does the doctor say?"

"I don't know. But you can still do the exorcism."

"Well, of course I can. Did your mother send you, Dinehle?"

Dineh thought about what she should answer. "My mother is sick. She cries all the time. I came on my own."

"Well, good, Dinehle. You go ahead and knit my sock, and I'll do the exorcism."

Soreh-Rokhl took the kerchief from Dineh and, feeling her way against the walls, went into the next room, where she stayed for five minutes. When she came out, she said: "Here you go, Dinehle. Tie it around his head, and may he get well."

Dineh took the kerchief with great care. She placed it under her dress against her chest and ran home.

Once she was back home she returned to her position by the Russian stove and waited for just the right moment.

Malkeh was giving Itshe spoonsful of medicine and arranging his covers. "Sleep well, Itshe. Sleep well."

Itshe fell asleep. Malkeh softly made her way to the table. She turned the wick in the lamp and left. Dineh slipped quietly down from the Russian stove and took the kerchief from her chest. She quietly approached Itshe, placed it around his head, and looked at him for a long time. He was breathing quietly. Dineh felt happy. The kerchief around his head was already making him feel better. Tomorrow, when he would be cured, she would ask him if he even realized that it was she who made him well.

Then Dineh recited the Shema bedtime prayer with great concentration and went to sleep. She dreamed that Itshe recovered and that she told him that it was she, in fact, who made him better.

The next morning his fever had gone down, but the doctor continued to prescribe medicinal heart drops. He said he would check back again in the evening.

Dineh got up, washed in a hurry, recited the blessings, and went over to Itshe's bed. His face was pale yellow. Only his eyes burned. He noticed her and called her over to his bedside.

"Itshe, do you feel better?"

"I don't know myself. You know what, Dineh? I'm going to tell you something, but you won't understand."

"Tell me, Itshe; I will understand. You'll see that I'll understand. You see, you're better today. Yesterday I went on my own so no one would see me, and I asked Soreh-Rokhl to do an exorcism for you. I put the kerchief around your head and you started to feel better. You'll be cured."

Itshe smiled: "What will become of you, Dineh? You're a big girl now—almost twelve years old—and you're still so silly."

Feeling insulted, Dineh responded: "How am I being silly? I want to make you better."

Itshe took her hand: "I'm going to die, Dineh."

Shuddering, Dineh said: "What are you talking about, Itshe? You won't die. After all, you can definitely get washed with Grandpa's soap and linen. That's a great remedy. Mama said that it was torn into pieces to be used as a remedy. You see? Everything's there under the beams above the Holy Ark."

Itshe's smile was full of pain when he said: "But I wanted to tell you something."

"What is it, Itshe? Tell me. I won't tell anyone. Of course you know that I won't tell anyone."

"Yes, I know. You'll make a good rabbi's wife."

Delighted, Dineh said: "Really? I'll be a rabbi's wife?" But her delight quickly turned to sadness. "No, I won't be a rabbi's wife. Motl smokes on the Sabbath. It's a great sin. Right, Itshe?"

Malkeh approached. "Go now, Dineh. I have to give Itshe his medicine."

Itshe weakly made a dismissive gesture with his hand. "It won't help, Malkeh."

"Don't be silly. You're doing better today. The fever's down. The doctor's coming back in the evening. You see? Today's Thursday. Mama baked challah. Tomorrow you'll make Kiddush."

ITSHE'S LAST KIDDUSH

The next day—Friday—the entire household was seemingly back on its feet. Itshe felt better. At dusk he asked to be washed and have his shirt changed. He wanted to recite the Kiddush blessing. "It's been so long since I said Kiddush."

Overjoyed, Dineh looked on at Itshe, and in her heart she blessed Soreh-Rokhl.

Two challahs were set down for Itshe. The table was moved over to him. He recited the Kiddush right after their father, and everyone answered amen. While eating the soup he grew tired and lay down. He began to shiver and had difficulty breathing. Having heard that Itshe was feeling better, aunts and uncles from the surrounding villages and everyone from Peyse's household came to visit.

But seeing him now, all of them stood there stunned. Some began to weep in the corners. The men ordered that the doctor be sent for straightaway. Vasil hitched the horses and left for Kapyl′.

Itshe was now having more trouble breathing. Choked-up wailing sounds could be heard coming from Peshe and the aunts. Peshe wrung her hands: What could she do for her child? Periodically, Malkeh came up to her, pleading: "Mama, stop. He's begging everyone not to cry."

Dineh sat in her spot atop of the Russian stove and shivered. She kept looking in the direction of the beam where the holy soap and the white rags lay—and she waited, surprised that they weren't being used. She couldn't stand it any longer and screwed up the courage to approach her mother. "Mama, why isn't Itshe being washed with the soap that you brought from Grandpa?"

"Oh, why are you bothering me? What kind of soap has suddenly popped into your head?"

"That soap—the one over the Holy Ark, under the beam, that was used to wash Grandpa when he died."

Peshe burst into a bitter lament: "Oh no, a sapling just coming up . . . they've gone and killed him . . . Father in Heaven, have mercy . . ."

She told Aunt Khashe to go and bring down the soap. "Maybe He'll have mercy on my child and because of your merit, Papa . . . You were such a saint . . ."

Aunt Khashe climbed up onto a chair and brought down the small package. A bowl of water was brought over, and Khashe took a piece of white linen and washed Itshe's face and then his hands. "Your grandfather, may he have a luminous stay in the Garden of Eden, will intercede on your behalf. With God's help, you'll get well."

Dineh stood behind Khashe the whole time, following her every move. Now Itshe would get better.

She approached the bed and took Itshe's hand: "Itshe, do you know who I am?"

"Why wouldn't I know?"

"And can you talk?"

"You can see for yourself . . ."

"And . . . and can you see?"

As if to free himself from her interrogation, Itshe responded: "Oh, why are you asking such silly questions? I'm dying—*that* I can see."

"No, you're not dying. If you can see and speak, you won't die. And you've already been washed with Grandpa's soap."

Malkeh returned. "Go away. The doctor's here."

The doctor examined Itshe. He sat down for a while and then left. Peshe was led out of the room. Malkeh, Sholem, Uncle Shimen, and Aunt Khashe remained around the bed.

Itshe was breathing with difficulty when he fell asleep. Everyone left the room. Only Malkeh stayed at his bedside. Her eyes wide open, Dineh sat in her position and stared at Itshe's face. Out of the blue, he started awake. He unexpectedly sat up and asked Malkeh for a drink. He drank a mouthful of water and fell back onto the pillow. Malkeh called everyone in from the other room, and a white sheet was pulled over Itshe's body and face.

Wailing erupted in the house and drifted out the windows and into the night beyond.

On Sunday morning Itshe was taken to Kapyl′ to be buried. Throughout the entire time Sholem didn't shed a single tear. He walked around with his mouth in a grimace. He fasted. That's what he'd been doing since his mother died. On every yahrzeit of hers he fasted. Now there would be another yahrzeit. While placing the shrouds on the corpse Sholem didn't take his eyes off Itshe. It was hard to know if this was because he wanted to make sure that everything was being done properly or because he couldn't take his eyes from the dead young face that he would now be seeing for the last time.

People slid over to the side to make room for Sholem. Someone handed him the white belt and, gesturing with their lowered heads, indicated that he should tie the belt around the shrouds of the dead. Sholem furtively approached the corpse's stretcher and, like a stiff, wooden marionette, tied the belt around the corpse with leaden hands. He moved over and resumed his silent watch over his son.

In the cemetery Sholem was given the shovel to shake the first three shovelfuls of earth onto the corpse. With stiff hands he poured the first earth onto his young son's face, and a gravedigger moved him aside. Sholem stood as if paralyzed and gazed at the grave. Then they told him to come closer and recite the first Kaddish. His black beard looked like a cloud around his pallor. His lips started to tremble. Everyone saw that Sholem wanted to say something—but that he couldn't. He started to wobble . . . and then he fell. A tumult ensued. "Water! He fainted! Hurry! Bring over a shot of brandy!"

Someone poured water over Sholem. They massaged him and poured some brandy into his mouth. His eyes opened wide. Remembering what had happened to him, he wanted to stand up. Men lifted him by gripping him under his arms. When he was standing, he recited the first Kaddish in a strange voice.

With the same degree of muteness Sholem returned home. Once there he got down on the floor, removed his shoes, and began the seven days of mourning.

In Sholem's house there wasn't much time to devote to a single calamity. Besides Peshe's ongoing moaning and fainting, and Sholem himself behaving like he was in a strange world, and bad news from Faytl and Leyeh—Leyeh was more in bed than out—Dineh took sick as well. The doctor didn't know what was wrong with her. When they allowed her rest she lay there as if she were dead. She became weaker and weaker and often fainted. She was driven to a prominent doctor in Slutsk and then to another in Minsk. She was sick for nearly the entire summer.

In the autumn the children were driven back to the shtetl—to work and to religious school. The atmosphere had quieted down somewhat. People began to take hesitant steps. Things were getting back to normal. Past events had to be covered up. Without saying a word mothers sighed and watched over their children—the ones who had survived. The youth was once again rendered mute, like someone utterly frozen stiff after a great fright.

When Soreh, Dineh, and Daniel were brought back to Kapyl′, a holiday atmosphere took hold in Roda's house. They were treated like welcome guests. With tears in his eyes, Shmuel-Arn caressed each child individually: "It was sad here without you."

Roda echoed his sentiment. Shprintse caressed Dineh's head. "Good Dinehle. I missed having you here. Now you can help me out a lot, Dinehle."

Motl was tender with Dineh, a confidante. He looked at Dineh with an adult's understanding of what was causing her pain. At dusk he would often call on her to walk with him in the forest to gather the leaves for Shmuel-Arn's bath. She gladly followed him, but quietly and sadly. Motl tried to draw her into conversation and get her to talk and tell him what was on her mind. "What are you thinking about now?"

As if in a daze, Dineh answered, "About the leaves we're gathering."

"What is it that you're thinking about the leaves?"

"I'm wondering whether such leaves grow in the cemetery."

"Of course they do."

"Will you show me where the cemetery is?"

"Why not? You know yourself where it is."

"I mean, I'd like for you to go with me to gather leaves and help me find Itshe's grave."

Motl was silent.

"Well, will you go with me?"

"I'll go with you sometime."

"I don't want to go 'sometime.' Let's go now."

"You're not allowed, Dineh. You'll get sick."

"No, Motl, I won't get sick. I just want to see his grave."

"I promise I'll take you there on the Sabbath."

"Good. The Sabbath it is." Dineh was silent again.

"What are you thinking now, Dineh?"

"Motl, why didn't Grandpa want Itshe to get better?"

"Which Grandpa?"

"Oh, Motl, you don't know . . .Why did God cause Itshe to die?"

"Come on, Dineh, you haven't gotten any smarter. You believe in foolish things."

"Foolish things—well, so be it. And your smoking on Sabbath—is that what you see as smart?" She remembered something and brightened: "You know what Itshe told me before he died?"

"No. What did he tell you?"

"He said that I'll be a rabbi's wife."

Motl laughed. "Well said. I say the same."

"I won't be a rabbi's wife."

"Why not? If you're as pious as you are now, you'll be a rabbi's wife."

Dineh considered this and responded, "Why do you smoke on Sabbath, Motl? It's a serious sin."

"You see, Dineh, if you believe in God so much, you don't have to be so worried that Itshe died. A pious person believes that everything God does is right, and a person must lovingly accept everything God does."

Once again Dineh reflected. "You're right, Motl. Itshe told me the same thing when Freydele died. Strange words he said. I didn't understand."

Sighing, Motl said, "He was a smart fellow. Who will settle the score for the young lives?"

Trembling, Dineh seized Motl's hand and said: "Say it again . . . Itshe said that same thing before he died . . ."

"Really? Are you sure he said that, Dineh?"

"Very sure, just as sure as I am that you just said it. I got scared. It seemed to me that Itshe himself was saying it . . ."

Motl thought for a while and said: "You know, Dineh, I'm not a Zionist anymore."

"Why?"

"Now's not the time for that . . . You wouldn't understand . . .Your mind is still full of women exorcists—good deeds and sins. You live somewhere up in the clouds, not knowing what's happening around you."

Frightened, Dineh looked at him as if she wanted to fathom his thoughts. But she remained perplexed and despondent. "I don't know, Motl . . . I don't know what you're talking about—just as I didn't understand what Itshe was talking about . . . Just as I didn't understand why everyone was beating and killing each other . . .You shouldn't tell anyone what you said before, Motl."

"What did I say before?"

"What Itshe said . . ."

"Why not?"

"No, Motl, you shouldn't! God forbid, you'll also . . ." The last words remained stuck in her throat.

"Who then will settle the score? If you want me to, I'll take you to the cemetery on the Sabbath—to a secret *sobranie*. Hershl will speak there, and so will I. Moysheh-Leyb is now in Cherven′. He'll be bringing news. There'll be updates."

Confused, Dineh said, "Motl, you just told me you'll take me to the cemetery on the Sabbath to find Itshe's grave."

"Well, yes, we know where his grave is. Do we ever! That's why we hold our secret meetings there. The regional police superintendent won't think to look there. And it's good to look upon the graves of the fallen. It gives us courage."

"Your mother knows about this?"

"She probably knows, but she pretends not to."

"And Shprintse?"

"Shprintse knows about all of it. She gives us literature and tells us what to say and how to say it. People write to her from Moscow and Siberia. She herself was in Siberia, and her husband died there."

"And she looks so quiet. Now I'll be afraid of her."

Laughing, Motl said, "You're a fool. Who could be afraid of Shprintse?"

"Yes, but the things you're saying about her."

"I'm not saying anything bad about her. But see to it that you don't breathe a word of this to her."

"I won't say a thing, but I'm afraid."

"You're as silly as a baby. You don't have any common sense."

"Why?" shouted Dineh. "What's Soreh doing then? Does she also go with you to the cemetery on Sabbath?"

"No. They're older. They meet in Yanetske's little forest. Let's go. It's already late."

Her mind racing, Dineh went home without a clue as to how to sort out these thoughts. A tangled cloud of a thousand colors rotated before her eyes. That night she couldn't sleep. Daniel slept on a sofa not far from her. "Why are you tossing and turning? Why aren't you sleeping?"

She recited the Shema bedtime prayer again and again, but still nothing became any clearer to her. What were strangers doing on Itshe's grave? How did he matter to them? They hadn't even known him. No, she wouldn't go with Motl to the cemetery on Sabbath. She would have to go by herself. She needed to be alone with him in silence, the way he was silent in his grave . . . What kind of speeches would they be giving? She would find the grave by herself. And if Motl asked her, she'd tell him that she didn't want to go to Itshe's grave with other people. And if he laughed at her? Well, let him laugh. It wasn't his brother who died. He couldn't know what that meant. His understanding of what she was going through was exactly like hers when he was talking to her about Zionism and other things . . .

The next day Dineh paid scant attention to the lessons in religious school. Her head was elsewhere. Instead of going home after school to Roda's house to sew she went through a back alley and kept walking, all the while glancing around her like a thief, until she reached the fence of the cemetery. Dineh turned around, looked through the fence, and heard people talking. Frightened, she went back. Not today. Another time.

She entered the house and went directly to Shprintse's little table. Work was already set out for her.

"Here you go, Dinehle. And by the way, now that you're quite the young lady, it seems to be that I need to use the formal mode of address."

"No, you don't have to address me formally," Dineh answered, repeatedly casting covert glances in Shprintse's direction so she wouldn't notice.

Shprintse sensed her uneasiness and looked up: "Is there something you want to ask me, Dinehle?"

"No, no. For some reason, my stitches aren't coming out very well."

"That happens sometimes."

Dineh accepted these words as if they weren't coming from the Shprintse she had known up until now but from someone else entirely, from a stranger she was hearing speak for the first time. Motl's words returned to Dineh and surprised her anew.

That Friday, when they were freed from religious school, it was still quite early. Dineh found her way to the cemetery. She crawled over the fence via a side path. She searched for a very long time until she found the board that read "The young man Yitskhok, son of Reb Sholem." A narrow, not yet overgrown mound. She stood over it in silence for a long time. She felt drops of rain fall on her, and she remembered that she had to go. Two tears fell on her hands. She quickly wiped them on her dress. With an ache in her heart, she quietly retreated from the small mound of earth and went home.

The next day, Motl quietly asked her: "Dineh, do you want to go?"

With a proud sadness, Dineh answered: "I already went. Yesterday, after school. And by myself."

Motl looked at her for a long time: "You're an odd girl, Dineh. So you don't want to go with us?"

"No. And I don't see why strangers should go to someone else's grave. He wasn't their brother. They didn't even know him."

Motl didn't respond. He just looked at Dineh and smiled gently.

LEYEH DEPARTS THIS WORLD

The children went home for the Sabbath and once again didn't return.

On Saturday evening a messenger rode in with the news that Leyeh was in the process of giving birth and that it wasn't going well. A pair of horses was hitched straightaway, and Sholem, Peshe, and all four children left for Pesatshne. They arrived there at dawn. Lamps were burning in Reb Yitskhok's house. The flames in the oven blazed. Pots of water were being heated. An obstetrician and a doctor went in and out of the woman in labor's room. Screams cut like knives through the night air. This continued for a long time until Leyeh commenced a wailing that sounded like the terrible baying of hounds. And so it went, through the whole night and into the next day.

Faytl sat by the door of his wife's room, black as coal. When the doctor asked him if he wanted to go into the room he started pounding his chest with his fists. "I have no right. I'm a murderer!"

The screams from the woman in labor diminished in frequency and intensity until the doctor opened the door and told Faytl to come inside.

Leyeh lay there like someone who'd been dragged out of the river. Next to her on the side of the bed the dead child was covered.

From under the cover Leyeh extended a deathly pale, childishly small hand and drew Faytl to her. Faytl fell on his knees and burst out loud into tears like a child. A smile appeared on Leyeh's face, like someone freed from a terrible seizure. She turned her head slightly to one side—and was still. The doctor put his ear to her heart, led Faytl from the bed, covered her face, and left.

The entire shtetl—Jews and gentiles—attended her funeral.

Faytl observed the seven days of mourning with Leyeh's family. A few weeks later Sholem drove to Pesatshne and took over the iron business in Faytl's name. Faytl remained in the business and lived with people he knew.

THE GLOOM DEEPENS

In Sholem's house the mood grew thicker and heavier. Everyone was silent, their heads lowered. And each fixated on the question they knew to be paramount in their own and everyone else's mind: What would happen now? Grief gnawed at the walls. Malkeh, the very foundation of the household, was often not at home. To Peshe's questions about her whereabouts, she only responded: "Where am I going? To work in the fields."

Peshe understood all too well that the sad walls of their village home were closing in on Malkeh. She also knew that Malkeh's behavior had to do with the fact that she had recently been receiving letters from America in the same handwriting as those that had once come from Odessa. Blond Isak with the black cape, who had bought his way out of military service and been an employee in an Odessa bank, had to flee with others and sneak across the border for political reasons. This upset Malkeh greatly. By nature she couldn't live with an urbanite. Born in the village, she was a vigorous girl, with an innate sense of deep devotion and loyalty, and she carried the weight of all the household responsibilities on her shoulders. When she fell in love with the urban cousin from Odessa she felt that she belonged to him until death did them part. But she couldn't form a clear picture in her mind of how and when they would be reunited. She waited for a miracle. She didn't want to speak with her mother about any of this. A certain pride didn't permit her to discuss this issue with her mother. She considered it all a secret that no one must know. Now that Isak had gone even farther away, her secret was buried even deeper, and the longing, which she so wanted to conceal from herself, grew sharper.

But things reached the point that when Peshe scolded her one day for hiding from Alter, a young man from a fine family from a nearby shtetl who was pursuing her romantically, a disconcerted Malkeh responded: "There's a boat ticket in the dresser . . . Send me to America."

Malkeh's words struck Peshe like a thunderbolt. She remembered the boat ticket and for whom her brothers had sent it, and she burst into tears. "We'll have to send the boat ticket back," Peshe said.

But the ticket wasn't sent back. Soreh was drawn to the wider world. When she was home one Sabbath, Malkeh told Soreh that there was a boat ticket in the dresser.

Malkeh's message immediately piqued Soreh's interest. She soon forgot about the messenger. She was convinced that the boat ticket would mark an auspicious beginning of a journey that would enable her to venture forth across the ocean and see the world. She immediately began to formulate plans. At the third meal on that same Sabbath, Soreh announced to everyone at the table that she wanted to go to America. The case she made was as follows: Uncle Shimen from Dakhtervitsh was about to go to America; his son Ruve who had fled Kapyl′ during an ambush was also in America and was writing letters saying that things were going well; and an entire contingent of girls and boys were leaving Kapyl′. Soreh declared that she wanted to go with them.

Malkeh responded that she wanted to go. Throughout her whole life, Soreh had been a free bird, never at home, while she, Malkeh, was shut in in the village, bearing the burden of all the household responsibilities. It was she who should go to America, she said. Besides, she was the older of the two. And they mustn't think that she would be going there to play. She would work hard there and send money home, just as other girls she knew did.

And so, sitting around the Sabbath table at dusk, the specter of America tore through a Jewish village home. Two years ago the idea that Sholem would send a child of his across an ocean somewhere out there in the world would have been laughable. But now the borders of faraway countries had moved closer in the minds of Jewish parents. Children had fled, and when word was received that they had arrived on the other side of the border, they thanked His Dear Name.

After a long period of stasis following the massive bloodbath, unrest was once again spreading. In response, pogroms began to break out in the small towns and villages. This was all happening after the big Kyiv pogrom. Police raids and ambushes in private houses resumed. In Kapyl′ the police surrounded Yanetske's forests, where a meeting was being held. The participants were arrested and banished.

Soreh was in attendance at that meeting with a packet of pamphlets under her arm. She herself didn't realize what a miracle it was that she managed to get out of the forest. But it was no longer safe to go back to Roda's place. It was far safer not to be seen by the police. They were keeping an eye out for her and, in fact, were actively searching for her. One of them had spotted her with the packet of pamphlets running through the forest. Like a demon, she had slipped through his bare hands. He had to get hold of her, he said.

So Soreh went home to Ugli.

The terror from the first catastrophe had not left Sholem's house. Itshe's image arose before everyone's eyes. But now Soreh's precarious situation prevented Sholem, Peshe, and even Malkeh from any peace of mind. The younger sister forgot all of her plans that she had not yet dared to execute. She now gave them up completely. In the face of the danger hanging over Soreh, Malkeh forgot altogether about herself and her dream. Her loyal nature, with all of its sensibilities, was aroused. Now there was nothing more to think about. Soreh had to be readied with a passport from the provincial government and sent, in the company of Uncle Shimen and other acquaintances, to America.

With the burst of energy that surfaces in the presence of danger, preparations commenced. Sholem traveled to Minsk for a passport. Peshe dried zwieback and cinnamon, along with hard cheese. Malkeh sewed blouses with lace. Roda and Shprintse sent a wicker suitcase for packing Soreh's things. In the suitcase they packed two beautiful dresses and a light-colored coat. On the Saturday night before the Sunday journey to the train in Horodzshe, aunts, uncles, cousins, and neighbors came to call. Each brought along some kind of care package for the trip and their warmest blessings.

As she was wont to do, Aunt Yakhe rode over in the light, old buggy harnessed to the dun-colored horse while Uncle Leybe followed alongside on foot. From a small, thin, tidy, white bag he removed two hard, dark triangular blocks of sheep's cheese and several heads of garlic on a string.

"Take it, daughter. When my Rakhmiel left I also gave him garlic. He wrote us that on the ocean voyage it really came in handy," said Uncle Leybe.

Roda also came to say goodbye to Soreh, to give her a farewell kiss.

"My child, I'm sending you to Itshe-Mendele. Kiss him for me. Tell him how much his mother misses him. It's good that you're going, Sorehle. May God grant you both long years. You're like one of my own children to me," she said.

Her maternal heart was searching for a way to make a match for her son across the ocean—although the idea had hardly even occurred to Soreh.

Sholem drove with the contingent. After sending Vasil home from Horodzshe with the coach, Sholem continued on with them until they reached the border. Thus Sholem's house became even lonelier—yet with its door open to faraway vistas.

Dineh now played quite an important role in Roda's house. Not only did she read and reread to Roda every letter from her sons, but with keen understanding and intuition she grasped everything Roda wanted to say in response. She wrote letters on Roda's behalf that Roda herself hadn't even thought to write. At Shmuel-Arn's bedside Dineh behaved like an adult. She did everything she could to make life easier and more bearable for the invalid. And Motl, despite the fact that he was older than her and said things that didn't penetrate Dineh's mind, became accustomed to looking up to her like to an older sister. While dedicating herself to help lighten their difficult home circumstances, Dineh grew very close to Motl.

But all calm retreated from Sholem's home. The house rattled as if before oncoming winds. A storm was bearing down, and there was nothing to stop it.

The family received a letter from Soreh. Their group had made it over the border and were now on the ship. As soon as they arrived in America, they would let everyone know.

So everyone carried on, waiting for a letter from America. Three weeks, then four, then five and six. No letter came. More often than not Peshe was bedridden. From the blows of the last two years she had become as creased as a bag. She hardly spoke to anyone. Her eyes had turned red from weeping and lack of sleep. Sholem walked with his head bent to the ground and never spoke. The choked sighs, seemingly ripped from him involuntarily, were the only signs of what Sholem was experiencing.

Finally a letter from Uncle Shimen arrived. In it he wrote that, thank God, he was finally in New York. His son Ruvn was quite a remarkable young man. With God's help he, Shimen, had found work. He was sweeping out a factory and earning six dollars a week. At night he slept in the factory. The boss was a caring Jew who let him sleep there. Shimen hoped to achieve his goals and would, with God's help, come home. Finally he asked if they had heard anything about Sorke, daughter of Sholem, because he had great heartache over her. They had probably heard through the newspapers that their ship had been hit and the passengers boarded onto small ones. In the great commotion that ensued Sorke's hand had slipped from Shimen's grasp. To this day he still didn't know what had happened to her.

Yes, they had read about this in the newspapers in Kapyl'. Motl, Roda's son, read the article. But he hid its contents from his mother and Dineh. The ship carrying Soreh struck an iceberg that hammered holes into its walls. Passengers drowned. Among them was a girl, one Soreh Kazhukofski. Soreh's family name was Zhukofski.

No one had any doubt that this was Soreh, the daughter of Sholem. People sighed and wailed. Only four months later a letter from Soreh arrived—in her own poor penmanship. Soreh described what had happened to her. She got lost on the night of the calamity. She was moved from the larger ship to a smaller one, which she rode for a night and a day. Then she was driven to Liverpool, where she roamed aimlessly for six weeks. From there a Jewish aid society sent her to America. Soreh had a stomach ailment for six weeks after her arrival. She didn't like America.

This was the piece of good news that helped to dispel the terrible thoughts that had recently reigned over the household.

"Thank God. As long as she's alive."

Several weeks later Roda also received a letter from Soreh. She wrote that she missed everyone so much. She had gone to Roda's son Itshe-Mendl and given him regards from home. Soreh had lost the shirts and the cheeses Roda had sent him in her care, along with her luggage, when the ship struck the iceberg. Itshe-Mendl had asked pointedly about each of them individually. He was handsome and polite but sad. He missed home so much. He too didn't like America.

With that letter, things got easier for Roda. Now her Itshe-Mendl wouldn't be quite so lonely. And the mother's brain spun plans.

Following Leyeh's death Faytl started coming home again. His main goal in coming was to see Mikhliye. She now worked in the forest, not far from Sholem's house.

Yet again, this match did not please Peshe. She drove often to Slutsk, where she had her eye on a girl, a good wage earner with a fine pedigree, and beautiful to boot.

MALKEH KHARASH

Malkeh Kharash was well known in Slutsk. People brought their finest clothes to her to sew. An orphan without a father, she was a shining crown to her mother. She never went out on the street without a hat. Her workshop was managed in an impressive manner. She kept a maid to serve both her and her mother. Malkeh Kharash was of middle height, full figured, with a delicate, white complexion and hair worn in a high coiffure that beautifully complemented her face. She dressed with elegance and taste, with all sorts of collars and little bows that she knew how to match to each and every dress.

Peshe, Sholem, and Malkeh seized on the idea that Faytl ought to come with them to Slutsk. Their pretext: business matters as well as a possible match for his sister Malkeh. They spoke to Faytl of a Kharash family in Slutsk and mentioned that one of its daughters, Malkeh Kharash, had a cousin. He lived in a village behind Slutsk. And since they had settled upon such and such evening, well, then, fine, he, Faytl, should come along.

Unwillingly, Faytl rode along with the family and returned betrothed to Malkeh Kharash.

But Malkeh came home without a groom. She refused to even consider the match.

A short while later Faytl got married and brought the urbane seamstress into the home of his first wife, Leyeh, who had died not long ago.

To her the house seemed narrow and sad. She felt like a prisoner there. But she was clever and loyal by nature. Her mother had died exactly a month before the wedding. Now she was entirely attached to her young, sad husband. Although Faytl was not cold to her, she tried a variety of means to reach his heart. When she set her high coiffure with lovely combs and perched a stylish new hat on it, donned the small suede gloves on her delicate hands, and they went out to take their Sabbath stroll, everyone—men and women—turned their heads as far as their necks would permit to gaze upon the beautiful, sophisticated, finely attired lady. Young folk sought excuses for briefly dropping in on Faytl to spend some time with the young couple. His wife warmly welcomed everyone.

In Pesatshne, Malkeh's life was difficult. But slowly it became bearable. During the summers a sister from Minsk and a niece, who was a doctor in Kyiv, came to visit. Acquaintances often came from Slutsk. Faytl, wanting to show that he was an expert in the treatment of a woman with delicate hands, even brought a young gentile woman into the house to do the dishes, polish the candlesticks, and wash the floor for the Sabbath.

Mikhliye sometimes came to visit. Malkeh received her warmly. This time the quiet Mikhliye thought that Faytl had found his true love and she, Mikhilye, had nothing to wait for . . .

Uncle Shimen was working hard in America. He continued to sleep in the factory, saving every groschen to send to his daughter Mikhliye for a dowry—a total of three hundred rubles. He wrote that if God would help him save enough on his expenses, and a few groschens on top of that, he would come home. America was not for him.

It wasn't long before a groom was found for the quiet Mikhliye. He was a worker from a poor family, a young man who had come back from America. She had a quiet wedding and lived with her husband for some two years. Faded before her time, she departed this world. Out of Mikhliye's quiet, pious mouth not even her mother, Khashe, ever heard a single negative word about her husband. Still it was clear that her husband had caused her death. People said he used to get drunk and that he infected Mikhliye with some kind of disease that proved fatal to her.

NO WORD FROM ITSHE-MENDL . . .

For the past few months Roda had not been herself. She was disconsolate, barely interested in sewing. Although outwardly calm and in good spirits, Shprintse had a premonition that Roda's anxiety was not without cause. It had been three months since they had received a letter from Itshe-Mendl in America. Hindl, Shprintse's sister in America, at whose home Itshe-Mendl lived and whom she treated like her own child, hadn't been sending any letters either. This could not be taken as an ordinary occurrence. In addition, Roda had been having a disturbing dream—three times now. She was even afraid to put it into words. In the dream she was sitting on a chair that had four legs. When one of the legs broke from under her, causing her to fall down, her son Itshe-Mendl entered and told her, "Mama, sit shiva for me and see to it that Kaddish is said."

When she first had this dream Roda fasted. After the second time she went to the cemetery to her parents' graves to weep and ask them to intervene on behalf of her dear son, the rabbi who, poor thing, was alone and desolate in the world.

After the third time she fasted again and went to the rabbi and asked him to interpret this dream for her. The rabbi, Hershl's father, who visited Shmuel-Arn at home and was a good friend of theirs, listened to Roda with great concern. He too was worried about Itshe-Mendl and his failure to write. Itshe-Mendl was his older son's friend. They had studied and received rabbinical ordination together. After listening to Roda's concerns he lightened her bitter heart by providing a positive spin.

Dineh now functioned in Roda's household as a dedicated nurse. At night Roda came to sit on her bed like someone seeking consolation. "What do you say, Dinehle? You're pious and good. What does your heart tell you?"

With a heavy heart made to look lighter, Dineh answered: "My heart is telling me that you'll get a letter this week."

For a moment things became easier for Roda, and like an old woman, Dineh added: "What should my mother do? Soreh's not writing either."

"It's different . . . If Sorkele were good she would write about my Itshe-Mendl."

"Why should she? He'll write to you himself. Don't forget—it's so far—across an ocean! Ships sink. It's on the other side of the earth, after all—so they say."

And her head began to spin. But Dineh didn't have time to think about incomprehensible matters. The realm of the concrete, the matters that were pressing so close to her, were now occupying all of her attention. She had spoken about this carefully to Motl one time and openly with Meyshe-Leybl and Hershl. She told them that something had happened to Itshe-Mendl in America. She had no doubt of it.

For a few months now Motl had been teaching in Keylye. He was teaching Reb Elye of Keylye's smaller children. With the money he earned he contributed to the household and studied on his own. He didn't come home until the evening. So how could they make sure that a letter about Itshe-Mendl did not land in Roda's hands? It was decided that at eleven o'clock each day Dineh would run from school to the post office and inquire after a letter. The teacher agreed, and so she went for the mail for ten days until the anticipated letter arrived. Dineh was too afraid to open the letter herself. So that evening she went with Hershl to the rabbi. The rabbi opened and read the letter. Sighing, he said: "Blessed is the True Judge. A mother's heart cannot be fooled. He came to her in her dreams and told her to observe the seven days of mourning and recite the Kaddish."

Dineh stood there frozen. She hung on the rabbi's every word, not knowing what to do.

"Here, Dinehle, read it for yourself. You've always been the one to read and write letters for her."

Her heart and child's hands atremble, Dineh accepted the papers and read them for herself.

There were actually two letters in one envelope. One was from Hindl, Roda's niece. She wrote how despondent and heartbroken everyone was. She was sick most of the time, and her small bit of livelihood had now quite declined because of her chronic illness. This calamity had utterly finished her husband off—he too was sick, suffering from a neurological disease. She had to send him away from home. And as for Itshe-Mendl—how could she have written earlier? How can you write a mother such news?

The other letter was a short one in Itshe-Mendl's handwriting. His lettering was nervous and rushed. "If I could only have helped you with my forfeited life, Mama, things would still have been good. But not only can I not help you, I am a burden to others. And who is she—this other? Hindl, a poor, sick woman with small children and a sick husband. I don't know if things are worse for her than they are for you. I shouldn't have come to America. My hands did not take to the work in the shop. They told me to stay home the next day. When I sold newspapers on the street, they laughed at my side locks. The boys ripped my coattails. And recently the thought about home—of Papa, and you—and then about Hindl and her life here and that I was taking up a bed in her house and taking away a piece of her bread . . . I struggled with my thoughts for some time. God will forgive me. I hope that you too, Mama, will forgive me. Sit shiva for me and see to it that Kaddish is said."

Large, thick tears rolled from Dineh's earnest eyes onto her cheeks and hands. "What should we do now?"

The rabbi understood what she was asking. "For now, don't say anything to Roda. Not a word. We have to wait."

"And to Motl?"

"You can tell Motl. And Leyb too. I'll tell Leyb today. He'll say Kaddish."

Dineh got ready to leave. "Rebe, keep the letter with you."

"Very well. It'll stay here."

From that point on Dineh found it hard to sit down with Roda. Both Shprintse and Roda began to scrutinize her pointedly. "What are you thinking?" Or: "Why are tears coming out of your eyes?"

"It's nothing."

Every other day Roda sat Dineh down to dictate to her what to write to America. Completing this task was terribly painful for Dineh. And when Motl asked her in the evening how she could do it, she answered: "Out of pity."

At this point Motl entirely lost his wise air, his man-of-the world sensibility. He started to look at Dineh as someone greater than himself.

A letter came from Soreh. She wrote that things were not going well for her in America, that things weren't going well for all poor people in America. No one even talked about revolution there. If things were going badly for someone and he didn't have the means to live—well, they had built a high, long bridge over a large river for that—it was called the Brooklyn Bridge—and you could throw yourself off from that high bridge that had cost millions of dollars to construct directly into the river. That's what Itshe-Mendl had done. Did Roda know about this? She didn't have the heart to write her.

That's how Motl, the rabbi, and the elder Leyb, Roda's brother, who said Kaddish for Itshe-Mendl, learned the details of Itshe-Mendl's death. Roda, certain that a misfortune had befallen her child and feeling that the people around her knew what had happened, racked her brains day and night, wanting to find out the secret. It was no use asking Dineh. Roda knew well Dineh's pious yet determined nature. "She's like an iron safe," she used to say about Dineh. When going about her day Roda was alert, wanting to see how people looked at her, to hear how they sighed when speaking to her.

Until one day—an evening, to be precise—Roda had an idea. She would go into the women's section of the synagogue and ask about Itshe-Mendl. There she might glean some information from a loose-lipped woman that would solve the riddle of what had happened to her son. She entered and waited. But while she was waiting it suddenly dawned on her. Her old, deaf brother, Leyb, was saying Kaddish! Yes, she was hearing it—right then and there! How was it that he was saying Kaddish? She knew all of his and her yahrzeits. He didn't have a yahrzeit to commemorate today! The prayer service had barely concluded when Roda descended from the women's section, pushed her way through the men, reached Leyb with great effort, and shouted into his ear: "Whom are you saying Kaddish for?"

He looked at her, utterly at a loss, and pretended he didn't hear her. She looked at him and realized instantly that everyone was staring at her in horror. "Why are you afraid to tell me? I know you're saying Kaddish for my Itshe-Mendl."

Disoriented, Leyb looked over at the rabbi: "Rebe, did you tell her?"

Roda lunged at the rabbi: "Rebe!"

The rabbi, seeing that Roda was about to fall, reached out to catch her. But she fell. A tumult ensued in the synagogue. Women screamed: "Water! She's fainted!"

Roda was revived. She opened her eyes and once again fainted.

The end of dusk. In some of the windows the lit wicks of the lamps were already flickering, casting dancing shadows through the panes. Dineh went to the window and looked out. "Motl!"

Motl approached. "What can that be?"

Shprintse, who was polishing a glass from a lamp and blowing her breath onto the glass so that it would be cleaner when wiped off, also approached the window, her petite steps audible in her high heels. "What are you both looking at?" Once she got there, she too looked out and asked: "A funeral? Now? So late? And no one died today. From some other settlement?"

The two small children, Noske and Rivele, also came to the window. "Oh no, a funeral! Who could it be?"

Shmuel-Arn shouted through the open door: "Why are you all standing there? What are you staring at? Light the lamp for me! Don't keep me here lying in the dark. I get terribly uncomfortable when I have to lie alone in the dark. Where's Roda? Why is she so late today?"

Dineh pushed her way past the children to the door, everyone following behind her. Quiet and frightened, Dineh said: "Don't shout. You'll scare your father."

Like a light suddenly kindled in her brain: Motl's mother! She must have found out.

A crowd of women, men, and children were coming down the hill. They were carrying someone. Four men were carrying the person. They were headed straight to Roda's house.

"A lamp! A lamp! Where is there a lamp?" A heartrending scream, then weeping, came from Shmuel-Arn's room. "A lamp! A lamp! Light a lamp for me! Why was I left in the dark? Roda!"

As if awakened from a deep sleep, Roda heard her name being called and tore herself from the four pairs of hands that were carrying her over the threshold. She called out to Shmuel-Arn in the dark room: "Here I am, my husband."

With a heartrending cry, she fell upon his bed: "Congratulations to you, my husband; our Itshe-Mendl has become a groom. Congratulations to you. You're the father, after all—and I the mother."

She fell into a fit of howling. Shmuel-Arn, more dead than alive, said: "Help! Help! Why are you keeping me in the dark? Give me a lamp. My Roda has gone out of her mind." And with his only healthy hand, Shmuel-Arn banged on the window. The clatter of glass shattering into little pieces falling both on the bed and on the cobblestones outside resounded in the air.

A lamp was brought in. Shmuel-Arn lay stiffly, with his twisted face and bloodied hand, bent and contorted. Roda lay over him and wailed convulsively.

That night, Shmuel-Arn passed away.

LISTEN TO ME, SHOLEML . . .

Once again an autumn, with its heavy, seasonal clouds, expanded over Sholem's house.

Marko, the neighboring Polish nobleman who held Sholem's fate in his hands, had taken quite sick—a sickness so terrible that when he opened his mouth to speak he would shriek like a young rooster learning to crow. He was constantly short of breath and choking. The specialist from Warsaw diagnosed him with galloping consumption of the throat and declared that it was too late for surgery. In his agony Marko took to drinking himself into a state of forgetting until convulsions shook him. He was a frequent guest at Sholem's house and always ordered something to be brought from the accursed monopoly store. Peshe would have to serve liquor and snacks. Over a glass, with one drinking partner or more, Marko lamented his life and spoke with great regret about Sholem's fate, which now lay in his dying hands and would soon transfer into the unreliable hands of his children.

When Marko became thoroughly intoxicated and fell over on the wide, long sofa reserved for passing travelers, Sholem offered him a glass of cold lemonade, helped him put on his overcoat, and seated him in the light wagon that was waiting for him. Marko would whisper secretively in his ear: "Listen to me, Sholeml. Pay attention. Because after my death, my detestable sons will not take care of you. My son-in-law, the Pole, is relentless. He says he hates the little Jews. Not while I'm alive. I won't let him do you any harm. I wouldn't replace—" But he ended his words with a crowing and was unable to finish what he was saying.

To the sick, drunk Marko Sholem offered these words of hope, "*Panie* Marko will get better." Privately, however, his mood was dark. He was convinced that the cloud was about to burst and thunder would soon crash down upon his head.

One Sunday morning the bells in all of the churches in the vicinity were set to tolling. That night Marko, the Polish nobleman, had died. After the three days, when the body lay in state and guests traveled from far and wide to pay the deceased their final respects, came the ceremonial *pohorony*, with priests and icons and long processions through the village to the graves. Everyone crossed themselves and praised the deceased for his good, pious deeds. Those who survived him—his sons, daughters, and a son-in-law—followed behind in closed phaetons. It was beneath their dignity to mix with the common *narod*. They sat stiffly and implacably in their phaetons. At the burial they stood like statues, without shedding a tear or expressing any grief whatsoever.

The most stricken of all was Sholem of Ugli. With the death of Marko, the Polish nobleman, the last support was pulled out of the ground beneath him. He went through his days biting his dry lips, tugging on his thick beard, and generally unable to come up with any viable options. What was to be done? Sholem walked past his buildings as if saying goodbye to someone close to him who was permanently departing for distant shores. He plowed his fields tearfully, fully aware that he wouldn't be harvesting them to the accompaniment of his own song. He knew that the hands doing the sowing would not be the ones doing the harvesting. And yet this year, like every year, Sholem plowed and sowed as much as he could with his own hands, together with the help of his workers, who shared the thoughts that were weighing so heavily on his spirits.

It was a mild winter, and spring arrived early. The crops in the field were outstanding. The hay in the meadows waved in the wind, swaying and reaching toward the sun. The velvet greenery of the young, growing rye field appeared as a wide sea breathing quietly and deeply. In the stables young calves butted against their mothers' full udders with silly heads. In the stalls horses stood with their small, young foals between their legs. With their narrow, long mouths the foals searched for the stiff teats of their mothers. Horses and cows stood with outspread legs and surrendered to the pleasure of the warm, suckling mouths of their new offspring.

Sholem was in the field when a rider from Marko's estate arrived. Peshe and Malkeh greeted the rider and asked if Sholem ought to be summoned from the field. But the rider just handed them a long envelope with a red eagle stamp and an adjacent red wax seal. He then returned along the path on which he came, leaving in his wake a thick cloud of dust generated by the hooves of the proud dun-colored horse.

The envelope scalded the fingers of those who touched it—first Peshe's trembling ones, then Malkeh's.

Malkeh took the letter from her mother's hand, assessing its weight in her own hands, like someone who understood that her life's fate was sealed therein. But not just her own life, Malkeh thought. Before her shrewd eyes pictures, one after another, began to extend in a dreamlike fog of smoke. She saw before her the long fields that were like a part of her, the meadows, and the trails so smooth and soft to the tread. Cattle, horses, sheep, hens, pigeons—all stretched before her in rows. They were out of the stables, the chicken coops, and nests, and their heads and wings were lowered. There was her father with his walking stick in hand, the shepherd who didn't know where to lead his flock. Or where he himself ought to go . . .

Malkeh started awake from her vision as if from sleep and saw her mother wringing her hands and looking out into the field.

"He won't be able to bear it," Peshe said.

Malkeh decided what to do: "Wasn't this all expected? I'll go over to Papa by the wells."

Malkeh went to Oliana and whispered to her: "Did you hear?"

"Heard and saw. If only he'd broken his legs . . . When I heard the galloping of the aristocratic hooves something tore inside my heart."

"I'm going over to my father at the wells. He's there with the woodcutters. Go and talk to my mother. Cheer her up a bit."

Oliana wiped her nose and her eyes with her apron. "Go . . . but how can I cheer her up when I feel so terrible myself? May they not live to tread on our fields. This is my home; I've put in my own sweat and blood here. I've practically raised you in this house. I nursed all of you children here with my own milk, rocked you with my own hands. Where will I seek refuge now? I'll get on my knees in church. I'll give to the charity of Saint Ulas. I'll ask the saints to help me curse their despicable bones so they won't live to move into these houses or eat from these fields."

She crossed herself and told Malkeh to go to her unfortunate father and comfort him. They'd all go with him and help the good Pan Sholem however they could. He was like a father to them all.

Malkeh left. At dusk she returned with Sholem. At dawn the next day Sholem harnessed the horses and left for Marko's estate. He returned even more dejected. The young Polish villain hadn't even wanted to speak with him, only repeating what was written in the letter. He was giving him six weeks to sell everything. He would pay him the promissory notes that his father, of blessed memory, had signed to him. He'd leave him the house, the orchard, and the garden, because he himself intended to build on the other side of the village. But Sholem had to leave the farmhands.

After another sleepless night Sholem harnessed the horses and went to see his lawyer in Slutsk. The lawyer explained to him that there was nothing he could do here. Marko's children had the right to do whatever they wanted, including driving Sholem out without paying the promissory notes. He could go to *sud*, but these days, things weren't working out well for Jews there. The lawsuit would drag out and cost money, and Sholem could still lose. Since Marko's children had offered to pay him well and allow him to remain in his large house with the orchard and garden, that would be the better option for him.

To move matters along Sholem emptied one stable and placed the cattle from both stables into one. Butchers and nearby peasants came each day to select cattle, heifers, and calves. With the sale of each animal there was a fresh lament in the house: this one they'd raised and tended, this one had given the choicest milk, this one was like a child when it was milked. Peshe wouldn't let them be sold to the butchers. "I'd rather they be let loose in the fields until the wolves tear them apart than send them to their slaughter with my own hands and then pocket the money," she said.

One of Marko's estate stewards came to ask if Sholem might want to sell the young animals and heifers to the new landowner who would be coming here. He could then just leave them in the stables. They wouldn't have to argue about the price. And *Panie* Sholem could leave two cows for himself and his family. They could remain in the stables along with the landowner's animals. He wanted to buy the horses too—the two dun-colored ones—along with the young red mare, and they too would stay there in place.

The typically reflective Sholem became incensed. His first instinct was to have a go at the ruddy, full-blooded steward and tear him apart limb from limb. But he didn't dare. He was now in their hands. But not a single one of his cows and not a single horse would he permit to remain in the stables in the control of Marko's children. That's for sure! "Let the nobleman know that as early as yesterday that merchants were here, and I sold them down to the last head."

The steward peered at Sholem with suspicion. "It's your business. I'll let him know."

After telling this lie Sholem immediately began to sell and divide up the cattle and horses. Uncle Yankl, who was now even more impoverished, took to speaking repeatedly about the two cows that Sholem gave to him. "No one will lack for milk anymore."

One day, when Yankl wasn't around, that wife of his, Kreyne, had packed up her rags and her three children and disappeared. She left him his own three starving children. They lived a life of extremes. Either Yankl celebrated a feast out of the blue with multiple courses and singing on the occasions when he'd somehow managed to acquire a few groschens or they went entire days without food, drifting like lost sheep and waiting for their father to come home. Now Yankl's hopes soared to the sky. He'd be a broker! He'd sell milk, cheese, and butter—all from Sholem's two cows.

Sholem was left without a single cow in the stable. Every day Oliana went to a neighboring stable and brought back a jug of milk for the household. Sholem sold all of the chickens in a nearby village. One night he crawled up to the roof of the barn and removed all of the pigeons from the coops that were under the roof. He tied them and carried them down into the barn. He then went back up and brought down every last one of the coops so that the pigeons, who had a tendency to return to their homes, wouldn't have a place to return to. The next day he led all of the pigeons—some eighty in total—to a faraway village and left them with a Jewish settler who had pigeons of his own.

Having cleared everything out of the stables and barns, Sholem's momentum collapsed. Whether sitting down or moving about through nights and days, he kept thinking: What next? Peshe's perennially worried talk now reverberated in his mind: America! From the moment he was born Sholem was welded to the earth, and any faraway place was incomprehensible to him. He bemoaned, and often disdained, the peddlers of secondhand goods, brokers, and others who changed their homes. His was the path of the peasant bound to the land, who didn't dream of the faraway. But now his step was that of someone in a fever dream. The land that for generations had been his was now suddenly his no longer. He was walking on alien soil. He had to flee it—far, far away, across the ocean, as a matter of fact. Peshe called it America. If it was America, then so be it.

And as if of its own accord the name "America" gradually rose to the tongues in Sholem's distraught house. A wagon was sent to fetch Faytl from Pesatshne. Malkeh went to bring Dineh and Daniel home. To Roda's question of who was leaving, Malkeh was unable to provide a clear answer. "We still don't know. My father's going. But because we can't let him go alone, I'm going along too. We don't know who else is going."

Terrified, Dineh immediately declared: "I'm not going. I'm coming back."

For three days and nights they deliberated. Who should go? For Sholem himself it didn't much matter one way or the other. He wasn't going to seek fortune in the "Golden Land," and his plight wasn't even comparable to that of his poor, pious brother Shimen, who had gone to America to earn a dowry for his daughter and then returned home. He was going out into the world to escape his very self. No plans or goals crept into his brain. Everything was decided without him, around him, and for him. Malkeh would go with him. In the meantime, since Mama would be going to Pesatshne to stay with Faytl and since Sholem and Malkeh would send for Mama immediately after arriving and getting settled in New York, well, then, maybe it would be better if they took the twelve-year-old Daniel with them. He would study there, and it would be more comfortable for Papa to have the boy with him.

They started to pack the wagons and sent copper, brass, bedding, and sacred books on to Pesatshne. Everything that remained behind in the old, well-established house was there for Yankl's taking when he moved in. The smaller front room was as grand as a palace compared to Yankl's hole-ridden hut in Dakhtervitsh. Let Yankl be the boss and keep an eye on all that was left over—until who knew when.

SHOLEM'S DEPARTURE

Sholem wanted to leave the village quietly, without any to-do. He requested in advance that Stepan come on Sunday night with his horse and wagon and take him and the two children to Slutsk. From there they'd travel by train.

But still early in the evening a swarm of people and coaches surrounded Sholem's house. There were riders on horseback, Jewish settlers, and gentiles from Ugli and nearby villages. Everyone came to bid farewell to their old friend and beloved boss. Sholem was moved to tears. They all wanted to extend their good wishes. He only left the village late at night, accompanied by wagons and riders. Stepan reported that at his departure in Slutsk peasants kissed Sholem's hands and wept.

Not having the will to come back on an empty stomach, Stepan stopped off at a tavern, where he got quite drunk. He cried his heart out until he fell asleep on the wagon. Only when the horses came to a full stop and the dog started barking did he wake up and find himself in his own yard . . .

Quietly, Dineh moved through Roda's house. Before her stood her father as she had seen him before his departure. She felt her face becoming inflamed and took care lest someone notice that she was turning red. Dineh was remembering how he had offered her his hand as he was leaving. This was the first time in her life that her father offered her his hand. Dineh's blushing was not just from that but also from the placement of his other hand on her forehead, lifting her long, thick hair, looking into her face for a long time, and bringing her close to him, as if he were seeing her for the first time in his life. "You're quite the big girl, Dinehle. I mean, really a big . . ."

He wanted to give her a kiss. This was something Dineh couldn't bear: a man! Her own father, to be sure, but still a man. She quickly turned from him, hiding her face in her hands. She turned to the wall and stood there. Sholem went over to her, placed his hands on her head, and as if in jest said: "Now I really know you're a big girl." And he kissed her on her hair. "Be well, my child."

And he left. Dineh stood there for a long time, afraid to budge from the spot, not wanting to dislodge what she was feeling at that moment, what she felt . . . until Daniel came over and tugged at her hand. "Dineh!"

"What do you want?"

"Why are you standing there like a rabbi's wife at candle lighting?"

"What do you want?"

"I don't want anything. I just wanted to say that . . . Faytl's going to take Goldetske to his place. Do you think he'll take good care of her? She's old. She can barely walk. Mama says she's already fourteen years old."

"Fourteen years old isn't so much . . . Grandpa lived for a hundred and two years." Dineh grew reflective. She remembered Itshe and was silent. She looked down at the floor.

"Dineh . . ."

"What?"

"I'm leaving for America soon . . ."

Dineh shuddered. "I don't know what that word is. Who thought it up? I don't know how people make it to the other side of the earth alive. Is it . . . You'll say Shema and *ha-Mapil* every night. You hear? Maybe you'll get there alive. Who knows how long it takes?

"You take a train and then a boat."

"And you roll around the earth until you roll to the other end of the world, where America is."

"You're a fool. Who told you that you have to roll?"

"How else can you roll around the world to the other side? Didn't you learn in geography how round the world is? Like an egg. How else can you get to the other side?"

His certainty plummeting but nonetheless determined to pluck up his own courage, Daniel said: "I'm a good swimmer. And I'll just do what everyone else does. Papa's a strong man. I'll be with him, so I'm not afraid."

Daniel started to leave, but Dineh called him back. "Daniel?"

"What?"

She extended her hand, just as her father had done. Daniel looked at her hand, thought for a moment, and then laughed: "Go on. You're crazy!"

Dineh was even more embarrassed, put her hand down, and hid it in the folds of her skirt.

"Why are you acting like a fool, Dineh? As soon as we get to America we're sending for you and Mama." He took hold of her hands. "Dineh, you're so silly!"

Dineh choked back her tears. But then she starting sobbing. Daniel also started to cry. Malkeh came over. "Go on. Hurry, Daniel. The wagon is waiting. It's late. Dineh, you stay here with Mama. Take good care of her. We'll send for you. At most in half a year's time. As soon as we arrive and get settled."

Malkeh approached Dineh and took her in her arms. "There, there. Hush, Dineh. You're a big girl. You'd better distract Mama so she doesn't cry. You won't be here long." Malkeh gave Dineh a kiss and was gone.

DINEH DOESN'T WANT TO LEAVE

With that scene foremost in her mind, Dineh walked around Roda's house as if in a dream state. Roda, Shprintse, Motl, and anyone who came into Roda's house treated Dineh like a very sick patient. They spoke to her quietly and politely, looking probingly into her eyes. Motl brought her along on his walks with his friends in the evenings. Motl bought her an instructional manual in English and Russian and started teaching her English. It was interesting. The words sounded so far away and weird, but you could find out how people on the other side of the world said that they were in love. They said it so weirdly that it made you want to laugh . . .

After one such lesson Dineh sat despondently, looking past Motl. Heavy sighs slashed a jagged path from her heart. When Motl asked, "Dineh, why are you sighing?" she answered, "I'm learning the American language. I like it, but I'm not going to America."

"You'll have to go. Your mother will take you with her."

"I'm not going. I like it here." And looking past Motl: "So then—you want me to leave?"

"You'll have to go, Dineh. You'll all be going."

"Well, does that mean I can't stay here?"

"Go, Dineh. If I could . . . If the whole world would become one country, you'll come back and we'll go there."

This didn't please Dineh. She went to bed feeling miserable, and she sighed there until late into the night.

Several times that summer Faytl and Peshe came to Kapyl′, pleading with Dineh to come with them to Pesatshne for a little while. But Dineh would hear none of it. For her part, Roda rallied to Dineh's cause: "She's learning the English language here. Motl's teaching her. Plus she has her friends here. And she's already sewing—a pleasure!"

For the holidays Roda sewed her a beautiful dress along with a fine, brown coat with wide sleeves in the latest fashion. "Dinehle really deserves it," she said. Through her sewing Dineh earned Roda some three rubles a week. She drew the most beautiful patterns on satin quilts and down blankets. The wealthy housewives didn't haggle at all.

Displeased, Peshe returned to Pesatshne without Dineh. As for the matter of going to America, it seemed to Dineh that somehow something would happen and she wouldn't have to go.

For the High Holidays, the Jews who settled around Ugli decided that, as in previous years, the prayer services would be held in Sholem's house. The house remained as it had been; the Torah scrolls still stood in the Holy Ark. Peshe had taken one set of the Talmud to Faytl's home, but the other one, along with other Judaica and High Holiday prayer books, remained.

Yankl lived in the front room. There was now more room than before. Uncle Shimen had returned from America and moved with his family to stay in Sholem's house in Ugli until after the holidays.

The holidays occupied a prominent place in Dineh's devout, aching heart. Dineh knew quite a few prayers by heart and said them with great concentration. As the learned woman, Peshe had recited the prayers out loud so that the women who didn't know the prayers could repeat them after her. Since childhood Dineh had sat at her mother's side and prayed with her. Peshe was proud of her: "The words come out of her mouth like pearls."

She would hand Dineh a holiday prayer book, sit her way at the other end of the bench, and the women sitting next to her would be delighted with her. "She has the mind of a man, may no evil eye hurt her."

Dineh would pray with her unique brand of piety. She understood that she was the vehicle for the prayers of the women who unfortunately couldn't themselves pray. At every available moment she read them the Yiddish translation that provided the meaning of the Hebrew prayers.

On the eve of that holiday Dineh's heart was heavy. She didn't want to go with Mama to Faytl's house for the holiday. She wanted to be in Kapyl′ with Roda. But when she remembered that this would be the first holiday in her life that she wouldn't be home, and the women wouldn't have Mama or her to follow in the prayer services, Dineh became very sad. If her pride had allowed it she would have gone home by herself for the holiday . . . But who was home at this point? How would her home look without any of the people who had once lived in it? Tears trickled down now onto her hands.

Two days before Rosh Hashanah Roda fitted Dineh in her new alpaca-cloth blue dress, with the dark red velvet collar and cuffs, which suited her quite beautifully. She also tried on the lovely brown light coat with the wide sleeves and collar. Shprintse wove wide, red satin ribbons through Dineh's long braids. They rotated her from one side to the other in front of the long mirror and beamed with joy at the sight of her. Dineh felt embarrassed and sad, like a Jewish bride who has just been ceremonially seated and whom the wedding jester admonishes and then predicts her fortune in humorous rhyme. Dineh saw how Motl was looking at her from the side, sitting over a book and pretending that he didn't notice—neither her nor the two women hovering over her to doll her up. She felt strange in the beautiful clothes, and she soon stopped paying attention to the prettifying that was happening to her. Once again she remembered last year's Rosh Hashanah and the Turkish-style dress with the flowers that Mama herself had sewn for her and how she stood among the burning candles and prayed before the women. A gnawing sadness gripped her heart. Feeling discouraged and dejected, Dineh removed the light coat and the dress, laid them both on the table, and went to sit on a sofa in a corner. The two long braids fell over her constricted shoulders onto her hands. She sat in despair and looked down into the depths of her aching heart.

That evening two wagons drove up to Roda's door. From one of them descended Velvl, Itke, Henye, and Peyse of Ugli's son along with his wife and older daughter. From the other came Uncle Shimen and Aunt Khashe and their two children, Hayem Motl and Khayke—twins who were the same age as Dineh. It soon emerged that both had come with the same demand: nothing other than that

Dineh travel home with them for the holiday.

When Dineh heard this she excitedly jumped up and down: "I knew they'd come!" She quickly caught herself and lowered her eyes. "I wanted a home for Rosh Hashanah so much . . ."

All of the people from Ugli chimed in: "What then? Without you, the women wouldn't even know how to start the prayers. You'll be a distinguished guest."

Roda and Shprintse were pleased to pack Dineh's new clothes and see her seated in Uncle Shimen's wagon that would take her home for the holiday.

She sat throughout the journey as if she were a mute. She hemmed and hawed in response to Aunt Khashe's questions. When the coach started to approach the village her heart began to pound so fiercely that she had to gasp for breath. It wasn't out of joy that her heart was pounding but out of fear . . . For the first time she would be going home without anyone from her own household there to greet her. People would look at her with pity. To whom over there did she belong? At whose table would she sit? She would be like a beggar woman among strangers. A feeling of forlornness gripped her. All around her Dineh sensed a terrible isolation. The trees along the road who knew her so well looked at her like an uninvited guest. The chimneys of her father's houses and barns, where now Marko's wheat and hay were stored, didn't recognize her. She was a stranger here.

IN THE EMPTIED HOME

The wagon pulled into the yard, up close to Sholem's former home. Aunt Khashe and the children got out of the wagon. Dineh remained behind, without any desire to follow them. She would have preferred to sit in the wagon for a long time until it took her away. A destination—a particular place to go—was not on her mind. The entire world was now alien to her. She didn't have a home anywhere. Her aunt affably called to her: "Come on, Dineh, get out of the wagon. Are you being lazy?"

Dineh reluctantly climbed down from the wagon, placing her feet on the ground as if it were made of broken glass. She looked around. It was late in the evening. Good thing it will be dark soon, she thought. No one would see her, and she would see no one. Hayem-Motl and Khayke helped her down from the wagon, and Dineh trudged with quiet, hesitant steps to their home. She stood frozen; a shudder ran through her. She didn't go in. Instead she walked past it and into the orchard. To the great pear tree that stood behind the window of her former bedroom. She would embrace it like a brother, like someone who felt what she herself was now feeling. She went past the cherry trees and looked, her heart pounding like a hammer: Could it be that the tree wasn't there? She raced to the tree's spot. Gone . . . A hole—where once the old pear tree had stood. She lowered herself to the freshly covered pit and wept racking sobs. All of her dreams, the stories of her sisters and brothers—all of it now hung in the air and on the branches of the pear tree. The pear tree had once provided seats for them all on its accommodating, wide branches. The children had installed cages on them with open doors, with various kinds of food, water, and saucers for the blue-necked and red-bellied birds that came to feed and drink as to their own nests.

She sat on the cold, damp ground, her head lowered to the hole, and whimpered like a child exhausted from crying. Until Henye came over, bent down close to her, and said: "It wasn't just that tree. They also uprooted other trees and replanted them in fertilizer where they're building their houses. There'll be nothing left of them. Come on, Dineh, it's cold. You'll catch a cold sitting on the ground. You'll eat supper with us tonight."

Dineh felt better and was pleased that she didn't have to go into her ruined home. "And will I sleep at your place too?"

"We'll see."

The warmth of Peyse's house embraced Dineh from all sides. She found herself seated at the table among children and adults who had the candor of children. Everyone spoke, asking questions and answering them. Blind Soreh-Rokhl, who sat with the children and who looked like a child herself, smiled upon all that she could not see. Old, diminutive Khishe, with her nearsighted eyes, offered Dineh a flowered plate and—before setting it down—lifted it close to her eyes and wiped it with her hand, because this plate was reserved for guests and mustn't have any dust on it. Itke, who leaned her still young, full body heavily upon the crutch under her arm, sprung from plate to plate, seeing to it that every child had their portion. "Eat it with bread."

Peyse, with his short, gray, rounded beard, sat at the head, with the pale Velvl at his right. Around the ordinary table a festive atmosphere of decent people welcoming a dear guest after a hard day's work prevailed. Henye had already spoken to Itke about Dineh staying over. Soon after the meal Itke said to Henye, loud enough for Dineh to hear: "You'll sleep with Dineh tonight, Henye. I'll bring some fresh sheets. The children will sleep by the oven."

Henye was pleased, and as for Dineh—well, of course she was too.

"Just don't talk in your sleep, Dineh, and then spill out all the secrets, like Aunt Soreh-Rokhl."

"That is, if I'll be able to sleep at all . . ."

"You'll sleep, Dinehle, you'll sleep. Say the bedtime prayer, both of you, and you'll sleep."

Dineh talked with Henye, whispering late into the night. She revealed to her friend all that she carried in her heart. The darkness was conducive to talking. For her part Henye told Dineh all of her hidden longings—how she wanted to go to a city to learn tailoring and read books . . . Here at home she couldn't achieve anything. But what could she do? Her mother was a cripple, and she had to help her at home and often outside of it by carrying the bundle through the villages. Because she was tall, people thought she was an adult. For the holiday her mother had bought her a jacket and galoshes. Tomorrow she would show them to Dineh. She'd wear it all to synagogue—to services—tomorrow. All the Jewish girls from the nearby villages would be there. She was embarrassed to beautify herself because everyone would laugh and say that she was about to receive suitors . . . and she blushed when people spoke about her in that way. Her grandfather also embarrassed her like that. Her face burned. So she'd sprouted up—was that her fault? For her part Dineh told Henye about her navy-blue dress with the velvet collar and cuffs and the brown light coat with the wide sleeves like the ones priests wore. When it was time both friends would dress up and go to synagogue and pray from one holiday prayer book together. Like big girls. In that way, their spirits light, they started to read the bedtime prayer, without prodding, in a quiet, clear tone. They hugged—and fell asleep.

The next morning Dineh woke up late. In fact, both girls overslept. Itke had to wake them up. "Such big girls shouldn't need to sleep so late. It's the day before the holiday. And there's still a lot of work to do. The candlesticks have to be polished, the children have to be bathed and dressed . . . Henye, get to work."

Dineh declared that she'd help. She polished the candlesticks, and with great proficiency and love dressed the smaller children, combed their hair, set their braids, tied ribbons, and looped a bow at the ends of the little braids, as if they were her own dear sisters for whom her child's lonely heart so pined. Once their work was finished both girls washed, brushed, and braided their own hair. After they put on their holiday clothes they didn't recognize each other. Dineh was radiant, as if born anew. She was no longer the quiet twelve-year-old girl but a beautified, urbane young lady. Everyone looked at her. Her entire outfit was draped on her as if it had been specifically poured and adjusted for her face and appearance.

Everything proceeded according to plan until they went to Sholem's house for services. Dineh dawdled with Henye until the last possible moment. She walked as if with someone else's feet. With each stride they buckled under her. Her heart pounded. How would she take the doorknob in her hand? How would she open the door and cross the threshold of the house that was so much hers, more than anything in the world, and to whose door she was now approaching as a stranger? As Dineh got closer to the door she maneuvered it so that she would walk in front of Henye. But she stood frozen. Henye shifted her over, opened the door herself, and then gently led Dineh in by the hand. Dineh crossed the threshold. The women quickly surrounded her. They hugged and kissed her. They took her by the hand and sat her on a bench opposite the tall, white stearin candles. Before her was a holiday prayer book; around her sat aunts, cousins, and good friends from nearby villages. Aunt Yakhe immediately requested: "Speak, Dineh, speak. They're about to start the afternoon prayers."

The women slid over to get close to Dineh. She heard the men get up to pray. She opened the holiday prayer book and also began to pray. The women caught each word of hers and recited after her. She forgot that this was no longer her home and that she was an outsider here. Dineh prayed in a loud voice, with concentration, both for God and for those who needed to recite after her.

After the service people once again surrounded her. They caressed her. They took in the sight of her, marveling at her beautiful dress and the ribbons in her hair. They took care not to cause her distress—and avoided speaking about private matters. They asked Dineh to stay and have supper with them—with all of the neighbors who were in Ugli until after the holidays—to partake of a feast of fish, everyone together around one table.

Dineh looked around her, searching for Henye to rescue her. But she couldn't find her, and she allowed herself to be led by her aunts and the other kindly women.

She went into the large synagogue chamber, where the men had just prayed. Now there were two long tables decked in white and topped with challahs under cloth covering. Delicious-smelling fish had been placed on long plates, and the men were seated around the table. At the head, where her father had always sat, now sat Reb Yoshe, the miller from Otkulevitsh, a learned man and her father's old friend. At the head of the other table sat Uncle Shimen. Reb Yoshe called Dineh over to her and asked her how she was doing and caressed her head.

Dineh was seated with the women and children of Dineh's age. She was offered the best portions on fine dishware. She felt as if someone else's mouth were doing the chewing. Sensing everyone's eyes upon her, she felt ashamed not to eat. She had to hold herself back from bursting into tears. She counted the courses and waited, as if for a liberator, for the last one to come . . .

After the meal she practically snuck out of the house. In Peyse's house she was once again embraced like a family member. She slept with Henye for another night, and in the morning she went once again to prayer services. After prayers she had to stay for a warm meal with her relatives. At the services and while reciting the prayers she wept, no longer ashamed to do so in front of the adults. Before her eyes she saw Papa at the synagogue lectern; Mama standing before the women, her earrings dangling from her ears, with the large, brown holiday prayer book; and her sisters and brothers . . . the chandelier with its twisted branches . . . All now floated unsteadily before her tear-filled eyes. And soon . . . the emptiness of the entire house, still crammed full . . .

Immediately after Rosh Hashanah she asked Uncle Shimen to take her back to Kapyl′. She couldn't be convinced to stay until after Yom Kippur. Uncle Shimen harnessed the little horse and drove her back to Kapyl′. Now she felt close to the shtetl. Sure, it wasn't her home either, but the pain that she felt here in Ugli, her once-home now rendered foreign, would be absent in Kapyl′.

Dineh entered the house with her cardboard box and looked from one person to the next like someone who had done wrong. Everyone was pleased to see her. Motl considered her in silence, but Shprintse said: "Good, Dinehle. Tomorrow you'll be able to help me stitch embroidery onto a woman's jacket. I was worried you weren't coming. My eyes are hurting from this fine stitching."

Dineh sensed how everyone in this house cherished her, and she felt warm gratitude toward them. That evening she sat up late with Motl after her English lesson and told him about her experiences during the last few days at home and about the uprooted trees. Motl listened to her quietly and hardly responded. He only told her that they'd held two clandestine meetings on both days of Rosh Hashanah. Dineh didn't pay attention to what he said. The holes left by the uprooted trees were foremost on her mind.

She went to bed, her heart aching.

IN SLUTSK

Soon after the holidays Peshe came to pick up Dineh. She had to travel with her to Slutsk to apply for a passport. And then there was the matter of the birth certificate documents. As a result of an error Dineh's name had been left off her certificate. It was necessary for Dineh to come along on the trip. That's what Peshe's lawyer had written her.

For Dineh, this was all completely unnecessary.

She didn't want to go for a passport. What did she need a passport for? Let Mama go by herself. And right now there was so much sewing to be done here. Dineh didn't want to abandon Roda in the middle of all this work after Roda had spent money and sewn such a dress and coat for her. Not to mention that she was eating and sleeping in Roda's house without paying room and board.

But Dineh had to go with her mother.

The journey was long and arduous. For the first time in her life Dineh was riding with strangers in a wagon driver's narrow covered wagon. The wagon felt to her like a muddy sack blocking off the breathable air. The driver's coarse words to the horses grated on her ears. The road dragged on for what seemed like an eternity. She imagined herself sentenced to a never-ending ride in a filthy wagon surrounded by revolting talk and people. She sat there preoccupied with herself and her own hazy thoughts. But for what? Why were they going from one place to another—what were they looking for? She felt a sense of mortification before such a display of beggary. The people riding with her now were beggars or Gypsies. Perhaps her proud father, the person of the free, open fields, also had to ride in just such a covered wagon with just such characters, with just such a driver . . . How far and how long did he have to ride? Rummaging through her mournful thoughts in this way, she fell asleep. In her sleep Dineh had a vision of herself swinging in a barn with her girlfriends from Ugli and Dakhtervitsh on a large board hanging from rope in the air. The more forcefully the wagon jolted and lurched on the road the higher she flew in her dream on the swing through the clean barn redolent with the smell of fresh hay . . . In the rush of wind her braids unraveled entirely and her hair spread out behind her like far-flung fans. Dineh's colorful, pleated skirt lifted up around her in a circle dance, and a vigorous, child's glee pulsated through all of her limbs . . .

When her mother lightly shook her shoulder and said to her, "Get up, Dineh. We're here," Dineh opened her eyes in fear, unable to take in where she was and what was happening around her. Mama repeated her message: "We've arrived in

Slutsk. Look outside. You'll see such tall buildings and beautiful shops."

The purpose of this trip to Slutsk gradually returned to Dineh: a passport. Silently she gazed out of the wagon.

In Slutsk they drove to the home of the lawyer Aba Raskin. He was a relative of Peshe's. He finalized the passport for Dineh.

The home was large and tidy, full of sons and daughters, sons- and daughters-in-law. There was a fortepiano—everyone played it and sang. They spoke all the languages of refinement: Russian, German, and among the very young French could also be heard. Hebrew newspapers, among other publications, were piled on a big desk. Verandas encircled the house and overlooked a vast garden with trees. And the discussions! Day and night they argued and debated. *Rusya! Anglia Frantsia Palestina politika!* It all seemed bizarre and unnatural to Dineh. Not a single Yiddish word in the air. Why so many languages when you could speak quietly and in Yiddish? Why play on the fortepiano and sing? Weren't they embarrassed to do that in front of strangers? A profound longing for her former home—for the quiet animals in the stables, for the song of the peasants as they went to and from the fields—once again seized her. How beautiful the song of toil and work now appeared to her in comparison with this debauched home, where people quarreled, shouted, and sang for no particular reason and without any sense or purpose!

Out of politeness the young girls of the house asked Dineh if she wanted to go for a *progulka* or sit on the veranda. She shook her head to decline their invitation and remained stubbornly silent. She wasn't interested in the gentile languages and the vacant chatter. She was reminded of Shprintse, far away, all the way in Siberia, where she had buried her husband and child, and who had returned, after all that suffering, to Kapyl′, where she read Russian books and newspapers—probably when no one was looking. How could she not have? How else would she have known all of the things she told Motl? Shprintse herself sewed at Roda's and helped her support herself and her children. She didn't play the fortepiano or sing for no particular reason. She spoke Yiddish. That's how people were supposed to be. That's just how Shprintse was . . .

They stayed in Slutsk for a week.

On several occasions Peshe took Dineh for a walk outside. She showed her the market and the great buildings surrounding it. She even took Dineh to a confectionary and bought her ice cream. But Dineh returned from such outings dispirited and complained of headaches. She hated all of the hullaballoo. "When are we going home?" she asked.

When Dineh was once again seated in the covered wagon she immediately felt better. She was going back. Not home—now there was no home anywhere. But at least she was leaving this place of fresh alienation.

This time, after a long, drawn-out journey over unfamiliar roads, the covered wagon stopped next to a small home in a yard. Once again Peshe nudged the half-asleep Dineh awake, letting her know they'd arrived—this time in Pesatshne. Peshe was living here with her son Faytl. Dineh looked out from the wagon—once again unknown, but at least a closer unknown. From the small house several women and girls came out to greet them. The only familiar face that Dineh saw was her brother's wife, Malkeh. And even her, Dineh hardly knew. But she liked her appearance. She wasn't tall but was well built, and now she appeared even ampler. "How are you, Mother-in-Law?"

She came up quite close to Dineh, offered her hand, and gave her a kiss. Dineh appreciated the refined, white skin of Malkeh's hands and face and the thin, silky, curly black hair that framed her white forehead in ringlets. Sadness emanated from deep within her. Dineh gathered this from Malkeh's eyes, and she quickly felt close to her.

Faytl lived in the apartment in a building belonging to the daughter of Peshe the baker. Peshe the baker had died two years before from cancer, leaving behind a sick husband, Volfke the blacksmith, and eight children. The oldest, Khafke, an irascible girl of twenty, now ran the bakery. She rented the apartment over the kitchen to Faytl. It was a small, three-room apartment.

Dineh liked the place. It was kept tidy. Everything—down to the last trifle—looked clean. When Dineh spent the night there she sensed that her sister-in-law's life was not going well. She noticed that although Malkeh was eager to comply with her mother-in-law's every request, Peshe still looked down on her. Her brother Faytl treated Malkeh like a stranger and gave her orders even when they weren't necessary. Such behavior greatly irked Dineh. She observed too that Malkeh was in the advanced stages of pregnancy, and it was difficult for her to perform excessive chores. Virtually unnoticed by the others and without being asked, Dineh began to lighten Malkeh's burden by performing various chores so that Malkeh wouldn't have to: sweeping the house and serving Faytl his meals. Malkeh quickly felt the understanding of her little sister-in-law, and she welcomed her with open arms. They were soon as close as two good friends or sisters. They did things together, laughed together, and at times cried together too. For example, sometimes there was a wedding in the shtetl to which Malkeh was not invited. After an exhausted Faytl had come home, eaten, and gone to sleep and Peshe had gone to visit a neighbor, Malkeh would put on her cape, comb her hair, and say: "Come,

Dineh, we're the most important guests."

Both of them would leave, stand far behind a side window where the wedding was taking place so no one would see them, and listen to the musicians play.

Sometimes in the middle of the day Malkeh would dress up and call Dineh to take a walk with her on the boulevard because "she wanted to show the ladies her hat done in the latest style and have them all look at her." She'd take Dineh by the hand and they'd go behind the house to sit on the earthen bench . . . In this way Malkeh laughed at her now-constricted life and her former big-city ways.

Dineh felt sympathy for her sadness and longing. When no one was around to watch Malkeh would show Dineh a drawer full of the dresses and blouses she was in the process of sewing. Dineh absorbed Malkeh's joy with a trembling in her heart, but without words. Only her eyes expressed the unsaid, only her warm, moist glances . . .

Dineh missed Kapyl'. She missed Roda's house. She received letters from Motl with postscripts from Shprintse. She wrote back, and in each letter she wrote that she missed them.

But she also was growing used to living in Pesatshne. She had become deeply connected to her sister-in-law and felt that Malkeh needed her. Malkeh was, by nature, refined and proud, but people came to her and she was on good terms with each of them. The neighbor women regularly sent someone over to her, asking if Malkeh would be so good as to read one thing or another for them. In the afternoons the women came themselves, asking if Malkeh would kindly read from fashion books and just show them how to cut out pieces for sewing. Yet for all the good will around her, Dineh felt that Malkeh told no one what was really happening in her life. She, Dineh, understood Malkeh . . . This gave her a sense of satisfaction, and she remained in Pesatshne after discussing it with Malkeh.

"You'll stay here, Dinehle, until I come to term. I'll go to Uzda to my sister the obstetrician, and if everything goes smoothly I'll bring you back a beautiful little girl, a special gift."

HAYEM-FELIKS'S CHILDREN AND HAVEHLE

Like every small town, Pesatshne had its own rich man. Hayem-Feliks was the rich man of Pesatshne. All of the orphans and widows deposited their wealth with him. Peshe also deposited the money that Sholem didn't want to take to America with him. He would pay interest. He owned a big stone building that stood on a mountain on the outskirts of the shtetl, as well as his own coach with horses from abroad. His two sons and daughter—his only daughter—all studied in St. Petersburg. For the holidays they all came home. But during their holiday time they didn't joyride around on their sleek, tall horses or their bicycles like others of their social standing. They spent their free time with the poor children in town and with peasants in the fields. They agitated, spread propaganda, and even called a strike in their own father's timber factory.

In another home in Peshe the baker's courtyard lived a pale, coughing, unobtrusive, and pious man, Zisl the teacher. His students were mostly girls and women whose husbands had left to go overseas and to whom they now, poor things, had to write letters. Zisl barely managed to earn a living from his female students, but he was invariably quiet and courteous. And he never complained. Quite the contrary. His wife, Dvoyrehle, wore a brown, thick wig and a white ribbon on her young, lovely head. In the evenings she plucked feathers to help her husband generate income. They had a daughter—their one and only child, the apple of their eye. The good Dvoyrehle never had any more children. Only Havehle.

And everyone in the shtetl knew Havehle—both for her beauty and for her gorgeous singing. When Havehle was twelve years old, Dvoyrehle sent her to Uzda to a good seamstress. For three years she studied the craft there. When Havehle returned home she bought a sewing machine, set it up next to the open window in her room—and sewed and sang. With her sewing, Havehle gradually started to help augment her parents' paltry income. As she grew older Zisl's house became brighter and more comfortable. Folks in town depended on Havehle for a higher level of fine stitchery. Although Malkeh Kharash of Slutsk had married Faytl and no longer directed a workshop, she still yearned for her profession and would often sneak over to her neighbor Dvoyreh's house and quickly pass her hand over the fabric or cambric spread out on Haveh's sewing table to mark it up with a piece of chalk. Then, looking at Haveh, she would gesture about this or that fashion in the fashion book. Soon Haveh became a seamstress with a reputation. People even came to her to order wedding gowns. All the while Haveh sewed and sang. She bought another sewing machine, and now several other girls from the small shtetl sewed and sang with her.

Hayem-Feliks's children were frequent guests in Zisl's house. Monye, the older son, was often preoccupied with Haveh. He taught her Russian, brought her books to read, and brought her along to all of the *sobraniia*. Zisl and Dvoyrehle would look upon the activities of their child with apprehension in their hearts. "Good children . . . but what do they want with our child? Why don't they go out with their peers? If only they would leave us in peace."

That's how they both felt, but they were afraid to put these thoughts into spoken words.

Havehle grew and blossomed like a flower—and she read the books Monye brought her: Turgenev and Pushkin and Gorky, as well as the small, thin booklets without covers that he wanted her to distribute to people who came into the house to bring sewing work or to the girls who worked with her. Haveh was delighted that she was helping Monye in his great mission to transform the world . . .

"Yes," Monye would say, "we'll transform the world, Haveh. Then your mother won't have to pluck feathers all night long, and my mother won't have to yell at and boss around more than ten maids. Your father won't have to choke during his coughing fits when he gives his lessons, and my father won't have to count the interest and bathe in someone else's sweat and blood."

After hearing such assurances Haveh would come home and, her large eyes shining with conviction, recite a few of Monye's words to her parents in a singsong voice. They would look at her and plead with God to keep their child unharmed by such talk, the wild words she was saying.

THE MURDER VICTIMS IN THE FOREST

One Friday evening at dusk, just after Dineh washed her hair and put on a clean dress and Faytl got dressed for the afternoon service in the synagogue, there was a banging on her bedroom window. Dineh went to the window and saw Haveh standing there. Her mother's shawl was wrapped around her shoulders, and under the shawl she was holding a package of books. Faytl and Malkeh came over and opened the window.

"I have to escape. I'll run to the forest. A patrol is about to come and search the house. They've already been to Feliks's. They took away everything they found there; they arrested all three of them. Through a message that one of the maids delivered, Monye urged me to collect everything in the house, burn it, and then flee to the forest for a day or two until everything calms down. Take pity, take it all from me, hide it. I wasn't able to burn it."

Haveh was trembling in absolute terror as she spoke. She immediately turned and fled behind the buildings, through the courtyard, and onto the narrow trail leading to the forest.

Her heart frozen, Dineh watched as Haveh beat a hasty retreat. She saw her wide shawl flying out after her on both sides like a pair of wings—until Haveh's figure disappeared among the trees. Dineh fell face down on her bed and sobbed, imagining Haveh terrified at night, alone among the wolves and who knew what other dangers . . .

Everything had happened so unexpectedly that they were all momentarily stunned. Only afterward, after Haveh had disappeared into the forest, did they start to blame themselves and others: "Why did we let her run to the forest?"

"We shouldn't have let her go."

"We should have hidden her here, in the attic."

"What should we do with these books? Where should we take them?"

"We have to hurry and let Zisl know. He won't be able to bear it."

"We have to run to the forest and look for her and bring her back."

A commotion ensued. Everyone came in from Peshe's house. Dvoyrehle, looking exhausted and weak, snuck into the house. For a moment everyone stopped to listen.

She didn't know where her Havehle was. She was afraid that, God forbid, something terrible had happened. She had been sitting by the stewed vegetables, with wet hair, and when she went out for a moment and came back—Havehle wasn't anywhere to be found. Did anyone see her? She could catch a cold, God forbid . . .

As she was talking they heard the galloping of horses. Patrolmen quickly filled the courtyard and proceeded to storm into Zisl's home. They turned over the beds, emptied the closets, and searched every corner of the cellar and attic. And from there they went to another house, and then through the fields to the forest.

The narrow alley filled with Jews. People forgot all about the Sabbath and synagogue. Everyone's eyes were turned to the forest. That's where they were in a rush to go.

The police raided and searched every other house. The children fled.

Late evening turned to night. People stood in the cold, dark streets, wringing their hands. Women wept. They tore their hair from their heads. "To the forest. We have to go to the forest!"

"Children . . ."

"Beasts with weapons . . ."

"It's nighttime. It's the Sabbath!"

"It's not the Sabbath! Fire! We should take lanterns! We need to get to the forest to look for the children!" The men left and returned with lanterns in their hands. Still wearing Sabbath kaftans with long coattails, they made their way through the fields and to the forest.

They thoroughly searched the forest, but except for the prints left by the horses' hooves they didn't find trace of a single soul.

But then a plaintive groaning was heard. The men pricked up their ears. They approached with care and with jagged, bated breath. The farther they proceeded the closer the groaning sounds. Finally they reached the spot where, under a tree and in a pool of blood, lay Berke the blacksmith, an orphaned youth.

He worked in Volfke's smithy and stayed in their house. People predicted that he would soon marry Khafke and take over the smithy because of Volfke's poor health.

The police had previously captured Berke in a larger city. He'd fled and hid here. So when the patrols came he got scared and fled into the forest . . .

Now Berke lay with glazed eyes, gasping, and a weak gurgling sound issued from his throat. He lifted an almost lifeless hand with difficulty and let it sink back down. The men bent down, holding their lanterns over him. The cold, green autumnal moon shone between the naked tree branches. "He's breathed his last breath."

"Blessed is the True Judge!"

After another few moments of absolute silence, bowed heads, and lowered lanterns, the figures again began to stir uneasily: "What's going to happen? We've got to keep going."

"We have to search. Where should we go from here?"

"Which direction?"

"There, in the direction that Berke pointed."

"What does a dying person know? So what if he made some hand gesture?"

"He knew more than we know. We have to continue in the direction he pointed in."

"What will happen to the body? You're not allowed to leave a corpse unattended."

"Let's have a few men stay and watch over the body until the others get back."

"Who'll stay?"

"Not me!"

"Not me!"

"Those who aren't looking for a loved one should stay with the dead."

A few lanterns were set on the ground. Several bearded men dragged over the trunk of a chopped tree and placed it by the head of the dead man. One man took off his coat and covered the corpse. They lowered themselves, sitting on the trunk now at the corpse's head, and began rocking . . . The light of the lantern's flames flickered before them onto the ground, sending long, trembling shadows over the bare trees. A resonant, wordless melody reverberated in the night: *Oy-oy-oy! Oy-oy-oy!*

The other group of men went off in the direction toward which the dying Berke had pointed. Their lanterns lighting the ground, they walked, searching and calling out. No voice, no echo. It was late. The search party members shivered from exhaustion and the nighttime cold. Soon the wicks would devour the lanterns' kerosene and they would be left in darkness. Where should they go? Where should they search? They would make their way back to the shtetl—maybe there was news there. Maybe the fugitives had returned home another way. They would go back to the men who were watching over the corpse. They'd go back on other trails. Maybe they'd discover something that way. They took care to stick close to each other.

In the midst of this discussion one of the members of the search party who had been standing off to the side screamed. The forest trembled. All heads turned to the lantern off to the side. The figure was on all fours and screaming like someone possessed. They all ran after each other, pushing, like in a narrow room when someone faints.

As they approached the lantern and got down on their knees they saw an outspread, bloodied shawl. A girl's naked leg extended out from under the shawl. Someone lifted the shawl. Underneath lay the torn body of a young girl—Haveh. Prostrate beside her, Zisl, her father, howled like a severely wounded dog.

ANOTHER HOME FOR DINEH

Dineh gained another home in Pesatshne. She went there every day and did what she had to do, what she could do. That home was Zisl's.

All of the sandy shtetl—the small market, a few shops, and several little side streets—now looked like a house after a funeral. Anguish hung heavily in the air and trickled down into everyone's heart. Some people passed by Zisl the teacher's house with grieving hearts. Others entered and left without saying anything. There was no place for words, much less consolation.

The only one who found a way to reach the unfortunate couple was little

Dineh. At first she came to them with a pot of cooked food that her mother had sent her to take over. She went to the closet with the utensils and asked if these were the ones for meat. She carried a plate of food to Zisl—and then to Dvoyreh—and waited, practically unnoticed, in a corner until they had put something in their mouths. When they were finished, she discreetly came back, took the plates and the spoons, and washed them. The next day she did the same until the grieving parents quietly responded to a "good morning" and a "good night" and, with the passing of days, grew accustomed to her coming and looked forward to seeing her.

Hayem-Feliks's children were released. The older one, Monye, returned home. One day, when Dineh was coming out of Zisl's house, he ran into her and asked her to stop for a moment. He wanted to ask her about the two fallen ones. He had a sharply pointed face. He spoke Yiddish poorly. He wanted to help them but didn't know how. He had money in an envelope. Perhaps Dineh could leave it in their house in such a way that no one would know where it came from. Monye said he knew he could depend on her.

With these words he placed a sealed envelope in her hand and closed it with his own.

Dineh didn't know what to do. Should she refuse him? He looked so unhappy and disconsolate that she wanted to do whatever he asked of her. "Well, good. For you."

"But no one must know."

With that, Monye left. Distressed, Dineh looked after his departing form, at how his brisk footsteps were taking him farther and farther away. At this point her options seemed limited. Where should she go? What should she do with the envelope? Where should she hide it?

Approaching the door of the house, dark Khafke stopped her and asked: "Well, any news over there?"

Dineh, as if just awakened from sleep, stiffly tightened her grip on the envelope that she'd previously been carrying like an alien thing you find but are eager to cast off. "What news should there be?"

Khafke sighed heavily. "What news could there be, you ask? Well, let me tell you. The ones rotting in the ground don't know about anything anymore. And those who are left behind have plenty to grieve about . . ."

Dineh understood all too well that Khafke was thinking about Berke. Berke, who was to have been her groom, was now lying in the ground, and she, Khafke, would have good reason to mourn . . .

Dineh looked sadly down and had no response to Khafke's anguished words.

Khafke was unable to speak openly to anyone about herself or her wound. So she spoke about the grieving parents who had been struck by such a catastrophe. "What will they do now—with both of them sick?"

Dineh shuddered, clutching the envelope in her hand.

"Winter's on its way," continued Khafke. "Haveh provided all of the life support for that house. Of course, Hayem-Feliks's sonny wasn't harmed in the least. He gets to walk around again free as can be."

Her words stung Dineh. Without audacity, she responded: "Who knows? Things are bad for him too."

Khafke pounced: "Bad? What's bad for him—what, tell me? Did they murder his bride? He wouldn't have married her anyway."

Dineh didn't even stop to consider this. She was too preoccupied with what she was holding in her hand. The door opened, and her sister-in-law, Malkeh, emerged. She had come to see why Dineh was dilly-dallying at Zisl's house—and here Dineh was chatting with Khafke. So Dineh gladly went into the house, quickly ate her supper, and went to bed. She kept the envelope in her bosom.

The next day Dineh hid the envelope under the feather comforter. Later she placed it back in her bosom, secured the belt around her waist, and headed off to Zisl's place.

Zisl had slowly started to drag himself out of bed, and one by one, female students reappeared. Young married women came to sigh over their harsh fates: life was paper-driven . . . and if only they could at least write down their desires and feelings by themselves—without having to ask someone else . . .

Zisl called Dineh over. "Dinehke, come here, daughter. You know how to write English. Please write down the address. These days, it's hard for me to copy these foreign letters. My eyes tear up, and my hands just don't move the way they should."

Dineh sat down and wrote out the address in English.

"Look at her hand go, no evil eye."

"I can also write a letter to America in Yiddish if it's hard for you, Reb Zisl."

"I know you can. I don't want to trouble you."

"It's nothing."

Dineh sat back down and read the letter that the young wife gave her and set out to write a response. The woman started to tell her what to write, but Dineh smiled. "I've already written the letter. I'll read it to you soon."

Dineh finished writing the letter and then read it out loud. Zisl listened attentively. Dvoyrehle remained seated, her head to the side, her hands lowered, and looked at Dineh. The young wife breathed quickly and swallowed a few words. Dineh finished reading and looked around. "Good?"

"Good? What a question!"

"You should write handwriting models. You should write a handbook of sample letters."

"Golden hands, no evil eye."

"She knows everything, no evil eye. It's so touching."

"My word, Reb Zisl. I myself didn't realize how bitter my life is. She captured on paper all of the sadness in my heart. May your hands only serve you well. What a letter—" And the young wife wiped her eyes.

Dineh was embarrassed. Throughout the writing she had been focused on all of the yearning that was this woman's fate, her lonely life. The pen in her hand had raced over the white paper like a sled over a smooth, slippery path. But now she was ill at ease. She stood up. "My mother definitely needs me at home. I have to bring Faytl his meal."

To the chorus of thanks, Dineh quietly answered: "It's nothing. You're welcome."

While closing the door behind her, Dineh remembered the envelope. She took it out from against her chest, set it on the ground next to the threshold, and then stepped on it several times. She then picked it up and quickly went back into the house. The young wife with the letter was already standing near the threshold, poised to leave. When Dineh opened the door, the woman left. Dineh closed the door and offered the squashed envelope to Dvoyrehle. "Take a look, Dvoyrehle. I was outside, on my way home, and I just saw this envelope lying on your doorstep."

"There's no telling what wanders into the yard. A child probably lost it, or a woman who came to my Zisl for a letter or an address."

"I'm in a rush. My mother needs me. The envelope is sealed shut. You should look inside before you throw it away." She saw that Dvoyrehle was looking toward the window and at the envelope. Dineh was sure she wouldn't throw it away before opening it. She quickly left the house and went home.

She insisted on bringing Faytl his lunch when he was in the shop and staying with him until dusk so that Malkeh could lie down and rest. By then it was quite difficult for Malkeh to move, and she was grateful to Dineh for the help.

It was a cold day, with an autumn drizzle. A damp chill seeped into the air. Throughout the week income had been scant in Faytl's iron business—with only a carriage from a nearby village coming for a pound of nails or a few pounds of rope. But Dineh stayed in the shop. If Faytl wanted he could lie down behind the wall, on the sofa in the warehouse. If someone came she'd wake him up.

"Fine," Faytl responded.

Dineh remained on her own behind the shop table, thinking about Zisl's house, the letter she'd written, and the envelope with the money. Had they opened it? How much money was there? Would they use it?

These thoughts filled her mind until she grew tired. Once again she yearned for all that had been—first for Kapyl′ and then for her former home, for the quiet village, for her father, for all that constituted her life as a child, filling each and every corner of her reality and child's fantasy. All of that was now shattered, dissipating away from her. The whole village stood before her. She saw its small houses now as if through a thin autumn mist. From the tall chimneys smoke was curling upward . . . The peasant women were busy combing the flax and preparing the wool from the shorn sheep for winter—to spin and dye and weave . . . The peasants were threshing in the barns . . . The smells of the village in all their variety returned to Dineh—and the physical ache of homesickness enveloped her . . .

PARASKA THE MADWOMAN

As Dineh sat at the front preoccupied with her memories, the door of the shop quietly opened. She looked up and standing before her was Paraska the madwoman. How had she made it here—all the way from Ugli? At first Dineh didn't believe her eyes. Was she dreaming? How could she possibly have gotten here? But in fact it was her. Paraska.

Behind the table Dineh stood up. Without saying a word she contemplated Paraska's bare, swollen-blue feet and hands; her face—fat and smudged, with chapped lips thickened from the cold; her stomach—big and neglected; and her entire body gave the appearance of an inflated, dirty bag on the verge of exploding at any moment. In addition to such an unfortunate presentation, there emanated from Paraska—veritably radiating from her person—the years of almost constant trudging through the villages and fields near Ugli. Her body, half naked, half covered in rags, appeared as a kind of reminder of how cruel life could be to humankind.

Dineh carried a chair over to Paraska and told her to sit down. Paraska sat down with difficulty and, without saying a word, looked ahead. With a distorted face, she then laughed soundlessly. Dineh spoke to her, but she didn't respond. In the small basket holding the food Dineh had brought Faytl, an apple and a small piece of bread were left over. Dineh offered these to Paraska, who lifted them to her nose, inhaled deeply, and commenced to eat with great gusto. Once again Dineh tried to speak with her, but Paraska acted as if no one were there and the food had descended from the air itself into her lap.

Dineh felt ill at ease in Paraska's presence. She went behind the wall and awakened her brother. Faytl entered the room, and as soon as Paraska spotted him she stood up and approached him. Without a prologue of any kind she launched immediately into the middle of her tale: "They beat me up—in the fields and in the forests. You see?"

She lifted her torn, filthy rag made to serve as a dress and showed Faytl a body marked by blue bruises. Faytl responded gently: "I'll show them, Paraska. They won't beat you anymore. Sit down, Paraska, right here, near the little oven. You'll warm up. I'll boil some water for tea."

Faytl sent Dineh to buy some food. She went out and came back with bread and herring. Dineh saw that he had already prepared the hot tea.

"She didn't want to say a single word to me, but with you she's completely at home. How did she get here? All this way!" said Dineh.

"She's been here a few times. One time she dragged herself here through the fields and then came across the shop. From that point on she just remembered it. Whenever she comes to Pesatshne she comes straight here. She doesn't recognize you. That's why she doesn't speak to you. She's the same age as me. I remember her from back when she was a little girl . . . I remember how she fell in love with Alyosha, who's now her brother-in-law. Paraska was the most beautiful peasant girl in the village. But her sister, Manka, also fell in love with Alyosha, and it was she who married him. And Paraska was left pregnant. I remember how she gave birth to a bastard, and she was driven out of the house . . . Manka, her own sister, was the one who drove her out. Their shared family background wasn't enough for her . . . And the father, Ulas the drunk—remember him?"

Dineh nodded her head. "Of course."

"From that point on, he started beating Paraska. And there was no mother. So Paraska started wandering, with her child in her arms, one place by day, another by night. A beautiful, blond bastard, who resembled his handsome creep of a father in appearance. But with her, with Manka, he didn't have any children. None at all! Paraska had enough children for all of them . . . After she suffocated her first child, she went crazy and started hauling herself around . . . always like this, with her belly reaching up to her nose . . . and she gives birth to them and suffocates them . . . and it doesn't bother anyone . . . Shepherds in the fields beat her up, she doesn't eat—and yet she lives on—as if to spite Manka and Alyosha . . ."

Shuddering and with tears in her eyes, Dineh absorbed every word coming out of her brother's mouth without saying anything in return. Paraska liked Faytl because he had a good heart. She came to him like a mute dog to a kind owner. Who knows, thought Dineh, given how bad things are with him . . . She remembered Mikhliye—what Faytl had said to Mikhliye when they were riding in the wagon on the way to his wedding with Leyeh . . . She looked from Paraska to Faytl and weighed each one's pain separately.

Warmed now, Paraska sat by the oven and, in her dozing, murmured incomprehensible words. Out of the blue she called out to Faytl: "Where's your father now?"

"Far, far away, Paraska. In America."

The distance didn't faze Paraska. "And your mother? And Sorke? And Itska died, right? I know! Why did they leave their home? They didn't get beaten up. They didn't suffocate any children. Why did they leave?"

"Marko's son-in-law drove them out."

"They should go back home. Marko's son-in-law, that Polish son of a bitch, kicked the bucket. They buried him along with his bastard. Your father should come back home."

Paraska's talk terrified Faytl and Dineh. They knew that these were the words of a madwoman and surely weren't reliable, and yet she spoke with such clarity that disbelieving her wasn't possible either. But when Faytl began pressing for details, she once again droned on about the shepherds in the fields and how they beat her. As if talking to himself, Faytl said: "Who knows? Maybe there's truth in what she's saying. We'll have to find out."

A gentile in a wagon drove up to buy something. Faytl gave him what he asked for and asked him to take Paraska with him to his village and let her stay overnight. The peasant took her. She left pleased: "That Polish son of a bitch—he's six feet under. Sholem will come home. Everyone will come home. I'll come home too."

That evening there was big news in Faytl's home. The passports and the boat tickets for Peshe and Dineh—along with a letter from America—had arrived on the same day. Papa wrote that Malkeh had the good fortune to become engaged to his nephew Isak. He was a good, fine young man, and with God's will everything would go well for them. He was an educated man and suited to American life. When Peshe, with God's will, reached America, they'd jointly celebrate Malkeh's wedding and Daniel's bar mitzvah. He wasn't fond of anything in America, but he had no say in the matter and he couldn't be picky either at this point. Peshe should do whatever she could to travel to America.

Faytl recounted what Paraska the madwoman had said about Marko's son-in-law. Malkeh reported that Zisl had been over twice that day looking for Dineh. In the stomped-upon envelope that Dineh had found on his doorstep and handed over to his Dvoyrehle was a brand-new banknote of a full one hundred rubles. They feared a new calamity. Maybe someone had left it at the doorstep to do them in. Zisl had already been to see the rabbi, and in the synagogue he asked people what to do with the money. In such a poor shtetl, how could hundred-ruble banknotes be lying around beneath your feet? And where of all places? At Zisl's place, at Zisl's home in the courtyard. Something was fishy. Who knew what else God had in store to punish him with? How had he so sinned against His Beloved Name?

Dineh felt pressed upon from all sides. As for the matter of the found money—well, she couldn't know how it would all turn out. But more than anything she was jolted by seeing official passports and the boat tickets. It meant she would have to leave home for good and make her way somewhere leading into an abyss. She couldn't think about the future because she couldn't visualize with any clarity something that was so far from home. It all seemed to her like a sealed state of unreality into which she couldn't peer. Dineh felt she was losing the ground beneath her feet. The earth, the world itself, was on the verge of slipping out from under her, and she was left outside, stranded in the air . . .

Dineh stopped eating and sleeping and became quite emaciated. Peshe summoned the medical practitioner, who gave her little packs of wormwood powder. It didn't help. Peshe traveled with Dineh to see the doctor in Uzda. The doctor discovered that Dineh was suffering from anemia and prescribed drops. But Dineh didn't get better. Until she overheard Mama talking to Malkeh about writing to the lawyer to extend the validity of the passport.

". . . To travel with a sick child in winter? What will I do if, God forbid, we're turned away at the port of entry? It'd be better to wait and then, if all goes well, leave right after Passover."

This helped Dineh more than the wormwood powder. A moment of reprieve was good too. She wouldn't worry about what would happen after Passover. For now she would remain on solid ground.

Dineh resumed her previous chores. Once again she went to Zisl the teacher every day. The whole issue of the found money had resolved itself. Dvoyrehle held it in her wrung hands for so long until she accustomed herself to the idea that God's ways were essentially mysterious. If it was right for Him to take away the one and only apple of her eye and allow her to walk about on sinful ground, then it was right for an envelope with a hundred-ruble banknote to wander into her courtyard. And here, such a golden child, no evil eye, as Dineh had brought the banknote inside and presented it to her and wouldn't even accept a few rubles to buy herself a light dress or a pair of shoes. Dvoyrehle cashed the bank note—through Faytl, as a matter of fact—and gradually started using the money.

Young wives and girls once again came to Zisl the teacher for letter writing in the hopes that Dineh would write them. And the responses to the letters that Dineh wrote were different from the ones that used to come. The men remembered their responsibilities. Grooms became homesick. Dineh acquired a reputation. People talked about her. They wondered what she would someday become. Zisl, who had been the letter writer up to that point, kept repeating that they ought to compile such letters into a handbook of sample letters, and people ought to use them as a model . . .

A LITTLE SOUL IS BORN

Winter set in. And one night a sled with soft bedding was hitched to two horses, and Faytl and Malkeh drove off to Uzda. After three days Faytl returned pale and exhausted but with a contented, bright smile reaching all the way to his high forehead. Following a long night and day of struggle, Malkeh had given birth to a daughter, a beautiful, tiny girl with a round face and minuscule hands.

Peshe baked pound cake, filled bottles with wine and jars with cherry brandy and preserves, and set out, with Dineh, to Uzda to see the new mother.

Lying in bed in her beautiful nightshirt, Malkeh truly beamed. To Dineh she smiled playfully and said quietly: "Now I couldn't care less about them, those Pesatshne big shots. Things won't be so sad for me now. I have a daughter. I'll spend time with her. And you, Dinehle, if you behave properly, I'll let you spend time with my daughter too. She's a young lady—not just anyone—cosmopolitan, born in Uzda . . ."

Dineh gazed upon Malkeh's beauty and maternal joy with warmth and affection.

Malkeh stayed in Uzda for a month. Then Faytl once again filled a sled with soft bedding and brought the young mother and the child—the beautiful little girl with luminous eyes—home. They named her Reyzele—after Malkeh's mother. Faytl's home shone with new life.

Another letter from Sholem in America arrived for Peshe. He wrote that Malkeh had the good fortune to get married and that he was lonely. He was now without a woman to run the household. Peshe really did need to finish her preparations and set out to travel.

Dineh's severe anxiety returned. Once again she looked for a way to hide from the reality that was rising up toward her. She felt that what had once been distant and uncertain was closing in and becoming unavoidable—this America that was somewhere on the other side of the world. She would have to uproot herself from the land where she was born and where she took her first steps. She would have to sever herself from her very existence, from everything that constituted her and her world. All that was beyond—whatever would come afterward—did not enter her imagination. She just felt that she was standing on the brink of an abyss, a darkness. At the very least she wanted to distance herself from it. She would return to Kapyl′. She needed to get to Kapyl′.

Peshe was extremely busy with preparations, and Dineh was just getting in her way underfoot. She decided to send Dineh to Kapyl′. Let her go. As long as she didn't get sick, God forbid. When Peshe went to Slutsk to buy new silver candlesticks to take along to America, and an assortment of silver spoons, forks, and knives—a wedding present for Malkeh—as well as two shawls, one for herself and one for Malkeh, she stopped on the way at Roda's house in Kapyl′ and dropped Dineh off there.

In Roda's house Dineh was the same honored guest she had always been. Everyone thought it was such a shame that Dineh was leaving for America. Shprintse sewed a dress for her made of batiste with a short jacket of green fabric so that she would be warm on the ship. While she sewed Shprintse looked at Dineh and repeatedly reached behind her glasses to wipe away her tears. "For some reason my eyes keep tearing up today. It's probably the weather."

Roda looked at Dineh and sighed. She "promised" her that she wouldn't stay long in America. She'd come back . . . America wouldn't suit her . . . As she talked heavier sighs kept tearing their way from her heart.

Worse off than anyone was Dineh herself. She sat like a mute—not speaking and not hearing what those around her were saying. Motl tried to comfort her by saying that it wasn't such a big world after all. There would come a time when countries would get closer to each other, and in a short time people would drive and even fly, like birds, from one country to another . . .

Hearing such talk from Motl, Dineh lost her patience: what foolishness he believed in! Flying like birds! And if they fell and, God forbid, got killed, what would happen then? It'd be better if he didn't speak such foolishness at all. Everything did have its limits!

Motl would smile sadly at Dineh's obstinacy. But none of this had a calming effect on Dineh. "It would be better if there weren't ships that could travel across oceans . . . No one would leave their homes, and no one would drown. You could drown if you go on a ship."

"But not with an airship."

"Oh, stop speaking such silliness, Motl. An airship! You could fall and get smashed to pieces, God forbid!"

Such conversations between Dineh and Motl took place at night, from beds set up on opposite sides of the room. They spoke in whispers so that Noske, who slept with Motl, and Rivele, who slept with Dineh, wouldn't wake up. They would speak this way until late at night until Motl told Dineh to go to sleep and Dineh started to recite the Shema bedtime prayer. Throughout her recitation she posed all sorts of questions to God and answered them herself with heavy sighs that tumbled down like stones from her child's heart.

Her mother lingered in Slutsk for two weeks. On her return trip she stopped at Roda's house to take Dineh back to Pesatshne. But with Roda's help Dineh managed to stay in Kapyl'. Still, the feeling that she would soon have to leave the very ground that supported her intensified within her. For that reason she was afraid. What was to be done? And if anything were to be done, it would have to be done soon. Mama could come and take her, and then it would be too late. She waited. Surely it wasn't possible that Mama would leave forever a home where she was abandoning her children in a cemetery—without even going to say goodbye to them. It just couldn't be. Dineh remembered as if it were today how sick Mama had been for a long time after the death of her little sister, Freydele. Itshe was, after all, already an adult when he died. And would Mama really go away and abandon the graves of two children, desolate and alone in the cemetery? Dineh waited. When Mama came to Kapyl', she would surely go to the cemetery and cry over the graves of her children so they would forgive her. Mama wouldn't have ripped herself away from them, but Papa had written that she must come. So it would be.

But Dineh didn't get to see her mother. Instead of Mama arriving in person there was a letter from her. She wrote that she was now going to Ugli and that on Friday Uncle Yankl was coming to take Dineh to Ugli. From there they'd be going to Pesatshne, and from there—to America.

The letter arrived on Tuesday. That gave Dineh all of three days to say goodbye to Kapyl′—to Roda's house. Mama wasn't coming and wasn't going to say goodbye to her two children whom she was leaving here in a state of eternal abandonment. At dusk that evening Dineh went by herself to the cemetery. Walking around the fence she saw that no one was there. She picked a spot where the fence was low and climbed over it. She found Itshe's grave and fell prostrate next to his tombstone.

She sat in that position until the coolness of the wind between the trees went through her. She looked up and saw the darkness of evening. With a heavy heart she got up and went to look for another grave. A little grave—but she didn't find it. She climbed the fence, walked pensively through the field, and returned to the shtetl, where the flames of the lamps flashed through the windows.

During the day on Friday a wagon came from Ugli with a letter from Peshe that Dineh should come for Sabbath, and that on the way back to Pesatshne they would stop in Kapyl′ to say goodbye.

Despondently, Dineh climbed onto the wagon. Vasil told her to sit next to him on a bit of hay packed into a small sack. He said it would be a softer seat for her.

Vasil chatted with Dineh, wanting to cheer her up a little—but his own voice was gloomy and things were going badly for him. Since Sholem's departure life had soured for him. He hired himself out wherever he could just to make ends meet. The walls of his sinking cottage, where his wife, the ample-bosomed Oliana, was busy with the white-haired, bedraggled, and barefoot children, were closing in on him. When she spoke with or shouted at them, she did so half in Goyish and half in Yiddish, as if she were still in Sholem's house. With forced cheer, Vasil said: "Well, Dinke, so you're going to America?"

Dineh answered glumly: "I don't know . . . If Mama says we're going, I guess we're going."

"You should talk to your father when you're there, Dinke. Tell him to bring me over too. I'll serve him the way I did up until now. Will you tell him?"

"I'll tell him. But why do you have to go so far from home? And what'll happen with Oliana and the kids?"

"I'll send for them. The way your father's doing with you and your mother."

"Don't go, Vasil. It's better if you stay here. I don't want to go either. This is our home."

Vasil responded heatedly. "Our home . . . a fine home—your father driven out like a dog from his own house and from his own property. That vile dog . . . the earth shouldn't hold him. Drove out your father, and now he himself is six feet under. Let him rot! I took up drinking. I drink from aggravation, and then I come home and I beat Oliana and the kids."

Dineh shuddered in horror. "You beat Oliana, Ustina, and Arkhip? It's forbidden, Vasil. My father wouldn't forgive you. Beating? Beating Oliana and the kids?"

"As God is dear to me," said Vasil guiltily. "Dinkele, you know me well, after all. I never beat anyone, have I? But this is from stress. I don't know what to do with myself. Promise me that you'll ask your father to send for me."

"If you promise me that you won't hit Oliana and the kids anymore, then I'll ask my father to send for you—that is, if I go there myself."

"What do you mean—if you go there? You're definitely going."

Pleased with herself, Dineh answered: "They can still turn me away from the port. They say that a lot of people are refused entry at the port because of trachoma or if they find any kind of marks on the body. And I have a big mark on the foot. Maybe they'll turn me away."

"May God protect you!"

"And I ask God not to let me get through."

"You're a silly girl, Dinke. What are you saying—that everyone will be in America and you'll be here?"

"That's nothing. Itshe is here all alone, and Freydele . . ."

Vasil crossed himself and said: "What are you saying, Dinke? In the name of the Holy Mother, they're dead, after all. How could they go with you?"

"That's even worse. If they're dead and can't come—well, you're not allowed to abandon their graves and leave them isolated forever. For all eternity."

Vasil considered this. "The things she says—you'd stay with Faytl if you stayed here."

"No. Not with Faytl. I'd stay in Kapyl′ at Roda's."

"As long as I live, I won't understand you at all. The things you say . . ."

The wagon stopped in front of the house that had once been Sholem's domain and Dineh's home. Now it stood mute and cold. The windowpanes looked stiffly and despondently out around themselves.

From a side room a door opened. Yankl came out, cheerful as ever. "Come in, Dinehle. Come, I'll help you. You'll warm up, get something to eat. Your mother is in Dakhtervitsh. She'll be back soon. Come in."

Dineh followed as if in a trance. She entered and sat down on a bench at the table. The building now looked like a neglected granary. Yankl's children sat in tatters around the old, low stove and amused themselves with pieces of yellow cheese that looked like coarse soap . . .

"That's expensive Dutch cheese, Dinehle, that Yankl the broker threw out because of the smallest defect. That's because the cheese sent abroad can't have the slightest blemish. And as soon as a cheese cracks or gets spots it can't be used. So thanks to the crazy people living abroad the kids and I live like emperors, with the most expensive cheese. But kids are kids, after all, and don't understand the taste or have any good sense. They want bread. I should give them bread. Isn't cheese tastier than bread? For one pound of cheese you can buy three pounds of bread . . . But you can't convince them. Bread is bread! But soon there'll be bread too. Soon Aunt Peshe will come from Dakhtervitsh. Then there'll be bread. And Aunt Khashe will send both bread and challah."

At these words the three individuals sitting around the oven with the pieces of old cheese in their hands turned to face their upbeat father. Their eyes shining and mouths half open, they turned and looked in the direction of those wondrous sounds—bread, challah. After such a valiant explanation, a contented Yankl started fussing with the oven. "I'll boil some water. And you, Hayem-Motke, pop over to Khishe and ask to borrow a little tea and a few pieces of sugar. Let Dinehle drink a glass of tea and a piece of Dutch cheese—expensive but really top-notch."

Hearing her name jolted Dineh back to reality, only then taking in what her uncle was saying. "Thank you, Uncle. I'm not hungry. I'll wait until Mama comes. Then we'll all eat together."

"Well, if you want to wait for your mother, so be it. There'll be challah and bread and fish. A Sabbath fit for a king."

STILL LIFE

Dineh stole quietly from the house. She'd go to Peyse's to see the kids. When her mother came she would return.

Closing the door behind her, she stood still. Throughout the day the sun had heated the large house, and Dineh placed her hand on it, like a mother feeling the forehead of a sick child when it was asleep. With her hand running over the warm wood, she trudged over to the door. She touched the warm piece of iron, the doorknob. Her legs shook. She tried the doorknob and the door yielded, opening with a faint, weak squeak. She stood at the open door and looked fearfully at the large desert, which for one terrifying moment looked to her like a distant, deep cave, where the sun shone through with a long, thin ray and cast a scant shadow on the bare floor. Her eyes followed the dancing, shimmering ray. She crossed the threshold, closing the door behind her. The spot that the ray of sunshine had previously illuminated was now gray and, for a moment, darker than all that surrounded it.

She looked around. Everything looked ashen and frozen, like a still life painting set behind glass. Dineh was gripped by a sense of unease. She left the large front room. She opened the door—like a thief checking to see if the residents were home—and crept quietly into the large room, the synagogue room. The same stillness, but here the rays of the sun, refracted between two tall trees growing by the fence around the yard, shone brightly through a window. The synagogue room abandoned as after a pogrom . . . The Holy Ark, its dusty green curtain adorned with two embroidered golden cherubs that had dust on their wings, stood as it always had. The carved pictures on the eastern wall—the ones with lions on either side as well as the large scene of Jerusalem that Malkeh had sewn back when she was a child, with its eternally green poplars and the dove with its lowered wings on the holy destroyed wall—all hung where they always had. But thin, trembling spiderwebs covered the frames of the pictures, and gossamer strands had been spun over the glass. The set of the Talmud and the long benches were still there. Even the chandelier, with its artfully turned branches, dangled from the ceiling as it always had. Only now a green, damp rust covered the once-gleaming, gold-hued brass.

Dineh stood frozen as if she herself were one of the lifeless things in the abandoned, spiderweb-covered room. The rays of light that sifted through the trees and illuminated the synagogue room had started to narrow, and the sun's glare was now cast over the door to the kitchen. Again Dineh followed the sun and felt her hand on the doorknob. She gave a gentle push, and the door to the large kitchen opened. The ray of sunshine extended in a narrow stripe over the kitchen floor. Dineh followed it. The door between the two rooms remained open. The shelves, on which the copper and brass pots had once rested and brightened the walls with their shine, now stood empty. By the wall between the window and the outside door was the large ritual washstand, now empty of its large copper water container and the water basin that used to stand next to it. There were greenish rings of mold where the utensils had stood with such assurance for so many years. Dineh stared at the green rings of mold for a long time. Tears began to form in her eyes.

Suddenly Dineh heard a faint, weak meow. Fearfully she started to look around. She turned to the wall with the built-in oven. She soon heard another meow, but this time more distinct and longer—as if in prayer. Dineh approached the oven and looked under the hearth into the winter chicken coop. But then the faint, pleading meow sounded from on high, above Dineh's bent shoulders. She straightened up, looked into the oven, and saw an exhausted, elongated gray cat stuck in its depths that seemed to her like an open, dark pit. Dineh found all of this deeply unsettling. But soon a tremor—both from fear and from joy—coursed through her: Grulya!

The supine, stretched-out, thin cat stood up, found its bearings, and began to exit the open oven. She approached the hearth and lifted her teary green eyes to Dineh. With trembling fingers she caressed the gray, ash-dusted, emaciated coat. The cat gave a nimble leap, landed at Dineh's feet, and proceeded to pace back and forth on her scrawny legs around her. Through her faint yet exuberant purring and meowing the cat then launched into a narration of all that she had experienced and suffered when the family forsook the house.

Dineh bent down and lifted Grulya from the floor. She stroked her and lay her head against the cat's fur. Then she left the house and returned to Uncle Yankl to ask him for a little bit of milk. Uncle Yankl looked at her enthusiastically. "Milk? Of course! As much as you want. Hayem-Motke, run straight to Oliana. Ask her for a little bit of milk. Well?"

This time Dineh didn't stop Hayem-Motke. The boy returned quickly with a small pitcher of milk and a message from Oliana. She told him to tell his father to come and milk his cow himself. That way he and the kids wouldn't have to be without milk or wait for her to bring it to them each day.

Dineh poured milk into a small saucer and placed it on a bench. She held the dusty Grulya over the milk. The cat lapped up the milk, fearful of missing a single drop of what she had long been seeking. After every few slurps she lifted her head and looked up at Dineh.

The door opened widely and Oliana entered, her arms outstretched. "Dinka! Just look—she's finally getting to see you, in spite of everything! It seems that she's only a cat—and yet she recognizes her owner's hand. No matter how many times I called her and took her home, fed her milk like a child of my own—and the kids coddled and comforted her, and they wanted to play with her—but nothing doing! Before you turned your back—she was already gone! Where's Grulya? It was no use. She'd already disappeared and was back in the oven. I felt sorry for the mute creature. A person has longings too . . . And then Vasil took to the bottle out of aggravation—drinking and crying and beating me and the kids. A man can do anything. Do I miss them any less? It tears my heart up when I think about everything that's happened. It was my home. After all, I raised the kids."

Oliana bent down to Dineh and gave her a kiss on her head. "Oh, Dinka, Dinotshka, the earth shouldn't hold him, that Polish dog. He brought us misery. Now he just talks, my Vasil—about going to America. To *Pan* Solom he says he'll go, to America. And leave me and the kids behind, to face my dark fate."

Oliana wiped her eyes. Dineh consoled her. "If he does go, Oliana, he'll send for you and the kids. He told me so himself."

"Good Dinkele, not for nothing did I carry you in my own hands and teach you to say *ha-Moytse* on bread when you didn't want to eat matzo on Passover. Remember?"

Dineh smiled in embarrassment. "I was little."

"Of course you were little. Now you wouldn't do that. Passover is Passover. You're a good, pious girl, Dinke. Don't I know it—good and pious."

Oliana sat down next to Dineh on the bench and turned to face her while she stroked Grulya. "Dinka, did he really tell you that himself? That he'll send for me in America? Tell me, Dinotshka."

"Yes. Today, on the way from Kapyl′, he told me."

"Good, Dinka, speak to your father. I'll ask your mother. I served them loyally, like my own parents. Vasil wants to leave here. A dog also has to have its own piece of the garbage pile. We're worse off than dogs here. We don't have a patch of our own field. This tiny cottage isn't ours either. When Marko's nasty son feels like it he'll throw us out just like he threw out your father."

Looking at the cat, Oliana was lost in reflection. "There, just like her, just like Grulya . . . left without a home . . . She'll lie in the oven until she dies . . . I brought her all the way to Dakhtervitsh to your Uncle Shimen. Your Aunt Khashe—tears poured from her eyes when she looked at us. She welcomed me like one of the family. She packed me a small bag of food and little things for the kids. She gave Grulya to the kids and told me to go home and not worry—they'd take care of her. She wouldn't lack for anything there, she said. It didn't take but two days—and Grulya was back in the oven. Found the way back herself. An unspeaking beast is more loyal than a person, more direct. Let her down, Dinka. We'll see if she goes to look for the way back to the oven."

Dineh put the cat down. But she didn't leave. Staying at Dineh's feet, Grulya purred contentedly and snuggled up to her.

PESHE COMES TO SAY GOODBYE

Footsteps and snippets of conversation could be heard behind the door. Peshe and Uncle Yankl entered. Yankl was weighed down with cups and packages, bread and challah. Uncle Shimen had brought all of this over with Peshe to Yankl's for Sabbath. That's what Peshe wanted. On the last Sabbath, she'd be in Ugli—in her own house. Aunt Khashe, all too aware of Yankl's homemaking skills, cooked and contributed fish, soup, stewed vegetables, challah, and bread—just as Uncle Yankl had, in fact, predicted. A Sabbath feast fit for a king.

Peshe immediately started talking things over with Oliana. It was already somewhat late, almost time to light the Sabbath candles. Tomorrow people would come for prayer services. It had been a long time since there'd been a quorum of ten men, and the synagogue room was covered with dust and spiderwebs. What would happen after her departure? Well, that was a lost cause. But for now Oliana should start warming some water and washing and dusting the synagogue room as much as possible. Oliana heard Peshe's requests—and a joy shone from her honest peasant eyes. She would do it right away. In fact she would do it immediately. She would also wash the floors and wipe the windows. It wouldn't take long. Her hands had been hungry for proper work.

Throughout Peshe's conversation with Oliana the cat stood at Peshe's feet, rubbed against her clothes, and purred with docile contentment.

At the Friday night supper Uncle Yankl beamed with joy. Reykhl's four tall brass candlesticks, previously hidden on a shelf in a side corner and covered with green mold, now stood on a table covered with a thin, worn, but very white tablecloth. Opposite them had been placed two not very large challahs with decorative braids on their spines. A tidy, thin cloth, bordered by extended fringes and embroidered with red, covered the challahs. On the cloth: the entire text of the Kiddush. This cover was a remnant of the fragile Reykhl, from her gifted, fine hands—sewn way back in the years of her girlhood. The brass candlesticks shone with a golden mirrorlike gleam, and the four burning candles, their flames shining downward, were reflected in them. Yellow sand was neatly spread on the floor. The three children had their hair washed and wore clean, mended undershirts and shirts.

The devoted Oliana had made all of this ready for the Sabbath. She'd wanted everything to look beautiful for her boss and the Sabbath to be a success. She also brought a fresh shirt to Yankl and cleaned his Sabbath kaftan, which he hadn't laid eyes on for quite some time. She told him to wear it because of the guests. Yankl sang the Song of Solomon in a loud, beautiful voice. During the meal he spun his colorful plans of everything he'd do when Beylke, his Beylke who would never forget her father, would send him a fifty. He would clothe the children and also have something made for himself for the winter, and he would hire a teacher for the children. He had to leave Ugli. What good was Ugli to him when he was born in Dakhtervitsh, where every peasant was like a brother to him and every stone on the path knew him, was like family to him? And he would cover the roof of his home, and all would be well . . .

Yankl's heart was filled with joy. It wasn't so bad here on God's earth, eh? What did she, Peshe, have to say? No, it wasn't bad at all.

And a bit of brandy stood on the table in a narrow-necked, round-bellied green bottle, and the ever-festive pauper didn't need much to forget himself. One glass and done. "To life, Peshe! To life, Dineh! To life, kids! Well? Be happy in your kingdom, guardians of the Sabbath, guardians of the Sabbath, guardians of the Sabbath."

The children sang along with their hoarse voices. Dineh forgot herself and started to sing along with the refrain, at first quietly to herself, then with more enthusiasm, together with the children: "Guardians of the Sabbath, guardians of the Sabbath."

While seated, Peshe doled out the portions and served the plates to each person in order of age. Grulya shuffled under the table around her feet, eating everything Peshe gave her and purring happily.

Oliana set up the only bed of superior quality in Yankl's home for Peshe. Henye and the other children came to bring Dineh over to their house to sleep. Dineh was delighted with this invitation. Peshe now felt homesick for her neighbors with whom she'd never been close—not out of hatred but out of caprice that stemmed from a traditional sense of snobbery. She now realized how childish and foolish her behavior had been toward good, decent folk. When you dwell securely in one place you sometimes allow yourself to indulge in such foolishness. Still, she couldn't speak openly about having given herself airs all these years. That would have been out of character. Entering their house, as she'd done during the last few days in the village, and speaking with them—that, yes. So she went over to Itke and Khishe and even drank a glass of tea with them, which both women offered with great humility. Khishe, whose eyesight was now quite weak, asked her daughter-in-law, Itke, who leapt about on a crutch, to check whether the glass was clean and to wash the spoon again. She wanted to make sure they were offering Peshe the jar with the better quality of little cherries. The first batch of jam had come out runny so she'd cooked a second one—hopefully they wouldn't need it;

in a house with kids, may they be well. But, God forbid, it did sometimes happen that they needed a spoon of jelly. Her Velvele, may he just be with her for many years, sometimes got tired, poor thing, after a bout of hiccups. They tricked him, mixing a spoon of the syrup in a glass of cold water, and it seemed to him that it had brought the color back to his face.

And Peshe drank the tea with the little cherries. She praised the syrup and pointedly avoided talking about the more intimate matters slithering from her heart on a direct path to her tongue, and that she had to gulp down . . .

Afterward the women and children spoke with great enthusiasm about how Peshe came to drink tea with them . . . and how she praised the jelly.

To that the elderly Peyse retorted: "A glory for the Jews! The noblewoman lowered herself, put aside her pride, and drank tea at the blacksmith's house. The Messiah must be coming soon. Nothing less . . ."

He said it without rancor, because in his home they all remembered the good heart that beat beneath Peshe's stiff ribbons . . .

In Peyse's small house, Peshe's footsteps still reverberated, echoes of a time of misfortune and danger when she, Peshe, had cast aside all her caprices, the way a child throws down a toy that he's sick of.

Peshe told Henye to thank her grandmother for inviting Dineh to sleep over at her place. But Henye replied: "We should thank you that she's coming."

That night Dineh slept with Henye again. They hugged and talked almost until dawn. For both children life was pounding on the door, as if through a fog. There was so much that was incomprehensible, so much painful sweetness laced with childish, nostalgic sadness! With their chatter each tried to explain to the other what was awaiting them so far away . . . and was so inconceivable. Until, tired of talking and all that hadn't been said, they began to recite the Shema bedtime prayer—Henye, faster and quieter; Dineh, slow, counting the words and thinking about their meaning—and they both fell asleep.

It was Itke who woke them up. "Henye, get up! Everyone's going to services." There was chicory covered on the hearth, and butter cookies rested in the small dairy cupboard wrapped in the red-bordered cloth. Itke told Henye to see to it that Dinehle had a taste.

When Peshe got up, Oliana had already been in Yankl's house and brought in hot chicory with boiled brown milk. Peshe had a quick breakfast and got dressed. She took a prayer book that Oliana had wiped so carefully and thoroughly that not a speck of dust remained and entered the synagogue room.

The abandoned room that only yesterday had been dusty, dark, and forgotten displayed an entirely new face in the Sabbath morning light. The floor—freshly washed; the panes—clear, sparkling. The pictures on the wall, the curtain of the Holy Ark, the benches, the long table, the chandelier were all revived like a once-parched grassy field after a good, sustained rainfall. A white tablecloth covered the long table. The bookcase gleamed with cleanliness; the spines of the sacred books shone with their old, lustrous, worn leather and with the etched, old, golden letters . . .

Peshe sat alone on a long bench at the table with a heavy heart and an even heavier mind as her thoughts jostled against each other like the currents of a river during a storm. Each tried to find a way to the bank but were flung back into the whirlpool.

The door opened and her sister-in-law Khashe's kind face appeared. As if pulling herself out of a heavy nightmare Peshe stood up to greet her with a friendly "Good Sabbath, Khashe."

"Good Sabbath to you, Peshe. I rushed over, thinking I'd be late. But—no one's here," she responded.

"Have a seat, Khashe. You must be tired from your walk."

"I'm not tired, but I do have to sit down. I'm no longer young, praise God." A deep sigh wrenched itself from her heart. "He probably knows what He's doing."

Peshe's face was covered by a dark shadow. She knew all too well what these words meant. The devout mother was surely remembering Mikhliye, her daughter, her sapling, who had died such an untimely death. Khashe's sorrow encircled Peshe's heart like an unyielding ring of fire. In recent days she'd had enough time to weigh everything she achieved in the thirty years she spent in this settlement. A powerful feeling of regret came over her as if she were responsible for the pain that now covered the face of her sister-in-law. Khashe's pious, weeping mother's heart was seeking the meaning of God's ways that lay behind a high iron door that the eyes of a sinful human being could not penetrate.

A squeak of the door lifted the two women out of their somber moods. Sholem's sister from Stanki entered. "Good Sabbath, all. The men are standing and chatting outside. It's time to start the service. By the time we make it all the way home, through the little forest—well, it's rough going now. The mud—it takes an hour just to find a passable road. It's high time they start the service."

Soon men and women started to congregate. People greeted Peshe warmly with a "Good Sabbath" and began the prayers. Uncle Yankl was called to lead the service.

TWO FIGURES IN BLACK

But before he could start the door squeaked, and all heads turned toward it. People went quiet. Two strangers entered: a young Christian woman and a four-year-old girl, both dressed in black. From the mother's young, refined, narrow, and soft face burned two large, terrified eyes. The girl, with the same terrified eyes as her mother, had bright, straight hair that hung around her scrawny child's face. The young woman made her way between the men and went directly to where the women were sitting. She scanned the faces and then approached the person she'd been looking for: Peshe.

"*Pani* Solomova, I came to ask for your forgiveness. Please don't curse us anymore by candlelight. My husband sinned—he drove you out of your home. And so you cursed him, and he was taken young from the world. And after him our son, Yoshka. On more than one night I soaked the pillows with my tears, pleading with him: they'll curse you. They have a strong God—He freed them from Egypt; He split the sea for them; He covered the sun for them. Look, be careful, I pleaded with him—remember what the Gospel says—my husband just laughed at me—but when a stomachache took hold of him he wasn't laughing anymore. He screamed, cried, and prayed for someone to save him. 'The Yids cursed me,' he screamed. He realized it was too late. His mother had predicted that they would light candles and damn him and his children—he had laughed at all of it—and my hands and feet trembled. He, the father, deserved it. But my child left the world an innocent."

After she said this she fell to the ground, her tears overflowing, to Peshe's feet and kissed the hem of her dress. "Have pity on me, *Pani* Solomova. You're a mother yourself—for myself, I don't care. My life is ruined in any case. But my one and only little girl, my Helenka, she coughs through the night and says strange, terrifying words. She talks to her dead little brother. During the day she doesn't eat and walks around in a trance. I can feel that she's cursed, that she'll be taken from me like my Makar, like my Alyoshka."

She fell into a fit of weeping, choking on her tears: "*Pani* Solomova, as your God is dear to you, let my daughter remain to me. It'd be better if you cursed me, but just don't take her from me . . . Let your husband return—take back everything that's yours. What do I need it for? I didn't lack for anything at my father's house." She continued to weep, becoming breathless in the process.

Peshe bent down to her and helped her stand—her whole body was trembling. She took her by the hand and led her out of the synagogue room and into the street. "Calm yourself. Don't cry. Please. We don't curse anyone over candlelight. We're not allowed to curse anyone by candlelight. We bless over candlelight. Go home and be at peace. I wish your child a speedy recovery."

The young woman again fell to her feet and kissed her hands. "If you could just imagine my nights, when she coughs and starts to call out to my Alyoshka. The lamp below the icon doesn't burn with as much sorrow as my heart burns then. The Holy Lord's Son, who hangs over her little bed, didn't feel greater pain at the crucifixion than I feel on those nights."

Once again Peshe eased her up from the ground. "Stand up, Makarova. Take the child to a doctor. He'll give you a remedy, and she'll get better."

"Makar's mother says that only you can help me. She knows. She's old. She knows sorcery too. She told Makar and me that you would curse us—and so it was. Now, she says, take your child by the hand and go to Solomova. Go on the Sabbath when they pray, when her heart is turned to God, get down on your knees in front of her, and ask for her forgiveness. And if she forgives you, your child won't die . . ."

At that, Peshe lay her hands on the child's blonde head: "May your child get well soon. I forgive you with all of my heart. May God forgive you everything."

When Peshe returned to the synagogue room people stared at her, their mouths gaping and their eyes filled with questions. No one said a word. Silently they started the prayer service, only the women sighed a bit more heavily and wiped their noses with the edges of their Sabbath shawls.

People had prepared a Kiddush after prayer services for Peshe at home. The whiskey and tortes were prepared yesterday and then sent to Yankl.

Everyone sat down around the long table. A few would have liked to say some suitable remarks on Peshe's behalf, something that would serve as words of farewell. But that didn't happen. The air around the table was leaden. Heavy and gray. The young mother's shadow was cast before their eyes. What everyone wanted to forget now swam back up—onto the long table, the walls, the Holy Ark, the sacred books in their cases. Everything testified to the rupture of a home, a family, lives, and banished souls. Suddenly the assembled were left seated around the table like mourners . . .

On Sunday morning the gentile men and women from the village, and also many from nearby villages, accompanied Peshe from Ugli, kissing and weeping—until Vasil roared at Oliana that it was enough. "Leave Dinka alone! Don't kiss her so much! You'll suffocate her! And the horses won't stand still!"

And he flicked the whip over the horses—but what did he have against them, the mute beasts? And besides them, did he have anyone? After all, he usually unburdened his bitter heart to them. But now the lash of the whip wasn't meant for them but for himself. Now he would have wanted to flog and hurt himself. Because how else could he spit out what was now causing his heart such pain? He wouldn't cry. Vasil was no Jewish woman. Over a glass of brandy—that was something else. When you get drunk you can indulge in crying. But now—with the tears choking him—he would have liked to utter the kind of word that would turn the earth upside down and swallow up everything, himself included. And as his tongue was mute and he felt smaller than an ant, and with everything that was causing him distress, the whip in his hand became something of a savior. The horses unexpectedly broke out of their very calm gait and left the group of people behind.

Through a thin fog of dust people looked at the wagon that took Peshe and Dineh from Ugli. Vasil soon loosened his grip on the reins, and the horses went back to their slow trot and rocked the light wagon from side to side. Their hooves knew the road well, and Vasil and his two riders were left to their thoughts . . .

As they left the village, saplings on both sides of the road bent like young gentile village girls waiting for their local young men.

In her heart Dineh bade farewell to each small tree. She saw every one of them bow their heads to her as they responded: "We'll miss you too."

GRULYA RUNS AFTER THEM

Lost in her dreams, Dineh thought she heard meowing . . . No way! But instead of counting and saying goodbye to the trees, she now cocked her ear in the direction of the squeaking wheels. Was she just imagining it? She decided to listen even more intently. And it wasn't long before she once again heard the meowing. "Mama, do you hear?"

But Peshe didn't hear anything. Neither did Vasil.

"Mama, I think it's Grulya!"

Hearing "Grulya," the cat felt at home and responded with a more confident and robust "Meow!"

Vasil stopped the wagon, got down from his seat, and saw Grulya right next to the back wheels. He wanted to strike her with his whip, but the cat looked him in the eye so directly that it cut through his heart. He spat on the ground and said: "That old carcass—she wants to go to America too."

They resumed their journey. Afraid of Vasil's whip, Grulya had fled behind a tree on her limber feet and again started running after them and meowing. So Peshe told Vasil to stop the wagon and bring Grulya inside. Dineh took the cat in her hands and caressed it until she fell asleep happily over her knees.

Peshe didn't stay long in Kapyl'. She said goodbye to all the members of Roda's household and told Dineh to do the same. Time was wasting. It was a long way to Pesatshne, and they would have to ride in darkness. With tears in her eyes Dineh stood silently, not knowing how to start. Peshe's rushing was making her even more upset—until Shprintse came to her rescue.

"Well, Dinehle, travel safe. But don't forget to write. You write such beautiful letters," Shprintse said. She gave Dineh a light kiss on both cheeks.

After Shprintse, Roda approached and, weeping quietly, kissed Dineh. "Travel safe, my child. May God grant you all you are worthy of."

Standing in a queue behind Roda were Noske and Rivele, whom Shprintse had sent over to say goodbye. They both offered her their hands and kissed her. They left the house, and the entire household followed them to the wagon.

With averted eyes Dineh moved to walk past Motl and proceed directly to the wagon. But Motl blocked her path and asked, "What, Dineh? You don't want to say goodbye to me at all?"

Her eyes now lowered to the ground, Dineh answered: "What's the use of saying goodbye?"

"You're weird, Dineh. What's that mean? Why does anybody say goodbye?"

"I don't know."

Motl offered her his hand. Dineh didn't take it. She stood and looked down.

"Well, Dineh? Travel safe."

"Maybe they'll turn me away from the port."

"Don't be ridiculous! You're healthy. They won't turn you away."

Dineh was sad and angry. "Don't you want them to turn me away?"

Motl pushed his hand closer. "Well, travel safe, Dineh. Give me your hand."

Dineh felt a hot blush spreading over her face. She lowered her head even further so that Motl wouldn't see how red she must now be. She gave him her hand—and immediately withdrew it, as if from a fire. She approached the wagon and sat down. Vasil handed Grulya to her. Dineh took the cat onto her lap and turned her face away so that no one would see the tears stinging her eyes. Motl shouted after her: "I'll write you letters, Dineh. And you write back."

The road to Pesatshne stretched out long before them, seemingly without an end. And if someone had asked Dineh if she wanted it to end she might well have said no. She was both saddened and gladdened when she thought about how Motl had spoken to her and how bashful she was when he took her hand—what a sweet shiver went through her body when her hand touched his for a moment. But he was bad, in any case, that Motl. He said that they wouldn't turn her away from the port. He wanted her to go. Why are people so strange that nothing bothered them? But here she was holding Grulya in her lap—such warm devotion, such longing for home, such not-wanting-to-be-parted. And all this from a cat, a mute creature who had more devotion within her than a person. With this thought the dozing cat became closer and dearer to her. Dineh snuggled up to Grulya positioned between her knees and caressed her with tenderness.

AT FAYTL'S

Their first joyful encounter at Faytl's was little Reyzele, a chubby baby with dimples in her soft, rosy cheeks and a happy, laughing face. Malkeh herself seemed much happier now. Faytl too looked more content and in a better mood. Peshe immediately began making preparations to leave. She baked and dried zwieback soaked in black beer and sprinkled with cinnamon. She also dried some cheese, baked fruit layer cake, and packed lemons, garlic, and onions.

To the extent possible Dineh tried to intertwine reality with dream. Surely something would happen and she wouldn't go. When Zisl the teacher's wife, Dvoyrehle, who now plucked the feathers even more quietly, reminded her "Dinehle, you'll write us? We'll miss you," Dineh felt as if these words were grabbing hold of her. What do they want from me? Why are they reminding me? Do all of them really want me to go? Who knows? Maybe I won't go.

But Dineh couldn't fool herself for long. Each day served to remind her more and more that the unavoidable was approaching. The packages and baskets around her seemed to be multiplying before her very eyes. When her mother asked which dress she wanted to wear for the journey and which she wanted to pack, something rent inside her heart. She didn't answer.

"What's taking you so long to answer?"

"It doesn't matter to me."

But when Peshe blew up at her—how can a girl be so careless and walk around as if she were at a stranger's wedding?—and when the poison dripped from Peshe's mouth, Dineh finally told her mother to leave the flowered dress and the flowered shawl unpacked and out for her.

"You'll be cold in such a thin dress."

So Dineh indifferently chose a warmer dress. "Will this one work?"

Dineh became very sad. It was true, then, that she would be going. Mama had said that as early as tomorrow they'd be going to Slutsk and from there—directly to Horodzshe and the train.

Dineh crossed the courtyard to Zisl the teacher's house to say goodbye to her two lonely friends. It seemed to her that only they could sense how heavy her heart was. They too were utterly desolate. How could they be left alone in their old age without a child, without anyone? She went in and sat down next to Dvoyrehle and waited for Zisl to finish his lesson. When the children went home Zisl went into the kitchen. Dvoyrehle stood up and asked: "Dinehle, you'll eat supper with us before you leave, won't you?"

Now Zisl was the one who wanted to lighten the heavy mood at the table. "Well, Dvoyrehle, did you cook a good supper? Dinehle is an important guest here today—no joke! She's going all the way to America. And who knows how rich she might be some day. We have to be good to her, Dvoyrehle. If we're not she won't send you a golden chain or write you letters in English . . ."

For a moment Dineh's heart became warm and light. What did she want more than to cheer up these two lonely people? "I'll send you. I won't forget."

With sadness, Dvoyrehle buoyed Dineh. "Of course, Dinehle. May God only give you what your golden heart deserves—but now, you're leaving."

Dineh's sadness returned, and she confided in her friends: "They might still turn me back from the port . . ."

In the same breath, Dvoyrehle and Zisl said: "What are you talking about? God forbid! You're a healthy child, no evil eye."

Dineh stood up, placed a foot on the bench, untied the sock band, pulled the sock down, and showed: "See, Dvoyrehle, I have symptoms on my leg."

Dvoyrehle took the lamp in her hand and bent down to look at Dineh's leg. "Do you want have a look too, Zisl?"

Dineh edged her leg closer to Zisl, as if he were an expert. She hoped that their verdict would come down to her detriment. They both looked at her leg, considering one side under the lamplight and then the other. Dineh looked up at them with a pounding heart.

Zisl straightened up, combing his meager beard between his gaunt fingers. "Who knows? Is it possible to know? Whichever way their whim moves them—that's what they do. Sometimes they let in one person with trachoma and send back someone else with the smallest dot on the body. Well, did your mother consult the doctor?"

"No. There they only ask about trachoma. He's not an expert in anything else. Reb Zisl, do you think they'll send me back?"

"God forbid!"

Dineh pulled the sock back up and realized that she had shown her naked leg to a man, an old man. A hot blush spread across her face. She quickly brought her leg down and hid it beneath her dress. "I have to go now."

"Be well, Dinehle. Thank you for coming. Tomorrow, with God's help, my old lady and I will come over to say goodbye to your mother."

Dineh quickly left the house. She fought back the tears.

In Faytl's home they didn't get to sleep until daybreak. They discussed how they would divide up everything left behind after Peshe's departure. Faytl said he'd take care of it all.

Dineh went to bed early—both because the wagon was coming early and they'd have to travel the whole day and also so that she wouldn't hang around looking sad and lost in thought like someone distraught. Peshe was quite upset by Dineh's indifference to the whole matter of America. "What will become of this girl there? I don't know. I wish we were both already settled there. I don't know what kind of scene she'll make during the trip. It's like dealing with a simpleton, and she barely hears what you say to her . . . And to set out with that onto the road. I just hope I don't mix things up and give the wrong answer at the border or the port of entry . . ."

TO THE OTHER SIDE OF THE WORLD . . .

Throughout the night Dineh tossed and turned in bed, unable to sleep. She recited the Shema bedtime prayer with tears in her eyes and again prolonged the words of *ha-Mapil* . . . Tomorrow she'd be leaving. Where and how were hard for her to imagine. But she would be leaving this place forever. What would happen afterward? That was something she didn't think about. Some kind of eternal, endless path led to the other side of the world . . . To get there you had to travel and roll in the dark forever, as if through concealed caves that she had read about in the Pentateuch . . . In her weary imagination Dineh envisioned the dark, long abyss . . . Her head turned. It seemed to her that she was descending, along with the bed and pillow, further and further into that abyss, where the endless road would need to start tomorrow . . . With these thoughts and with her hands clutching the pillow she fell asleep. It was Peshe who awakened her.

"Wake up, Dineh. The wagon is coming at 7:30. They shouldn't have to wait for us."

Dineh started awake and quickly sat up, gripped by fear. At first she didn't understand what her mother was saying to her, but gradually she remembered everything that was happening here. A shiver went through her body, cutting down to the bone. She had to get dressed. The wagon was coming soon. There was no time to think.

She got dressed, washed, and recited the blessings in a whisper. The table was set. She didn't linger long at the table. She needed Faytl to give her the key to the store. She'd forgotten something there. She had to go back but would soon return. Faytl went with her to the store. He sensed what was drawing Dineh so abruptly to the store. After he opened the door for her, Faytl stayed outside. Behind a wall in the iron shop, little white-furred Goldetske was spending her last years, moving around with difficulty on her thin little legs. Mostly she lay there the whole day, only looking up with her teary, red little eyes when Faytl brought the saucer of food. Or when someone called her name.

Now Goldetske lay in her corner, bedded down on a blanket and breathing heavily in her sleep. Snuggled up against her was Grulya, feeling like a vagabond who had found a slice of home and rest after a period of long, lost wandering. Grulya made sure that a mouse's rustle was never heard through the walls or the floor of the shop. Old and tired, it was a bit hard for her to move around and, like little Goldetske, Grulya dozed during the day in the warmth that spread from the oven or—on the warm days—in the rays of sun that were cast into the back room of the store through the cracks in the wall. Now they were both lying in the sweet sleep of early morning. Dineh got down on her knees before them. The two small creatures were as dear to her as the days and years of the childhood she was now leaving behind like a dream in tatters. She bent her head toward them, snuggling her face in the warm fur of their slumbering forms. Tears poured from her like a warm rain on a summer field. The cat stood up, raised its back like a shaft bow, and stretched its front, then back, legs. She straightened up and considered Dineh, as if in surprise. Then Grulya began rotating around Dineh's knees and purring, as if to say: it is a bit early, to be sure, and you did take me from my sleep, but still, you are an important guest . . .

For Goldetske, given her age, Dineh's early morning visit came more as a dream than reality. Her teary eyes blinked and opened through her sleep. Then she drowsily grumbled and once again closed her eyes. Dineh positioned herself on her knees and felt the warmth of her two old friends . . . until Faytl's voice jolted her as if from a trance: "Come, Dineh, it's getting late."

Startled, Dineh stood up, like someone caught in the act of theft.

When they entered the house, Yisroel the wagon driver stood with the whip-cane under his arm. Peshe scolded Dineh: "What got into you—running off like that into the shop at the crack of dawn? And here people have to stand and wait."

Without a word Dineh got dressed. Malkeh took her by the hand. "Come, Dinehle, let's kiss each other goodbye."

And she covered Dineh's face with tears and kisses. Like two good sisters who understood each other without having to say a word, they embraced and bid each other farewell. Then Malkeh, arm in arm with Dineh, entered the bedroom. There little Reyzele lay awake in her cradle, flailing her baby hands and feet into the air, cooing like a young dove to herself and playing with the early morning rays of sun over the cradle. They stood for a moment. But Reyzele quickly noticed the guests and picked herself up as if she were ready to jump out toward them.

"Reyzele, do you see? Dinehle is about to leave. Say goodbye to your aunt."

Dineh took the child with trembling hands, kissed her, and then put her back. But Reyzele didn't want to stay lying down. She pulled herself toward Dineh and squirmed. Malkeh took the child in her hands. "Well, all right, Reyzele, we'll take you out. We'll walk Grandma and Dineh to the wagon."

Outside, small groups of neighbors and acquaintances were gathered to say goodbye. Dvoyrehle held something in a small, white bag.

"Here you go, Dinehle; you'll have a bite to eat on the train. To make the nausea go away. God forbid, I've never ridden on a train, but they say that it presses under the pit of your stomach and makes your head spin. No joke, how it races forward the way that it does. Here you go, Dinehle; give some to your mother too. A little bit of gooseberry preserves. It's cut up. You can eat it like a candy. It's cooked stiff. And a bit of hard cheese and two lemons."

Dineh heard everything as if from a great distance. Her head was spinning—these two poor, good people had surely taken from the savings set aside for their daily needs to buy all of this. In the commotion around the covered wagon she drew Dvoyrehle a bit to the side and told her with bashful, quiet words: "You've spent money on me. You shouldn't have. But if they turn me away from the port, I'll sew at Roda's house in Kapyl′ and I'll be able to help you."

"May God protect you, my child. May you and your mother arrive in good health as you join your father in America. You'll be respectable there, God willing.

My Zisl always tells me that you, Dinehle, would have been a great rabbi if you hadn't been born a sinful woman. Write us a letter—you'll bring happiness to our dark hearts . . ."

Suddenly she remembered something. "Do you hear, Dinehle? It's good that I remembered. I had it on my mind the whole time, but my head, I wouldn't wish it on anyone, is distracted. Do you hear, Dinehle? You'll arrive in Horodzshe, where you'll stand at the station by the track and you'll wait for the train . . . Do that, all right? Look, Dinehle—like this . . ."

She pushed apart the fingers of both of her hands and spread them along the length of her face. She inserted her two thumbs in her ears and, with the longest finger, firmly closed her eyelids.

"Do you see, Dinehle? You can do this? Well, try right now. I'll watch . . . Good, Dinehle, that's the way . . . Well, did you hear anything?"

"No. I didn't hear a thing."

"And did you see anything?"

"When you close your eyes with your fingers, you don't see anything . . ."

"Good, Dinehle. Will you remember? When you stand by the train tracks and hear a faraway whistling and sustained banging, you'll know that the train is coming . . . If you close your eyes right away and stuff up your ears just like I showed you, you won't get scared, God forbid. When the train came to Horodzshe for the first time some twenty years ago, we went to have a look. When we were all standing there, one of us, a young married woman, kept her eyes open. When she saw how such a huge, black mass was flying and turning so quickly like a snake and with its whistling and banging, she was so terrified that she fainted. Wow, did that create a commotion! But if you remain standing the way I showed you, God willing, nothing will happen to you."

Voices rang out: "Dineh! Dineh!" Faytl and Malkeh came up to her and took her by the hand. "Mama's already in the wagon! Hurry!"

They quickly said goodbye, and Faytl lifted her up into the wagon. Peshe made room for her.

Everything spun around Dineh like a ring of fire. Vertigo seized her. Her heart felt like pounding hammers. The image of the train, sliding like a black snake and whistling and banging from a distance, now roiled her frightened imagination. Through closed eyes Dineh saw large, black, clattering monsters flying upon her with terrifying speed, squeezing her and swallowing her whole. She did what Dvoyrehle had told her to do when the train came. With clenched eyes and ears she leaned against Peshe's shoulder. In that way she rocked in the large, dark covered wagon, utterly adrift, like someone reading the Book of Job during the period of mourning.

In Slutsk, Yisroel the wagon driver brought the horses to a stop near the home of the lawyer Aba Raskin. In early evening his grand courtyard and red-brick edifice looked like a great, dark specter, with thousands of fiery eyes flashing through the many windows and between the tree branches to the darkness outside.

Peshe went in and immediately came back out, accompanied by Raskin. "Everything will go well. And the stagecoach will come at around nine."

OUTSIDE OF THE CITY, IN THE WIDE-OPEN FIELD

Next to a long structure without walls, Yisroel's covered wagon once again came to a stop. Under an extended red roof supported by four wide, quadrangular pillars, people waited—and all around them and at their feet were packs, bundles, and bags. Women wrapped in shawls stood over the packages and guarded them fiercely. They kept repeating the names of their children, who were either sitting on the packages like hens on their perches or running around the legs of the adults. The mothers anxiously maintained their vigilance so that, God forbid, a child wouldn't vanish out from under them before the stagecoach arrived and so the packages wouldn't get mixed up with someone else's—their neighbor's—packages.

Dineh crawled out of the covered wagon. Peshe told her to sit on the large basket and to keep an eye on the packages. She'd settle the bill with the wagon driver. As if sleepwalking, Dineh sat down on the large basket. She felt nauseous to the core. She felt a physical revolt at the scene all around her—like Gypsies without homes . . . but with one key difference—the Gypsies roamed freely in the forest and fields, while today there was such restriction, with all of the packages and bundles and the filthy covered wagon. And now here they were under a long roof with strange women and children . . . What connection did she have with these people and everything that was happening around her? Her innate pride revolted within her. It caught in her throat, in her nostrils, and in her heart—like after a bad meal . . .

Peshe came over to where Dineh was sitting to rest. "I wish we were already there. This ordeal can drain you of all your strength. Are you hungry, Dineh?"

"No. Who can eat?" She felt a suffocating odor around her and started shivering.

"Are you cold?"

"No, I'm not cold."

"That's all we need, for you to get sick, God forbid. As if I don't have enough to deal with."

"I won't get sick. Don't worry."

Shortly thereafter the heavy clopping of horseshoes on the paved road could be heard. Everyone made for their bundles and hastily dragged them from under the long red roof and closer to the road. A high, long wagon with long benches up above was harnessed to four large, beautiful horses. And on the coachmen's seats—two drivers with round caps and sparkling visors, blue short jackets with brass buttons in two rows. They brought the long, high wagon to a clamorous halt. The echo of the bells on the horses' harnesses resounded for a few minutes. Once again the image of the train as Dvoyrehle had painted it for her rose before Dineh's eyes. The stagecoach was nevertheless an image closer at hand: the wheels, the harness . . . in her childish imagination she saw herself flying on a chariot with four gray horses—not massive, landbound horses but rather silver-maned horses on supple legs, their heads held high. They were carrying her way up into space, through paintings of silver clouds . . . And the chariot on its light wheels had rose-blue wings . . .

The stagecoach was comprehensible, even though it had heavy wheels and larger, broader horses with heavy horseshoes on their firm legs, strong as brick buildings. But the train that would rock like a black snake and fly like a ghost, whistling and banging—of that she was afraid. Her whole body began to tremble. Peshe pulled Dineh close to her. "What's the matter? Are your legs paralyzed? Are you sick?" She placed her hand nervously on Dineh's forehead.

Dineh sat on one of the benches up above in the oddly long wagon, resting her head against Peshe's shoulder and holding on to her with her hand. With the harness bells clanging, the stagecoach jolted into movement. All of the riders abruptly rocked back and forth. Then the road stretched smoothly before the eye between two long rows of poplar trees, and the long, high wagon rocked with the rhythmic steps of the horses. Inside the mood became more relaxed. Children fell asleep in their mothers' laps, others on the packages at their mothers' feet, still others sitting on the benches, their heads rocking sleepily on their shoulders to the rhythm of the wagon that rocked like a cradle . . .

Those who were awake talked among themselves, at first quieter as between strangers. Then they chatted long enough to find out who was going where, on which ship, with how many children . . . They talked and sighed with pious anxiety, invoking God's help in reaching their destination. From the few younger men and youth came more secular talk. They spoke of politics . . .

They rode all through the night. Dineh dreamed of Ugli's green fields, blossoming orchards, and a full barn of hay—and a swing on a rope. She and her girlfriends were swinging and laughing through the wide-open gate of the barn, and the wind lifted their light skirts with every whoosh through the air.

She was jolted awake from a sudden shaking of the stagecoach. She couldn't remember where she was. But soon everything became clear to her. The stagecoach had come to a stop. Women started waking up their children, and a commotion ensued. Everyone looked for what was theirs. Soon the high covered wagon arrived. As if from a nocturnal cave women and children and bags crawled out of it. More wagons drove up and came to a stop in the cold, gray dawn. They sat snuggled together in the cold, each seeking warmth in the person seated next to them. Gradually they adjusted to the situation at hand and began dozing once again while looking with half-open eyes to the doors of the small depot that stood like a fortress with closed shutters and doors.

The station was scheduled to open shortly. Inside they could buy their tickets and, at the same time, warm their chilled-stiff bones a little. As a result, everyone kept an eye on the station.

The period of waiting around the station while seated on luggage seemed to stretch out like an eternity. The dawn meandered in gray fog and didn't want to emerge. The moist air weighed on everybody's heart. Sleep, hunger, and thirst gnawed at the smaller children. They demanded what was owed them. The mothers couldn't find enough hands and words to quiet them all—placing a hand on one child's mouth, yanking the sleeve and body of another. "This isn't home. We're on the road . . ."

Only the little ones didn't understand clearly what their mothers meant. They repeated the same demands but this time with stronger protests against the injustice being perpetrated against them. Now people waited as if for the Messiah himself—until a light cart approached. Someone with yellow buttons on his coat and cap descended. He haughtily passed the luggage and people and, without even looking around, unlocked the door, went inside, and closed it again. People made a dash for the door, but it was now locked from the inside. Still, their mood lifted. They paced back and forth in front of the train station door—until another wagon—more beautiful than the earlier cart—approached, and a man, whose uniform buttons were made of brass and larger than those of his predecessor, exited. This second man had prickly whiskers and wore sharp spectacles. A barbed cockade adorned his round, blue cap. His predecessor opened the door wide for him and immediately undid the shutters from the tall, dusty windows. Once again the group made a dash for the door, but a vulgar word shouted by the man with the smaller buttons pushed them back.

A clock chimed hoarsely. With a tinny, croaking voice the station clock chimed six times. The door now stood wide open. People pushed their way into the station. Mothers shouted to their children to guard the packages and not step away. And they untied their stiffly knotted-together little bags hanging from their necks on thick bands and rummaged through them with trembling fingers for a banknote or a coin. "When your brain is frazzled . . ."

The clerk with the sharp spectacles and whiskers was now standing without his cap. His head was bare and his forehead was ruddy. His even ruddier, fat neck spilled over the stiff, bright blue, velvet collar of his uniform. From a distance, his gaze in and of itself generated such fear that you found yourself drenched in sweat . . .

Their fingers shaking, they approached the small window. The man with the sharp spectacles now stood like an important, precious bird in a cage behind heavy yellow bars, forever reaching out a fat red hand. Like rings around a barrel, three wide gold rings encircled each finger. With this hand he grasped the money that was ready for him. Without looking anyone in the face he spewed out the question consisting of one word and sounding like a stern command: *"Kuda?"*

The little door to the golden cage slammed shut. The man with the smaller buttons commanded everyone to leave the station and head to the tracks. The travelers nimbly did as they were told. Again they took their bags and packages and set them in a long line next to the gleaming, narrow rails of the train track. They got in line, each person behind their baggage, and ordered their children to hold on to their mothers' dresses and not to let go of each other or get scared when the train came.

Everyone stood up straight, like soldiers at their post in the battlefield, ready to meet the enemy's attack. A long roar bellowed from a distance. The ground trembled beneath their feet. Dineh trembled forcefully like a thin tree in a storm wind and rocked forward. Peshe grabbed her by the hand and looked her in the eye: "What's wrong with you? Act like a human being! Look—there are little kids who aren't afraid. Look at how pale she is! Buck up! It's nothing. You'll hear the train coming closer. Close your eyes with your hands, stuff up your ears, and you won't see or hear anything. When we get on board and sit down I'll give you some cherry brandy. You'll feel better."

For a moment Dineh recovered. But with the second roar of the oncoming train, accompanied by a long, ear-piercing whistle, she was again struck with terror. She lowered her head deep into her raised shoulders, like someone in a moment of danger who feels that something is about to fall on her head . . . She stood there, her hands over her face, and plugged up her ears with her thumbs. The sighing and heavy breathing of the train wheels and the locomotive came closer and closer. The whistling rent the dawn air into pieces. The din and banging of the wheels, like the enormous wings of flocks of birds, the heavy panting—all of it scalded the ground beneath Dineh's shaking feet and squeezed tightly like hoops around her heart and around her temples. With a terrible crash the train shook—and went quiet. For a moment stillness reigned all around. The echo of terror and clamor shook the air. The locomotive breathed heavily, like someone expiring, until its last breath was muted.

Peshe pulled on Dineh's arm. "Well? How long are you going to stand there like a pious Jew during the Amidah? The train is right there and ready."

Dineh took her hands from her eyes and saw for herself a kind of wagon made of cast iron with a roof, doors, and windows, something like a house, really, with high steps and set on wheels. The fear slowly ebbed from her heart. In its place unfolded a sense of surprise: it was like a long, black home that flew on wheels over shiny, narrow rails, and it whistled, sighed, and shot out smoke and steam. Was it not then a living thing? Where did it come from?

Turning her head out, like someone suffering from a cold and stiff neck, her gaze devoured the chimney of the locomotive and the locomotive itself. Once again Dineh found herself surprised. In the meantime a stampede around the train was underway. People began to push toward the little stairs of the cars. Peshe took Dineh by the hand. "Come!"

Dineh followed her as if not with her own legs. Peshe pushed her onto the high, narrow little stairs—and up into the train car. Dineh was walking, but she felt as if her legs were about to buckle.

"Walk faster!"

Like a blind person, Dineh felt where she was stepping on the floor with her feet. In the half-dark gray train car, the air was smoky. The bench she sat down on was dusty and filthy. She looked down and saw spit on the floor. In disgust she raised her feet under the bench so they wouldn't touch the floor. Peshe sighed heavily. "Thank God. At least we're in the car."

Dineh choked on the foul, smoky air. A chill emanated the bench she was sitting on and went through her clothing to her body. She shivered lightly, as if from the touch of a cold, alien hand.

The din of the surroundings—the mothers and their children pushing each other, eager to grab seats—settled down somewhat. By now people were sitting on the cold, filthy benches and somehow beginning to make themselves comfortable and feel at home. Mothers took food out from the white bags and offered it to their children—this one an apple, another a piece of a roll. And soon they all sat quietly and expectantly. A many-buttoned conductor walked through, calling out to the riders to be ready.

The mothers again embraced their children, telling them to hold on to each other, not to be afraid. At first a slow, then rapid, slapping sound was heard, as if from heavy wings, and then there was the locomotive's rumbling, along with its heavy breathing and sighing. And suddenly—a long, resounding roar and whistle. This mixed with the terrified cries of the children. The train tore away from the earth, beginning slowly but then with ever-increasing speed, power, and roar, slapping its path into the distance, into the infinite distance . . .

Trembling, Dineh held on to the bench with both hands. Her head was spinning. Everything before her wobbled. Like the train itself, she was tearing herself from the earth. It was now carrying her on its thousands of crazy-wild wings, accompanied by its terrible, ghastly noises, somewhere far, far away, into an infinite, inconceivable distance . . .

(Completed Mont Roland, Québec, 8/22/39)

(White) Russia and Beyond: On the Art and Life of Ida Maze

An Afterword by Yermiyahu Ahron Taub

"My mother really never left Russia," said Ida Maze's son, Irving Joseph Massey.[1] In *Dineh*, her posthumously published autobiographical novel, we learn why.

Dineh is a pastorale laced in beauty and sorrow and a bildungsroman told from the point of view of a devout girl. Maze's friend, the Yiddish poet M. M. Shaffir, typed the book from Maze's handwritten manuscript and prepared it for publication. Additionally, Shaffir was the secretary of the committee formed to publish the book. The original Yiddish version appeared in 1970. Set in what is now Belarus, Maze's heroine is fueled by her hunger for learning; connection to faith, family, and community; and love of the natural world. The interior mindscape—dreams, visions, fantasies—of the young person occupies a primary place in the book. Throughout one senses the interplay, the creative conversation, between the perspectives of the author looking back on her life and the title character/fictionalized self in the in situ moment. It is particularly in the dialogue spoken by Dineh that we see Maze bringing the voice of the child to the fore, where we can most easily forget the Ida/Dineh divide. Interestingly, *Dineh* contains very few surnames. That absence underscores the book's essential hybridity and lends to it a kind of folkloric feel. We know this is the story of the author's childhood and early youth, and yet . . .

Maze artfully interweaves Dineh's story with portraits of relatives, neighbors, and members of the community, many of them women and girls. We meet the mysterious seamstress Shprintse; Beyle, who leaves home to work as a maidservant in Minsk; and Hinde, who falls in love with a young nobleman, among numerous unforgettable others. Each of their lives takes unexpected turns, and Maze distills these stories to their essential core to heighten the inherent drama therein. In her unflinching examination of the lives of women she writes powerfully about class stratification, thwarted romance, violence (domestic, state-instigated, and otherwise), and the perils of childbirth. Maze's women protagonists are forces to be reckoned with. They work as seamstresses, teachers, field workers, and homemakers even as they

1 YAT telephone interview with Irving Joseph Massey, April 29, 2019.

grapple with oppressive arranged marriages, domestic violence, financial hardship, ailing spouses, and many other trials. Her portrayal of women's lives is remarkable in its candor. Given that the manuscript was completed in 1939,[2] Maze was arguably ahead of her time as well. Today, as societies around the world confront entrenched misogyny and gender oppression, *Dineh* has much to say to contemporary audiences about these themes in an earlier time. Taken as a whole *Dineh* provides a vivid portrait of rural, village, and small-town life in White Russia in the last decade of the nineteenth and early years of the twentieth centuries.

Propelling the novel forward are the tightening noose of tsarist anti-Semitism, the increasing restrictions on Jewish economic survival, and the rising tide of revolutionary movements. The restrictions enacted by the state ultimately lead to the emigration of Dineh and her family and others in her community. The aforementioned Shprintse; Itshe-Mendl and Motl, the sons of Roda and Shmuel-Arn; Haveh, the daughter of Dvoyrehle and Zisl; and Dineh's siblings Itshe and Soreh are just some of the characters who are swept up in the call for social change. Maze depicts the profound systemic injustice that prompted the movement, and she is clearly deeply sympathetic to its goals, yet the novel can hardly be read as an appeal to revolutionary arms. Rather her focus is on the terrible costs the movement takes—the young lives cut brutally short and the loved ones left behind to mourn. In the aftermath of viciously suppressed political demonstrations Maze writes, "Only instead of young footsteps resounding with song there now came stooped, wailing mothers and fathers in search of the torn remains of their children. It was difficult to identify your own child. Most went unidentified." At one such demonstration Dineh's brother Itshe is fatally injured. When Motl speaks of holding a political meeting near Itshe's grave and the importance of looking upon the burial places of fallen comrades, Dineh wonders, "What were strangers doing on Itshe's grave? How did he matter to them? They hadn't even known him."

Maze is also concerned with the lives of non-Jews and relations between Jews and non-Jews. She writes about the lives and traditions of the peasantry with great eloquence. The dire living conditions of peasants is the principal factor that spurs Itshe and others to revolutionary activity. Oliana, who lovingly raised Dineh and her siblings, and her husband, Vasil, play critical—and complex—roles throughout the

---

2 Irving Massey recalls that his mother wrote the bulk of *Dineh* in their apartment in Montreal during a period of prolonged illness, possibly as early as 1936. The "Completed Mont Roland, Québec, 8/22/39" note at the end of the book refers presumably to when and where Maze concluded the draft rather than when and where she wrote the entire book. (Email from Irving Massey to the translator, July 30, 2020.)

novel. The story of Maria Andreyevna and her daughter, Paula, is one of the most harrowing in the book. Their narrative begins with such warmth and beauty and in just a few pages spirals tensely down into hell. Maze innovatively presents the story from the mother's perspective, a distance that only adds to the ultimate devastation. Paraska the madwoman ("the most beautiful peasant girl in the village"), whose lover marries her own sister, leaves home, baby (born out of wedlock) in hand, to escape her father's blows. On the road she faces new and continuous violence in the fields. With his tender care, only Dineh's brother Faytl can break through the layers of Paraska's trauma. Faytl gently leads Dineh to overcome her initial revulsion over Paraska's physical decay.

Maze's book displays, and is arguably predicated upon, a deeply felt gendered analysis. From a very early age the title character has to navigate and struggle against the realities of a patriarchal society. When Dineh asks her brother Itshe what he's studying, Itshe asks, "Would you understand if I told you? A girl is not allowed to know what boys study." Upon her emigration, Dineh's friend Dvoyrehle reports that "My Zisl always tells me that you, Dinehle, would have been a great rabbi if you hadn't been born a sinful woman."

And yet despite obstacles Dineh, with the help of others, finds her way. Even if male characters who care deeply about her, such as Daniel, Itshe, Motl, and Vasil, sometimes tease or disparage her, Dineh charts her own course and remains true to the specificity of her own perspective, her way of seeing and being in the world. Dineh's father, Sholem, recognizes her aptitude for learning. Dineh's educated mother, Peshe, teaches Dineh and her younger brother, Daniel. For all the tension in her relationship with Dineh (that begins seemingly from the moment of her daughter's birth), Peshe clearly takes pride in her daughter's scholasticism. Maze makes clear that it is Peshe who has Dineh stand up in front of the class to recite the Psalms with Yiddish translation. Dineh's drive for Jewish learning surpasses those of her own peers, and her academic talents earn her the admiration of children and adults alike. Her deep religiosity, the anchoring of her very self in the realm of the spirit, is also esteemed by many around her. Dineh, like Peshe before her, comes to read the prayers at services for the women who cannot read. She crafts letters for young wives whose husbands have emigrated, drawing upon her awareness of what lies within the hearts of these women who themselves cannot write.

Thus the reader joins the young protagonist as she moves into knowledge and as she shares her knowledge. And as the novel progresses, what is considered "knowledge" changes—or rather expands. By the book's end we come to see that Dineh's *bildung* stems not merely from her deep scholasticism but also from a growing mindfulness of the harsh realities of life confronting so many in the tsarist realm, as well as from her connection to her family, Roda, Shprintse, Soreh-Rokhl, Zisl and Dvoyrehle, Malkeh Kharash, Henye, and all of the beloveds around her.

In contrast to the many novels on the migration experience that focus on the challenges of adjustment to and acculturation in the New World, the central action of the novel takes place in the Old World. Of course, the fates of the characters who reach America and the letters they send back are crucial factors in the book. Still, when taken as a whole, *Dineh* is arguably more of an emigration, or a pre-emigration, novel rather than an immigration one. Readers experience the love that the title character feels for her world, her profound reluctance to leave it, and indeed the emotional devastation caused by the rupture of emigration. The final chapters of the novel take us deep within Dineh's psyche as she dreads (and resists) leaving the people she loves, the sacred burial ground of her siblings tragically buried so young, and the natural world that has nurtured her so deeply. The current historical moment that is the backdrop to the preparation of this English translation is characterized by profound population upheaval and displacement. Dineh's resistance to departing her home, which for all its numerous challenges and problems she loved so much, offers contemporary readers a fictionalized glimpse of the terrible losses undergone in an earlier historical moment of emigration.

Hayeh Zukofsky (also rendered as Zukowsky and Zukovsky, among other forms) was born to Shimen Zukowsky and Muscha Govezniansky Zukofsky in 1893 in the village of Ugli (also rendered as Ogli), White Russia (now Belarus). She was one of eight children, two of whose deaths are so powerfully depicted in *Dineh*. After emigrating from White Russia in 1907(?),[3] she lived briefly in New York City and then settled in Montreal. She married Alexander Massey (Elyohu Maze) in 1912,

---

3 There is some divergence on the date of Maze's emigration. As of 2021, the article on Maze in the Jewish Women's Archive placed the date as 1905. A paper written in Maze's own handwriting in Maze's collection in the Jewish Public Library of Montreal states that she "came to America with her parents in 1908." Maze's biography in *Idishe dikhterins antologye* (Chicago: Farlag L.M. Shteyn, 1928), which includes some of her poems, also notes that Maze "came to America with her parents in 1908." The *Leksikon fun der nayer yidisher literatur* (*Lexicon of New Yiddish Literature*; New York: Congress for Jewish Culture, 1956) states that she was fourteen years old when she emigrated. The ship's manifest for the S.S. *Noordam* on August 10, 1907, notes that passengers Musche Zukowski (wife, age 54) and daughter Chaje (seamstress, 15) came from Rotterdam. Their last permanent address was listed as Ugli. Their final destination was listed as New York. The evidence for 1907 seems definitive to me, but I modify the date with a parenthetical question mark to indicate the ambiguity.

and they had three sons, Bernard (Ben-Tsien), Earl (Israel; Yitskhok Mordkhe), and Irving Joseph (Yisroel Yoysef).

Ida Maze was a central figure in the realm of Yiddish letters, and her generosity was the stuff of legend. The letter-writing talents displayed by the young Dineh in this autobiographical novel were no less prominent in Maze's adulthood. Indeed, the reader can imagine Maze building and honing her epistolary (and literary) artistry during letter writing done as a girl for women who were unable to do so themselves. According to Irving Massey, she wrote approximately ten letters a day,[4] and certainly her vast collection at the Jewish Public Library of Montreal (JPL) attests to that wide epistolary reach. There one can find letters on a wide range of personal and professional topics. Much of the correspondence centers around Maze's support of other writers. She helped refugees navigate the complex Canadian immigration system and advocated for writers in many different ways.

Maze proved to be a deft and dedicated editor of the books of other poets. She edited and released the poet Yudika's book *Vandervegn* (*Paths of Wondering*; Montreal, 1934) with illustrations by Bezalel Malchi. From 1935 to1937 she edited volumes of *Heftn* (*Notebooks*; Montreal and Detroit). She edited M. M. Shaffir's *A stezhke* (*A Footpath*; Montreal, 1940). In 1943 two of her edited books appeared: S. Z. Shneirson's *Bay dayne toyern* (*At Your Gates*; Montreal) and, with assistance from the poet Benjamin Katz, Freydl Charney's *Freydl's lider* (*Freydl's Poems*; New York). H. Leivick wrote a foreword and Maze wrote an afterword to *Freydl's lider*. In that afterword the thoroughness and emotional intensity that Maze brought to her work is evident. Maze wrote, "I spent a year reading the poems of Freydl's manuscript, and I also wrote out and gathered the poems that appeared in various journals and newspapers, and I can honestly say that this was sacred work for me. There were days when I felt the grandeur of Freydl's poetry upon me more than anything else around me." Maze's[5] efforts on behalf of Freydl Charney's work did not go unheralded. In a review of *Freydl's Poems*, Sh. Tenenbaum writes, "A special thanks to the Canadian Yiddish poet Ida Maze who, for an entire year, carefully transcribed the poems. Her afterword is written with great love and tenderness to a sister-poet."[6] In her own book *Naye lider*

---

4 YAT telephone interview with Irving Massey, May 16, 2019.

5 Ida Maze, afterword to *Freydl's lider* (*Freydl's Poems*; New York: A Committee of Writers and Activists and Freydl's Family, 1943), 343.

6 Sh. Tenenboym, "*A heldin in dikhtung*" ("*A Heroine in Poetry*"), *Di shtime* (*The Voice*), April 15, 1944.

(*New Poems*), Maze wrote a poem for Charney entitled "*Freydl Tsharni'n*" ("To Freydl Charney"; "I never saw you with my own eyes / But through your poems I knew your life as I knew my own").[7] She edited and wrote an afterword to Hanah Shteynberg's *Bleter in vint* (*Leaves in the Wind*; Montreal, 1944).

In taking stock of the accounts of the time, one is struck by how Maze's largesse must have occupied much of her days. In the years 1936 to 1942 she read stories to children in the Jewish Public Library on Saturdays. In an article written a year after Maze's death the poet and writer Rachel H. Korn observes, "Although she herself possessed a fine, refined taste for the slenderest nuance of authentic art, she was always more interested in drawing close the strange, unsuccessful poems, stories, and portraits than the best works of our most eminent artists. She sought to embrace those unsuccessful creations with maternal warmth in order to keep them away from the cold draft winds of the inevitable sharp criticism to come."[8] In his report on Yiddish writers in Canada and America, Hersh Fenster reflects, "From her, Ida Maze, shines infinite goodness, tender motherliness, and her home is always a community council for writers. There is not a single Yiddish writer or poet who comes to Montreal who does not find a way into the home of our poet. She, Ida Maze, stands in consistently warm and friendly contact with a number of Yiddish word artists. She keeps several of them on her mind, is interested in their lives and their creativity. She worries over their suffering and rejoices, like a devoted mother, in fact, in their joy." Fenster also discusses the many letters from "spiritual-creative Yiddish persons" in Maze's possession that serve "as a cultural-historical document of an entire time period."[9] It is striking to me that Fenster chose to highlight Maze's correspondence in his article. Even during her lifetime, then, it is clear that Maze's personal archive—letters written and maintained—and the many acts of magnanimity that took place between (and that indeed fueled) their writing were considered worthy of celebration. As Irving Massey tells it, no one at that time would have used the word "salon" when describing the gatherings at their family home. It was just a matter of people dropping in. There was no such thing as making an appointment. One walked in the door. The telephone was not used. Maze never went to bed before midnight.

7 Ida Maze, *Naye Lider* (*New Poems*; Montreal: Leyen-krayz ba der Idisher folks bibliotek, 1941), 113.

8 Rachel Korn, "Ida Maze," *Der Keneder Odler* (*The Canadian Eagle*), May 26, 1963, 5.

9 Hersh Fenster, "*Mayne bagegnishn mit yidishe shrayber in Kanade un Amerike*" ("My Encounters with Yiddish Writers in Canada and America), *Undzer shtime* (*Our Voice*), Saturday–Sunday, October 26–27, 1957, number 232 (3726), 3.

People were there until 11 p.m. for a "*serye glezlekh tey*" ("a series of cups of tea"). Those with no place to go stayed over at their apartment. Massey does not remember a time when this was not the case.[10] The visual artist Rita Briansky remembers that slabs of chocolate were on offer, with a knife beside them. While people were talking they would scrape away at the chocolate. Briansky remembers that Maze was always "Ida" while her husband was "Mr. Massey." He made tea and chopped liver, and he called his wife "*mayn altitshke*" ("my old lady").[11] Ira Robinson, the historian of Canadian Jewry, noted that "on the one hand, Ida Maze was a remarkable writer, and on the other, a nurturer . . ." Regarding the latter, he stated that "Maze kept an open house for everybody . . . Everybody and their brother's cousin showed up."[12]

Maze's support of Yiddish writers extended far beyond the realm of her apartment and is evident throughout her aforementioned correspondence. Calling her a "great woman among the Jewish people" ("*gedolah be-Yisrael*"), Miriam Karpilove, author of *Tagebukh fun an elende meydl* (*Diary of a Lonely Girl*),[13] expressed thanks to Maze for her "warm interest in an almost unknown person such as myself."[14] Another example of support can be found in letters between Maze and the poet, folklorist, and translator Naftoli and his wife, Zina Gross. In 1941 Naftoli Gross thanked Maze for her beautiful book *Naye lider*. He writes, "I am reading these poems with true pleasure."[15] In a letter to Maze some eighteen years later, and a testament to the longevity of Maze's support, Zina Gross writes, "I thank you warmly for your check of $15 and for all of your struggle and hard work on the distribution of the book of poems by Naftoli Gross. I don't have the words to express my acknowledgment and gratitude for your warm and friendly reaction."[16] Abraham Sutzkever (Avrom

---

10 YAT telephone interview with Irving Massey, April 29, 2019.

11 YAT telephone interview with Rita Briansky, May 19, 2019.

12 YAT in-person interview with Ira Robinson, September 16, 2019.

13 Jessica Kirzane's translation of Karpilove's book was published by Syracuse University Press in 2020.

14 Letter from Miriam Karpilove to Ida Maze, May 15, 1947(?), Ida Maze Collection, JPLM, Correspondence, Miriam Karpilove.

15 Letter from Naftoli Gross to Ida Maze, August 15, 1941, Ida Maze Collection, JPLM, Correspondence, Naftoli Gross.

16 Letter from Zina Gross to Ida Maze, February 8, 1959, Ida Maze Collection, JPLM, Correspondence, Zina Gross.

Sutskever), the renowned poet and editor of the prestigious literary journal *Di goldene keyt* (*The Golden Chain*), called Maze "the keeper of the books for all of Yiddish literature in Canada." He writes, "At the same time, I want you to know that I admire your dedication and friendship to Yiddish writers. If we had more Ida's, we would all be witnesses to a new Yiddish renaissance."[17] During his visit to Montreal in 1959, Sutzkever too spent time in Maze's home: "It will soon be a year since I ate that delicious lunch at your home."[18] Upon the death of Maze's husband, Alexander, Sutzkever wrote her a letter of condolence: "I've only just recently learned of this loss. The news of your husband's death upset me greatly. Just last year we were often together, after all . . . He was a dear, kind man. I don't know how to console you . . ."[19]

A dramatic series of letters from A. Ajzen (Avrom Ayzen; 1909–1958), author of such works as *Shtam un tsvayg* (*Trunk and Branch*; Vilna, 1935) and *Mentshn fun geto* (*People of the Ghetto*; Mexico: Yiddish Culture Center in Mexico,1950), is particularly instructive. In reading these letters, one can see (and sense) the great efforts Maze made to help a Yiddish writer. Her work had life-altering effects. Ajzen reached out to Maze to help him emigrate from Mexico to Canada, and she proved to be a lifeline for him. Ajzen writes, "First, I want to express my deepest thanks for your friendliness and promise to help, if possible, with my coming to Canada . . . Perhaps a Montreal school would bring me as a teacher (I worked for several years in Vilna and Mexico in the Yiddish schools)."[20] In a letter some two weeks later, Ajzen shared some of the realities of his personal situation, his professional goals, and the lengths to which he would go to emigrate: "I don't have any relatives or friends in Canada. Still, I hope to get a job as a teacher of Yiddish or of history, which you will see in the enclosed papers. I could also teach Hebrew. As a last resort, I'll take anything . . ."[21] Throughout their correspondence regarding Ajzen's emigration

---

17 Letter from Abraham Sutzkever to Ida Maze, July 3, 1959, Ida Maze Collection, JPLM, Correspondence, Abraham Sutzkever.

18 Letter from Abraham Sutzkever to Ida Maze, November 24, 1959, Ida Maze Collection, JPLM, Correspondence, Abraham Sutzkever.

19 Letter from Abraham Sutzkever to Ida Maze, April 23, 1960, Ida Maze Collection, JPLM, Correspondence, Abraham Sutzkever.

20 Letter from A. Ajzen to Ida Maze, February 14, 1950, Ida Maze Collection, JPLM, Correspondence, A. Ajzen.

21 Letter from A. Ajzen to Ida Maze, March 2, 1950, Ida Maze Collection, JPLM, Correspondence, A. Ajzen.

from Mexico, the two writers exchanged warm opinions regarding each other's books. In a letter of July 3, 1950, Ajzen asked Maze to intervene on his behalf with a book dealer who had stated his unwillingness to sell his books.[22] Later that month Ajzen writes, "My legal situation is such that I can be banished from the country."[23] Ajzen's mounting desperation reverberates from the courteous, sometimes formal tone of his correspondence. In a letter from November of that year Ajzen notes, "I can't bother you anymore . . . You've already done so much."[24] Ajzen eventually did make it to Canada. He died in Toronto in 1958. These brief excerpts from the extended correspondence between Ajzen and Maze demonstrate the kind of work Maze performed on behalf of Yiddish writers.

Maze's encouragement and support extended beyond the realm of Yiddish letters. Rita Briansky was the recipient of such support. Briansky met Alexander Massey when they were living in a small town in northern Ontario. Massey was a traveling salesman who brought news of Jewish Montreal and read his own poems to Rita's family. When her family moved to Montreal, Briansky walked over to the Mazes' home on Esplanade Avenue to introduce herself. Briansky recalls her first sighting of Maze: "Near her courtyard, I met her, a small black figure, like a bird, bent, and smiling through heavy eyelids, and I fell in love with her at sight; and from then on the Massey home became my second home."[25]

Briansky's family pressured her to study bookkeeping for practical reasons when she wanted to pursue her love of the visual arts. When Briansky became upset at their insistence, her mother called Maze over to intervene. Maze asked Briansky what she herself wanted. She replied that she wanted to finish school and study art. Maze said she could get Briansky babysitting jobs, secondhand books, and an art teacher. Maze arranged for Briansky to meet Alexandre Bercovitch, who became her first art teacher. Briansky called Maze her mentor and surrogate mother.[26]

Maze's generosity is lovingly remembered within her own family as well. Maze's

---

22 Letter from A. Ajzen to Ida Maze, July 3, 1950, Ida Maze Collection, JPLM, Correspondence, A. Ajzen.

23 Letter from A. Ajzen to Ida Maze, July 14, 1950, Ida Maze Collection, JPLM, Correspondence, A. Ajzen.

24 Letter from A. Ajzen to Ida Maze, November 12, 1950, Ida Maze Collection, JPLM, Correspondence, A. Ajzen.

25 Rita Briansky, "Ida Massey—the Person," *The Canadian Jewish Chronicle*, June 14, 1963, 13.

26 Op. cit.

grandson Ephraim Massey shared his memories of his grandmother. Ephraim called his grandmother "Babe" (pronounced BAA-beh) and his grandfather "Zeyde." He visited his grandparents every year at Passover. The seders were long and elaborate, attended by relatives and others he only knew from that one time of year. In Montreal in the 1950s, Ephraim remembers that streetcars ran on Park Avenue, milk was delivered in horse-drawn carriages, and chickens were bled at the market. Maze kept many different foods in the refrigerator. She made blintzes; her husband made chopped liver. When the Masseys were living in Boston, Ephraim's grandparents sent them boxes of food that included such delicacies as pickles, horseradish, Montreal bread, and homemade chicken soup with egg yolks. When his grandfather died in 1960 Ephraim attended his funeral. In the fall of that year the Massey family moved from the Boston area to Montreal. Ephraim spent time with his grandmother during that time. He sometimes stayed overnight in her apartment on Darlington Avenue. He watched television shows, including *The Twilight Zone*. Maze served smoked meat sandwiches and ginger ale. She gave Ephraim money to buy food and candy that he liked. For Ephraim, his grandmother's home was a haven. The last time he saw her was at the Jewish General Hospital. She called him "*mayn kind*" ("my child").[27]

Maze's poems, widely admired in the Yiddish literary realm, were written in a pared-down voice that, with its great depth of feeling, lingers long after reading. Maze authored four books of poetry: *A mame* (*A Mother*; 1931), *Lider far kinder* (*Poems for Children*; 1936), *Naye lider* (*New Poems*; 1941), and *Vaksn mayne kinderlekh* (*My Children Grow*; 1954), which was awarded the prize in children's literature by the Congress for Jewish Culture in 1955. After Bernard's tragic childhood death, Maze wrote a sequence of deeply moving poems that formed the basis of *A mame*. One reviewer asked, "Can one review a mother's grief?" and, regarding several lines from the book, later wrote, "In these lines, the purely personal and private are at last elevated to the poetic."[28] In her debut book the poet expresses her grief in all its fullness and variety. Within its seemingly traditional forms is a joltingly modern undertaking. Beneath and between the elegantly composed lines roils the choreographed howl of an anguish that will not abate. There is no talk of redemption here, no glib consolation. In the poem "*Yortsayt*" ("Yahrzeit") the poet declares, "Today I have a yahrzeit for my child / and light no candle for his soul." Her assertion of the day's significance moves into active "not taking of action": "I weep no more and search no more / and

---

27 YAT telephone interview with Ephraim Massey, June 28, 2019.

28 *Globus* (Warsaw), June 1933, 84.

light no candle for his soul."[29] In her not weeping, not searching, and not lighting a candle, the poet finds a path of nonaction within a whirlpool of grief seemingly without borders.

In this poem questions swirl around the practice of commemoration that the poet refuses to take for granted. Does she find the practice of candle lighting inadequate? Misleading? Furthermore, the speaker's use of "today" make us wonder if on a later day in a later year she did, in fact, light a candle. Perhaps these questions are beside the point. Even as the speaker decides not to light the candle, her naming that decision—the poem itself—becomes a form of yahrzeit.

If in "Yahrzeit" Maze revisits conventions around time, the poem "*Nit keyn blumen*" ("No Flowers") finds her confronting the matter of place (and space). The poet juxtaposes absence ("No flowers, no grass / grow on the grave of my child) with presence ("A small monument—mute stone / stands and looks into gray space"). After a transitional moment, the poem moves from the descriptive to the prescriptive. She calls forth: "Let his grave remain raw / as the wound in my heart / as my child in his black pit / as his shadow is in my home . . ."[30] Like the candles not lit from "Yahrzeit," the flowers and grass function as a forceful absence, a presence outside the borders of the poem. Once again we see Maze refusing the conventions of mourning, resisting any adornment of her sorrow. Given what we know from *Dineh* of Maze's love of nature, this insistence seems particularly wrenching.

The uncertainty of response recorded by that early reviewer of *A Mother* reverberates down to this day. In reading the book we too feel uncertain, unsettled. And yet, in their precision and candor, there is a kind of spartan splendor in the poems of this collection. Even as she calls for rawness Maze locates a motherlode of truth that renders conventional notions of ornamentation irrelevant, even superfluous. Like Briansky, Rachel H. Korn noted the "bent" form of Maze's body in her remembrance. In Korn's conjecture, that positioning of the physical self, that way of moving through the world was a reflection of Maze's acute connection to her dead. Korn writes: "Both her [Maze's] head with its expressive eyes and her body she held bent, as if she wanted to be closer to the earth, to hear the voices that were underground, the voices of her dear ones—her younger little sister Freydele and her eldest son who were cut off from her too early."[31]

---

29 Ida Maze, *A mame* (*A Mother*; Montreal: Idisher kultur gezelshaft, 1931), 34.

30 Ibid., 39.

31 Rachel Korn, "Ida Maze," *Der Keneder Odler* (*The Canadian Eagle*), May 26, 1963, 5.

As Maze continued her writing, her tone expanded considerably. Some of her most delightful poems were for children. In the poems in her second book, *Lider far kinder* (*Poems for Children*; Warsaw, H. Bzshoza, 1936), Maze takes us deep into the inner lives of children, the mother figure often nearby. In "*Mame iz shuldik*" ("It's Mama's Fault"), the child cleverly blames his inactivity (laziness?) on his mother's constant scolding. The speaker of "*Red ikh tsu mayn berele*" ("I Speak to My Teddy Bear") finds solace in his toy when adults do not listen to him. In "Yosele's fraynt" ("Yosele's Friend"), a little boy finds company with an imaginary friend when his mother, with whom he loves to play, is too busy. In "*Ikh bin a kapitan*" ("I'm a Captain"), a child imagines himself traveling as a captain of a ship on a journey to a land of wonder, with his mother alongside him.

In what will come as no surprise to readers of *Dineh*, children speak directly to animals in some of these poems. For example, in "*Af a rayze mit mayn ketsl*" ("On a Trip with My Kitty"), a child imagines faraway voyages with his kitten only to be brought rudely back to reality. In "*Yingl un ferd*" ("Boy and Horse"), a boy engages in conversation with a horse stuck outside in the rain. The poems are often charming and yet sharply observed, poignant, with filaments of keen psychological insight glittering beneath their whimsical exteriors.

Maze's children's poems were well received by her intended audience. In a letter to Maze the Yiddish educator Yosl Mlotek wrote about the joy her book *Vaksn mayne kinderlekh: muter un kinder-lider* (*My Children Grow: Mother and Children Poems*) had brought him and his son. "I read the whole book. Then I read it to my Zalmen, and I must tell you that no other poem has so pleased him as much as '*Mayn kleyninke meydele Suzi*' ('My Little Girl Suzi'). He knows it by heart and takes so much pleasure from it. He also liked the poem about the three little bears very much. In general, the book makes a very good impression." He added, "I hope to be in Montreal this summer. We'd like to spend time with the family in your mountains. We'll certainly see you."[32] The Zalmen that Mlotek was, of course, speaking about was his son Zalmen Mlotek, the future conductor, pianist, and artistic director of the National Yiddish Theatre Folksbiene. In *Vaksn mayne kinderlekh*, Maze included children's poems written throughout her career and published in earlier books. In her preface she stated, "the child was the reason for my origins as a writer. It was to children that I wrote both my joyous and my sad poems."[33] Heightening the sheer pleasure of the *Vaksn mayne*

---

32 Letter from Yosl Mlotek to Ida Maze, June 22, 1954, Ida Maze Collection, JPLM, Correspondence, Arbeter Ring (Workmen's Circle).

33 Ida Maze, *Vaksn mayne kinderlekh: muter un kinder-lider* (*My Children Grow: Mother and* Children's

kinderlekh experience are lovely illustrations by Bezalel Malchi, H. Daniels, and Y. Shaynblum. In reading Maze's poems, one marvels at her capacity to inhabit both the mother and child roles with such totality. It is to the latter that she seems to let go the most, to give free rein to her innate wonder and glee.

Of particular interest to readers of *Dineh* may be the poems from *Naye Lider* (*New Poems*) that Maze wrote about her beloved father. In the novel Maze portrays Dineh's father Sholem's connection to the land, the earth, and the ground beneath as a kind of spiritual love, his true home. Sholem's happiness in nature mirrors and perhaps inspires Dineh's own and seems to deepen her devotion to him. Several poems in this book underscore the daughter-father bond so evident in *Dineh*. In the poem "*Vi sheyn*" ("How Beautiful"), Maze once again brings a fresh perspective to a timeworn topic. Instead of bemoaning the decline of the aging body, she finds beauty. She writes, "How beautiful the footsteps of old age / Careful, slow, and still / . . . Each step an accomplishment on the way to the goal." With that introduction Maze brings the reader to the figure on her consciousness. She declares that she wants to be like her father, "to live and die as he did." She invokes his eighty years "so fruitful, so full." Later, in the poem's final stanza, the speaker expresses a longing "to go as he went, with faith to the sunlit shore." Far from flinching from the inevitable twin embraces of old age and death, Maze reaches for them . . . if they can only be akin to those of her father. The movement of the poem—from the small triumph of each aged step to the sweep of a life fully lived—is rendered possible by the patriarch's "faith and love all the way to tears."[34]

In "*Fun Feld un vald iz dayn shtam*" ("From Field and Forest You Emerged"), Maze charts her father's life path with breathtaking tenderness. The poem, written in twelve four-line stanzas, is startling in its compression. It begins with the speaker passing her father on distant paths, yet his words follow her like "golden rain in a dream." She has absorbed deeply within herself the rustle of thin sounds when her light child's steps followed him. Her father, she notes, tended to his children, cattle, and horses only to find everything slip from his grasp. He swam across oceans in search of his children and his home, leaving behind his way of life, "*di shtam fun dayn gebeyn*" ("the origin of your bones"). At this point in the poem we can visualize the action beyond the borders of *Dineh*, a kind of sequel revealed in verse. Now we observe the impact of uprootedness on someone so dear to her. For here, in a land of "hurry and sway"

Poems; Montreal: Kanader Yidishn kongres, 1954) [9].

34 Ida Maze, *Naye Lider* (*New Poems*; Montreal: Leyen-krayz ba der Idisher folks bibliotek, 1941), 15.

("*impet un shvung*"), he hid his own language beneath his own tongue. And yet, like Job, he never blasphemed, never lost himself in his sorrow.[35] The speaker addresses her father directly; each "he" above is written as "you" or "your." Her homage to her father is constructed in a rhythm of tremendous musicality, an incantatory singsong. Maze's language embodies the twin perspectives of child and adult simultaneously present with us all. While depicting suffering, the poem ultimately finds its equilibrium. Even as the patriarch is uprooted from home and land, he remains rooted in his faith and, as the speaker suggests by extending back to the biblical Job, in the sweep of Jewish textuality and history. By poem's end, as at *Dineh*'s, the reader is welcomed, like the needy and the poor of Montreal, into Maze's circle of light, where family, community, and society—and time itself—are necessarily entwined.

I touch upon some of Maze's poetry in this afterword to give readers of *Dineh* a brief taste of her poetic concerns and voice. I see her poetry and prose as complementary engagements on a spectrum of creative production. In both the poet engages themes of nature, family, class, aging, vulnerability, and gender. In both we see her deep engagement with the interior lives of children. In both her characteristic courage, grace, and artistry are readily apparent. Maze's commitment to and connection with her poetry was absolute. In the homage to her friend cited earlier Korn recalls, "She [Maze] was anxious about each new poem, trembled over its fate, its destiny, when it would go forth alone and unprotected into the cold faraway world. She used to minimize the significance of her poems so that her disappointment would not be so bitter and harsh if the poem did not receive the expected recognition."[36]

If Maze is celebrated for her accomplishments in the city of Montreal, the Laurentian Mountains too figured prominently in her life. Year after year she and her family spent their summers there. Irving Massey recalls that the Jewish population in the Laurentians was more scattered than in the Catskills. Artists and literary figures of various kinds, such as Rokhl Ayzenberg and Melech Ravitch, came to visit them.[37] Rita Briansky often stayed with Maze and her family in the Laurentians. She would sometimes accompany Maze to the creek when she went there to wash clothes. There Briansky painted the poet while she was at work.[38]

---

35 Ibid., 110–111.

36 Rachel Korn, "Ida Maze," *Der Keneder Odler* (*The Canadian Eagle*), May 26, 1963, 6(?).

37 YAT telephone interview with Irving Massey, September 16, 2020.

38 YAT telephone interview with Rita Briansky, May 19, 2019.

In the Laurentians, writing was a vital pursuit for Maze. Once, while she and her son were walking on a back road in the Laurentians, Maze decided to sit. She told Irving to go ahead. By the time he came back, she had written a poem. Irving would go over Maze's poems with her, offering feedback, discussing their sequencing and grouping. During the off season Maze and Irving traveled to the Laurentians to work on her poems.[39]

There has been ongoing interest in Ida Maze over the years. In his 1934 book *Idishe dikhter in Kanade* (*Yiddish Poets in Canada*), H. M. Caiserman-Wital looks at Maze's early poetry. He notes that "There hasn't been a single anthology, literary journal, or special pamphlet that has appeared in the last eight years in Canada and at time in the United States, in which Ida Maze's poetry did not offer blessings with the piety and modesty of her talent." In Maze's poetry, Caiserman-Wital highlights the themes of sadness and stillness and "maternal motifs, children motifs, love motifs, nature and social motifs [. . .] in all, one senses, above all, poetic truth."[40] In analyzing Maze's first book, *A mame*, Caiserman-Wital notes, "Therefore, it is clear that she brings no peace to mothers, but a thin, quiet sadness that completely penetrates the consciousness."[41]

Irving Massey has written an extensive, wide-ranging essay on Maze's milieu, her role in sustaining other writers, and an analysis of her overall poetic contribution. The essay includes translations of some of Maze's poems. Massey highlights Maze's work in "four major genres: the elegiac poem, the children's poem, the nature poem, and the realistic poem of maturity." Massey argues, "Her poems are meant to contribute to a community rather than to set her apart from it. As she herself insists, they are the poems of a servant, not a master; the title of 'The Unpaid Maid,' 'Di nit batsolte dinst,' is one that can be worn with pride, not only with resentment. That is, perhaps, her greatest originality, and an attribute rare in modern poetry: she fulfills the ideals of her community while yet retaining her identity as an individual poet; she is a writer whose work, even at its most private, is subordinate to community."[42]

39 YAT interview with Irving Massey, May 16, 2019.

40 H. M. Caiserman-Wital, *Idishe dikhter in Kanade* (*Yiddish Poets in Canada*; Montreal: Farlag "Nyuansn," 1934), 76–78.

41 Ibid., 86–87.

42 Irving Massey, "Public Lives in Private: Ida Maza and the Montreal Yiddish Renaissance" in *Identity and Community: Reflections on English, Yiddish, and French Literature in Canada*, Irving Massey (Detroit: Wayne State University Press, 1994), 96–98.

In a recent essay highlighting the work of Esther Segal and Ida Maze, Rebecca Margolis provides a thorough survey of this scholarship on Maze. Margolis problematizes the trope of "mother" that has surrounded Maze. She writes, "Maza's legacy of inspiring and helping others has in so many ways superseded her legacy as a poet." And then: "In the contemporary discourse about Segal and Maza, their relative literary merits appear to have little bearing on how they have been remembered." Margolis notes further that Maze's "visibility as a nurturer and helper and characterization as a 'mother' created a persona that extends beyond the corpus of Maza's Yiddish writing."[43] Undergirding Margolis's essay is a call for the return to the literary text in the Yiddish original and in translation.

In an undated dispatch entitled "A Call to the Friends of Ida Maze, May She Rest in Peace," M. M. Shaffir asked for support for the publication of *Dineh.* In it he writes, "We are therefore appealing once again to Ida Maze's hundreds of friends and to everyone touched by the luster of her wonderful personality to subscribe to this book—*Dineh*, an autobiographical novel of Ida Maze's childhood, that will surely take an esteemed place among the autographical novels in Yiddish literature."[44] I fully share Shaffir's belief in the novel's importance in Yiddish literature, and I honor his extraordinary work in bringing his friend's manuscript to publication.

In some ways, *Dineh: An Autobiographical Novel* itself is a bridge between the twin roles of "remarkable writer" and "nurturer" outlined by Ira Robinson. Within its pages one sees the many ways that Dineh/Hayeh nurtured others—the help she provided to Shprintse, the careful tending of Shmuel-Arn that she offered, and the love she gave to Dvoyrehle and Zisl upon the tragic death of their daughter, Haveh. In *Dineh* we see kindness depicted in a remarkable literary structure with sparkle, with precision. The book, an homage to those whom Maze had to leave behind but whom she always remembered, feels itself like an extension of the kindnesses offered by its title heroine. *Dineh*, it seems to me, is a novel that melds art and ethics or, rather, that refuses to separate them. In the words that grace its pages, art is an ethical act; ethics so presented is itself an undertaking in artistry.

I am delighted, then, that the publication in English of *Dineh: An Autobiographical*

43 Rebecca Margolis, "Remembering Two of Montreal's Yiddish Women Poets: Esther Segal and Ida Maza" in *Women Writers of Yiddish Literature: Critical Essays*, ed. Rosemary Horowitz (Jefferson, N.C.: McFarland & Company, Inc., 2015), 264–265.

44 M. M. Shaffir, "*A vendung tsu di fraynt fun Ayde Maze, a.h.*" ("An Appeal to the Friends of Ida Maze, May She Rest in Peace"), not dated, Ida Maze Collection, Jewish Public Library of Montreal, Group II, Biography, Box 1.

Novel will acquaint new audiences with Ida Maze's literary work. Here readers can immerse themselves in the rural world of White Russia evoked with care and wide-eyed clarity. Here they can view an intimate, rich portrait of a vanished world that nurtured and shaped a beloved Yiddish literary figure. Here a poet, writer, editor, and cultural activist who devoted so much of her time to promoting the work of others is the object of extended focus, a focus that she herself sculpted. Here is the artist, anchored in love, under the proverbial spotlight. Here is her creation, her vision. It is a virtuoso performance in poetic prose that I hope will garner Ida Maze a broad and new readership.

Glossary

Amidah ("*Shimenesreh*" in Yiddish; "*Shemoneh Esreh*" in Hebrew): the central prayer in the Jewish liturgy, recited with the feet planted firmly together and preferably facing Jerusalem

Batiushka (Russian): father, also used as a religious title and for the tsar

bolnitsa (Russian): hospital

darmoyeda (Russian): human parasite, sponger

eruv ("*eyrev*" in Yiddish): the wire border that enables Jews to carry objects on the Sabbath

Fonye (Yiddish; pejorative): Russian, the Russians, the government in tsarist Russia

"God of Abraham" ("*Got fun Avrom*"): Yiddish prayer recited by women and girls marking the conclusion of the Sabbath while the males are in the synagogue reciting the Mayrev prayer

goyim (Yiddish, from the Hebrew; plural form of "goy"): non-Jews

goyish: adjective, referring to something or someone not Jewish

gymnasium (plural: *gymnasia*): a type of secondary school in some European countries that typically prepares students for university

Havdalah ("*Havdole*" in Yiddish): the ceremony performed at the close of the Sabbath and festivals to mark the return to workdays

Kiddush ("*kidesh*" in Yiddish; "*kidush*" in Hebrew): proclamation of the holiness of the Sabbath or of a holiday, recited with the blessing over the wine at the family table; communal celebration with wine and food in a synagogue after morning prayers on the Sabbath

"Kuda?" (Russian): "Where to?"

Lag BaOmer ("*Lagboymer*" in Yiddish; from the Hebrew "*Lag ba-Omer*"): a Jewish holiday celebrated on the 33rd day of the counting of the Omer, the 18th day of the Hebrew month of Iyyar, believed to be the anniversary of the death of the Mishnaic sage Rabbi Shimon bar Yohai

maftir: reading in the synagogue of the Haftarah (text from the prophets); person called upon to perform this reading

ha-Mapil (Hebrew): the Hebrew blessing recited after the Shema bedtime prayer and right before falling asleep

matushka (Russian): a combination of "*mat*" (mother) and the suffix "*-ushka*" (expressing endearment); a term with multiple meanings, such as mother (archaic and colloquial); a woman, usually elderly (archaic and colloquial); a nun or the wife of a priest (colloquial)

ha-Mavdil (Hebrew): Hebrew blessing said at the close of the Sabbath

Meyer Baal ha-Nes (Hebrew): Meyer, the miracle maker; a Jewish sage in the time of the Mishnah known for the miracles he performed; in times of crisis, Jews give to charity in his name

naplevat (Russian): literally "you can spit on it"; here, never mind, no matter, let's not worry about it, it's not important

narod (Russian): folk, people; in the 19th and 20th centuries, often used by intellectuals to refer to the peasantry as "salt of the earth"

Ninth of Av (*Tishebov* in Yiddish, *Tish'ah Be'av* in Hebrew): the Jewish day of mourning commemorating the destruction of both Temples in Jerusalem

obysk (Russian): police raid and search

Pan (Polish): "Mister," "Sir," or "Lord"

Pani (Polish): "Madam," "Missus," or "Lady"

Panie (Polish): plural of "*Pani*"; "Ladies," "Miladies," or the vocative case of "*Pan*," used when addressing people, as in "*Panie!*" ("Sir!" or "Milord!")

"Pavorozhim, matushka" (Russian): "Let's tell the future, mother."

podruzhka (Russian): girlfriend

pohorony (Russian): funeral

pozharnaia komanda (Russian): the firefighter brigade

progulka (Russian): a walk, a stroll

ruskii narod (Russian): the Russian masses, the Russian people

Shavuot (Hebrew; "Shvues" in Yiddish; "Pentecost" in English): holiday celebrated seven weeks after Passover to commemorate the revelation of the Torah at Mount Sinai; feast of first fruits

"Shivtekha u-mishantekha, hemah yenahamuni" (Hebrew, from Psalms 23:4): "Thy rod and thy staff, they comfort me."

shiva (from the Hebrew "*shivah*"): "*shivah*" means "seven"; the seven days of Jewish mourning that begin after the burial of the deceased

sobraniia (Russian; singular *sobranie*): organizational meetings

sud (Russian): court

svoboda (Russian): freedom

Tsyganka vorozhilka (Russian): Romani fortune teller

uchitel (Russian): teacher

ukaz (Russian): decree

Vide (Yiddish; from the Hebrew "*Vidui*"): confession of sin (collectively on Yom Kippur or individually before dying)

"Volki!" (Russian): "Wolves!"

"Yey Bogu, Panie Shiye, ne znaiu" (Russian): "Dear God, Mr. Shiye, I don't know."

Translator's Notes

Minus the diacritics, I generally followed the American Library Association/Library of Congress (ALA/LC) system for the transliteration of Yiddish throughout this book. Words accepted into English (e.g., *Amidah*, *Havdalah*, *Kiddush*, *Shavuot*, and *yeshiva*) are not italicized and follow the standard English form or spelling rather than the ALA/LC transliterated one (*Shimenesreh*, *Havdoleh*, *kidesh*, *Shvues*, *yeshiveh*). Of course, the individuals upon whom the characters in *Dineh* are based would not have pronounced them this way, and in at least one case (*Amidah*) would most likely not have used that word.

In most cases I used the ALA/LC system for the transliteration of Yiddish forenames of Hebrew and Aramaic origin. Readers familiar with the YIVO system of transliteration will notice some differences between the two systems. Thus the title character is transliterated as Dineh and not Dine (YIVO), and her older sisters (as well as other characters with those names) are Malkeh and Soreh, not Malke (YIVO) and Sore (YIVO). When I thought the YIVO system aided pronunciation, such as "Rokhl" (YIVO) rather than "Rohl" (ALA/LC), I departed from my usual practice.

For the names of Yiddish authors, I mostly utilized the headings established in the Library of Congress/Name Authority Cooperative (LC/NACO) File. Thus, I chose A. Ajzen, Rachel H. Korn, and Abraham Sutzkever rather than Avrom Ayzen, Rokhl H. Korn, and Avrom Sutskever respectively.

When I was certain that the geographic name found in the original Yiddish text was the same place noted in the LC/NACO Authority File, the JewishGen Communities Database, or other English-language resources, I used the forms found in those resources. In cases where I did not find an authoritative Latin-letter form or where there was residual uncertainty about whether the Yiddish form found in the novel was indeed the same place mentioned in external resources, I used the systematic YIVO transliteration of the Yiddish place-names.

The name "Ida Maze" is a hybrid formulation. The forename is the standard Latin alphabet spelling. If one were to follow a systematic transliteration of her forename as it appeared in Yiddish one would end up with "Ayde." Because "Ida" appears in almost all English-language sources and because of the challenges "Ayde" would pose to English-language readers, I did not choose "Ayde" as her forename. The surname "Maze" is a systematic transliteration of the Yiddish form. I employ the form "Maze" for several reasons. For one, it most closely represents the Yiddish last name the author herself used as a writer. Significantly, "Ida Maze" also appears to me to be the predominant form in most English-language resources, including references such as *Encyclopedia Judaica* and the *Jewish Women's Archive.* Other renderings of Ida Maze's last name (pronounced MAA-zeh) are Maza and Massey. Irving Massey told me that the name Mazeh comes from the Hebrew "*Mi zeh Aharon ha-Kohen?*" ("Who is Aharon ha-Kohen?").

I used the term "Gypsy" in the book only after considerable deliberation. Many consider it to be highly pejorative and prefer the terms "Roma" or "Romani." In a compromise effort to be both respectful of evolving cultural expectation and faithful to a historical text, I did consider using "Roma" in the nondialogue parts and "Gypsy" in the dialogue. However, in discussion with others and upon further reflection, I decided to go with "Gypsy" uniformly throughout. I thought it would be too jarring to have "Roma" in some cases (nondialogue) and "Gypsy" in others (dialogue). Additionally, it seemed to me that "Roma" or "Romani" felt too contemporary, too "presentist," even in the nondialogue parts of the novel, and that they would have removed the reader from an immersive experience in a book describing life of well over a century ago.

The translations in the afterword of this book are my own. All newspaper articles cited in my afterword were read as clippings in the Ida Maze Collection at the Jewish Public Library of Montreal.

Appendix

Readers of the original Yiddish-language book (Montreal, 1970) will note the absence of three brief passages in my translation. In this appendix I provide the passages from the Yiddish book whose translation I did not include in the English-language book. I also include the translation of the passages and the justifications for the omissions.

On the bottom of page 18 and the top of page 19 in the original Yiddish book, the following sentences of dialogue between Malkeh and Vasil appear:

—Iz shlogstu dayn Nastusyen mit di kinder. Iz vos kumt aroys fun dayn trinken?

—Bist gerekht, gerekht: ikh shlog, un nokh dem fardrist mikh. Un der hezk vos ikh makh on in shtub yedn mol, iz oykh nisht keyn kleynikayt.

Translation:

"And then you hit your Nastusya and the kids. What good comes from your drinking?"

"You're right, that's true. I hit them and then get upset. And the damage that I do at home each time is no small thing."

This exchange raises several issues. Who is Nastusya? If she is Vasil's previous girlfriend/wife (prior to Oliana), why is there no mention of her or their children later in the novel? Perhaps more important, consider the later (retained) exchange between Dineh and Vasil:

Dineh shuddered in horror.

"You beat Oliana, Ustina, and Arkhip? It's forbidden, Vasil. My father wouldn't forgive you. Beating? Beating Oliana and the kids?"

"As God is dear to me," said Vasil guiltily, "Dinkele, you know me well, after all. I never beat anyone, have I? But this is from stress. I don't know what to do with myself. Promise me that you'll ask your father to send for me."

It seems highly unlikely that Vasil would have lied so baldly to Dineh at this crucial moment when Dineh is about to emigrate and he is asking her to put in a good word about him to her father. Furthermore, if he had a history of domestic violence, Dineh would surely have known about it. Therefore she would not have been so taken aback by his admission of beating Oliana and their children, and she would have called him out on his obvious lie. For those reasons I did not include in my translation the exchange between Malkeh and Vasil that appears on pages 18–19 of the Yiddish text. I carefully considered the importance of domestic violence this early in the novel as a means of foreshadowing later manifestations, but given the problems outlined above I ultimately decided that it did not warrant retention and would negatively impact the reader's experience.

I changed the "Petrak" that appears on page 21 of the Yiddish book to "Vasil" and removed the clause "*a kurts-geviksik, shtil, dershlogn poyerl.*" The description "a short, quiet, dejected little peasant" simply did not apply to Vasil. Who was Petrak? The name "Petrak" does not appear again in the novel. Nor is his fate ever mentioned.

On page 140 of the Yiddish book, the following two sentences appear:
Un az Marko iz in a zuntikdikn tog geshtorbn, iz nokhn pokharon, vos hot gedoyert gantse finf teg, Sholem tsurikgekumen vi fun gor a noenter levayeh. Zayn hob-un-guts iz itst geblibn in di hent fun an unerlekhe zin un tekhter un an eydem Markos.

Translation:

"After Marko died on a Sunday and after the funeral that lasted five days, Sholem returned as if from a funeral of someone very close to him. His worldly possessions were now in the hands of the dishonest sons and daughters, and a son-in-law, of Marko."

I did not include this passage in my translation because this plot element occurs again on page 207 of the Yiddish book, where it is discussed at greater length. That later occurrence seemed to me to be the more appropriate location, and that is the one that remains in my English translation.

Due to the uncertainty they generated, I changed several name iterations in the book. On page 132 of the Yiddish book, Peshe refers to a "Shmuel the son of Uncle Ruvtshe from Odessa" as Malkeh's love interest. This character is later referred to as "Isak." Given the intensity of Malkeh's love for the cousin from Odessa, it seems highly unlikely that Malkeh would be in love with two different cousins from Odessa, let alone without any explanation of that situation by the author. Alternatively, this figure might have had two different names. Finally, this might have been an error. Given that we cannot know for certain, I changed this one "Shmuel" to the more predominant "Isak" in my translation. Similarly, on page 180 of the Yiddish book, a "Mrs. Razovske" complains to Sholem about Itshe as if her own child were in danger. This is the only time that the name "Razovske" is used. I take this character to be the "Haneh Yoshelyevitsh" who appears earlier in the novel. Certainly her description and concerns match those of Mrs. Yoshelyevitsh. Of course, Itshe might have moved and Mrs. Razovske could be another character entirely, but that is not depicted in the book. For ease of reading, I therefore changed "Razovske" to "Yoshelyevitsh."

Given that *Dineh* is a posthumously published novel and that Maze did not make final edits on her manuscript, I believe these changes are warranted. I did not make any of them lightly. It is my hope that they enhance the overall reading experience—and that Ida Maze would not have been displeased.

For any and all errors in the book that are my own, I ask for the reader's forgiveness.

Acknowledgments

My first debt is to Ida Maze's son, Professor Irving Joseph (Iossl) Massey, for his support of my translation project. During telephone interviews and email correspondence, Iossl munificently shared his knowledge of and experiences with his mother. Additionally, he connected me to his son Ephraim Massey and the visual artist Rita Briansky and provided crucial information that led me to William Shaffir. During a visit to Iossl's home in Buffalo, New York, in November 2019, he offered additional reminiscences and showed me numerous photographs and works of art.

I thank William Shaffir for granting permission to publish his father M. M. Shaffir's prefatory note to *Dineh.*

I am grateful to the generosity and hospitality of Maze's aforementioned grandson, Dr. Ephraim Massey, and her mentee and friend, Rita Briansky. Ephraim and Rita shared their knowledge of Maze in telephone interviews. During a research visit to Montreal in September 2019, I was fortunate to meet them both in person. Ephraim drove us to the graves of Maze, her husband, Alexander, and son Earl (Israel). We also saw the facades of the buildings where Maze and her family had lived. In the evening Rita treated us to a delicious dinner in her home, and there we continued our celebration of Ida Maze. It was the capstone to a magical day.

The gifted staff of the Jewish Public Library (JPL) of Montreal provided vital support. Jessica Zimmerman and Nicole Beaudry of the JPL Archives went far beyond the call of duty in their assistance to me during my September 2019 research visit. Jessica provided careful guidance to the vast Ida Maze Collection and welcomed me warmly into the JPL Archives. Employing masterful research skills, Nicole offered extensive help in locating genealogical information on the Zukowsky and Massey families. Nicole located the 1907 ship's manifest demonstrating the arrival of Musche and Chaje Zukowski. Librarian Eddie Paul of the JPL and genealogists Stanley Diamond and Mark Halpern provided various kinds of aid as I was tracking down information cited in the afterword. I am grateful to all of them for their congenial professionalism and indeed to the extraordinary communal treasure that is the Jewish Public Library of Montreal.

I would also like to thank others who made my time in Montreal so special.

Professor Ira Robinson generously shared his knowledge of Jewish Montreal and offered warm support and inspiration. My niece Feigie Moses, her husband, Avner, and their children, Mordechai, Yissochor, Levi, and Tova, welcomed me into the familial fold. Chomie and Zev Rosenzweig provided an evening of stimulating conversation and convivial fellowship.

I offer profound thanks to Norman Buder. With great thoroughness and precision, Norman answered numerous questions regarding challenging Yiddish linguistic concerns and generally offered vital feedback and helpful insights. Norman offered sage counsel on the structural matters raised in the appendix. Norman's extraordinary erudition has greatly enriched this text, and his enthusiasm about this project and his encouragement mean so much to me.

I am extremely grateful to Elżbieta Pelish for her prompt responses to queries on Russian and Slavic linguistic matters and the eastern European cultural context. Ela's generous and spirited engagement with questions of language and culture animated my translation journey. I thank Oksana Klebs and Paul Crego for checking my Russian transliteration and translation.

Allen J. Frank grappled with questions I posed to him on the issue of the translator's editorial reach and responsibility and offered thoughtful feedback.

A translation workshop at the 43rd American Literary Translators Association (ALTA) conference proved most beneficial. I thank workshop facilitator Antonia Lloyd-Jones and participants Jane Bugaeva, Maia Evrona, Deborah Kim, Kristen Renee Miller, Emma Roy, Tania Samsonova, and Samantha Schnee for their insightful comments on a brief excerpt of my translation. Thank you also to ALTA's Sebastian Schulman for his enthusiastic encouragement of my translation project.

Members of the literary translators' community presented helpful responses to thorny translation issues and offered welcoming and supportive fellowship. I thank Indran Amirthanayagam, Nancy Naomi Carlson, Keith Cohen, Mindl Cohen, Barbara Goldberg, Paula Gordon, Anne Henochowicz, Aviya Kushner, Wendy McBurney, Yvette Neisser, Carol Volk, Sergio Waisman, and Deborah Wassertzug.

I thank Cecile Esther Kuznitz and Amanda (Miryem-Khaye) Seigel for research procedural insights and help.

I am extremely grateful to Lisa Newman, Jeff Hayes, Gregory Lauzon, Yankl Salant, and the team at White Goat Press for their belief in this book and for so gracefully shepherding the manuscript to publication.

Pearl Gluck's wisdom and support were instrumental to me throughout the process of bringing this book to life. For your faith, friendship, open ear . . . and heart, thank you, dear Pearl.

I would like to thank the colleagues and friends who have nurtured me in so many ways: Angelika Bammer, Andrew W. M. Beierle, Bella Bryks-Klein, Cindy Casey, Ellen Cassedy, Jim Feldman and Natalie Wexler, Michael Gasper, Ken Giese, Reiner Gogolin, Paula Goldberg, Peter Goodman, Ada Gracin, James Hafner, Janice Hamer, Miriam Isaacs, Kate James, Deborah Kalb, Julia Spicher Kasdorf, Eitan Kensky, Oksana Klebs, Barbara Krasner, Cecile Esther Kuznitz, Amos Lassen, Elizabeth Goll Lerner, Laura Levitt, Ashira Malka, Erin McGonigle, John N. Mitchell, Elżbieta Pelish, Rita Rubenstein, Nancy Sack, Yankl Salant, Paul Edward Schaper, Faye-Ann Schott, Jeffrey Shandler, Harvey Spiro, Jonathan Sunshine, Michael Swirsky, Phil Tavolacci, Deidre Waxman, Rivka Yerushalmi, and Sarita Zimmerman.

My sincere apologies in advance to anyone whose names I have accidentally omitted in these acknowledgments.

About the Author

Courtesy of Irving Massey

Born Hayeh Zukofsky (also rendered as Zukowski, Zukowsky, and Zukovsky among other forms) in 1893 in the village of Ugli (also rendered as Ogli), White Russia (now Belarus), Ida Maze (pronounced MAA-zeh; also rendered as Maza and Massey) was an important figure in the world of Yiddish letters. After emigrating from White Russia in 1907(?), she lived briefly in New York City and then settled in Montreal. Maze's generosity was the stuff of legend. She helped refugee writers navigate the Canadian immigration system, edited the books of other poets, and advocated for writers in many ways. The doors of her home were kept open, and many Yiddish writers gathered there. Maze was an acclaimed author of poems for adults and children. In addition to *Dineh* she wrote four books of poetry, *A mame* (*A Mother*; 1931), *Lider far kinder* (*Poems for Children*; 1936), *Naye lider* (*New Poems*; 1941), and *Vaksn mayne kinderlekh: muter un kinder-lider* (*My Children Grow: Mother and Children Poems*; 1954), which was awarded the prize in children's literature by the Congress for Jewish Culture in 1955. Ida Maze died in Montreal in1962.

About the Translator

Photo by Tamar London

Yermiyahu Ahron Taub is a poet, writer, and Yiddish translator. He is the author of six books of poetry, including *A moyz tsvishn vakldike volkn-kratsers: geklibene Yidishe lider* (*A Mouse Among Tottering Skyscrapers: Selected Yiddish Poems*; Library of Contemporary Yiddish Literature, 2017) and two works of fiction, including *Beloved Comrades: a Novel in Stories* (Anaphora Literary Press, 2020). His most recent translation from the Yiddish is *May God Avenge Their Blood: A Holocaust Memoir Triptych* by Rachmil Bryks (Lexington Books, 2020; Lexington Studies in Jewish Literature series). Please visit his website, yataubdotnet.wordpress.com.

White Goat Press, the Yiddish Book Center's imprint, is committed to bringing newly translated work to the widest readership possible. We publish work in all genres—novels, short stories, drama, poetry, memoirs, essays, reportage, children's literature, plays, and popular fiction, including romance and detective stories.

White Goat Press Titles

- *Sutzkever Essential Prose* by Avrom Sutzkever
  translated by Zackary Sholem Berger
- *Seeds in the Desert* by Mendel Mann
  translated by Heather Valencia
- *Warsaw Stories* by Hersh Dovid Nomberg
  translated by Daniel Kennedy
- *In eynem: The New Yiddish Textbook* by Asya Vaisman Schulman,
  Jordan Brown, and Mikhl Yashinsky

Forthcoming

- *From a Bird's Cage to a Thin Branch: The Selected Poems of Yoysef Kerler*
  translated by Maia Evrona
- *Childhood Years* by Peretz Hershbein
  translated by Leonard Wolf

To learn more visit yiddishbookcenter.org/white-goat-press